STRIVERS
ROW

During the 1920s and 1930s, around the time of the Harlem Renaissance, more than a quarter of a million African-Americans settled in Harlem, creating what was described at the time as "a cosmopolitan Negro capital which exert[ed] an influence over Negroes everywhere."

Nowhere was this more evident than on West 138th and 139th Streets between what are now Adam Clayton Powell and Frederick Douglass Boulevards, two blocks that came to be known as Strivers Row. These blocks attracted many of Harlem's African-American doctors, lawyers, and entertainers, among them Eubie Blake, Noble Sissle, and W. C. Handy, who were themselves striving to achieve America's middle-class dream.

With its mission of publishing quality African-American literature, Strivers Row emulates those "strivers," capturing that same spirit of hope, creativity, and promise.

SIMON SAYS

A NOVEL OF

INTRIGUE,

BETRAYAL . . .

AND MURDER

SIMON SAYS

COLLEN DIXON

STRIVERS
ROW

VILLARD | NEW YORK

Library of Congress Cataloging-in-Publication Data

Dixon, Collen.
Simon says: a novel of intrigue, betrayal—and murder / Collen Dixon.—1st ed.
p. cm.
ISBN 0-8129-6881-6
1. African American men—Fiction. 2. Washington (D.C.)—Fiction.
3. Mayors—Fiction. I. Title.

PS3604.I94S58   2003   813'.6—dc21   2003041134

Villard Books website address: www.villard.com

Printed in the United States of America
24689753

First Edition

This literary effort is dedicated to all of us still searching. . . .

Always be grateful . . . never be satisfied.

*Follow your dreams, pursue your hopes, and
always keep striving.*

*Never be limited by your color, gender, or
physical disposition.*

*We are the sum total of our life experiences and
we all have a story to tell.*

One love . . .

For what shall it profit a man,
if he shall gain the whole world,
and lose his own soul?

MARK 8:36

THROUGH the eyes of a young black boy growing up in Washington, D.C., vision is comprised of dreams, nightmares, and realities.

You see, just outside the hallowed halls of Congress, a stone's throw away from the Lincoln Memorial, and beyond the Washington Monument's shadow, throbs the real heartbeat of Chocolate City. Native Washingtonians, namely black folks living in the District and those who sought refuge in nearby Prince George's County, coined that phrase to enlighten the world of their fierce pride. The pride of being one of the few majority-black cities in America with a black mayor.

The real D.C. is a deceptive mirage neatly placed between two distinctively different realities. It is a place where legislators refine the art of talking out of both sides of their mouths. They practice what they are paid for both under and above the table, within and outside the law. It is a place where criminals and politicians make for strange bedfellows, and are sometimes one and the same.

In the 1970s, an era of prosperity thrived after the tumultuous 1960s, and urban growth and gentrification emerged. With a high-

profile, boisterous black mayor at the helm, D.C. was like a newly
christened ship riding the waves of change and prosperity into the
decadent, free-love new decade.

The seventies were a time of change and inspiration. Music
found deeper roots in funk and soul, as the mellow Motown
sounds gave way to the reign of the hard-thumping, strong lyrics
of innovative bands such as Parliament and the Ohio Players.
Even James Brown changed his tune. His style evolved from
pleading "Please, Please, Don't Go," to demanding "Say It Loud,
I'm Black and I'm Proud."

Skyscrapers grew out of the debris of the riots. Power-brokering
deals were conceived during frantic, backseat liaisons between
friends and enemies. These deals celebrated the birth of the new
downtown, while orphaning densely populated residential areas
that became throwaway societies and seedy concrete jungles.

Yet the more vocal, well-heeled block areas thrived, the ones
with the political pull and clout of Capitol Hill and the Sixteenth
Street Gold Coast. For these communities, the future seemed
promising. Where firebombs, massive demonstrations, and police
activity had created a virtual ghost town for the impoverished
masses, suddenly neon signs were cropping up. They illuminated
the streets with glaring new enterprises and opportunities, and the
city folk rejoiced.

Two separate dichotomies coexisted. Where the Black Power
movement encouraged the youth to fight the power, the older, settled middle class felt that the seventies signaled that the struggle
was finally over and that *their* time had come. They were holding
on to promise and hope, and finally prospering from the opportunities created by affirmative action. Unemployment was low, and
good government jobs were easy to claim. Entry-level positions in
corporate America were being offered and accepted at a rapid pace.
Educational grants were plentiful, private scholarships were being
offered like pouring rain after a long drought, and the American
dream of going to college was not only rocking the rich to sleep,
but even the lower middle class. The federal purse strings opened
and cash flowed freely from the guilt-ridden white masses that

had little or no desire to repeat the destructive experience of the riotous sixties.

Where white folks had their baby boomers, the black youth were the booming babies. The product of urban decay and of the troubled men back from 'Nam, they possessed an incomparable demonstrative pride. They turned a deaf ear to the pleas of the civil rights movement and found strength and freedom from the Black Panthers. "Negroes" became "blacks," and Angela Davis, Huey P. Newton, John Shaft, and Superfly were transformed into heroes.

Welcome to D.C., Dark Country. Chocolate City. Where black folks were unaware of Jim Crow or racial polarization, for they held the positions of power. Or at least that was the illusion.

Welcome to D.C., circa 1974. Where a little boy's dreams can become reality, and that reality can often become a nightmare.

SIMON
SAYS

CHAPTER 1

ALEXANDER "Chip" Baxter stood near the middle of the long line that stretched from the pharmacist's counter, in the back, to the front of the cramped drugstore. People's, the only drugstore within a ten-block radius of Shaw, was on overload as usual. Shaw was a desolate place, full of decayed remnants of days gone by. Days and times when people took pride in where they lived. Now they just took.

Despite it all, it was Chip's home. And this was one of the more upbeat days, the first of the month, or Mother's Day, as it was called in the 'hood. Everyone was in high spirits, laughing and joking. Mother's Day was the busiest day of the month, as the welfare recipients conned, coerced, and cajoled in order to make their monthly pittance stretch against the rules and the sky-high prices of the Establishment. Children scurried about, begging their mothers to buy the dime-store toy of their dreams. Meanwhile, adults tried to make a dollar out of fifteen cents, using their modest windfalls to purchase diapers, Kool-Aid, cigarettes, and Similac—the staples of a struggling community.

Shifting his weight, Chip clutched the prescription until his nails left deep indentations in his sweaty palms. The perspiration smudged the doctor's signature to the point of illegibility, but that was okay. He'd gotten so many prescriptions filled there that the pharmacist knew exactly what he needed. Unless there was an evil clerk aching to give Chip a hard time. He dreaded the aggravated counter girl going off on him. He'd seen her do that often enough.

Chip tried desperately to suppress the loud yawn straining his small ten-year-old body, but it was a losing battle. The yawn forced his bloodshot eyes shut, like the snap on a mousetrap. He had deep bags and dark circles etched under his eyes, and he looked like one of the drunks or sleep-deprived addicts who hung out on the corner. His "Feed the Children" poster-child appearance was a direct result of last night's disturbing nightmare and the intense migraine that followed. The dream had been exceptionally vicious, and it was lingering longer than most. Almost two hours had passed since he'd left the ratty old free clinic over on First Street for a temporary fix and rushed over to the drugstore, just to hurry up and wait. The line had barely moved, and the few times that it did, some bigger person would bogart his way in front of Chip. There was nothing he could do about it, so he just waited for relief to come.

The yawn brought welcome tears to his dry eyes, and he stretched while carefully guarding his place in line. Sleepy tears dribbled down his gaunt cheeks, and Chip nearly gagged. Nausea was one of the side effects of the migraines, which were sometimes unshakable. Sunlight and noise also heightened his discomfort. Needless to say, time served in the chaotic drugstore only made them worse.

The dank, shabby store was stifling in the extremely humid July air. Instead of being a place that offered refuge for the sick, it was dark and depressing. Fighting the urge to simultaneously vomit and cry, Chip leaned against a rack of feminine-protection products and instead yawned again. Eyes shut, he prayed.

Chip's thoughts drifted back to his bad dreams. As young as he was, he remembered when they had started. It was right after his mother's death. For a while, they had occurred every night, and then they had become less frequent. Sometimes they were confusing, but most of the time they were scary, until his mom appeared. She was a calming presence, and offered him comfort he didn't get in his waking moments. In the midst of utter turmoil, she'd wrap her arms around him, and he'd often awaken reaching for her, only to be met with the raucous snores of his older brother, Ivan.

At the end of one of these episodes, Chip would be dazed and drained. His pajamas would be soaked with sweat, damp through to his rumpled cowboy sheets. Only snippets of the startling visions remained, enough to leave him disoriented, trembling, and afraid.

Ceiling fans hummed and stirred the suffocating air. Chip rubbed his aching head. Last night he had awakened Ivan, and to Chip's surprise, he'd been pretty sympathetic. Normally, Ivan was kind of grouchy if his sleep was interrupted. So it had made Chip feel a whole lot better when Ivan talked to him until Chip drifted off to sleep. It beat the times Ivan mumbled incoherently, uttering gibberish and snoring in the middle of Chip's sentence.

Chip scanned the line. A teenage mother was at the front, engaged in a heated dispute with the pharmacy clerk. They were truly going for it. With a baby hoisted on her hip and a toddler playing with a colorful condom display, she cussed and shouted as she and the clerk argued over the expiration date of her public assistance card. Folks in line were getting restless, and the noise level rose as they began shouting at the clerk and the mother to hurry the hell up. Impatience, poverty, and the choking humidity of the D.C. summer made a volatile mix. Chip squeezed his eyes shut even tighter in a futile attempt to block out the heat and the brewing turmoil, an ugly vortex that threatened to suck him in at any moment.

Suddenly, the back of the line surged forward, shoving Chip and sending his prescription fluttering to the floor. He quickly leaned down to pick up his precious piece of paper, as a commanding voice rose above the rumblings of the crowd. Chip stood motionless, too frightened to even breathe.

"Everybody get your asses on the floor! Get on the damn floor! Right now! This is a stickup!"

"Don't nobody move, or else you gonna get some of this heat!" another guy yelled from the front of the store. His tone was also deep and extremely agitated, and he sounded like he was itching to shoot somebody. Anybody.

"Everybody drop they purses. Now!" the first robber yelled, this time even louder. "Don't nobody try no stupid shit and try to be no hero."

Pandemonium erupted and most folks dove for the dirty floor, scattering their unpaid merchandise all over the cramped aisles. Knocking over displays, mothers grabbed for their children, and screams resonated at a feverish pitch, yet Chip's feet were nailed in place. This had to be another bad dream. Except it wasn't. This was a living nightmare.

Trembling like a wino down to the last drop of his Wild Irish Rose, Chip just couldn't move. Fear riveted his maypop tennis shoes to the floor, and his knees knocked like the rhythmic drumbeats from the go-go bands that played at the free concerts in the park. Two hooded gunmen wearing black ski masks rushed toward the pharmacy counter, demanding cash and drugs.

A wet, warm sensation trickled down Chip's pants. He had wet himself in front of all of these people, but he wasn't ashamed. This wasn't a matter of social protocol or embarrassment. It was reality. The intense fear that caused his bladder to release was real. Witnessing an actual armed robbery was nothing like what he had seen on his black-and-white TV or in the Technicolor-enhanced movies.

One of the gunmen yelled, his lips spraying spit at the hysterical clerk, and she cried fitfully as she tried to get the cash register open. Yet Chip couldn't hear anything. He saw their mouths moving, but everything was muted. There was a rapid succession of bright lights and gunfire as the man blasted her in the chest; blood and guts splattered everywhere. He mercilessly shoved her lifeless body aside and grabbed the contents of the cash register.

Chip's eyes stuck on him like cheap tennis shoe soles on hot asphalt. He knew he risked his life by looking, but he couldn't help it. Chip was mesmerized, yet acutely repulsed. He'd never seen bloody body parts splashed before his eyes, and while his mind said *run for your life,* his feet and soggy briefs said *no way.*

Swearing at the store's sweltering heat, the murderous gunman snatched off his mask and hurdled over the counter. He stopped dead in his tracks when he noticed Chip, standing in the pool of urine and staring straight at him. In a split second, Chip's abbreviated life flashed before his eyes, and he swore he saw the angelic apparition of his mother. The gunman had blood in his eyes, and he looked at Chip as if he were going to be next on his hit list. But in the distance sirens began to sound, and the other gunman yelled for the murderer to run. Calmness swept over Chip, for he knew that his mother was looking out for him as his life precariously hung like laundry on an overloaded clothesline. The murderer laid a long finger next to his throat and made a slicing motion. It was code for what would happen to Chip if he ever recalled the gunman's face. Squealing or dropping a dime on him would mean certain death. Running past Chip, the robber nearly slipped on the slick trail of pee. Angrily, he took a moment to exact revenge on Chip, with his wet pants and a splitting headache. The robber slammed him into the row of tampons and sanitary napkins.

When Chip awoke, EMTs were shaking him into consciousness, as he lay sprawled out on tiny pillows. As they assured him that he was going to be okay, some snaggle-toothed old lady shouted out that Chip had seen the robbers.

He hauled ass before the cops could catch him. As the smudged prescription slipped through his fingers, all he could think of was escaping. Energized, he slipped under the yellow police tape and past the numerous policemen.

Chip had proven he was a survivor. He had stared down death and survived. From that point on, he'd trust his instincts.

Later that evening, a still-breathless Chip, now freshly changed, waited anxiously on the fire escape for Ivan to come from basketball camp. The window fan barely stirred the suffocating heat in the Baxters' modest apartment; Chip often sought refuge on the escape during the summer's sweltering heat. When Chip finally saw Ivan kung-fu fighting down the block with his best friend, Fortune, Chip crawled through the window to run to the door to meet him.

With perfect timing, he swung the door just as Ivan was about to open it. "Hey, Ivan, you'll never guess what happened to me today."

Ivan shot him a dirty look as he nearly tumbled through the doorway. "Hay is for horses. You're right. I'll never guess, because I don't care. But I bet you'll never guess what happened down at the drugstore." Ivan tossed his gym bag onto the sofa and karate-chopped his way into the kitchen. He opened the freezer and refrigerator doors and stuck his head inside the freezer compartment. "Man, is it hot in here. I swear we need an air conditioner or something."

Chip ran into the kitchen and stood behind the refrigerator door, the cool air blowing on his skinny ankles. "I bet I do know. I was there."

"You're lying." Ivan jerked his head from the freezer section, then rummaged through the rest of the refrigerator.

"I'm not, Ivan. I was."

"You saw all that killing and whatnot?" Ivan looked at Chip and stuck an apple in his mouth. He bit off a big chunk and shook his head. "That's far-out, dude." He grabbed a bottle of orange juice and shoved the door closed.

"Yeah, I guess. But it was kind of scary. I even wet on myself when I saw the guy that shot the clerk. And the cops tried to stop me, but I ran."

Ivan nearly dropped his apple. "Don't feel bad. I would've probably shit a brick if I'd seen it. But you didn't say nothing, did you? You know you can't do nothing like that. They'll come after you if they even think that you'll drop a dime on them. You catch my drift, Chip?"

Chip nodded with widened eyes. "But I feel bad about the girl. She was mean sometimes, but it's still sad that she got killed like that."

Ivan took another bite of the fruit, and looked at Chip with a sad expression. "That's cold, but there's nothing you can do about it. It's just like that. You can't help yourself if they kill you too. So you can't never tell nobody, okay? Not even Dad. Especially not him."

IVAN'S ADVICE PROVED helpful. As time passed, the robber's face was erased from Chip's memory, only occasionally materializing in his nightmares. But even then he'd quickly blot it out, and awaken with the face just a blur. Eventually, it became a distant memory for Chip. His life again became focused on his little world, which included reading and hanging on to every one of Ivan's words. A big brother in every sense, Ivan was Chip's hero. Chip had spent many a warm summer evening at the local playground idolizing Ivan while watching him as their father taught him how to play basketball. Yet the enjoyment Chip derived from watching Ivan play barely offset the isolation and loneliness that were his constant companions, as he sat among the broken beer bottles, usually trying to read a book. Normally, he could devour one in a day, and reading was one of the few joys he had.

Everything came so naturally for Ivan, and he was awesome to behold. Even at his young age, Ivan was athletic, smooth, and confident, all the things Chip could only imagine being, since he was just a little bookworm. On a daily basis, every bully in the fourth grade constantly reminded him of it. And no one did it better or with more vigor than Calvin, the ringleader for the thugs-in-training.

"WHAT'S HAPPENIN', CHUMP? What's goin' on? Your brother can't play no ball. My uncle'll whip his ass any day!" Calvin sneered and rolled his beady eyes at Chip.

He was being challenged by his nemesis, a nappy-headed, pigeon-toed jerk who got his jollies by being a bully. A handful of dirt cascaded over the basketball court's fence and landed on the open pages of the book Chip was reading, and he quickly brushed it off.

Calvin always lurked around, ready to sucker-punch Chip or

double-dare him to fight. He'd sometimes draw an imaginary line across the sidewalk and taunt Chip to cross it. In school Calvin always showed out to get some attention and embarrass Chip, even if it meant being sent to detention. That would make him even more bent on getting Chip. The constant battle between Calvin's brawn and Chip's brains usually resulted in name-calling, and the winner was whoever got the better of whom. In Shaw, when confronted, you had to come back and come back correct. No halfstepping. Any comment hurled in your direction was an invitation to scrap. It was a juvenile version of the classic adult game of the Dozens, a tactical tool developed for coping with the tragedies of everyday life.

Chip sometimes chose to ig Calvin, but today his interruption was particularly annoying since Chip had just gotten to the best part of the latest Encyclopedia Brown mystery. The book had taken almost two months to arrive at the cruddy public library, and every day he had anxiously trekked over, checking for it. The librarian always greeted him with the same icy expression, until yesterday, when she'd shoved the book at him before he even asked for it.

"So what, Calvin? That guy wasn't your uncle. That was just your aunt's boyfriend. And I bet he hasn't even been around since that day he was here." Chip cut his eyes and turned the book over and shook the dirt out.

"So? He's a guard for the Bullets. And he's got boo-coo money and lots of clothes and a big purple Cadillac. Plus, he told me to call him Uncle Ray. So there."

"Forget you, Calvin."

"Forget you, forgot you. I never thought about you," Calvin said.

"So what. All that guy does is ride the bench. I checked. I may not watch sports, but I read the paper, and he never gets any points. None. And plus, he just *ought* to be able to beat Ivan. He's only thirteen. And that man, well, he's probably like fifty years old. That's not even fair." Chip sucked his teeth and went back to reading his book.

Calvin cut his eyes over toward Chip's dad. "You just a little cross-eyed fool," he said under his breath. "And I ought to kick your ass like I did the other day." Calvin licked his tongue at Chip and stuck his middle finger menacingly through the chain-link fence.

Chip glanced toward his father, and was relieved to see him engrossed in showing Ivan how to put a backspin on the ball. "You don't scare me, Calvin. You talk a bunch of trash, but you're just simple and jealous because you can't read like me. Now leave me alone." Chip slammed his book closed.

"Your momma's simple. Oh, but dag-on. You ain't even got one, you jive turkey. Ha!" Calvin snickered and hawk-spat on the sidewalk.

At that same moment, Chip's father glanced at them with a look that stopped them cold.

Chip was quick-witted and always easily pummeled Calvin with a few biting words. What he lacked in size and strength he more than made up for in cunning and intelligence. But in the presence of his father, he was tongue-tied and too afraid to respond.

"Later, bamma," Calvin said, and took off running down the block. Chip jumped to his feet, a deflated expression creasing his forehead.

A skinny foot with a holey shoe two sizes too big jutted out from the shadows of a tenement building and sent Calvin tumbling headfirst onto the concrete. Rubbing his bloody hands, Calvin formed his mouth to cuss out whoever had tripped him, but before he could utter a word, he spotted the culprit. His jaw immediately dropped and he did a double take when he recognized the tripper's menacing face.

It glared down on him with cold, red, empty eyes. Eyes that had seen far too much for his youthful age. The old man's face on the young boy's body conveyed an undeniably threatening message. The notorious Fortune Reed hovered over Calvin like a hungry spider eyeing a fat fly entangled in his web.

Calvin was visibly frightened. The bully was being bullied, and

Chip enjoyed every minute of it. It was nice not to be on the receiving end for a change. Redemption sure was sweet.

Fortune was as cruel as he was mean, and Chip was frightened of him too. Even though he was protected because Fortune was Ivan's best friend, he was still a menace. Momentarily, Chip felt sorry for Calvin. Yet when he thought about what Calvin would probably do to him later, the feeling passed quickly.

"You better watch your step, cool breeze. Next time, you might not be so damn lucky. It be like that sometime." Fortune glared and gestured condescendingly to help him up, but Calvin's eyes welled up and he jerked away. Like an alley rat beaten by a more ferocious alley rat, he scurried off, muttering cuss words.

Fortune pimped over to where Chip was standing. The pimp was an acquired walk he had worked hard to perfect, the ghetto swagger. But Fortune's was even more pronounced, since he also had a slight limp. As Chip watched him walk toward him, he wondered about how Fortune had got that way. No one knew, not even Ivan. That was a rarity, for everybody knew everything in the ghetto, or either they made it up.

A few years ago, Fortune had disappeared briefly, and not even Ivan knew where he was. When he had returned, he was afflicted, or " 'flicted," as they say. He wasn't even straight with Ivan about what had happened. Everybody asked, and depending on the day of the week or who wanted to know, Fortune had altered his story. One time he'd claimed that it was caused by a shot he got in a fight, and the next time he'd said that the foot got broken when he kicked somebody in the butt. Whatever the real deal was, eventually no one cared.

"Tha-thanks, Fortune. I, uh, appreciate it."

Fortune lit into Chip. "Don't. The only reason I looked out for you is because you're Ivan's little brother, and I don't like to see little punks like that get too big for their britches. But you just let these clowns play you all the time.

"Dag-on. What's wrong with you? You always got some book in your hands. Some old dusty-ass books ain't gonna teach you nothing about life. Ain't you figured that out yet? You best put that shit down and get real. You best be learning how to deal with these cats out here. Or else you'll be living the rest of your life being stepped on. And trust me, the older you get, the bigger the foot gets that steps on you." Fortune mashed his holey shoe on the ground to accentuate his point, and cussed as he stepped squarely into Calvin's fresh wad of spit.

"But I'm too little to be fighting—"

"Just because you little don't mean you can't have heart. You dig?"

"You know what, Fortune?" Chip said, and then paused. Fingering the frayed edges of his book, he looked away. "Never mind."

Chip turned his back to Fortune and sulked. Fortune had a lot of nerve, always instigating something that usually got either him or Ivan in trouble. Fortune really got on his nerves, but Chip was afraid of him. He hated to see Fortune coming, pimping and putting him down. It was that pimp walk that Chip really disliked, the way that Fortune slinked around to intimidate people.

Seeing Fortune do some wild things, and hearing about him doing even more, really irked Chip. Yet even today's act of tripping Calvin surpassed anything Chip had seen Fortune do to date.

"Oh, I know you not trying to break bad with me. I'm not the one that was all in your face. Don't you know nothing about ghetto etiquette? You don't never let nobody get the best of you. You always get the best of them, so they have to give you your props. That's a given. Even if they don't like you, 'least they respect you. Not like that little clown. I can't believe that you let that nigger roach-talk about your momma like that. You don't never do that," Fortune said.

Everybody in the ghetto had a mother, even Fortune. And it seemed that every time Calvin couldn't think of anything else to crack on him about, he'd say something about Chip's mother. That happened at least once a week, while Chip's nose was either meeting Calvin's fist or when a rock whizzed by his head.

"I, uh, I was getting ready to say something to him," Chip said, clutching his precious book. "But he ran away. Plus, I get sick of always fighting with him."

"Well, sick best get well. You ought to be tired of having folks wolfing in your face all the time. Chumpin' you. You know your daddy don't like that little punk stuff. You better learn how to defend yourself. Don't nothing shut nobody up like a fat lip." Fortune uppercut with his right hand.

He lit a partially smoked cigarette and puffed. At age twelve, Fortune had mastered the art of survival, and was gaining a hardcore reputation around the way. With his swaggered walk and hip, broken street slang, he was a hoodlum ahead of his time, the epitome of the ghetto man-child to be feared. Chip's father couldn't stand Fortune, and made no secret that he felt Fortune was a bad influence on Ivan. He did all he could to prevent Ivan from walking, or limping, down that same path.

As the smoke billowed, Chip got nervous, and motioned toward his father, who was still engrossed in coaching Ivan. "You better put that out, Fortune. My father might see you smoking, and you know he'll come over here. And you know he doesn't like that." Or you, for that matter, Chip thought.

Fortune dragged on the cigarette butt, and smirked through his characteristic chapped lips. "You said the right word, little dude. *Your* dad. Not mines. I do what I want, when I want. You the one that's got to worry about him breaking his foot off in your ass, not me. But one thing's for damned sure: he may not like me, but he knows I ain't no punk. And I know he don't want one living up under his roof."

Chip had learned early in life to abide by his father's wishes. His father wasn't a violent man, but when he said something, he meant it, and he would not hesitate to whip out his belt and put a hurting on him or Ivan. A hurting that could be felt for days. "Yeah, well, you might want to put that away before he notices. And don't blow any smoke on me. I don't want to get in trouble for smelling like that. Plus, I don't really care what you say, Fortune. I haven't had to fight anyone yet, and I'm not going to start now."

Fortune laughed again, as he rubbed the ashes off the used cigarette onto the bottom of his holey shoe, a trick used to preserve the cigarette. He was clearly unashamed that his shoes were worn thin.

"I'm just tryin' to hook you up, but you're just a trip. You always somewhere trying to think about something. But that don't work all the time. It's like you ain't even from 'round here. Like you from another planet or something. You better act like you know. Boy, I'm telling you, these streets is gonna eat you up, 'cause you gonna be too damned scared about what your daddy say. These muh hunchies around here don't care nothing about what your daddy say. He ain't gonna fight your battles for you. Shoot, they kick his ass too." Fortune swung his windbreaker open and revealed a knife stuck down in the waist of his pants. "This the only thing that's gonna make somebody listen. This tells the punks real quick, 'Don't start none, won't be none.' You best toughen up, or you is gonna get your ass kicked every day the sun rise."

Chip's jaws tightened, and he gritted on Fortune. The grit was the equivalent of staring someone down, and not dignifying him with a response. Your look did the talking. Fortune's words stung him, but he couldn't let on. He dreaded this game—an advanced version of the mind games he played with Calvin—in which Fortune would put him down because of his size or lack of street smarts. But Chip didn't like to match wits with Fortune. He was too sharp, so Chip just sucked it up.

"That may be how you make it, but I'm not. I know that you're a real bad dude, but I'm going to be smart one day, you'll see. And I'll be okay."

"All right, Thurgood Marshall, Junior. Whatever you say. But you should take my advice, shorty. Books is okay, but knowing the streets is what's gonna make you survive. And since you can't play no ball like Ivan, you best get some skills you can use. You'll see. You could learn a lot from me." Fortune laughed again, and began pimping away. With his tattered, oversized jacket swinging in the wind, he shrugged Chip off. Fortune flashed the peace sign. "Tell Ivan I'll get up with him later."

Chip sucked his teeth as he watched Fortune strut away. Chip felt a mix of fear, envy, and relief at his departure, his words echoing in his ears, and it angered him that Fortune was right. Chip feared Fortune's anger and devil-may-care attitude, yet he envied Fortune's freedom. His freedom to cut class and to do what he wanted to do. In all the time he'd known him, he never seemed pressed about anything. No rules. Nothing. Chip could only imagine how sweet that must be.

His father had rules for everything. Rules for getting up in the morning. Rules for coming home in the afternoon. Because they had no mother, Chip and Ivan shared chores, but Chip usually got stuck with the most; Ivan was not above flexing his big-brother muscles when necessary. And Fortune would come over, put his feet up and create a mess, and conveniently leave just before his father got home. Chip had become accustomed to the fire drills required to keep their dad off their backs.

Being the youngest son of Gerald Baxter and his late wife, Elizabeth, Chip had a difficult time coming of age. There were no hard-and-fast rules for the lone bookworm in a sports-loving family, especially at a time when little boys were expected to be rough and tough, even downright obnoxious. He was none of the above. He just didn't fit in.

Leaning on the fence and staring out at his meager surroundings, Chip felt a deepening sense of despair. Rusty chain-link fences, broken beer bottles, and crushed cans were strewn over the raggedy playground. Basketball hoops were absent of nets. In Shaw, toughness and athleticism ruled the streets, yet Chip wanted more, much more.

On his block, there was no such thing as scholars, only hustlers. Cats gained fame for being bad and thorough, taking no mess from no one. But Chip was an anomaly. He didn't act up to be one of the gang, and was subjected to the wrath of Calvin and others like him. At home it wasn't much better.

He was relieved that Fortune had left before he'd gotten him into trouble with his father. That was Fortune's gift. He had a knack for getting everybody else in trouble, and he'd slither away scot-free. It was the main reason Chip didn't like him very much. That and the fact that Fortune always called him a goody two-

shoes or an Oreo. Chip knew better than that. He knew he had resolve. He knew that hidden behind his meek facade was a mighty
tough skin. A skin tough enough to make it out of Shaw, without
having to be like Fortune.

"JUST POSITION YOUR fingers on the seams of the ball, son, and
let it spin off your tips. That's how the pros do it. Just like Wilt
and Bill. Bend your knees and relax. Put a backspin on the ball,
and just arch it. Come on now, you can do it. You've done it a
thousand times." There was a slight edge in Ivan's father's voice,
and a strained look on his face. It served notice: *Don't keep screw-
ing up.*

Ivan toed the faded free throw line, anxiously churning his
father's advice repeatedly in his mind. He caught a glimpse of
Chip's anxious face in his peripheral vision, and he sighed. He had
already missed six baskets in a row, and he could tell his father's
patience was wearing thin. If he blew it again, he could predict his
father's reaction. His eyes would roll up to the sky, then he'd shake
his head in disgust and start cursing under his breath.

His father was a good man, especially in a time when fathers
were scarce. But patience had never been one of his strong suits.
Reared in a time when black men had to hold their tongues and
bow their heads in order to survive, when it came to family, Gerald Baxter's tolerance was all but used up.

A short fuse ignited every time he slipped behind the wheel of
his cab, especially when he had to drive Mr. Charlie to the private
clubs that still didn't allow blacks in the front door. To the businesses where he hadn't been allowed to work, even though he was
just as smart as they were. It was expected that he transport these
folks day in and day out, tempering his anger at the cards life had
dealt him. It was a constant reminder for him, a constant pain to
endure. A pain he had no problem heaping on his family.

Chip crossed his fingers, and Ivan twirled the ball and prayed.
He wanted to finish this practice session so that they both could go
home and escape the falling darkness, which made it difficult for
Ivan to see the basket's rim. Only one dim streetlight shone near

the court, and it emitted as much illumination as a flashlight with a weak battery. Ivan had to practice in the evening because his dad drove a cab and was late getting home. He and Chip were forbidden to leave the apartment when he wasn't there. It just wasn't safe on the street for two young boys, and he didn't want them to get into trouble. Their entire social existence consisted of nosy Mrs. Owens from down the hall, and Fortune.

Gripping the ball in his sweaty palms, Ivan fondled it gently, then sank his free throws. On that muggy August evening, in his thirteenth year on this earth, Ivan knew that he'd make it. He grinned brightly and glanced over to Chip, and flashed the peace sign. It was a victory of sorts for Ivan, especially in Shaw, where every day was either feast or famine. On a clear, windy day, you could still smell H Street going up in smoke and flames. If Ivan could master this game, he could get the hell out of Shaw, before the hell in Shaw got him.

Feeling like he needed to prove something to the rest of the world—the "world" being the cats from Seventh and T, and the others who thought he couldn't hang—Ivan was extremely determined. They had called Ivan an L-7 square since the streets hadn't turned him out. He might not be a great student, but he wasn't a dummy either. He wasn't the ball-bouncing dumb jock that stereotypically ruled the b-ball courts and failed miserably in the classroom. Ivan was different, thanks to the iron hand of his father. His dad was a strong presence that overrode the lure of the streets, and encouraged Ivan to achieve in spite of the obvious pitfalls. Plus, Ivan had the overwhelming advantage of having Chip as his biggest fan. The three-year age difference wasn't that great, but since Ivan was nearly a teenager and Chip was still just a little kid, it was the difference between being cool and being a pest. But they spent a lot of time together, and whether they were doing chores or just hanging out, Chip loved to be in the company of Ivan, and even Ivan didn't find being around Chip too tough.

EARLY THE NEXT morning, Gerald Baxter had his sons in the alley behind their apartment building washing his cab. As the two boys sloshed around in the water, spreading soap bubbles across the hood of the yellow cab, Ivan shoved a brush at Chip.

"It's your turn to do the rims," he said, scooping a cupful of suds and tossing them onto the ground.

"Why do I always have to do the rims?" Chip asked as he kneeled down on the damp asphalt, getting his Toughskins wet.

" 'Cause you're closest to the ground." Ivan dipped a towel into the bucket and slung it onto the hood of the cab.

"I guess I'll always be the smallest. You know, I get tired of folks always picking on me, Ivan."

Ivan vigorously scrubbed some baked-on bird droppings and kept washing. "It won't always be like that. You'll get bigger, you'll see. And until then, if someone bigger than you gets up in your face, you come get me. Me or Fortune."

"Yeah, right. I'd get you, but not him. Shoot, he always picks on me too. Why does he always mess with me so much?"

"Oh, he's just jivin'. He really digs you. He has to. You're my little brother."

"Yeah, but you're his friend, not me. I know he's cool and everything, and so are you, but he scares me sometimes."

"Well, don't be scared of Fortune. He's just buck-wild like that. But he's good people. Don't sweat it. You know I'll always look out for you." Ivan took some suds and flung them onto Chip's head.

"Stop it, Ivan. That's not funny." Chip giggled as he brushed the foam from his brow. "I know you'll look out for me, but sometimes I just wish it wasn't so hard."

They kept washing, the subject matter turning a little mellow. Chip felt good knowing that Ivan was there for him, but something was missing: his mother and father. The sole purpose of their father's life was to get Ivan's basketball game together, and Chip often felt alienated and alone. Their father had big dreams of Ivan going to college, and Chip tried to understand his devotion. After all, he wanted to see Ivan succeed too. But for a motherless, misunderstood child feeling unwanted and unloved, it offered little solace.

"Don't sweat it, Chip. You'll be okay. Just wait and see."

"I guess. But you know what I mean. You can say that, but you don't have anything to worry about. You got looks, and you're athletic, and you're tall. Look at me. I'm none of those things. I can't even dribble and walk at the same time. Plus, Dad loves you. He doesn't even like me."

Ivan laid his towel on the cab and kneeled down beside Chip. "Don't say stuff like that, Chip. Dad loves you. You look too much like Mom for him not to."

"Sometimes I think that's why he doesn't like me. Maybe I remind him of her too much."

Ivan shrugged. "Quit trippin'. And don't be worried about playing ball. Everybody's not supposed to be able to do that. I'd have too much competition." He winked at Chip. "It's hip to be smart. And if anybody ever tells you otherwise, tell them to come see me. Now, get back to washing so I can get down to the court."

A FEW YEARS flew by, and Chip watched in awe as Ivan hustled and practiced, honing his skills. His game gradually went from good to outta sight, and he grew taller, leaner, and meaner. Chip even got in the game, sort of, and helped by being the ball boy and keeping Ivan's stats.

Over time, Chip grew comfortable growing up in Ivan's shadow, and despite their age difference, they were friends. Many older brothers played their younger brothers off, but not Ivan. He took time with Chip. He always made him feel special.

He also made sure that Chip knew about their mother. Ivan eventually told Chip the real story of how she died. The topic was taboo in their household, until Ivan broke the silence when he felt that Chip was old enough to understand.

One warm Saturday morning in October, he and Ivan snuck off for the first time without telling their father. Swearing Chip to secrecy, Ivan didn't even tell him where they were going; they just got on the bus and headed across town. On the way, with Chip

nervous about taking his first bus ride, Ivan told him all about
their mother, and he hung on to every word.

"You know what, Chip? I always had a lot to tell you about
Mom, but I wanted to wait until you were a little older. Plus, I figured that Pop would never tell you anything about her.

"She was really cool. And believe it or not, I remember a lot
about her. She was strong and really creative. She was kind of
ahead of her time, you know? Back when we were really small, did
you know she was part of the civil rights movement?" Ivan paused
and looked at Chip with a quizzical expression.

Over the years, Chip had pieced together the fragments of his
mother's life from the bits and pieces Ivan had shared with him
then. But Ivan had never provided so many details before. Chip
had a million questions he'd never felt comfortable asking. "Yeah,
I kind of knew," Chip said quietly.

"Well, she was the joint. And she really knew how to make Dad
do a lot too. Boy, you should've seen him around her. He used to
smile a whole lot, and they loved to laugh. I think I even saw them
dancing and listening to music too.

"But Dad didn't want her to actually go down South. I'm pretty
sure that they used to send money and stuff to support Dr. King,
and he was cool with that, but they had it out about her going
down South. But she didn't let up until he let her travel to Al-
abama, I think, to be in one of those demonstrations. When she
came back, she was really fired up about it. She'd seen the dogs
biting, and the firemen's hoses on people, but she was fine. She
even worked here as part of the movement, and Dad was real
proud of her."

"Wow," Chip said, his eyes wide in amazement. The thrill of
his first bus ride paled in comparison with Ivan's story.

"So, when she wanted to go back, he was okay with it. She was
going to be a Freedom Rider. Midway through her first trip, she
and two other bus riders were killed. Though the official report
was a automobile accident, it was just a coverup."

"How—how do you know? Who said something? Wh-why

didn't somebody do something about it?" Chip tugged on Ivan's sleeve, as the other passengers glanced in their direction.

"Shhh, Chip. Be quiet." Ivan's eyes darted around the bus, and he lowered his voice. "I heard Dad talking to someone on the phone a few days after Mom's funeral, a man who had been on the bus with her. And I overheard Dad saying that it wasn't an accident. That a car full of rednecks had run the bus off the road. When the man had tried to tell the police about it, they didn't even investigate it." Ivan dropped his eyes and turned away.

Chip could tell that it bothered Ivan, and now he felt overwhelmed with confusion. "But why didn't Dad ever do anything about it? Why didn't he?"

Before Ivan answered, he yanked the cord to signal the bell. "Come on, Chip. This is our stop."

When they stepped off the bus, they stood in front of Fort Lincoln Cemetery, where their mother was buried. They walked silently over to their mother's grave. Ivan whipped out a penlight.

"What are you going to do with that?" Chip asked.

Ivan hit a button on the bottom, and a razor-sharp switchblade popped out. He plucked a blade of grass and swiftly sliced it with the knife in midair.

"Aww, you're going to get in trouble. What if Dad sees you with that?"

"He won't," Ivan said as he leaned down to their mother's grave. He took the blade and trimmed the overgrown grass from around the headstone. "He'll think it's just a light. And you won't tell him the real deal."

Chip picked up the clippings and admired the way the grass now surrounded the marker. It was neat and even. "You know I won't, Ivan. That's really neat."

"Yeah, I got it from Fortune. Anyway, what you asked me about earlier—I think that when Mom died, Dad was just, well, his heart was broken. So was mine. You were too young, but it really hurt. And I know you miss her like I do. And I wanted you to know more about her."

"Well, gee. Why doesn't he ever talk about her? Why does he

make me feel like we can't talk about her?" Tears welled in Chip's big brown eyes, but he choked them back.

Ivan rubbed Chip's head, and hunched his shoulders. "It's just his way, that's all. I know he loved her so much, but I just think that's how he is. And I think that's why he treats us the way he does. He wants us to be tough, and I guess he doesn't know any other way."

"Yeah, but it's not that easy. Sometimes I feel like he can't stand me. Like he's disappointed in me, just for being me."

"I don't think so, Chip. Remember a long time ago I told you that you look a lot like Mom? Well, you do. I know you remind Dad more of her than I do, and that might make him sad sometimes, but that's probably good too. With you around, it's like she'll always be around too."

"And that's good? I feel like I'm being punished because of it. He makes me feel bad because I'm not good at sports, and because I'm just a shrimp. I can tell."

Ivan sighed and continued cleaning the now immaculate grave. "Well, you just have to believe me. I know you'll be all right. It may be rough now, but it'll get better." His face brightened and he added, "Plus, I remember hearing Mom say that the boys on her side of the family are late bloomers. So, since you took after her, maybe you're going to wake up one morning and be bigger than me." He grabbed Chip by the neck and put him in a mock wrestling hold. "Naw, I doubt it."

Chip felt better knowing that he and Ivan shared a common feeling of loss regarding their mother, and the anger at being unable to mourn properly. Even though their dad would chauffeur them out to the cemetery on her birthday and Mother's Day, dressed in their Sunday best, all they were allowed to do was say a prayer and leave flowers for her. That's what made the first and all of the subsequent trips to the cemetery Ivan and Chip took by themselves so special. It was their time. Their time to be with their mom, and their time to talk.

Though Ivan tried to fill the void, in the lack of an emotional outlet for Chip was the seed of an illness that plagues so many black men. The burial of emotions. The denial of feelings. It causes so much internal damage that they usually suffer from irreparable injuries without ever knowing it. Chip tried to fill the deep, gaping hole left by their mother's absence with books, while Ivan tried with basketball.

But discounting feelings was only one of the many spoken and unspoken rules in the Baxter household. Although their father kept a tight rein on them, Ivan got bold in his teenage years. He was getting streetwise, and enjoying his good looks and coolness. He even showed Chip a thing or two about life.

Things like three-card monte, shooting dice, and being hip. He schooled Chip about the things that went on in the big Ford Econoline vans that had the airbrushed murals on the side. Things that only a big brother could teach. Invaluable lessons that Chip never forgot.

They shared a close bond that consisted of mutual admiration, respect, and trust. Although Chip didn't completely understand it at the time, Ivan respected his book smarts. He didn't laugh at his clumsiness or when Chip cried out in the night because of bad dreams. Ivan encouraged him to be smart and even told him it was cool to want to grow up and be somebody. He taught him that it was okay to be different. That's what Chip loved about him. He was always there for him.

And Chip was there for Ivan as he became more worldly and mature. Ivan became more and more adept with his knife, often imitating the slick, knife-wielding Superfly or The Mack. Even though he was a good ballplayer, he wanted something more to made him look and feel bad. When he flashed the knife on the courts, some of the tougher dudes stopped calling him an L-7. The bigger bonus was that he could carry it right in front of their father, and he'd never be the wiser. It was their little inside joke, and after the initial apprehension wore off, Chip loved to see Ivan imitate the macho John Shaft with it. Chip had to admit, Ivan did look tough with a knife.

Chip adored Ivan and his growing popularity. He was everything that Chip hoped to be one day: cool, confident, and charming. Although they were different pages of the same book, together they made sense. Chip gained a real sense of confidence and determination from Ivan. Enough to not bother him about any more silly nightmares, especially the night before the championship game. Chip was so fired up about Ivan's big game, he really didn't pay much attention to the dream. Not like before. When he woke up and heard Ivan snoring below him, he smiled. For the first time in his life, he felt he could go back to sleep without one of Ivan's pep talks. It was a good feeling. Chip was finally growing up, and he had his big brother to thank for it.

CHAPTER 2

CARDONZA High's gymnasium was filled with a raucous, rowdy crowd. Just a few moments before, the standing-room-only hordes of fans had been hushed. The bleachers hadn't even creaked, as it seemed no one wanted to disturb the silence by drawing a breath.

Ivan had won the city championship for the school when he sank two free throws with seven seconds left in the game. Folks went wild, jumping from the bleachers when the buzzer rang. Cardonza had won its first championship in over fifteen years. The school was long overdue to throw down.

The security guards, frustrated at trying to contain the revelers, quit trying to clear the floor for the presentation of the trophies. Even Gerald Baxter could barely contain himself as Mayor Simon Blake presented Ivan with the MVP trophy. The mayor half-heartedly tried to quiet the crowd, but then pumped them up by declaring it a day of victory for Cardonza. The gym roared glee-fully as he yelled the names of Coach Simms and the basketball team into the scratchy microphone. A lump rose in Chip's throat as he proudly watched Ivan beaming under his mighty Afro, the same Afro that Chip watched him pick and shape meticulously for at least a half hour every morning. Funny, tonight it looked bigger and better than it ever had before.

It was a day of sorely missed pride in Shaw. Ivan was a real hero, and carried himself like a real pro. He had scored calmly and coolly, proving that all of those hours of practice had paid off royally. *Swoosh,* all net. With one shot, he had clinched that elusive scholarship, his ticket to escape from the troubled streets of D.C. to the safety of the little college down in Winston-Salem, North Carolina. He had survived. As Chip watched him in his crowning moment, he knew that Ivan was on the brink of making it. All he had to do was walk across the stage and collect his diploma. That would be another major accomplishment, and June would be here before Chip knew it. The light could be seen shining brightly at the end of the tunnel, and from the look on Ivan's face, it must've felt really good. He wasn't a statistic, and he was riding high.

"Eye on You" and "Eyes on the Prize" posters were being waved by every available hand. Everyone wanted to congratulate the star, from Mayor Blake, who mainly showed up in the neighborhood around election time, to Mrs. Marshall, who owned the corner store where everyone hung out after school. She was a big, warm, friendly woman who still spoke in a thick Southern dialect, even though she had left the South many years earlier. Mrs. Marshall was a generous woman who loved gossip and boys she deemed good, and she always gave Ivan and some of his boys free fried-fish sandwiches on Fridays, and cherished him as one of her special boys.

Ivan's friend Max and his teammates hoisted Ivan up on their shoulders so that he could cut down the net. As a boom box filled the air with Parliament's "Knee Deep," the crowd rocked and swayed with joy. Ivan was headed for the big time. He would be one of the few neighborhood kids and the first Baxter to go off to college. The dream was at last becoming a reality.

Their father was speechless, and Chip was stunned over his inability to talk. Gerald Baxter was never one to bite his tongue, and now he was just stymied, with a sheepish look on his face as he and

Chip moved onto the court to embrace Ivan. They both grabbed him from every angle, and uttered words of praise for their star.

Ivan's main squeeze, Stacey, came running over, with her long leather trench dragging on the floor behind her. She was really foxy, even Chip could tell that. "Oh, Ivan," she cooed, reaching for him.

Chip and his father reluctantly relinquished their collective grip on Ivan as Stacey bogarted in and kissed his sweaty face. He hugged her, and wiped the joyful tears from his eyes.

"YOU DID SO great. You were wonderful," Stacey said as her good girlfriend Gail stood behind her. Gail was Max's girlfriend, and the four of them usually hung out together. Gail nodded, then dashed off looking for Max.

"Thanks, sweet thing," Ivan said without a second thought. Normally, he would've never let his dad hear him speak so casually, but tonight he didn't care. Tonight was *his* night. His father didn't notice; he was too busy shaking hands and beaming from ear to ear.

Stacey pulled Ivan closer to her, oblivious to his sweaty uniform. She grabbed him like he liked, like he was her man. She whispered deeply in his ear, dampening her red lips with his salty sweat.

"I'm so proud of you, Ivan. You played your butt off tonight. Umph, umph, um." She shook her head in admiration. "You are just too much for words, boy. I can't wait to see you later. You know I have something very special for you," she said, licking her lips seductively.

Ivan's body tingled. He loved Stacey's dirty drawers. She was fine, foxy, and shaped like a brick house. She made him laugh, and he could talk to her about anything. They'd been going together since junior high. After several years of celibacy and saying no, Stacey had finally given in to his constant cravings after Fortune had loaned him the money to buy her one of those flashy mood rings. That night of passion had opened a door that had been blown off its hinges, and every opportunity they had, they ventured through that doorway. Many an afternoon they had coaxed Chip into play-

ing lookout on the fire escape, to warn them if he saw their father's
cab careening around the corner. Despite Chip's best efforts, they
had nearly got caught a couple of times.

They had quickly discovered the beauty and physical gratification of making love. Stacey, quite athletic herself, readily met Ivan's
constant cravings. One afternoon, with Chaka Khan and Rufus
playing softly in the background, they had a serious pillow talk.
Stacey loved Ivan with all of her heart, but she was focused, and
had dreams of her own, and they did not immediately include
having children. They had even talked about her going to North
Carolina with him. She was slightly afraid that Ivan would go down
there and meet somebody else, but she wasn't too worried. Those
little country girls had nothing on her. But for now, they had to be
careful. She even made sure Ivan used protection whenever they
were together.

"Oh yeah, tonight," Ivan whispered. "Your folks are still gonna
be out of town, right?"

"Yeah, we'll have the place all to ourselves because Skip and
Benny won't be around either. But they know what's up. They're
cool," she said, sliding her hands down his firm butt. "After the
party, we'll really celebrate." She pressed her soft body against Ivan's
groin, and his nature rose.

Ivan spotted his father over Stacey's shoulder, and abruptly
stopped hugging her, and she drifted from his arms. Kissing her
forehead, he uttered, "Solid. I can't wait for later."

"I know that's right," she said in a way that gave him goose
bumps.

Stacey and Gail volunteered to help Ivan's dad prepare for the
party. No one could get over the fact that he'd actually offered to
have guests over to their house. It was something that had never
happened before, and everyone was looking forward to it. Ivan
looked down and caught Chip's eye and grinned. As Ivan handed
his MVP trophy to his father, he knuckled Chip's head and draped
the basketball net over his little shoulders.

"That was dy-no-mite, Ivan. Dynomite!" Chip said, clinging to
his sweaty uniform.

"Cool, Chip. Cool. Now, let me boogie. I'll be home in a few."
He flipped Chip the peace sign and he ran off to the locker room.

IN THE LOCKER room, Coach Simms grabbed Ivan's shoulders
and shook them forcefully. "I'm so proud of you, son. You struggled every day, but you made it. You worked hard, and I'm just so
proud of you."

"Th-thanks, Coach. I owe you a lot too," Ivan said, blushing
slightly.

"You don't owe me anything. I never had any disciplinary problems with you, you're mindful, and you don't cuss. Well, at least
not that much. I knew you'd make it." He stared Ivan straight in
the eye. "I knew you'd do the right thing."

Ivan could only grin, a lump lodged deep in his throat. He
knew that Coach Simms had taught many talented boys, but most
had descended into bitter disappointment. Either they'd become
kings of the playground courts, been carted off to jail, or, worse
yet, killed in their prime.

"I got high hopes for you, Ivan. I know you'll go on, but you
won't forget where you came from. Just keep your head up, and
don't let nobody steer you wrong. And I mean nobody. Especially that criminal-minded Fortune. I know you're not perfect,
but you're about as straight as he is crooked."

"Thanks, Coach. I really appreciate it," Ivan said as he looked
down bashfully. "I know you mean well, but you don't understand. Fortune's really all right. He's like my brother."

Just like his dad, Coach didn't condone his friendship with Fortune. But that was minor. Ivan always knew he could count on
Coach, and even though he and his teammates sometimes gave
him hell, Coach took it all in stride. He'd been a true friend to
Ivan, and even his father liked him. It was Simms who had hooked
him up with Coach Wilcox down in Winston-Salem. Wilcox had
offered Ivan a full scholarship. Coach even went with Ivan, his father, and Chip for the exploratory visit. Even though Fortune had
been kicked out of school, and was told never to set foot on school

property, Coach still let him hang around at some of the practices. He did it as a favor to Ivan, but he had one condition: no monkey business. No hustling or recruiting, or acting a fool.

"I know him good enough, Ivan. He's about a half a step away from being like his brother Al. Just a bad seed, caught up in evil. But he paid the price for all of that robbing and stealing. And look at Fortune. I know what he's doing. And you do too."

Coach tossed Ivan the game-winning ball. "Just remember what I said, Ivan. Fortune may be your friend, but you know he's not right. And one day, it's going to catch up on him. I just don't want it to catch up on you. On Judgment Day, you're the only one that's going to be standing there. He won't be nowhere around. You got that?"

Ivan nodded his head slowly. One of the players threw a dirty towel in Coach's face. "Hey, watch out there now," Coach said as he vigorously patted Ivan on the back. A proud look spread across his face. "Good job, son. Just hang in there a few more months, and you'll go as far as you want."

FORTUNE SLAPPED IVAN five as he stepped out of the locker room. "What it is, Ivan. You kicked some serious butt in that bad boy to-night. And to top that, you just made me a c-note fatter, blood." He was tall and cocky, sporting the latest fashion, an expensive-looking, bright red, Indian-style suede jacket. The fringes on his arm jiggled as he whipped out a stack of bills and flapped them in Ivan's face.

Unfazed by Fortune's extravagant gambling habits, Ivan bounced him his hard-earned basketball. "It figures, man. So, where's my cut? Break me off a piece of that bread. You know I'm a little short."

Fortune dribbled the ball and twirled it on his finger. "You too tall to always be so dag-on short. You best get your ass a real *j-o-b*."

Ivan swung a pick from his pocket and proceeded to puff out his Afro. He elbowed Fortune in the ribs and said, "You know, I can't hang with your kind of *j-o-b*. It ain't happening. Plus, I know I wouldn't be jack shit if you had just lost a hundred."

"Sho' you right! But that's cool. I got a little surprise for you."

Ivan feigned surprised. "For me? What, you got me one of these jackets?"

"Be for real. I promised I'd get you one, but not until you get outta your old man's eyesight. He'll never cut my threads up. Anyhow, I got me some wheels."

"What? You got a ride?" Ivan was genuinely surprised. "That is too funny. You never blow money on anything." Ivan laughed loudly.

"A ha-ha hell. I gotta good deal on a bad-ass burgundy Cutlass Supreme and couldn't pass it up."

"Well, then, the only thing I want to know is when I can take it for a spin."

They laughed heartily as Fortune grabbed Ivan's gym bag and they walked toward the door. "Come on, let's roll. I may let you drive it tonight if you're lucky. So come on. You know your old man broke down and is throwing you this party. He's got to welcome Dr. J home the right way.

"Yeah, him and—what's her name—yeah, hot-to-trot Mrs. Owens got it together. Maybe since you be leaving soon, he'll finally shack up with her. Break down and give her some." They cracked up at the fact that after all these years, his dad still called their neighbor, Mrs. Owens, by her surname whether they were alone or in front of folks. She'd been after his dad ever since Ivan could remember, but he'd never seemed really interested.

Wiping off a spot of talcum powder from his precious letterman's jacket, Ivan smirked at the notion of his father and Mrs. Owens messing around. That was just too much to imagine. After all, Ivan had barely gotten his first piece this year from Stacey. He just couldn't imagine his pop doing the do.

"Yeah, I'm telling you. She'd do just about anything for Pops, and he doesn't pay her no attention. I know he ain't knocking boots with her." Nose wrinkled in disgust, Ivan snickered loudly.

"You gotta lot of nerve." Fortune mockingly sniffed in Ivan's direction. "What's that I smell? Nigga, you still got milk on your breath, except it ain't dairy I smell. It's brand-new twat, and I can still smell it on you a mile away. Pe-yew."

Ivan playfully jabbed at his best friend. "Negro, please. Shut up, will you? I'm talking about my dad, not me. He don't play that. Man, I remember the time me and Stacey was up in the cut, coolin' out. You know, kind of like getting ready to get in the mix. He walked in on us and started throwing haymakers at me. Right in front of my girl."

"We all know yo poppa don't take no mess. But, hell, it wasn't like you was going to get nothin' anyhow," Fortune chided. "Nothin' but a hard johnson and a wet dream."

"You don't know jack," Ivan said, rolling his eyes.

FORTUNE DID KNOW that Ivan hadn't got laid until a short while ago. It wasn't that he couldn't, but Stacey wasn't giving it up, no matter how many Isley Brothers records they grinded to. Fortune had tried to coerce him into getting with a girl who would give it up, but Ivan was too chicken to screw anyone else. He was too afraid he'd get the clap, and then his father would really kick his ass.

Despite his fairly decent looks, chicks really weren't Fortune's forte. Yeah, he screwed them when his nuts talked to him, but he was careful, and always, always wore a jimmy. He figured that all they wanted was his money, and he wasn't giving that up, not the greenbacks. He wouldn't spend a dime on a bumper of malt liquor or for some coochie. He didn't care how good either one of them was.

Yet, despite his nonchalance, there was something really gnawing at Fortune. He couldn't relate to the father concept. Especially since he and his seven brothers and sisters all had many different ones, and knew none of them. He couldn't understand what it was like having a worrisome old man like Ivan's dad around. In Fortune's eyes, Ivan's dad was like the Grinch who stole Christmas, every day. He forced Ivan to do all kinds of dumb crap, and never gave him nothing but a hard time. He had to study and take care of Chip, and even do chores. That was some sissy stuff.

So, it was Fortune's duty to protect Ivan from his overbearing father, because if Ivan wasn't careful, he'd probably end up sweet or something. From Fortune's perspective, Ivan needed him in his life, just to be sure he wouldn't go soft.

As they approached the gym's exit doors, the mood changed from upbeat to melancholy. As happy as he was for Ivan, Fortune had the sudden realization that this was the last time they'd be waltzing through the doorway as running buddies. Even as Ivan rambled on about how hyped he was, Fortune was feeling pangs of discomfort.

Caught up in a world of his own, he barely heard Ivan's banter. Fortune was having a moment of his own. He was going to miss his good friend. Fact was, Ivan was more than a friend. He was a brother.

Looking off into the distance, Fortune turned serious for a moment and spoke to his lifelong friend. For as much bravado as he brandished, he was deeply affected by Ivan's pending departure.

"Man, you got it goin' on. It's all getting ready to bust loose for you. You'll be rolling with the hot sauce. In August, you'll be outta sight." There was enthusiasm in Fortune's words, but a hollowness in his tone that made Ivan look a little guilty.

"But it's cool," Fortune said softly. "Now that I got my ride, I'll be down there to check you out. Holler at you for a minute. Make sure the coons and crackers is treatin' you right."

DAMN, IT FEELS good, Ivan thought. Yet Fortune's sobering words brought his heady disposition back down to earth. This had been the moment he had prepared for all his life. To win. To be a winner. While this was a monumental feat and he was truly ready to move on, it dawned on him why Fortune sounded so melancholy.

"Fortune, I'm glad you're going to come down and see me. I don't want you to think that I'm gonna go off an' forget about you, man. You're like my brother, you know?"

"Yeah, I hear you."

"I'm serious as a heart attack. You've always looked out for me, and I appreciate it. But I'm not gonna lie. I'm kind of worried about you."

"What? What you talking about? You ain't got to be worried about me. You the one going down there in the sticks. You gonna be in some hillbilly-country hick town where they probably still wear high-water Levi's and shit."

"It's not about all that, Fortune, and you know it. We've been hanging ever since I can remember, and now things are going to change. We always had each other's backs, but we're going to be a little far apart to help each other out. You know what I'm saying?" Ivan stopped and stared at Fortune, who just shrugged.

"Whatever, man. I ain't scared of that. I'm a grown damned man, and I can take care of my damned self."

"Yeah, okay. But I'm telling you, I'm concerned because I know what's up. You're dealing, and these niggers out here are rough. I just don't want nothing to happen to you, that's all."

"I'm gonna be all right, Ivan. Believe that. You just do your thing."

As they walked together, they knew that already their lives had diverged. The bridge between their two worlds was getting longer and longer. The two had cast dual shadows since the fourth grade, when some kid wanted to beat Fortune up after calling his mother a welfare ho'. Fortune, wiry for his age, commenced to kick the boy's butt, as Ivan, putting down his ever-present basketball, joined in as two others tried to beat Fortune. Fast friends they became, both with a kindred spirit for survival.

Fortune fiended for money so much that the nickname stuck. "I'm gonna be rich. Big car. Get my momma off welfare. I'm gonna make a fortune," he said so often, folks started calling him that. The child born Fletcher Reed was now forever Fortune, and so the legend began.

Ivan and Fortune. So much alike, yet so different. As their shadows had grown and changed, so had their personalities. Fortune was a slick, street-smart kid, yet he could almost handle the ball as well as Ivan. For obvious reasons, their lives couldn't continue to parallel. Fortune was the fourth oldest of eight kids, who grew up in the violence-filled projects at Seventh and T. All of his older brothers had done a stint in jail by the time they had reached puberty. Al, the eldest, had been killed at the age of sixteen in a robbery gone bad. Fortune had managed to stay relatively clean until his ninth-grade year; then the seduction of the streets and the encouragement of his alcoholic mother finally got to him. Studying and adhering to Coach Simms's rules weren't an option for him. He didn't have an authority figure at home, and there was no way he'd ever listen to some old potbellied basketball coach. Running numbers and selling dime bags of weed were enough to hang a fine leather jacket on any poor boy's back, and quiet the loose change in his pockets with silent bills. The limp he had mysteriously acquired as a child was now even more menacing.

Ivan's father seriously disapproved of Ivan's close association with Fortune, but the childhood friendship had withstood the pressures and the tests of time.

"We have had some good times, haven't we, Ivan? Man, we had it going on." Fortune's lips spread in a sly grin, and he stroked his chin.

"You ain't never lied. Except for the times you got me in trouble, you chump."

Fortune fired up a cigarette, and gazed at the burning match before blowing it out. "You know you owe me. You would've never had no fun without me around. So don't get so high and mighty. Remember, I was the one that gave you your first jimmy and your first joint."

"You know you're wrong. You left out one key item. That joint almost made me jump out the damned window. I liked to lost my mind."

Fortune covered his mouth and laughed loudly. "Oh, snap. You would remember that. But I didn't know that thing was laced with dust. But that was too funny. Your ass really thought you was Superman and could fly."

"It wasn't funny then. You had me tossing my guts up at Wanda's house, and then like a fool, you had me crawl out the bathroom window and climb down the fire escape. Then you even left the door locked."

"Yeah, but I couldn't let everybody see you all fucked up like that. Boy, Wanda and them was mad as hell. They couldn't even use the john until somebody broke the damn door. But hey, I fixed that punk that gave me that shit, didn't I? I opened up a can of whup-ass on him·that he'll never forget. Even when he sees me today, his ass'll cross two streets to get away from me."

Ivan waved the cigarette smoke away from his face. "Uh-huh. Well, I guess I can also thank you for scaring me off drugs. I don't think I ever even thought about that again."

Fortune grinned and blew a huge smoke ring in Ivan's face. "Yeah, but that angel dust proved to be my ticket to ride. Weed's at a whole other level. And trust me, making goo-gobs of money ain't bad."

"Money ain't everything, Fortune. You got smarts. You could go to school, and get a good job. It might take a little while, but it can happen." Secretly, Ivan envied the flashy clothes and wads of cash Fortune had. But he knew that nothing in the drugstore would kill him quicker than if his father even thought he was selling drugs. Fortune was his friend, and despite everything that was new and exciting in the late seventies, good friends were still very hard to come by.

The championship was the evening's highlight, but Fortune had a way of getting in the spotlight too. His bright red jacket made heads turn. It had been a splurge, but it was worth it. Fortune's reputation had grown by leaps and bounds; he was making a name for himself as the man to go to for dust, one who was progressing up the ranks of the illicit corporate street structure. He had endeared himself to the bosses by aggressively working the streets and keeping his lips sealed and his eyes averted. The organization, headed by a mysterious figure known only as Moses, gave Fortune many opportunities to prove himself. He was quick, ruthless, and very bright, and he could run numbers in his head with the best of them. Fortune quickly went to the head of the class of the soaring number of intelligent brothers on the street whose textbooks and blackboards were the concrete sidewalks and corners that held their fate.

Turning to his friend now, he said, "Ivan, school ain't for everybody. And I don't have time for all that minimum-wage shit. I got a plan, and I'm making bank. I've even been thinking about getting my own crib in a few months."

"You're joking, right? I thought you said you'd never move out."

"I know, but I'm thinking about going into business for myself, so I got to get ready. It's cool living there, you know, but it's a little cramped. Plus, I don't want my folks getting into my stash, you know what I mean? Product is product, and I'm not trying to support nobody's habits.

"But I ain't about to leave Shaw. This is home, man. Where else can I treat a whole block of kids to the second-run movies down at the Lincoln Theater, or flag down the Good Humor truck, and let them buy all the Bomb Pops and choc-cows they want? Plus I get 'em young. Everybody knows me. Money's power, baby."

"And you have the power to do better. But that's on you."

It was on him. This was his turf, where he was exalted. Fortune was the man, and had the admiration of his peers, and the fear of many others who thought he was a wild boy. People now saw him differently. They noticed him from down the street, and made it a point to nod their heads and say, "What's up." He finally had their respect. No longer was he the skinny kid trying to shake off the shame of being dirty and poor. Just as Ivan had his world at his fingertips, so did Fortune. He was as ambitious as Ivan, just in a different way. He was not to be outshined by anyone, not even his best friend. He'd already figured out how to make his dreams come true. Fortune had cast the dice and set his plans in motion.

Just a peon in the game, he knew that he'd be promoted if he played his cards right. From a runner, he could get his own territory, and eventually have a crew working for him. He wanted the big-time. He'd gotten a taste of it, and that made him crave it even more. But it hadn't been coming fast enough. Long on nerve, yet short on patience, Fortune had expedited the process by methodically skimming both money and product. He wanted to accumulate just enough cash to buy a stash of weed and branch out on his own. Extremely crafty, he had squirreled away the stolen goods. It had only been a few months, but he had managed to take about three grand and an ounce of dust and reefer. But he had to play it cool. He couldn't move too fast. Right now, he was just a nickel-and-dime dealer, and he couldn't just pop up with a stake. It was too risky. He figured it would take about a year to get enough cash, at least twenty grand, and until then, he'd keep a low profile. As long as he kept his little secret, and continued to work hard for the organization, no one would ever notice.

Ivan signaled for the ball back, and tucked it under his arm. "But anyway, check it out. Don't forget you promised me one like this. Only I want a black one." Ivan toyed with the frills on Fortune's sleeves, and shouted over the honking horns of the cars and Metro buses on Florida Avenue, which heralded Cardonza's thrilling victory.

"I'm hip to what you saying, but you a greedy muh hunchy, ain't you? First you wanna drive my ride, now you want a jacket like mines. Ain't no thing. In fact, I tell you what. You can wear mines till I get yours, and I'll hang on to this one," Fortune said as he fingered Ivan's letterman's jacket.

"Nah, man, I don't know. Dad'll wear me out if he knew I took this off. Plus, he'd kill me for wearing yours. You know he can't stand that kind of stuff." He caressed the leather letter C that covered his heart.

"Uh-huh. Well, lookie here," Fortune said soothingly. "We'll just switch for tonight. Your old man is so happy and whatnot, he probably won't even notice."

Ivan shook his head, declining weakly.

Undaunted, Fortune conned on. "Dig it. We'll switch before we get to your crib. Cool? But you ain't drivin' my ride."

Fortune would never let Ivan know that for all the trash he talked, he'd gladly, even if only temporarily, shed his facade and become a gifted, celebrated athlete like Ivan. The momentary fix was cool, and Fortune enjoyed escaping into the fantasy. Even if it meant that he'd have to get it off before he got within Ivan's father's sight.

It didn't take much to convince Eye. It was a thrill to think about wearing the coat, especially on this, his most triumphant night. It was such a rush, almost as great as the first time he came. Almost.

As he slid his jacket off and slid Fortune's on, his body tingled. At that moment, he felt brand-new. He was a winner, and now he looked like one. No one would look at him and consider him a punk daddy's boy who could play ball. As hard as he pushed himself, he could never outshoot the shadows of not having a reputation on the street like Fortune's.

"Solid, Fortune."

"You know you my ace boon, Ivan."

They exchanged a few more lighthearted words, partners in crime riding high. This night was the stuff dreams were made of, and both were enjoying their moment of glory.

CHAPTER 3

B LINKY really regretted this part of the job. The boss always got so pissed, and usually reacted very swiftly and very violently to any threat to his domain. One of the street lieutenants, who Blinky thought was questionable, reported to him that one of the runners had been skimming money. According to the source, the runner was brazenly throwing it around, and had even talked trash about it. This young buck was trying to play the operation and the boss for a fool. Enemies had tried to get the best of Moses and failed. No one in his crew had ever tried this before, and it was incredible to think that somebody like this little punk would. Blinky normally wouldn't have bothered the boss with such trivial shit, but he knew that if Moses were to find out about it later, it would be his ass.

As he walked across the floor of the dimly lit room, he could see Moses, seated and staring out the window, gazing at the inner city he helped to infest with drugs. The city he considered his personal playground, and its residents his toys. Blinky's eyes started fluttering rapidly as he struggled to find the right words that wouldn't set his boss off.

"Speak, damn it. This had better be important," Moses said, the air turning to ice as he spoke. He drummed his long fingers on the desk. "There's a lot happening tonight, and you know that I don't like being interrupted. Especially on such short notice. Heaven help you if this is something you could have and should have taken care of yourself."

"I—I could've taken care of it, Moses, but I think that it's your call. The word's out. Too many people know the deal and are waiting for your take-down. Too—too many know about it. A street lieutenant reported that one of the boys been ripping you off. You know they want to see how you gonna handle it, and I didn't want to be the one to make the call."

Moses continued to stare out the window, ignoring Blinky. He remained silent, and it seemed as if hours passed as he deliberated. Blinky's pulse raced, and he gulped deep breaths to keep his heart rate down. He really hated this part of the business.

Finally speaking, ever so calmly, Moses inquired, "Who is it?" He hesitated, squinting as if he were making a mental scan of who might possibly be foolish enough to run a game on him. "Who is this roguish bastard? I can't imagine who in my crew would have the balls to try to play me for a fool."

Fidgeting, Blinky anticipated the worst. He knew Moses had a soft spot for the young hustlers. But the soft spot was for the young 'uns that showed him respect, not disrespect.

"It's that Fortune boy, Moses. But hear me out. Don't be too hard on 'em. He's just a young'un. The money's got too good to him, I guess. He probably just got a little big-headed, is all. I'm sure if you talked to him, brought him down a notch or two, he'd get his act together." Blinky, hardened like a callus over time, also still cared for the young boys under his care, but he knew the inevitable: Moses would be forced to retaliate, even though he knew the young buck posed no real threat. He had to prove a point. Moses had to protect his reputation for running his business with an iron fist.

His voice cool and lucid, betraying no emotion, Moses methodically began his dissection. "What's the damage? How long has this been going on? Exactly how many greenbacks are we talking about?" Very detail-oriented, he could be reasonable, to a certain degree. Moses wanted to know just how ballsy this little punk had been.

Blinky really hated reporting the degree of offense. No matter what, the punishment was usually the same: harsh. "Seems like for the past six months or so. It's around two, three grand."

Picking up a pen, Moses tapped it on the desk, his nostrils flaring. "Haste makes waste, and I've got to send the right message. I've got a reputation to protect. A man with no rep ain't shit, at least not in these circles. Moses is not to be fucked with."

He tapped the pen with a vengeance. "What's up? Is his mother sick or something? He need some extra cash? Or, let me guess. He just start using the product, right?"

Shaking his head no, Blinky blinked and stuttered. "No, no. Rumor has it he was trying to get his own thing started. Trying to be a player—"

Sticking his hand in the air, Moses cut him off abruptly.

"Ah, so I get it. He's just an enterprising little poor-ass ghetto bastard. Trying to screw me to get his. Ain't that some shit? You know, I had a feeling about him. We should've never let him in. He should've done that little job for us, and that should have been it. I always knew that he was just too damned hardheaded and thought he was just too damned smart. But I'm a whole lot fucking smarter, and have been for a whole lot longer. I'll show 'em. Nobody fucks with me and gets away with it."

Nodding in agreement, Blinky relented. There wasn't any point in arguing with Moses. He'd known him too long, and the point was moot. Instinctively, he moved toward the door. "So, what's the word, Moses?" No one tried to take Moses down without feeling the wrath. He earned his reputation by swinging low, and swinging high, and anyone challenging his position knew the outcome. "I just can't understand how he'd try to do what other, mightier foes have tried and failed. Maybe you could teach him a lesson—rough him up a little, help him to better understand the way we do things."

Moses stared through him so coldly that Blinky's eyes even stopped blinking. "Enough, Blinky. There's no shame to my game. You get somebody to take him down. And take him down hard."

"Moses, don-don't you think—"

"Just do it, Blinky. Quick and clean. Leave my calling card, so everybody'll know I mean business. This is no exception. I can't let him get over, or else everyone will want to try me. We got to let 'em know. Don't start none, won't be none. So, if the young buck wants some of me, well, give it to him. Let him now be known as Fortuneless or Unfortunate. And make sure everyone knows that'll happen to them if they try to cross me. Leave just enough of him so that the casket will be open, so I can be sure to pay my respects."

Lowering his head and turning the knob slowly, Blinky slinked through the doorway. "And shut the fuckin' door behind you," Moses said, his words slicing through the air like a knife.

CAREFULLY MANEUVERING HIS prized possession through the wading crowds, Fortune drove and Ivan waved and worked his charms on the many admirers who flocked to the car as it approached. Earth, Wind and Fire pumped on the stereo, and Ivan and Fortune rocked to the rhythm. The Cutlass with its bright chrome wheels was waxed to the max, glistened under the streetlights, reflecting in the eyes of the well-wishers. The whole neighborhood seemed to be out and about for the celebration. The inner-city championship had finally returned to the 'hood, and folks were proud to have taken it back from that siddity crosstown school.

Ivan, in the midst of all the celebrating, checked his watch. "Man, I, I mean *we,* better get on home. I ain't about to have Pops waiting with streamers and balloons, gettin' all fired up 'cause I'm still out here trippin'.'"

Fortune shook his head, ignoring Ivan and enjoying the revelry. "Boy, I can't believe on one of the biggest nights of your life, you still talkin' about your pops." Rolling his eyes, Fortune reluctantly slowed down and pulled over to the curb. He drifted down to the front of a corner store. "We right down the block from your house, Eye. Cool out. Just hold up a minute. I wanna get some smokes."

Fortune slipped out of the car and headed toward the store. "I tell you what. You in such a hurry, you go on. Drive it on down the block. But be careful."

Ivan grinned, and immediately leaped at the chance. Then he hesitated, and leaned out the window. "What about my jacket, blood?"

Fortune waved Ivan off. "Go on, boy. Quit trippin'. Leave your bag in the car, and I'll bring it in when I gets there. Or you could just wait for me."

Ivan quickly slid under the steering wheel. "Naw, that's all right. It's cool. I'll leave yours in here too."

"Whatever. I'll be there as soon as I get a few puffs in 'fore I get to your crib. I know your pops don't allow no smoke blowin' up in his prison—I mean sanctuary."

Jerking the car into gear, Ivan leaned on the armrest and cheesed. "Screw you, man. Just finish before you get there. And don't get that smoke all up in my jacket, either."

Fortune spit on the sidewalk and turned on his heels. Heading toward the store, he shouted back, "You want anything?"

Grinning, Ivan replied, "Yeah, and she's fine as wine and waiting for me at my house. But you can get me some more rubbers."

Ivan slowly drove the car down the block and took a few moments to parallel park behind his father's cab. It was kind of hard for him, since he hadn't had much practice.

At that precise moment, a black deuce and a quarter rounded the corner. The frills on Fortune's bright red jacket jiggled as Ivan manually adjusted the driver's-side mirror.

"Slow down! There he is! Ain't that his ride?" the rider in the passenger seat shouted to no one in particular. He quickly answered his own question. "Yeah, that's that showboatin' bastard."

The driver slowly eased up on the accelerator. The huge V-8

engine roared loudly, and the gears shifted down as they crept up on their target.

AT THE COUNTER, Fortune reached for his wallet. "Damn," he muttered when he realized he wasn't wearing his jacket, and he knew Ivan didn't have a dollar to his name. "Wait a minute, man," he said to the balding, elderly man behind the counter. "Hold them for me. I'll be right back. Got that, old man?"

The old man cursed aloud as the cash register *cha-chinged* with the purchase.

Hoping to catch Ivan, Fortune hustled out of the store.

PERCHED ON THE fire escape, Chip was anxiously awaiting Ivan's arrival. Chip had been up and down, looking and leaning, for what seemed to be hours since the game had ended. Knowing that Ivan was hanging out with Fortune, Chip had hoped he'd come home soon. The only thing moving was a car that someone was trying to park in front of the building. Chip was fearful that his father would get upset over the fact that Ivan hadn't yet arrived, and he cautiously looked into the apartment. Chip was pleasantly surprised to see his father and Stacey joking around.

As Chip turned back to the street, his heart jumped. He instantly recognized Ivan, even though he was wearing Fortune's jacket. Ivan had just slammed his car door shut and was walking around to the sidewalk. Chip was elated to see him, but confused about whose car he was driving. He quickly dismissed the feeling as he caught Ivan's wide, bright smile as he opened the passenger-side door. Chip could barely contain himself. Ivan looked up, saw him on the escape and waved, grinning broadly. It was the moment Chip had been waiting for, and he almost wanted to leap over the rail. Except he thought better. He was up two stories.

That moment in time was all that mattered. Ivan was his hero, long before anyone else had realized he was a hero. Chip's little chest swelled with pride, and he was euphoric. No longer able to restrain himself, he ran to the rail, and started gleefully yelling to his brother.

The window of an approaching black deuce and a quarter low-ered, just far enough for a gun barrel, and for two bloodshot eyes to peer out. The car was rolling down the street, and Chip tried to flag Ivan, who was waving to somebody up in one of the other apartments. Chip also spotted Fortune, who was wolf-whistling, trying to get Ivan's attention.

Fortune, usually suspicious, assumed that the car's slow ap-proach was just someone trying to holler at Ivan. It's just another well-wisher, he thought as he yelled and whistled, "Hey, Ivan!" Then his eye caught the gleaming gun barrel pointed at his best friend.

Chip also saw the big car pulling up and the gun barrel pointed at Ivan. Then he noticed Fortune, arms flailing, starting to sprint toward Ivan.

Running frantically, Fortune's feet barely touched the ground. As he moved, he mouthed words, but no sound came out. In slow motion the barrel cocked, a gloved finger on the trigger. Fortune's eyes bulged as if they would pop right out of the sockets. Ivan swung around with a grin on his face, oblivious to the peril that faced him. The barrel, aimed at the chest of that garish red jacket, emitted a flash, and it rang out rapidly.

"I-van!!" Chip shouted at the top of his lungs as the bullets fired out into the evening air. The crackling *pop-pop-pop* and rapid flashes of light made his heart leap to his mouth. They were sounds and sights he knew too well. Far too well.

Tears of shock and disbelief streamed down Fortune's face as he ran toward Ivan's convulsing body. As the crimson blood flowed onto the sidewalk, Fortune's heart stopped. Chip passed out, and the world faded to black as the loud Electra 225 sped off in a cloud of thick, black smoke.

THERE HADN'T BEEN a rainier day as far back as Chip could re-member. The day of the funeral, the heavens wept, just like nearly everyone in Shaw.

There were a few who seemed to relish the thought of a fallen hero. Either out of personal despair, regret, or just downright evilness. Lies were generated, and rumors swirled throughout the 'hood, circulating like wildfire. Each one was increasingly outrageous. Thugs whispered that Ivan was running drugs, just like Fortune. There were several different versions of that far-fetched tale. Someone swore that he'd seen Ivan selling drugs, and some even claimed to have bought from him. Chip quickly learned that the only thing better than a hero was one who had fallen from grace. One minute Ivan was the star, the next a slain common criminal. Ivan was unable to defend himself, and Chip was too young and too devastated to step up to the task.

The few people Chip knew didn't have much to say. There was just a lot of head-shaking, and "isn't it a shame"–type talk. Mrs. Marshall grabbed and smothered him with her bosom every time Chip dragged past her store. She and others who knew Ivan knew that he hadn't been messing around with drugs.

The truth would remain elusive as a shroud of uncertainty clouded Ivan's death. Just as Chip's father had lost his mother, he now had also lost Ivan to forces unknown. Forces who would more than likely also go unpunished. No one knew exactly who had killed Ivan, and no one seemed overly anxious to find out. All fingers pointed to the only one who did know, Fortune, and his whereabouts were as mysterious as the truth. No one had seen or heard from him, and most everyone believed that he was the one with the price on his head, not Ivan. It stood to reason that Fortune would be the cause of Ivan's downfall. Yet, too many questions remained unanswered. Why had Ivan been wearing Fortune's jacket? Had he been set up? The questions and lack of answers nearly drove Chip crazy, and caused his father to completely shut down. Chip also became more withdrawn, with the only person in his life he could ever talk to gone.

He found a surprising ally in Calvin, who was uncharacteristically sympathetic. On the afternoon before Ivan's funeral, Calvin shimmied up the fire escape and joined Chip, who was reading a book.

"Hey, Chip. I think it was pretty messed up what happened to your brother. Especially because of that damned Fortune."

Expecting a hassle, Chip shoved the book under the stair and said nothing.

Calvin leaned against the railing and pointed to the spot where Ivan was gunned down. "Is that where it happened?"

Chip nodded, and Calvin hawk-spit with precision accuracy, landing the loogie in the location where the white police chalk was now fading. The effort made Chip smile.

"I heard somebody said they saw Fortune down on Fourteenth Street, high and out of his mind, talking to himself, and still sporting Ivan's jacket. They say he stole some money from the wrong folks. It figures." Calvin took out a pack of Bubble Yum and offered it to Chip.

Chip hesitated, then took the gum. "I don't believe that. Fortune's not crazy. He's too smart for that. Knowing him, he probably took the money they said he stole and got out of Dodge. But he couldn't have gone far, since he's never been anywhere. He's never even left D.C., and even northern Virginia's like another country away. I swear if I ever see him again, I'll get him."

Blowing a huge pink bubble, Calvin offered Chip five. "And I'll help you. You know I can't stand him from way back in the day."

FOLKS CAUGHT CABS or piled in cars to get to the services. They were motivated either to pay their last respects, or to get an opportunity to gossip firsthand. Chip's father wanted a private funeral, but the throngs, spearheaded by Coach Simms, talked him out of it. Coach, a churchgoing deacon, wanted Ivan to have a proper homecoming, and after some sincere prodding, Gerald Baxter relented. But it had to be on his terms. He wanted the viewing and the funeral to be combined, and no repast after the burial. Coach Simms got his wish, but it was bittersweet. Ivan finally made it to his church, Shiloh Baptist, unfortunately under devastating circumstances.

The church was filled to capacity, standing room only. As the soloist sang some hymn that Chip barely heard, tears welled in his eyes but refused to fall. They burned his lids, feeling as if they were searing holes in the sockets.

Nestled between his dad and Mrs. Owens, Chip sat stiffly, still in a state of shock. He felt like he was a spectacle on display, sitting uncomfortably on the first pew in a church that he'd never been in before. The oversized black suit he wore and the shoes that dangled from his heels served only to make him more miserable. The tears continued to burn and a knot rose in his throat from the words crying out from within, yet nothing happened. He wanted to scream, to cry, but his tongue was thick and his mouth was dry and cottony. Sounds were muted, voices clouded. He could barely hear his father mumbling for him to be strong. He was too distraught not to try like Ivan would've wanted him to.

His father took his own advice, and sat like a stone statue. Not a tear or an expression of sorrow crossed his face. Even as Coach Simms choked up and openly wept during the eulogy, Chip's dad showed no signs of emotion. Chip was dumbfounded. Steadfast and stoic, his father's body was present, but there was no sign of life. Mentally or physically.

As Chip tried to digest what was going on with his father, he heard a murmur that pierced his pain-induced deafness. It was Stacey, as she unsteadily walked down to Ivan's casket. Her mascara was streaked, and she held a bunch of carnations. She was sniffing and weeping more loudly with every step.

Chip had almost forgotten about her. Over the course of the week, when Coach Simms was planning the services, Chip couldn't recall if Coach had even talked to her. The phone at their house had rung off the hook, and his father had refused to answer it. Most of the calls were from reporters wanting to run a human-interest story, from the sensational to the mundane, and his father was not participating.

Weeping quietly at the casket, Stacey trembled as the tears streamed down her slack cheeks. Placing red carnations into Ivan's hands, she swayed back and forth, speaking softly under her breath.

She was having her own private, final conversation with Ivan. Out of respect, the funeral director held everyone else back. She was draped over the coffin for what seemed to be an eternity, until one of her brothers finally came up to get her. Almost afraid to interrupt her, he whispered something, and she took his arm as he slowly led her away from the casket. After taking a few steps, she stopped abruptly and then collapsed. Her brother carried her back to their pew as the white-uniformed nurses, with the handheld fans, flocked to her side.

This time the local dignitaries again showed up, not to celebrate, but to mourn. Mayor Blake and Principal Harris were in attendance to extend their condolences. Mrs. Marshall even closed down her shop for the day, out of respect for Ivan. She grabbed Chip's father, and hugged his rigid body. In her thick Southern accent, she wailed about what a good boy he was.

"I never heard him cuss or nothin'. Never even spit on the sidewalk. He was just a good boy. Such a good boy. Paid the price for hanging around that no-good Fortune," she said, her makeup running. She sobbed as if Ivan had been her own. Chip felt her cry the mammoth tears he was unable to shed. His gaze was fixated on the casket where his brother lay. The entire scenario was a bit much for him, a fourteen-year-old boy, to handle, and he thought he was going to lose it.

Rivals from Eastern and other crosstown basketball teams came to pay their final respects. Chip was surprised, yet pleased by their appearance. It made him feel good to know that most people hadn't bought into that nonsense about Ivan going astray. Chip was even more surprised that the illustrious Mayor Blake had made an appearance. But his presence collided with the memory of the mayor presenting Ivan with the MVP trophy, such a joyous time. It was the most triumphant milestone of Ivan's life. Now the mayor was here to mark Ivan's final milestone.

Greeting people as he made his way up the aisle, the mayor paused somberly at the casket. One of his bodyguards spoke briefly to the funeral director, who inconspicuously pointed to Chip's fa-

ther. The mayor immediately walked over to him with a grim expression on his face. As he extended a finely gloved hand to his father, Chip wondered how much a glove like that cost. And the
expensive-looking cuff links and the monogrammed shirt. Chip
felt even more self-conscious sitting in his brother's stiff, starched
shirt, two sizes too big.

Gerald Baxter stood, his face still void of emotion. Chip could
see the different toll the world had taken on each man. They were
about the same age, probably from similar backgrounds, yet so
very different. His dad, barely able to finish high school, had spent
his life laboring and sweating to eke out a living. Mayor Blake, on
the other hand, wore tailor-made suits and Italian-leather shoes,
and appeared vibrant and polished. He conveyed an effervescent
wave of confidence, cultivated by years of hobnobbing and rubbing elbows with the elite. He had gained his acclaim and wealth
by working his mind and panache for a living.

Suddenly, Chip could hear very clearly. As the words "tragic"
and "shame" fell from the mayor's perfect lips and straight white
teeth under that neatly cropped mustache, Chip was mesmerized.
The words were tempered with just the appropriate amount of
sympathy, yet they seemed slightly rehearsed. He must have spoken those words on thousands of occasions, to thousands of grieving families, Chip thought. But he did have style.

It was then that Chip plotted his destiny. Suddenly, Chip knew
what he wanted to be. Successful, polished, and refined like Mayor
Blake. He spoke so effortlessly, just like he did on television. He
glided away, with his special-agent-type bodyguards at his elbows,
and Chip's future passed before his eyes.

THE RAIN POURED down on the grave site in hazy sheets. Chip
and his father stayed until the last mourner left. It was then that
his father pulled a stack of letters out of his pocket, and threw
them into the grave. Puzzled, Chip asked his father what they
were. "They were letters for your brother. His SAT scores, his acceptance letters, all of that. They're worthless now."

Dazed and reacting without thinking, Chip did the unspeakable. He grabbed his father's arm. "Why did you throw them away, Dad? Huh? Why can't we keep them? Can't I have something of Ivan's? Can I, please?" he begged with all of his heart. A ten-ton weight had been thrust onto his chest, and he felt crushed by the impact of his brother's death.

Jerking his arm, his father shoved him away. "I don't want to be reminded of what might have been. I'm tired of thinking about what might've been. First my wife, and now my son. I want them buried with him, just like his dreams."

Finally, the burning sensation in his eyes gave way and Chip wept, tears cascading freely down his cheeks, as if floodgates had been pried opened and walls of water came gushing out. The tears unbridled his tongue and his fears as he heard words being spoken that he never knew he had within him. Not only had Chip harbored resentment toward Fortune, but toward his father too.

"You don't want any reminders, Dad? Well, then, I guess you don't want to be reminded that I'm Chip. A chip off the old block. Ivan's block." Chip glared at his father, who stood motionless over the grave. Chip knew it was too late; a beating or whipping was inevitable, so he continued. His body was swelling, and his eyes bulged with hurt and anger. "Just call me Alexander or Alex from now on, because I don't want to remind you of what might have been."

Thankfully, his father didn't strike him. But the newly christened Alex kind of wished that he would. It was worse that he ignored him. Once again his father had robbed him of his feelings, even the bad ones. Turning away, he acted as if he hadn't even heard Alex's bitter words as he began walking across the soggy ground toward the limousine. A few steps from it, his father paused and motioned for him to come. Again, Alex was apparently an afterthought.

The driving rain continued, and Alex did a double take. He could've sworn he'd seen a tall, ghostly figure duck behind a tree. He wanted to grab his father, but better judgment prevailed. As they pulled off, Alex knew he saw the shadowy figure run toward Ivan's open grave. It had to be Fortune. He blinked again, and as the words choked in his throat, the figure vanished from sight.

SLAMMING HIS FIST on the desk, Moses snarled, "I ought to kill all of those simple motherfuckers myself. How in the hell could any three people be so damned stupid at the same time? Are they related or something? Is it some kind of genetic defect, or are they just that fucking dumb? I refuse to believe that I had three complete idiots working for me."

First nodding his head in agreement, Blinky then dissented. "I—I understand what you mean, Moses, but they said that the boy did have Fortune's jacket on. It—it—it was an honest mistake."

Moses would not be consoled or cajoled. "Honest, my ass. There is no honesty in stupidity, and no mistakes without repercussions. How could they have killed the wrong boy? And worse yet, the goddamned hero of the city basketball championship. Probably the only one that might have done something with his otherwise wasted life. When you fuck up, Blinky, you really know how to fuck everything up."

Blinky sighed, knowing that the blame would fall squarely on his shoulders. "They've been taken care of, Moses. Permanently. The word is definitely out that you don't play that."

Grunting, Moses cracked his knuckles. "Yeah, same as always. The message is out. I got a bunch of tackheads working for me that don't know their assholes from their heads. I'm looking like a sucker that can't even take care of business. You know the hell I've gone through to build my fucking rep, and I'm going to risk it all on the hide of a worthless punk? Where the fuck is that two-bit Fortune anyhow?"

Blinky shrugged. "Nobody's seen him. Every lead I had turned up squat. He must have left town, or crawled up a gnat's ass, but he's disappeared."

Standing up, Moses cut an imposing figure as he circled the room. "Anyone can be found, for a price, but I don't think that he's worth it. He's probably more worse off alive than he is dead. Sometimes you can do more damage by not offing the bastard, but by icing someone he's close to." Moses snapped his fingers, as if this disaster had taken a sudden turn for the better. "Yeah, yeah. That'll work. Fuck Fortune. He's worthless now anyhow. He's scared so shitless, I'll lay money that we'll never see his sorry ass again. And if we do, he'll probably be some thieving junkie on the street, so strung out that the mere image of him will keep everyone else in check."

Moses plopped back down in his high-back leather chair, stroked his chin, and grinned. "You know what, Blinky? This may be the best thing. We got rid of two coons with one buckshot. A mediocre ballplayer that probably would have gone to school, dropped out, and been on the streets within a year, hustling with his buddy. And a two-bit punk that would've ended up in jail or dead before the year was out. Or either out here making a whole lot of babies that he couldn't support. In fact, what you did was better than just killing his sorry ass. Death is easy. Living is the shit that kills you slowly. Hell, you probably killed someone he loved more than himself. He'll carry that shit around with him forever. That lasts longer than jail ever would and hurts more than death." He folded his arms across his broad chest. "Yeah, Blinky, this may actually work out for the better. No joke."

Moses sneered and snapped his fingers at another thought that crossed his mind. It was another certification of his supreme intellect and superior street smarts. "And, as an added bonus, you've shut that punk kid up forever. He knows that his silence is his ass, and I don't think that he'll be so inclined to flap his gums about shit. In fact, he'll probably forget his momma's name. He doesn't have the balls to show his ass around here again." Moses leaned back in the chair. "You done damn good, old friend. Damn good."

CHAPTER 4

ALEX'S life was empty after Ivan's death. The only things he had left to remember Ivan by were a few worn girlie magazines and his treasured switchblade. Alex treasured it too, now more than ever before, and he vowed to keep it with him always. It was the one thing his father couldn't take away from him, and a small, yet sweet, secret revenge for the callous way in which his father had emptied Ivan out of his life. Alex made a makeshift key chain out of the knife, and savored the memories that it rendered. Their secrets would live on, despite Ivan's death. Alex decided to dedicate himself to keeping Ivan's memory alive, at least inside himself, until he was able to do something about it publicly.

As Alex grew older, he often found himself walking extra blocks just to avoid passing the old court where Ivan had played. Even the thumping sound of a bouncing ball would move him to tears. Eventually, he mustered up enough nerve to continue his and Ivan's secret tradition of visiting the cemetery. Now, instead of going with Ivan, Alex was visiting him too. Sometimes he'd even cut class to go and sit between the smooth headstones of his mother's and brother's graves, one of the few places Alex felt cared for.

For the longest time, Alex would catch himself searching the faces in the crowds on the street, looking for Fortune, or slipping and thinking that somehow he'd see Ivan. Sometimes he'd even see someone and do a double take, but he'd look again and realize it was just an illusion. A living nightmare.

Alex suddenly had some serious growing up to do. At fourteen, the anxieties of youth were blurred by the frightening thoughts and challenges that lay ahead of him in adulthood. Alex had to be his own hero, with no fans.

After Ivan passed, it was as if his father had died too. Gerald Baxter saw no point in living, only in dying. He started living to die, and no one in the neighborhood could believe that such a still-young man could be so consumed with death. Hoarding money became his passion. He worked constantly, saving to build a great, big mausoleum. He'd move Alex's mother and Ivan there, and the plan was to have enough room for him and Alex when the inevitable came. It was the only planning Alex saw his father do for him, which was pretty discouraging.

From Gerald Baxter's point of view, it was just a matter of time until he perished, so he had to be prepared. Nothing was going to prevent him from attaining this goal, especially not Alex. As he retreated further into his world of isolation, he left Alex to fend for himself.

Gerald Baxter was so busy scrimping and saving every dime that even his lust for discipline dissipated. That was the best thing that resulted from the tragedy. Alex no longer had to fear his father's demeanor, because they rarely even talked. The only contact his father had with the outside world was with the undertaker, to discuss the mausoleum, and with Mrs. Owens on very rare occasions.

The only conversation he and his father had was futile. As small as Alex was, he was outgrowing his clothes. When he asked his father for some new clothes, he told him no.

"Go wear some of your brother's. There are plenty in there, just go get some."

"They're too big, Dad. I can't wear them. All I need is a few pairs of pants and a couple of shirts."

"You got a good funeral suit, don't you? That's all you need. I'm not buying a whole lot of clothes for nothing. Wait until you can wear your brother's, or you can get Mrs. Owens to take them in for you."

Alex was flush with anger. He had enough problems, and it was not hip to be a tackhead at age fourteen. You couldn't be seen wearing last year's maypops, and not the bad Nikes with the swoosh on the side. It didn't matter if you were poor, you still had to be fashionable.

Alex's mind raced. He decided to start hustling.

But not the kind of hustle you'd expect. While most boys were learning to hold their private parts in public, Alex learned to hold down a job and obtain straight A's. He convinced Mrs. Marshall to let him work in her store delivering groceries for old folks and fish sandwiches to the lazy. Alex sweetened the offer by telling her that he'd work for tips until he could prove to be of some benefit to her. Eventually he did. Alex's math skills helped get her shoddy accounting books together. He could calculate figures quickly, and although she acted like she didn't care a lot about money, she was quite shrewd. She was extremely appreciative when Alex got the IRS off of her back, and even shared with him the depth of her wealth. She had real estate holdings in her hometown of New Bern, North Carolina, and even owned the building her store was in, and she wasn't "beholdin' " to anyone. It was a bit of wisdom that stuck with him. Money meant power, and Alex learned that as long as he was getting paid, new worlds opened up to him. Instead of just borrowing books, now he was actually able to buy some. He devoured everything from Maya Angelou to Socrates to Shakespeare and acquired an appreciation of culture and the arts.

Alex's only indulgence was a few new threads. He might not be cool, but at least he could look cool. He bought a pair of fashionable Nikes and wore them with Levi's with creases so sharp that they'd cut you. That was the style. He was growing up, and gaining respect in his own little way.

He was still pretty scrawny for his age, and a lot of folks tried to chump him for his money when Alex made deliveries. But he was determined to get out of Shaw as soon as he finished high school, so he made his mental strength compensate for what he lacked in physical capabilities. This was cast into play the time Doc, that drug addict, tried to beat him up and steal the money he'd just gotten for making a big fish-sandwich delivery to the barbershop down on Tenth and U.

Alex had just run out of the shop, and was heading down the block when Doc clotheslined him. He dragged Alex, kicking and screaming, into a deserted alley. In broad daylight, Doc clutched a jagged piece of glass, and pushed it under Alex's skinny ribs. He threatened his life if he didn't hand over the fifteen bucks.

Alex had to think fast. He wasn't about to die for fifteen bucks, but he wasn't about to give it to Doc either. Though Alex always carried Ivan's knife, he never thought about actually using it. Too many times he'd heard about someone getting killed with his own weapon.

Instead, Alex always kept an open bag of pepper in his pocket, just for these types of incidents. All he had to do was figure out a way to get to it, and he'd be set.

"Let me get it, please. Just don't hurt me," Alex pleaded.

"Hurry the hell up, boy. I know you better have at least five dollars, or I'm a slice you up."

Doc loosened his grip on Alex, and he reached in his pocket and threw a handful of pepper in Doc's face.

"You little fucker," Doc coughed and wheezed, rubbing his eyes. "I'm goin' to get your little scrawny ass."

A jittery Alex laughed and ran down the street. Strangely, he'd proven a theory that would haunt him the rest of his natural life: You didn't need to kill in order to survive, not even in the ghetto.

MONTHS TURNED INTO years, and eventually Alex's childhood nightmares and rumors about Ivan's death faded. They were replaced with the thoughts and concerns about the escalating violence, murders, and deaths, both tragic and expected, that shrouded and basically gripped the city, and especially Shaw. As the 1970s became the eighties, things changed, unfortunately not for the better. There was a new wave of drugs and crime as weed and reefer became nearly obsolete and PCP—angel dust, Lovely, or the "Love Boat"—charmed and titillated users both recreational and habitual. Eventually these narcotics bowed down to a new lord and master named crack. Alex watched with detached interest as the winos became hardened and desperate, and women not only turned tricks to support themselves, but also began offering up their children as collateral for a hit of the pipe that promised a high like never before. And ensured a low like never before, too.

Go-go still reigned supreme on the music scene, but it was being replaced with a new brand of music, aptly named rap. Run-D.M.C., The Sugar Hill Gang, and Whodini mixed street beats with catchy phrases filled with tales of humorous, and occasionally edgy, life stories. Suddenly, everyone wanted to emulate these rap impresarios, and started sporting thick gold rope chains, Adidas sneakers, and Kangol hats. Everyone except Alex.

The remainder of Alex's teenage years proved uneventful and fleeting. With his eyes focused on the ultimate goal of escaping Shaw, little captured or maintained his attention. Alex very rarely spoke to his father, and tried to see him as little as possible. Outside of cursory hellos and the occasional "good nights," their interactions were few and far between. Though tempted on some occasions to question his father, Alex simply learned to live without his intervention. On a positive note, his father wasn't the strict ogre that he had been when Ivan was alive. As long as Alex kept their home neat, his father never said a word. In fact, Gerald Baxter was an apathetic mummy who barely acknowledged Alex's existence.

So, Alex pretty much reared himself. With his father's emotional absenteeism, Alex had free reign to do as he pleased. But that meant nothing exciting. He hit the books hard, and worked a part-time job, in the evenings and weekends at the public library, and when time permitted, he still helped out Mrs. Owens. Alex visited the grave sites of his mother and brother more and more sporadically, instead using his time and energy to cement a permanent place on the dean's list. He maintained a 4.0 grade point av-

erage, yet denied his academic prowess to anyone who recognized
his skills.

While his contemporaries reveled in the transition from their
junior high to the coveted high school status, Alex remained status
quo. While his classmates blossomed and bloomed, sprouting fa-
cial hair, experiencing rampant growth spurts and changes in their
voices, estrogen and testosterone raging, Alex remained the smooth,
baby-faced little guy that the fellas no longer picked on and the
girls overlooked.

It really didn't matter too much to him. Alex had no real interest in girls. His diminutive size, inability to keep up with the latest
fads, and chronic shyness prevented him from ever approaching
them, and although he was involved in most of the student orga
nizations that sponsored the junior and high school dances, he always worked the concession stand. He was amazed at the *Soul
Train*–like, fluid movements of the cool boys and the jocks, and
how the girls were starting to fill out and get curves. He'd watch
couples as they tongue-kissed and slow-grinded on the dance floor,
at least until one of the administrators broke them up. It occurred
to Alex that he would never be part of the "in" crowd, so he just
stayed focused on academics.

He was the quintessential student, excelling in every one of his
classes. When his father's mailbox got crammed with offer letters to
colleges around the country, Gerald Baxter acted like he didn't notice. It hurt Alex's feelings, but it also made him more determined
than ever to succeed.

Alex was offered many other scholarships—full, partial, Ivy
League, even one from the Naval Academy—but he didn't choose
any of those. Not that he didn't think that he could hang aca-
demically; he didn't want to stray too far from his roots. He
wanted to get away from, but not forget, where he'd come from.
He felt strongly that he needed to be in a place where he could be
accepted for who he was, without having to compensate for the
color of his skin. So, he knew he wanted to go to a historically
black college. Up to this point in his life, Alex's interaction with
whites had been very limited. Although it was 1982, D.C. was still

pretty limited, especially for a poor black kid who had only ventured out to the Maryland suburbs in Prince George's County.

So, Alex selected Hilliard, because of its historical significance,
and its generous, full four-year liberal arts scholarship. It was a
record achievement for a student of Cardonza High, and in order
to prepare himself for the rigors of college life, Alex attended junior college at Prince George's Community College. He had mentally outgrown his peers, but socially, he was still quite stunted.
Even though he was on the prom committee, and Mrs. Marshall
offered her niece as a date for him, Alex graciously declined. He
spent his prom night taking a self-paced course in Latin.

As graduation approached, Alex invited his father and Mrs.
Owens, and she had to nearly twist Gerald Baxter's arm to get him
to say he would come. Even the thunderous applause Alex received upon being awarded valedictorian fell upon deaf ears: Alex
searched the crowd, and was disappointed by his father's stoic reaction. No matter how many honors or accolades Alex earned,
they were lost in the dimly lit world of Gerald Baxter. It finally angered Alex, and he was suddenly weary of trying to reach his father, and felt that he would never try again. He was more than
ready to get out of Shaw and leave all of the bitter and empty
memories behind.

CHAPTER 5

SADE'S smoky, sultry voice boomed "Smooth Operator" out of the window of a low-riding black 280-Z with the personalized New York tag, FLY GUY. The slick car captured the eyes of everyone on the yard as it passed by just as Alex walked up the ivy-hung stairs to the front doors of Livingston Hall. Lugging a tattered Samsonite and a worn duffel bag filled with shoes, books, and registration materials, he had arrived. He was at Hilliard Institute, a pillar of black bourgeoisie education with a warm Southern accent.

Okay, take a deep breath, Alex said silently, trying to compose himself. His first day at H.I. conjured up familiar feelings of uneasiness, fear, and loneliness. Feelings that had been his constant companions after Ivan's death.

The doors to Livingston Hall were old and creaky. The brass doorknobs had long lost their shine, but to Alex, even the worn knobs were profound. A whole lot of history had been made behind that door, through which numerous doctors, politicians, businessmen, and other major contributors to society had passed. H.I. was the cultivating field for many of the nation's top black

leaders, and although Alex was still painfully shy, he had keen aspirations. He was going to be somebody. He was finally going to
be like them. Tingling with excitement, he faced the open doors of
his new home, and was both excited and scared witless. Even
growing up in the harsh reality of Washington, D.C., had not prepared him for the mystical and frighteningly different world of
college life.

The campus was filled with late-model cars, beautiful girls, and
fly guys. He was feeling really uncool as he stood there wearing
less-than-fashionable high waters and played-out shoes. He had
long ago given up the idea of being a clotheshorse. But it didn't
matter. Alex was at H.I. Now academics would level the playing
field, or so he hoped. He had to believe that out of all of these
folks, there'd be others like him, about the books and not the
looks. Even if it was just a handful. H.I. was among the crème de
la crème of black universities. Just like Howard, Spelman, Hamp-
ton, and Morehouse, Hilliard Institute was considered the joint. It
was the place to be, and Alex was here.

Freshmen struggled with their overstuffed black-and-brass foot-
lockers and bags, as mothers and fathers uttered tearful good-byes.
Alex felt a tinge of jealousy as he stood there, alone, since his father had dropped him off as if he were a bag of dirty laundry.
There'd been no long, lingering good-bye for Gerald Baxter, just a
strange sense of relief that Alex was finally gone. And his relief
was matched only by Alex's delight. The delight of being free
from the mental and physical chains that bound him in Shaw. Alex
inhaled the excitement that crackled in the air and savored the
chaos of his first semester.

It had been a struggle, escaping from the suffocating despair of
Shaw to the sanctity of Tidewater, Virginia. But Alex was determined. He had beaten the odds by getting out relatively unscathed.
Bearing the emotional scars of being victimized personally by
crime, and standing witness as countless others had been, had left
him jaded and hollow. Since that frightful day of the drugstore
robbery, cold, hard crime had become a common aspect of his life.
In order to survive, Alex had learned how to blend into the back-

ground. He was introverted, yet safe, and he had trained his eyes to see little and his mouth to repeat even less.

At home, the sound of gunfire could be heard more often than cars backfiring. Alex could even distinguish between the different calibers of guns, just by the sound. From purse snatching, to shoplifting, to prostitution and drug pushing, he'd seen it all in a very compressed period of time. Death had been as much a part of his life as living, if not more. But it hadn't been enough to stop him, to ever tempt him into a life of crime. And today, he stood validated. A slight smile crept across his face, baring the even, white teeth he rarely showed. As he gripped his worn suitcase and stood on the hallowed grounds of Hilliard Institute, he was at the beginning of a long-awaited dream. Lifting his eyes to the heavens above, Alex silently thanked God, for now it was a reality.

His life had been given a needed infusion of hope, and he had a lot to prove. Alex wasn't supposed to have gotten this far, but he was going to make something of himself for his mother and Ivan. He figured that it was the least he could do, especially since he was the one who had survived.

Alex looked at the wrinkled piece of paper from the housing office, noting his dorm room number. Although he had looked at it a thousand times before, he still trembled. He was away from his stigmatized life, and the landscape was different now. On this canvas, Alex was going to use a broad brush and repaint his life. He was finally free to be himself, whoever that was. He guessed it was time to figure that out too.

Just as important to Alex was the fact that he didn't want to be a sell-out. He despised the thought of being one of those pseudo-brothers who got educated and began to speak really nasally. That would never work if he ever had plans to go back to Shaw and vindicate Ivan's death. He'd be dubbed an Oreo and kicked to the curb before he even got his point across.

So Hilliard was his starting point. And there were many mountains to climb.

As Alex walked through the halls and saw many of his fellow freshmen, well groomed, with matching luggage, he realized that he was still on the fringes. Even with his academic successes, he still had to climb out of a deep hole. Watching mothers hug their sons, and seeing the sons pull away, embarrassed at the sentiment, made him feel the familiar emptiness of being motherless.

But Alex still had his imagination, and even his dreams. Perhaps if his mother had been around, she would have encouraged him to step out and enter a world he wasn't so familiar with. Maybe he would've gone to a predominately white university. She would've been right there with him, arms locked, strolling up the hallowed stairs of Yale. She'd probably still have been wearing an Afro and dashiki, and would have quizzed students on black history as she passed them. Or at least that's how Alex imagined she would have been, from the fragments of information Ivan had told him about his mother. Her image again flashed vividly in his mind. Had his mother lived, his life surely would have been different. His dad would have probably been more of a father, more of a man. She would've made sure of that.

Caught up in the moment, Alex didn't realize that his feet were pointed at the front of his dorm room. Loud rap music blared inside, indescribable words ran together in rhythmic verses, and the door pulsated from the wicked beats. Alex reached for the knob, but the door swung open before he could grasp it.

"You must be my room-dog! What's up, my brother?" Standing before Alex's eyes was a huge mountain of a boy, with a broad grin and a shoulder-length, hanging gherri curl. He looked like the Kool-Aid character with a wet, black mop on his head. He grabbed Alex's belongings with one hand, and swung a ham of an arm over his shoulder. "You must be Alexander, right?" Gauging the weight of his bags, his roommate added, "You must be traveling light." He was talking so fast, his words ran together. It took a little effort for Alex to decipher the country accent, and before he could respond, the husky boy had hoisted his stuff on a flat little narrow bed on the opposite side of the room.

"My name's Rudy, man. But my friends call me Foody." He grasped Alex's hand warmly. Alex didn't have to wonder how he got that nickname.

"You can call me Alex. I don't actually have a nickname." He grimaced, recalling the cruel nicknames kids used to call him. That was all behind him now. He quickly surveyed the room, noting that the best thing about the pea soup–colored walls was that they were close to the bathroom he and Rudy would have to share with three other rooms.

"No sweat, Alex. I'm down with the program." Foody shrugged. "Let me show you the room. This ain't Ho Jo's, but I guess it's not too bad. I haven't seen those big flying roaches everybody's been telling me about yet." Alex couldn't tell if he was joking or not, but the thought of flying roaches was instinctively repulsive. They had "friends" at home, but none of them could fly.

Foody had nearly every high-tech electronic gadget known to mankind, including all kinds of stereo equipment—speakers, turntables, mixers, headphones, and records. But Alex had to give him credit. For as much stuff as he had crammed in, every cord was neatly wrapped and labeled. It looked like a professional had sweated hours, maybe even days, on the installation.

"I'm going to be a big-time rapper one day, man," Foody shouted over the loud, thumping music. He pointed to a poster of a leather-clad, thick-gold-chain-wearing man that was neatly taped to the wall. "I'm going to be as big as Kurtis Blow one day."

"That's cool," Alex replied, thinking that Foody was already bigger than the rap star, at least twice as big, weightwise. Alex wondered how much time he was going to spend in the library, because he'd probably never get any work done in here. Not unless he planned to write on one of the turntables.

"I'm from Tennessee, man," Foody said. "I say I'm from Nashville, but it's really a little town right outside of it." He paused, and looked at Alex with big, warm eyes. Foody smiled like he'd known him his whole life. "You know, it's a little hole, but it's a nice place if you like the country. Maybe you can come home with me sometimes." Foody paused, looking at Alex curiously as Alex carefully removed his clothes from his suitcase and hung them in the little cubbyhole of a closet.

"You know, you sure are kind of slim, Alexander, I mean Alex.

You mean to tell me your momma sent you off to school this puny? What you gonna do when you fall on hard times, and you really ain't got nothing to eat? Dry up and blow away? What's up with that?"

Alex knew the subject would come up eventually, but not so quickly. He figured that now was as good a time as any to tell Foody about his folks. But Foody gave him no time to reply. He kept right on talking.

"But don't sweat it. My moms'll hook you on up. In fact, she hooked me up before she left. Bought about two hundred dollars' worth of food, and cooked me up a trunkful of shit. Good eats." Foody opened one of his numerous trunks, and proudly displayed his food. "And I'm hungrier than a mug."

The locker was crammed with all kinds of succulent goodies carefully wrapped in crinkled aluminum foil. Sweet scents of home-baked pies arose, and a big country-ham bone protruded from one of the packages. Alex's mouth watered as he recalled the last home-cooked meal he'd eaten. It was courtesy of Mrs. Owens, and that had been an extremely long time ago.

Settling comfortably on the bed, Foody scrutinized Alex as he unpacked the rest of his meager belongings. He couldn't help but be slightly disappointed. He assumed that since Alex was from D.C., he'd be a really cool roommate. A real yo boy. Although D.C.'s rep didn't carry the weight of New York's or Chicago's, it sure beat that of his little hick town. As he checked out Alex's rags and lack of a gherri curl, he realized that being from the country wasn't all that bad. After all, he was in style, whereas Alex, the homeboy, was kind of tired. Real tired. He decided then that if Alex was going to be his roommate, he was was going to have to get cool, and quick. He wasn't about to get his face cracked since he had told too many of his homeys that he had a big-time, big-city roomie.

Alex seemed aware that he was being sized up, but didn't seem affected by it. Foody watched him meticulously fold his clothes, and silently hoped that Alex wasn't a fag. He could deal with a nerd, maybe, but sissy, no way. That was too ill.

Thankfully, Alex said, "Hey, wait a minute, now. Don't get the wrong idea. My pops was kind of a stickler for neatness. He'd have a fit if my room wasn't clean. Plus, without a mom, I was stuck doing all that housework stuff."

Relieved, Foody struggled to get off the bed, and lumbered over to Alex's dresser. Taking both huge hands, he proceeded to mess up his clothes.

"That was then, and this is the here and now, dude. You a long ways from home, kid, and guess what?" He swung his bulbous head around, comically surveying the room. "Your pops ain't here, so chill out. You probably got a lot of catchin' up to do. As long as he pays the tuition, who gives a damn what he thinks?" Foody noticed that whatever he said was having no effect on Alex. "Take a chill pill. Try to enjoy life for a change." He shrugged. He sure had a lot of work to do to make Alex cool.

The misfits spent the rest of the afternoon talking, both expressing their interest in being in school, but for diverse reasons. Alex wanted to get ahead, and Foody wanted to make his mark as an Omega man, and become a rap star. Foody, the Rapping Que. He could move pretty good for a boy his size, was awfully light on his feet. That was until he landed on yours, as Alex quickly discovered in their cramped little dorm room. Foody demonstrated the latest dances, like the Smurf, and showed off his prowess as a human beat box. An extremely loud human beat box.

"What's a Que, Foody?" Alex asked, unwittingly setting himself up for a dissertation on the fundamentals of campus life.

Again Foody looked at him like he'd said something sacrilegious. "Get outta here. What's up with that, dude? You from one of the blackest cities in the country, and you act like you don't know. Boy, with Howard University and all them honeys runnin' around up there, you mean you ain't never seen no Greeks before?" Foody shook his head. "The Ques are only the baddest frat on the yard." He lumbered over to another trunk, which was stuffed with vibrant purple-and-gold clothes.

"They wear these colors. I already got 'em for when I pledge. You mean you never thought about pledging? See, when you

pledge, you get to wear those Greek letters, and step like this—"
Foody performed his best imitation Que step, and barked like they
did. "Woof!"

Barking? Alex was smart enough not to let on that he really
didn't know a whole lot about frat life. Honestly, the frats had
never crossed his mind. He'd been offered scholarships from
nearly all of them but he never realized that they had their own
mini-empires at college. He figured that anything that deviated
from studying would only be a waste of precious time. Alex cali-
brated his thoughts before speaking. "I figured that I wouldn't
have time for it. After all, I have work-study, and I'm taking nineteen hours this semester."

"Nineteen hours! What's up with that? You trippin' or what? I
didn't even think they let freshmen take all those classes. Not me,
I'm taking as many fundamental bullshit classes as I can take. Basket Weaving 101. Give me some time to have some fun. Think
about it. When you gonna have time to party and shit? What about
gettin' laid? Gettin' paid? That's part of school too, you know. A
very important part."

"Yeah, I know, but I'm on a full scholarship, and I've got to
maintain my GPA no matter what."

Foody squinted at him, hardly believing that someone could be
so dedicated. Or so stupid. "Well, knock yourself out, 'cause I ain't
even trying to perpetrate like I'm taking all that crap. Yo, you must
have some hellified grades to even be thinking like that. But damn,
you gotta have some fun. And if we gonna be room dogs, you got
to loosen up a little. I ain't gonna have no reputation on the yard
for hanging out with a nerd." He ripped open a bag of barbecue
chips and cranked up the volume on his stereo.

As the afternoon passed, Alex told Foody about his mother, but
didn't go into a lot of detail. He had quickly surmised that Foody
probably had a big mouth, and anything that he shared with him
would probably be recounted to everyone else. Maybe not mali-
ciously, but told anyway. It was clear that Foody enjoyed being the
life of the party.

Surprisingly, Foody was sympathetic. "I—I just couldn't imagine, man. I mean, growing up without a moms to cook for you and whatnot. Unthinkable." Even Alex had to laugh. He'd never heard it broken down like that before. It was the only time that he'd ever thought of his mother humorously. At least Foody could make him laugh, even if the subject matter wasn't all that funny.

They learned a lot more about each other. Even to the point that, despite his initial misgivings, Alex was actually growing comfortable around Foody. He was a jovial spirit with a comical personality that disarmed and embraced you. With his offbeat sense of humor and curious observations about life, they were soon laughing and joking like old buddies. It was a relief not to be bogged down by the weight of his past. Alex actually felt befriended.

Foody's booming system and the sounds of Run-D.M.C. lured the other newcomers to their room, and Alex met other freshmen and made more friends. They shared a camaraderie that he'd never felt, and it was a nice change of pace. Alex now brimmed with hope.

One of the first upperclassmen they met was their residence assistant, Kerry. He warned them to keep the noise to a minimum, or he threatened to confiscate the stereo equipment. It was an empty warning, but to a wet-behind-the-ears freshman, it was law. It never occurred to them that he was just pulling Foody's leg because he didn't have a stereo that nice of his own.

It was Saturday, and there was still plenty of time to have fun before orientation and classes on Monday. Hilliard was located in Tidewater, which had a great reputation as a congenial seaside military town. They ventured down to the water's edge, and lulled by the glimmering lights on the bay, the motley crew of freshmen made their way around the yard. Desperately trying to look like upperclassmen, they failed miserably. It was as if the girls could smell the milk on their breath from a mile away.

A serenity engulfed the university. It was so heavenly that Alex almost heard harps accompanying the cries of the seagulls. Gone were the loud sirens and erratic sounds of the city. Hilliard was brand-new and exciting, yet peaceful and relaxed. It was a place where he was prepared to do what he did best: busting out A's.

Sitting by the river, some of the braver freshman dared whistle at the array of beautiful sorority girls as they passed by. Visions of loveliness, they were every hue, wearing different letters and colors, with different nicknames and numbers, but they were joined in the common spirit of looking down their noses at the lowly freshmen, although some of the guys were singled out as being cute or having potential. Good black men were hard to find, and one could never be too presumptuous. College girls realized long ago that you never knew who would pledge the following year and become the big men on campus. But the general consensus was that this group were still very much freshmen, with big-time dues to pay. And over the next four years of their lives, pay dearly they would.

CHAPTER 6

PERHAPS Foody had been right, Alex thought. He stood in front of the registration board that listed class after class of closed courses. But of course not, Foody couldn't be right. In the two whole days Alex had known him, he'd been incorrect on just about everything they talked about, with two exceptions—rap music and pledging. Two things that Alex really didn't care about.

Alex was getting panic-stricken. What ever had possessed him to take nineteen semester hours? It was evident that anything worth taking was already filled. So, unless you had a hookup with one of the students working registration, you stood an ice cube's chance in hell of getting a good professor. That is, if you knew who was good.

Kerry had hipped them to a couple of profs to avoid, and a couple to definitely take. Professor Brown's English lit, the bomb. Forget Tucker's Calculus 101, it was a real ball-breaker. Alex quickly discovered that, for freshmen, the best classes had prerequisites that were the weeders, which left him with the Professor Tuckers of academia.

Scrambling his choices, their availability, and the hours, Alex finally managed to combine nineteen hours, ranging from eight-o'clocks to evening courses, as he stood in the never-ending registration lines, which was constantly being cut by the upperclassmen. A feeble security guard snoozed in the corner, and a definite aura of chaos was erupting. Voices rose as friends greeted each other for the first time since the spring, and seniors howled in dismay as that one final class they needed to graduate closed right before their eyes.

Alex was constantly shuffled from one mismanaged area to another. He was always barraged with a bunch of impossible questions. Did he have this slip of paper, this form, this receipt, this copy? Did he have the appropriate signature on the appropriate document? Did he go to the financial aid office first? Did he have the bursar's stamp on this document? Did he have the proper signature to attend this class? If not, it could mean being sentenced to the back of another endless line. It was all so frustrating. By the time Alex finally reached the registration area, he was exhausted. There was no book that could prepare you for such an experience.

However, within this maze of confusion and turmoil, there was a tranquil group of students. They weren't the harried freshmen, the worried seniors, or the well-taken-care-of athletes. They were the Greeks.

They wore the latest fashions, hairstyles, and had the flyest looks. Noble Alphas donned their black and gold. Pretty-boy Kappas strolled, with their patented good looks. And then there were the Ques. They were big, strapping, burly guys, and athletes. There were smatterings of Sigmas and Iotas. Every guy on the yard appeared to be either in a frat or longing to be in one.

These were the folks with the connections. They had a hierarchy of inclusion that began with their own organization, then extended to their sister or brother organization, and then finally to the other Greeks. It separated them from the mere mortals.

They were brightly adorned in their colors, with mystifying letters and all types of cute names, some indicating glamour and beauty, and some posing threats. Names such as Haze Master X and Precocious reflected the unique characteristics and creativity of each of the members. They seemed to treasure the mere sight of each other. They happily grabbed and hugged one another, clearly oblivious to the perils and pains of registration. They had their own little system. A brother or a sister working registration would hook them up. They wouldn't even have to stand in line. He or she would slip them the form in advance, and they'd receive a printed copy of their classes at another social function. Closed classes? Not a problem. There was a magic override key he or she would hit and, *poof,* they'd be in there. Being Greek meant being well connected, both on the yard and off.

Alex absorbed the scenario with childlike awe. So this is what Foody was always talking about. Suddenly Alex understood. They were the campus leaders, the athletes, and the most popular people on the yard. And even if you were just mediocre, wearing a specific combination of colors and adorning three Greek letters across your chest elevated you head and shoulders above the crowd.

Alex got firsthand experience of just how much clout the Greeks wielded. When it was finally his turn to register, a big, strapping guy wearing black-and-red PKO letters and sporting freshly scabbed brands jumped in front of him, his knapsack jutting into Alex's face. The guy coolly stepped over to the open registrar, scattering Alex's precious registration papers to the floor. A feeling of inferiority swept over Alex as he turned red with humiliation. The Greeks snickered in their sacred corner, and he turned a deeper shade of crimson.

As he reached down to gather his papers, his eyes beheld the loveliest sight he'd ever seen. She was fine. Five-feet-five, maybe -four, with a lovely frame, silky, cinnamon brown skin, hazel eyes, and a gorgeous smile. Alex committed all of that to memory with just one glance. She wore no colors, but she had an air of self-confidence that had everyone taking notice. She reached down to help him, but before she could pick up a piece of paper, another thick-necked PKO stomped on the pile.

He reached for her arm. "Don't waste your time messing with this little bamma, doll." He whisked her away, leaving a bold Nike footprint on Alex's papers.

Alex stared at them, even as the Greek escorted her over to a group of AKAs in a sea of pink and green. They graciously made room for her. Who was she? What was she? How could he find out? He was so consumed that he didn't even notice that another registrar came open until she yelled for him to come to her counter.

The first couple of weeks passed without any major incidents. While Foody conducted his nightly game of Spades, Alex settled into his work-study job at the library, which was perfect. He was able to study and work, in addition to getting paid. His thoughts often drifted back to the day of registration. He hadn't seen that fine young lady since. That wasn't all that hard to believe, since Alex rarely looked up when he was walking around on campus, and was in the library the rest of the time. He barely even saw Foody, except in passing. They left notes for each other frequently, with Foody usually informing him of some "be there or be square" social event that Alex always intentionally missed.

It wasn't until a Saturday in early October that they really got a chance to talk, during one of Foody's finer moments, dinner.

"Bro-heem, you really got to start living. You're missing everything," Foody said. He stuffed a foot-long sub, literally, into his mouth. As they sat in the café, Alex reluctantly considered the possibility that he might be right. Foody continued eating and talking, and mentioned homecoming, smokers, fall rushes, and even midterms.

The mention of rushes caught Alex's attention. He had noticed colorful posters splashed around the yard, but never made the connection. He even had to ask Foody what a smoker was; Foody promptly shook his head in disbelief. Nearly a month on one of the most happening black campuses in America, and Alex truly didn't know what a smoker was.

"It's just what its name says, smoke-er. It's when the Greeks throw a set, invite potentials, and smoke 'em over." Foody sucked his teeth until he freed the hot dog bun that was lodged in one of the protruding gaps, and advised him that all of the Greeks used the same process.

Foody reveled in the opportunity to share his knowledge. His tutorials on college life were becoming a part of their daily ritual. "You gotta be careful," he said. "You can't go running to everybody's set, 'cause they watch you. The last thing you want to do is go sitting up in an Alpha smoker, and then pledge Kappa. They'll bust your ass for even considering another frat." He eyed Alex with amusement that dissolved into suspicion. "I know you can't be considering pledging?"

"No, well, I mean I don't have time. I just wanted to know what you knew about the Psi Kappa Omicrons." Alex shrugged.

Foody turned his nose up a little. "Well, they ain't the Ques, but they are known for being like leaders and shit. They're heavy into law and political science. And they don't step all that well. But I heard they do get down over there. They bust ass, that's why their colors are red and black. For blood and black eyes or black-and-blue bruises or something like that. That's why they're really known as the PsiKOs. Get it? Psychos. Why you want to know?"

Alex relayed the registration story. "I saw this girl, and—"

"And she kind of digs the PsiKOs," Foody said. "Pro'bly a sweetheart or frat ho' something." He chuckled to himself at the infinite wisdom he possessed after having been at school for less than a month. "Well, partner, if she is into them, you might as well hang it up. Any time they do that shit, that's all they affiliate with. That's why when I pledge Que, I'm going to get all the honeys." He went off on his usual Omega tangent, arching a hefty arm in their trademark frat sign, and Alex went back to thinking about that chance encounter with the vivacious beauty. Somehow he'd meet her again, Greek or not, and he'd at least find out who she was.

THE SEMESTER CHARGED forward like a runaway locomotive gaining momentum. Freshmen adjusted, bombed exams, and learned the art of cheating. Knowledge was acquired through association, networking with the upperclassmen in hopes of getting old exams. For the more sociable of the newcomers, this was an easy feat. For the more timid, like Alex, it meant that you studied a little bit harder.

Midterms and homecoming were quickly upon them. The semester was going smoothly, without any major incidents or displays of socially inept behavior by Alex. Unlike Foody, who was majoring in fraternity and minoring in socializing, Alex was about the books. If it hadn't been for the onslaught of general housekeeping and the announcement that several prestigious alumni would be descending on the campus, making endowments and meeting potential pledges, Alex might not have even noticed the general euphoria that gripped the yard like that of people on a drug-induced high.

It was during homecoming week that Alex finally saw the girl from registration again. She was as radiant as ever, and she was running for Miss Freshman. She had numerous people campaigning hard for her, passing out buttons and flyers all over the yard. Alex made sure he grabbed a button with her face beaming on it.

Posters decorated every wall in the freshman dorms. It was from the posters that Alex finally learned her name. She was Tiffany Renee Blake of Washington, D.C., and her lovely image adorned the dreary corridors of Livingston Hall. "Man, she is so fine," one of the guys drooled. "Wow, I'd like to get with that," someone else wishfully said. "I already did," a pimply face in the crowd lied. Everyone knew she was a shoo-in to win. She was the only one, from the freshman to the senior class, who had used colored posters.

One quiet afternoon, Kerry caught Alex daydreaming in front of one of the posters. Devilishly, he slid up behind him and bent his knee into the back of Alex's stiff, unsuspecting knee, causing him to lose his balance.

"Funky chicken!" Kerry howled as Alex emulated the dance of the same name from the late sixties, lost his balance, and stumbled with his books. Kerry slyly held out a hand to help him regain his composure. Alex shot him a hateful look, but allowed him to help anyway.

"That's your homegirl, man," Kerry said, nodding toward the poster. "She's a little honey, isn't she? A fine specimen of a woman, if I say so myself. I wouldn't mind tapping that ass my damn self."

Alex nodded in agreement, still a little miffed at being had by one of the oldest tricks by one of the oldest students on the yard. And Kerry had just gotten him last week.

"Well, nod on, my brother, 'cause you might as well get off on that poster. That's about as close as you're gonna get to that. She's talking to one of the biggest PKOs on the yard, this dude out of New York named Big Sid, and I heard that he got with her when she came down here for orientation. Shoot, they've even got her locked up as a sweetheart."

It must've been Big Sid who swept her away that day in registration.

"And on top of that, her dad's the mayor from D.C., Simon Blake."

Alex widened his eyes. "What do you mean, that's Mayor Blake's daughter? I grew up there, and never even knew he had a daughter."

Kerry laughed softly. "No kidding. Yo, I heard he kept her under wraps. Way under. You know, she was rarely seen in public. Went to a private school somewhere and shit. You know he didn't want his pretty young thing around you common Negroes." He slapped Alex loudly on the back of the neck and walked away, laughing.

Alex rubbed his neck. He couldn't believe that Mayor Blake had a daughter who was at Hilliard with him. Small world. No wonder she was the only candidate with the fly color posters. Alex was thoroughly enchanted by her je ne sais quoi.

"THE WINNER FOR Miss Freshman 1982 is—drumroll, please—Ms. Tiffany Renee Blake!" the announcer proclaimed, and the crowd broke into a frenzied roar. Even the football players crept back onto the field just to get a glance at Hilliard's beautiful Miss Freshman. It appeared that she garnered more attention than the seasoned upperclassmen. This was the type of girl who was raised in charm schools, and had cut her teeth on the etiquette lessons of Emily Post.

Waving merrily to the crowd, Tiffany acted as if she had prepared for this moment all of her life. As the elite alumni and the crowd rushed to garner her with praise and adoration, her dad seemed to stand head and shoulders above everyone else. "That's my girl!" he boasted, and proudly stuck his chest out and shook hands. Even Ray Charles could have seen he truly doted on his little girl. He wore a bright letterman's sweater with PKO insignias and designs across it. No wonder they all loved Tiffany. By virtue of her legacy, she was already a sweetheart, an honor rarely bestowed upon any girl. Unless, of course, a few of the frat had bedded her down. She was totally and completely the exception. She was destined to be their queen.

As her father gave her an enormous hug, the adoring crowd wolf-whistled and called her name. Finally, a girl had perforated Alex's outer shell. Her smile had penetrated his dull surface, and touched a spot he had never before acknowledged.

From the nerdy corner of the bleachers, reserved for the lowly lower classmen, Alex wistfully beheld the dynamic figures who symbolized life at its finest. Foody and the guys from the dorm were great company, but out there was an exciting new world going on, and he wanted to know more about it. Suddenly, he had aspirations that hinged on more than the purely logical—this was quite different. It was emotional.

FALL PASSED WITHOUT incident. Midterms were a distant memory, or a recurring bad dream, and now everyone braced for finals. Alex picked up additional hours in the library, and had begun to see faces there he hadn't seen all semester. Somehow you could just tell the end was near. Finals were coming soon, too soon.

Working at the library provided many advantages. Alex got a chance to study late, sometimes overnight if he fell asleep. And he had the grades to prove it. His lowest grade so far was an A-minus in Tucker's calculus, and with all of the overtime he was getting, he was saving up a good piece of change.

His unassuming and grateful manner had endeared him to the custodians, especially Mr. Miles. He always allowed Alex to stay late and come in early if he needed. Alex even made friends with some of the upperclassmen who needed to cram before an exam. It was around this time that Alex became buddies with one of the more popular upperclassmen, Horace White.

Horace was given the nickname Hoho because of his many sexual conquests. Hoho hailed from Detroit. Too smart to be limited to one fraternity, he only affiliated with organizations that had political ties. He was known as a sharp campus leader with a good future, but he could procrastinate. He was notorious for his smooth-talking ways. Late one evening, HoHo bum-rushed the door just as Alex was on his way out.

"*As-salaam-alaikum,* my brother." Horace was notorious for his ephemeral greetings.

"*Alaikum as-salaam,* Horace," Alex replied, genuinely glad to see him, but dreading the inevitable request that was about to reach his ears.

"Brother Baxter, I am in desperate need of a little assistance. I have been beseeched with the toils of my study, such that I've been unable to arrive here, at this institute of research, to complete a very necessary section of my pending sociology term paper." He paused for effect. Now the pitch. "Can you see your way through to help a brother out?"

Alex flipped the light switches back on. "All right, Hoho. But only for an hour." He glanced hesitantly at his watch. It was already eleven-ten, and he hadn't even been to his dorm room since he'd left for his eight o'clock poli-sci class.

As Hoho sauntered leisurely through the doorway, Alex sighed and prepared himself for what was sure to be a long night. He was so engrossed in thought that he didn't feel the slight push on the door as he settled his weight against it.

"Excuse me, but is it okay if I come in too?" a sultry voice whispered breathlessly, as if the speaker had just sprinted across the yard. Startled, Alex swung around, and was barely able to focus. It was a dream. His dream, talking and actually in his presence. It was Tiffany Blake.

She stared at him, waiting. Unable to speak, and breathless in his own way, Alex bobbed his head. "Thanks so much," she said. "I really appreciate it. I have a ten-page paper due tomorrow, and I've just started on it." She brushed by him, Louis Vuitton knapsack on her back, filling the air with heady perfume.

"N-n-no problem," Alex stuttered, his voice cracking like ice when warm soda is poured over it. Damn, he thought. One of the rare opportunities he'd have to talk to Tiffany Blake, and he'd choked. He watched as Tiffany walked over to the reference stacks and began skimming through the titles. Even off the field and without the crown, she walked like royalty. Erect back, perfect posture. Wow, he couldn't believe his luck. He'd only seen her in the library a couple of times during the semester. When he did see her, she was always with an entourage of groupies, Greeks, and other hangers-on. There was never a great deal of studying going on, but rumor had it she was busting out A's left and right. That stood to reason. Being the mayor's daughter kind of reserved you a spot on the upper end of the curve. Alex smiled. Hoho's intrusion proved to be a blessing in disguise.

After checking the lock on the door, Alex resumed his comfortable position behind the reference desk. He could see Tiffany occasionally scurry between the stacks, gathering dust-covered books, and Hoho was nowhere to be seen. Alex hoped he wasn't somewhere asleep, or setting a political fire that would cause the fire alarms to go off. He decided to find Hoho if he didn't appear within an hour.

Alex reviewed his calc homework again. It really bothered him that he was struggling with an A-minus in Tucker's class, and it always seemed to be due to careless mistakes. Tucker was such a son of a bitch, yet Alex respected him. Despite his grousing, Alex knew that he'd push himself to get an A. It was a challenge he'd win.

Closing his eyes, Alex daydreamed. He chuckled as he thought of how he'd tell Professor Tucker to kiss his ass after he got an A on the final. Alex was so consumed with the pleasure extracted from his dream that again he didn't notice Tiffany standing in front of him. When his eyes opened, she startled him with a curiously amused look on her face.

"I didn't mean to disturb you again. You looked like you were having a pretty good dream. So good I hated to interrupt you. I guess you're going to think I'm just a pest." She smiled demurely.

"I'd ne-never think that." Funny, Alex would've thought her to be anything but coy. But she was charming. With her rich brown hair flowing fully over her shoulders, her presence was radiant, and Alex was exhilarated just to behold her.

"That was very kind of you to let me in. I was wondering if you could help me find some books on sixteenth-century politics." As she spoke, her perfect teeth gleamed brightly behind her polished lips. Alex was truly mesmerized.

"Sh-sure," Alex said, struggling to keep his voice even. Nervous energy popped off of him so loudly that she must've heard it. He stood up and clumsily knocked his homework onto her feet. He blushed. If only a hole would open up in the floor and swallow him.

She politely bent down and reached for his papers. "I see your name is Alex. I'm Tiffany. It's nice to meet you. But you know what, I think we've met before. During registration. Under similar circumstances," she said, smiling. She noticed his papers. "So you have Tucker too. A lot of people don't want to take him because they think he's too difficult, but I don't think he's all that hard." Alex stared at her. Either she was very bright, or so well insulated that she hadn't noticed the man was a major ball-buster.

"You must really know your calculus, Tiffany," Alex said in half belief, half disbelief. She nodded as they walked through the stacks.

"Yeah, I guess. I took advanced-placement calc in high school. From what I can remember, it was actually kind of boring." She hesitated in her tracks, waiting for him to take the lead as part of the natural order. The male leadeth, no matter how inept he may be.

"Yeah, it's usually pretty boring to me too," Alex said. "But Tucker's got such a twist on his that he's even got me a little spooked about it. I make dumb mistakes, and he takes off so many points for little things. Like on my last assignment, he took two points off because he didn't like the type of parentheses I used in an equation." Alex felt a little more at ease. He was talking about something that didn't make him stutter: academia.

"Well, if you ever need any help, let me know. I'm always look-ing for a decent study buddy," Tiffany said.

She was not only beautiful, but smart too. But she was probably just being gracious so she could stay in the library. When they finally reached the section where the government books were housed, they talked about growing up in D.C., from two totally different perspectives, naturally. Amazingly, though, they still shared a lot in common. They both possessed a love of culture and the arts. They also recognized the burden and the blessing of being from the nation's capital. It seemed like they talked for hours, until Hoho interrupted them.

"Yo, my brother, I thank you for your fine nouveau Southern hospitality. But I must be off. If I can ever return the favor, please be sure to make me aware." Hoho eyed Alex and Tiffany with raised eyebrows.

"Ms. Blake, always a pleasure." He extended a gloved hand, and kissed Tiffany lightly on the back of hers. Hoho then gave him the soul brother number-five Black Power handshake. "Until we meet again. *As-salaam-alaikum*."

He strolled off into the maze, and Alex called out to him, "Make sure the door is locked. I don't need campus security com-ing down on me."

Tiffany frowned. "Is he always so dramatic? And so chatty?"

For the first time that evening, Alex felt comfortable enough to laugh freely. "Always."

Before they could resume their conversation, heavy footsteps thundered throughout the silent hall. Alex thought it was Hoho returning to drop another bit of knowledge, but then he heard the sound that made his stomach churn. The voice needed no introduction.

"Tiff! Tiff!" The agitated tone invaded their solitude.

"Sid?" Tiffany's soft voice, barely audible. The footsteps drew nearer and nearer, and before Alex could turn around, a hulking figure towered above him.

Not even acknowledging his presence, the gherri-curled Sid spoke directly at Tiffany. "Why didn't you tell me you were coming down here? I had to go by your room and the stupid-ass guard in your building told me where he thought you were. What's up with that? I almost had to knock that nigga Hoho out to get in here." He looked around, obviously irritated. "What's he doing here?" he said, finally noting Alex's insignificant presence by flipping a mammoth thumb in his direction.

"He was nice enough to let me in. Sid, I have a paper due tomorrow, and I've got to get some more information before I can even begin typing it. I'll be up all night."

Sid folded his arms in a huff. He looked like a disgruntled parent confronting a defiant child. "Whatever. I tell you what. I've got something that'll keep you up, and you know what that is." He shot Alex a nasty smirk. "You've got exactly twenty minutes to get what you got to get, then we're leaving. I've got some things to do, and I can't wait around here all night long."

Backing up silently, Alex wished not to be a witness to this spectacle any further. Sid treated Tiffany like a trophy. His prize. A pet that had the audacity to defy him by doing something without his authorization.

Back at his desk, Alex tried earnestly to concentrate on his books, yet his mind drew back to the stacks. Glancing at his wristwatch, he noted the time. It had been exactly ten minutes since he'd slipped away, yet it seemed like an eternity. He rued the fact that Sid had interrupted his and Tiffany's rather pleasant conversation. Alex had long forgotten that Kerry had said they were seeing each other. Chances were that if it didn't occur within the library's four walls, Alex was oblivious to it. And Foody never talked about anything but the Ques.

There was something so familiar yet so repulsive about Sid. He reminded Alex of the thugs from Shaw. So big and bad. Ready to exploit anyone deemed weaker. Alex wondered how Sid ever made it to college, especially since he was better suited for the streets. But Alex had greater concerns. Finals, Christmas, whatever. Thoughts that eventually led back to Tiffany. He didn't even hear Sid charging out of the stacks in a huff, with Tiffany walking frantically behind him, stuffing books and papers into her designer knapsack.

"Good night, Alex," she said, clearly out of breath. As they approached the gates, the alarm sounded.

"Wait, wait, Sid. I've got to check this out," Tiffany said, quickly removing a book from her bag.

"Fuck that. Do it some other time." Sid grabbed her hand and jerked her through the gate.

With a remorseful expression on her face, Tiffany called back, "Oh, Alex, I'm so sorry. Can you check this out for me, please?"

Sid was still loud-talking to Tiffany outside. Alex heard him ranting at her for apologizing to a lowly nobody. Tiffany looked back, shaking her head, as Sid manhandled her across the yard to his waiting car.

Alex peered out the glass doors. As he watched Sid squeal out of the parking lot, he felt the full effect of the unfairness of life. Here, this total jerk was considered a prize. "Nice guys truly do finish last," he said, safe behind the locked doors of his empty haven.

Alex never mentioned the events of that evening, fearing no one would believe that Tiffany Blake had even talked to him. That was until Hoho breezed through the dorms and asked if Sid had busted the conversation and him that night.

"Oh, snap. I would have never guessed that one," Matt from down the hall said, throwing a smudged Mr. Goodbar wrapper at Alex. "She actually talked to you."

Foody looked up forlornly from a bag of pork rinds, and pointed a greasy finger at him. "Puh-leeze. What's up with that? Boy, I bet

she was just batting those long lashes, tryin' to get up in that library after hours. Don't be fooled, yo, 'cause it don't matter none.
Big Sid'll kick your butt if he even thought that you were tryin' to
rap to his girly. And besides, she was probably only being nice to
you so she could get somethin' from you." He licked the barbecue-
flavored salt from his fingers. "Come on, city boy. I know you know
that much about the ladies."

"Naw, it might have been like that initially, but we actually
rapped. And she's really cool people." Hanging around Foody had
definitely expanded Alex's vocabulary.

"Yeah, whatever." Foody continued eating, then grabbed a
green bottle of Golden Champale and washed the midnight snack
down with finesse. "Look, D.C., don't kid yourself. Face it, she's
in a different league than us. Besides her daddy being the HNIC in
Chocolate City, she's a PKO sweetheart and whatnot. She's got all
of the sororities sweating her, and she's seeing the baddest PsiKO
on the yard. How you think you rank? You better slow your roll,
'cause on the real tip, I heard that nigger is straight up crazy."

Foody regurgitated everything he'd heard about Big Sid. "Big
Sid, or Sidney Lewis, is one of the main reasons they call them
psychos. He's from the Big Apple, the boogie-down Bronx, and is
one hazing, sadistic mother. And I heard he runs the honeys. Plus,
you know he's been here, like, forever. At least five years. And
everybody's scared of his ass.

"He's got everything. He can probably bench-press three-fifty,
he sports a huge gherri curl, and an even huger black Oldsmobile
eighty-eight. I heard he even used to be part of a gang back in the
borough, stabbing folks and robbing bodegas. He came down here
with such a reputation, none of the frats would touch him, except
the PKOs. That was because they got such a rep for drawing
blood, especially the old heads. They like that hard-core stuff.

"When he pledged, Sid had more wood broken on him than
anyone on any other line, except their charter line, the Blood-
thirsty Four. They said that anyone who pledged after him had to
deal with the same fate, and no one dared to challenge his authority or reputation. Not even his frat."

Alex absorbed Foody's words with detached concern. Sid was legendary, like Goliath, and even as Foody told the story, the room fell silent in fear.

DRIVING RAIN ALWAYS made Alex think about his past. It took him back to the day Ivan was buried. The claps of thunder reminded him of how the gunshots sounded as they struck Ivan down. As the years passed, things got better, but every now and then, a thought, an incident, or a sound would snatch him right back. Back to being that timid little boy who was without a figure to hide behind. So Alex created his own shadows to disappear into. All of this awareness was draining him, he thought, as he shifted uneasily in the reference-desk chair.

As the Christmas holiday approached, Alex was in a quandary. It had dawned on him gradually: he actually hated the thought of going home. He was concerned about the strides he'd made during his first semester being wiped away by the few weeks he was scheduled to be there. About being constantly reminded of the things that he tried to forget. D.C. His old life and the old him. If the campus hadn't been shutting down for the break, and students prohibited from remaining, Alex would've chosen to stay. But he had to go.

Although Alex was busting out his grades, he still felt like he wasn't making as much progress as he'd hoped. In many respects, he still saw himself as a huge disappointment. He wasn't cool like Ivan would've been at this age, and he was still awkward and unsure around girls. Sure, Alex had some friends, and the fellas from the dorm were cool, but something was still missing.

It was Ivan. Alex could envision him encouraging him, forcing him out of the shell he'd created. "Get up, man. Act like you know," he'd say, playfully knuckling him in the head. He'd tell him to live his life, and stop being so hard on himself.

Once again, Alex was so immersed in thought, he didn't notice that someone had walked up to his desk. Until he heard that soft voice say, "I'm so sorry about the book."

Alex looked up and smiled.

"Thanks for being so cool about it. Anybody else would've had me written up by now." She paused, then smiled triumphantly, handing him the misappropriated book. "You're Alex, right?" She stood before him, bundled up against the brisk December air. She looked rather fly in a tan fur jacket.

Alex stared down at the hardback reference book. "Yeah . . . yes, Tiffany." As usual, he stuttered nervously.

She brushed her lambskin-gloved hand across his arm. "You can call me Tiff. After what you did for me, I'd really like to consider you a friend."

Alex blushed. It had been almost two weeks, and he'd figured he wouldn't see Tiffany, or the book, ever again.

"Thanks, Tiffany, I mean Tiff. That's very kind of you." He picked up the book, expecting to hear her offer a gratuitous goodbye, and walk off into the sunset. Instead she came around the desk.

"So when are you leaving?"

Alex was caught completely off guard. "Leaving?"

"Yes, leaving. Like in leaving to go home?"

Home. The subject of his deep thought process prior to her arrival. "Oh, I'm sorry. Home. Probably this weekend."

"Oh, well, that's nice. Are you driving up?"

Alex suppressed a chuckle. Only she would consider that to be a legitimate question. Freshmen weren't even allowed to have cars on campus, yet she had one. He'd even heard that it was a neat little red convertible Mustang, the color probably indicative of her future sorority, Delta Sigma Theta.

"I wish. I'll be riding Greyhound." Alex swept the books from the desktop and began placing them on the reference cart.

Tiff's brows knitted, and then an idea flashed across her face. Her eyes lit brightly as a smile spread, displaying a set of polished, even, brilliantly white teeth. "What about this? Why don't you let me return the favor for you? Why don't you ride home with me?"

Alex had to be dreaming, and if he were, he didn't want to be awakened.

CHAPTER 7

ALEX leaned against the fence, exactly where Tiffany had told him to meet her. She'd said Friday at four-thirty, and he was early. He had kept this burning little secret from everyone, especially since he'd questioned his hearing when she'd offered him the ride in the first place. The gig was up when Foody asked to share a ride to the bus terminal and Alex had declined, stammering.

"Yo, why not?" Evidently, Foody wasn't looking forward to shelling out the five-dollar fare all by himself.

"Well . . . I got a ride home." Alex had turned his back on Foody and hoped he'd shrug it off and maybe eat something. Instead, he probed.

After several moments of badgering, Alex had finally told him who had offered him a ride, at which Foody immediately burst into peals of laughter.

"What's up with that? You are tripping. Ain't no way Miss Honey gonna give you a ride 'cross campus, more or less all the way to D.C. You better carry your tripped-out ass down to Greyhound with me and squash that notion. Chop-chop. Boy, you be bugging."

Alex's face became flushed with anger. He was many things, but not a liar. "I don't care what you think, Rudy." The only time Alex called him that was when he was extremely pissed off. "Tiff offered."

"*Tiff?* Who the hell is *Tiff?* Ohh, snap! So now you're calling her *Tiff?* Ain't that a blip. Are you even on a first-name basis with girly, or is that some made-up shit too?" Once again Foody had cracked up, his stomach jiggling.

"Look, you don't have to believe it. She said to meet her at four-thirty by the gate, and I'll be there." Jaws tight, Alex had slammed his suitcase closed and glared at Foody with a vengeance.

"All right for the gonads. I'm scared of you. Well, I'll tell you what," Foody had said as he sauntered out into the hall and approached the phone. "I'll call the grey dog to see what time they have a bus leaving for D.C. Mine doesn't leave until six o'clock, so you can still share a ride with me, if you need it."

Alex had listened to Foody's heavy thuds as he lumbered down the hall. He'd thanked God the dorms were empty, for if any of the other guys were around, the party would definitely have been on him, and at his expense.

He'd finished packing his bags, busily tossing a combination of books and wool sweaters into his aged suitcase. He didn't break stride when Foody sauntered back into the room and announced that Alex could catch the six-twenty grey dog with him, if he wanted to.

He'd closed the squeaky dorm room door in a dry good-bye to Foody and hustled down to the front gate. It was four-fifteen, and barely a five-minute walk to the gate, but he'd wanted to be prompt. He'd nervously wiped the face of his watch with a gloved finger. His body tingled. It was almost too good to be true.

The dial on his watch now approached four-fifty, and Alex began to feel a little antsy. He moved around to adjust to the chill of the setting sun. The winds were blustery, blowing off the river.

As each car approached, he looked up optimistically, only to be disappointed. Carload after carload of upperclassmen zoomed by. Alex couldn't believe his luck—bad, of course.

Shaking his head in disgust, he chastised himself. Only he could be so gullible. It wasn't until Foody walked by at five past five that Alex realized how much of a chump he was.

"Yo, D.C.," Foody hollered, with a grin so wide, the darkness lit up. Alex scowled as he continued. "What's up, man? Where's ya ride, homey?" Foody glanced down at his watch, a pretty effortless task since he had taken to wearing a clock around his neck.

Alex waved him off, aggravated that he'd even have to discuss this again. It especially bothered him that Foody might actually be right for a change.

"You know, it ain't too late to catch a ride on the grey dog, homeboy." Foody wheezed by toward the gate where the cabs picked folks up. A few students were milling around, waiting for a jitney or some other mode of transportation.

A lone Checkered Cab clanked to the gate, and the swarm of students attacked it, each desperate for a ride. This momentarily distracted Foody, who had led the charge. It looked like he would have someone to share the cab with after all.

Before Foody could get away, he had the opportunity to reach back and twist the knife once more. "I hope your girl shows up, Alex. It looks like it's going to be a cold night tonight, but keep hope alive, my brother."

It took an eternity for Foody to leave. At least six riders ended up in the cab, with Foody crammed in the front with some other unfortunate soul. Coattails and belts hung from the doors, with luggage overstuffed in the trunk. What a picturesque sight. Alex might be stranded, but at least he wasn't one of the Negro Beverly Hillbillies.

Alex didn't even notice that the glistening red Mustang had pulled up until a sweet voice called out, "Oh, Alex. I'm so sorry we're late."

Stunned, Alex stepped back on his feet. *We?* Only then did he hear the brusque grunting. It was just coherent and loud enough

to be audible. It was some kind of a put-down from Sid. Quickly
Alex surmised that he'd been sucked into the Twilight Zone. It
was his dream, Tiffany, smiling brightly, and his nightmare, Sid,
behind the steering wheel, with the driver's seat reclined until it
almost touched the backseat. Tiffany got out and gave him a gentle hug, rubbing his frigid shoulders, while Sid shot him a con-
temptuous look.

"Please forgive me, Alex. I'm notorious for being tardy. You'd
think that I'd know better by now. It drives my father absolutely
mad. You know, I'm so sorry. The trunk's full, so you'll have to
keep your bag in the back with you." She smiled cheerfully, her
eyes flashing apologetically. Alex clung to his tattered bag. Maybe
it wasn't too late for that bus.

The music was blaring a scratchy mix of New York house
music and rap verses, which he didn't bother to turn down. Alex
had to squeeze into the tiny backseat, and at that point, he noticed
how really huge and how rude Sid was.

"Sidney, please turn the music down." Tiffany slid her seat up
and turned toward Alex. "I know it's cramped back there, but I'll
try to make it a little more comfortable for you." She again smiled
brightly and twirled her hair around her ear.

Alex tried to relax when they took off. He and Tiffany did all of
the talking, while Sid remained sullen. They discussed their traumatic semester, current events, mutual interests, and goals for the
future. No subject, no matter how esoteric, went without their
point-counterpoint approach.

Tiffany was as brilliant as she was beautiful. She was so well
versed that talking with her was profound. Evidently there was a
lot more to Tiffany than the air-head perception that many people
had of her. Being around politics for all those years had taught her
a lot.

Shifting in her seat to face him, Tiffany voiced her opinion on
the subject of a black man, Doug Wilder, the first black man to
consider running for governor of Virginia. "Grist from the rumor
mill is that he's a shoo-in once Robb's term expires. I think it'll be
great if he runs. He seems to be very conscientious, and I think

that he'd be a great ally for the blacks in Virginia. And for the nation's political process as a whole."

Alex nodded. "I agree. He seems like he's pretty heavy, and he's
got a great reputation. If he decides to run and wins, he could par-
lay the governorship into something else. Like congressman. You
never know what the future may hold. I'm sure your dad would
appreciate some additional support in the region, especially if he's
going to seek statehood."

"Statehood is definitely a hot topic, but if Wilder gets in, it's
going to take him a while to get acclimated. But I'm sure he'll want
to see D.C. flourish." After further dissecting the campaign, she
added, "My opinion is strictly my own. I don't speak for my father,
and he doesn't speak for me."

Alex smiled slightly. "Caveat noted, Tiffany. You sound like you
have great potential to get into politics yourself."

Tiffany lowered the sun visor and checked herself in the mirror. "I'm concerned about my home, but not to that degree. My
dad's providing great leadership, but those folks can be a bit much
for me sometimes."

Sid cranked up the stereo and yelled over it, "What do you
mean, D.C. can be too much? D.C. ain't shit. They'll never be as
thorough as New Yorkers, Tiff. You know that."

Tiffany applied lip balm and cut her eyes at Sid. "That's not
what I meant, Sidney. I'm just saying I'm not interested in dealing
with people regarding political issues. People are just too mali-
cious when it comes to that. I'd rather work on cultural and social
concerns, that's all."

"Whatever," he snapped. "Ain't nothing goin' on up there.
Compared to the Bronx, D.C. ain't nothin' but a little hick town
anyway." He cracked the window and started to light up a cigarette.

"Sidney, put that out. You know I don't like you smoking
around me. And especially not in my car."

Alex averted his eyes, and gazed out onto the darkening highway. Despite Sid's juvenile mind games and intimidation tactics,
Alex was truly impressed with Tiffany, and felt blessed to be in her

presence. They continued conversing about everything from mysticism to world religion.

A brooding Sid shut off the heat and began playing chicken with passing cars until Tiffany shot him a look. "Sidney, will you calm down?" She reached over and turned the heat on.

He wildly veered off to a rest area and jumped out of the car. He left his door ajar so the frigid air could rush in.

After the arctic air jarred them back to reality, and they noticed where they were, Alex offered to get Tiffany a drink. He figured her throat was just as parched as his from all of their talking.

Stretching, Tiffany made a sound like a small, fuzzy kitten might if you stroked her stomach. She finally asked for a Diet 7-Up and reached for her purse, but Alex remembered the few crumpled dollar bills he had in his pocket. "Don't worry about it. I'll get it for you."

He crawled out of the backseat and looked around the dark parking lot. "Be sure to lock up. It's pretty dark out here."

"What's going to get me—Bambi? I'm just terrified of him." Alex locked the car door anyway.

Tiffany seemed strong, but she also seemed fragile. Behind her womanly eyes lay the innocence of a little girl, and that little girl seemed vulnerable to someone like Sid. But Sid was her man. One ride home was enough to show Alex what really transpired between them, and it was pretty unsavory.

Alex chose three drinks, including one for Sid. Alex wasn't sure if he'd like it; they didn't sell Bull or Mad Dog out of the soda machines. He laughed at his wit. Alex settled for a caffeine free soda. After all, the brother was hyper enough.

Approaching the car with his arms full, Alex saw that Sid had returned. He caught Sid's eye, and the devilish gleam that Sid cast in his direction sent a chill up Alex's spine. Sid was trying to push his hand under Tiffany's skirt, and she was obviously not too thrilled. Alex was mortified by the disrespect he displayed, and he figured that if he tapped on Sid's window, he'd stop. But Sid completely igged him.

Alex's thinly gloved fingers had stiffened from the arctic air and cold cans of soda. He gripped them even more tightly as his anger grew. How could Sid treat her like that?

Alex pounded harder on the window when he heard Tiffany say, "Why don't you let him in?" Finally Sid, without bothering to even look around, opened the door.

Once again, Alex crawled over Sid's seat to get in. When he offered Sid the soda, he snatched it without even a thank-you.

"Thanks, Alex," Tiffany said with a sheepish look on her face. "He's so crazy sometimes."

There was an eerie silence in the car. Alex shrank back in his seat. Sid adjusted the rearview mirror and smirked at him. Suddenly, Alex didn't feel very talkative.

From that point, Sid pretended Alex wasn't there. He monopolized the conversation with Tiffany, alternating between belittling her comments to trying to slob her down while driving eighty miles per hour. Over the next two hours, it became even more painfully obvious that Sid had little or no respect for Tiffany. Clearly, she was just a piece of property to him. He probably felt like Mr. Big Stuff in front of a little nobody like Alex.

Alex was angered that someone as special as Tiffany would subject herself to a lowlife like Sid. Yeah, he was what girls considered attractive, with a body that proved he spent way too much time in the gym. Yes, he was Greek, but what was the big deal? Was it enough to compensate for his barbaric behavior? Alex shuddered to think just what he was capable of doing behind closed doors.

It all seemed to make sense now. Alex recalled the library scene when Sid acted a fool, and the other times he'd seen them together out in public. Sid always seemed to dominate her every move, one minute playing the doting boyfriend, and the next ignoring her and playing her off to his frat brothers. Alex cringed at how Sid manhandled her. The grope session from earlier that evening caused the pit of his stomach to churn. Alex already had no respect for Sid, so he couldn't possibly have had any less. But as much as he tried to dismiss it, Alex had to question Tiffany's character. How could anyone who had so much going on deal with Sid? He was just toxic. Surely not for love alone. But that must be the answer. Could love be so powerful, and feelings so strong, that they eliminated common sense from the equation?

Alex was quite ignorant in the ways of love, and he wasn't overly anxious to learn. Seeing Tiffany and Sid's sad and twisted relationship was enough to make him thank God he hadn't ever gotten that close to anyone. He didn't want to know love if it meant self-destruction. He didn't have enough of himself to lose.

WHEN THEY ARRIVED on the outskirts of Shaw, Sid started singing "The Ghetto," and made offhand, offensive comments. Tiffany ignored him and asked, "When would you like for us to pick you back up, Alex?"

The thought of spending time in Tiffany's company was appealing, but Alex couldn't stomach the thought of another moment with Sid the miscreant. So Alex politely declined. Before Alex could close the car door securely, Sid pulled off from the curb, nearly yanking Alex's arm out of the socket.

Tiffany rolled the window down and shouted to him, "I'll see you soon, Alex. Take care." A gloved hand waved into the busy night. Somehow Alex felt that she was the one who would probably need to be taken care of. He was left with an uneasy realization that he'd probably never see her in the same light again.

But the memories of the tempestuous ride were quickly replaced with the familiar sights and sounds of Shaw that greeted Alex as he slowly walked up the stairs of his old apartment building. He slipped his key from his pocket, but stopped before he placed it in the lock. Something warned him to press the doorbell instead. As he waited for his dad to open the door, Alex wondered just how many kids returning home felt compelled to knock. He assumed not very many. But not many had the uniquely strained relationship Alex had with his father.

They had never reconciled. Though Alex had decided not to reach out to his father, it still bothered him.

Gerald Baxter never called him at school, and whenever Alex phoned home, his reception was lukewarm and indifferent. Black men always had a difficult time demonstrating affection toward each other, and toward their families. It was a job most fathers had given to the mothers, who generally had a tendency to over-shower their sons with love and attention. The old saying "Mothers love their sons and raise their daughters" was a well-known fact. However, what was the idiom that described motherless sons?

Alex could only imagine how it would be if his mother were still around. She'd be happy to see him, greeting him warmly with a big old hug. So proud of him, her strong black son, that she'd help him with his bags, filled with his aspirations and dirty laundry.

Instead, Alex was abruptly awakened from his reverie by reality. "Uh, hello, Alex," his father said, and greeted him with an awkward handshake.

"Hello, uh, Dad." As Alex entered the living room, the somberness of the small apartment brought the walls in even closer. Alex shrugged it off; after all, he was home.

"I think there's a few leftovers in the box. Mrs. Owens said for you to come down to her place; she fixed you, um, us, some food." His father reached for his cap and headed for the door. "I'm heading out now. I'll see you."

His father ducked out the door, and Alex was relieved that the few tense moments of strained conversation were over. He slowly walked back to his old bedroom. He suddenly remembered that his father hadn't gotten rid of Ivan's clothes. It was a little spooky. As much as Alex loved his brother, he didn't relish the idea of rifling through his old things. It was still too painful. They had shared a closet, but his father never allowed him to remove any of Ivan's things. Alex didn't want to tempt fate. He decided to leave his clothes in his suitcase, so he wouldn't have to confront any additional ghosts or memories.

The two weeks at home grinded by slowly. A momentary bright spot occurred when Alex braved the ten-degree weather to visit Ivan and his mom. Hovering over their snow-laden graves, he prayed, and reaffirmed his vow not to let Ivan's death be in vain. He practically froze to death, but it was worth it. Alex felt warmth there that he'd never find elsewhere, especially at home.

His father said little to him, and never offered any type of support. He didn't ask about what Alex was doing, how he was doing, or *if* he was doing at all. There were never any conversations about his life, especially regarding his future. Despite Alex being home, his father continued to work exceptionally long hours. Alex felt like an intruder. He had hoped the personal distance between them would change with his being away. But he was wrong. They were no closer than before.

But Alex also realized that he'd never considered what his father had been going through. It was something that Alex owed to him. He couldn't imagine how much he must have suffered, first losing a wife, and then a son. Gerald Baxter's wife had been everything to him. He'd worked hard to help her get through school, and although he was reluctant to let her follow her dreams, he was proud of her and her accomplishments. Her gregarious personality was complemented by his quiet strength. But with her brutal death and then the even more heinous public death of his firstborn, that quiet strength had been converted to a sullen existence.

But it was still difficult for Alex to understand. Deep inside, he craved support, love, and understanding, and he needed it, but he didn't feel worthy of it. Perhaps it was because he had lived, and his mother and brother hadn't.

Unlike other fathers, who had deserted their families, his father was there, but in a state of emotional desertion. Alex didn't know if it was anger or uncontrollable anguish that kept his dad locked in that state of mind, but he knew it was beyond his comprehension. He didn't have a lot of time to waste on supposition. He had to deal with the here and now.

At home, Alex was quickly assaulted by the failure that had swallowed his old neighborhood. Next to none of his old friends had gone to school. Those who weren't having babies or living off the system either worked in the government, went into the service, or had gotten in the revolving door of the criminal justice system. His old nemesis Calvin had become a statistic, arrested and paroled numerous times for increasingly violent crimes. He was in and out of Lorton Penitentiary on a regular basis. That came as no surprise to Alex. Career options were limited for most first-time offenders, and worse for repeat offenders, and the majority chose to climb the rungs of the criminal ladder.

The stroll around the neighborhood was less than fulfilling. Alex made the grievous mistake of passing Ivan's old court. For so many years he'd avoided that spot, and being suddenly confronted by it now brought back all the memories of Ivan's death.

Drugs were becoming the national pastime, and were ensconced in his environment. Cocaine moved out of the luxurious penthouses and condos of Georgetown and Dupont Circle and crept into the mean, crowded streets of lower Northwest, and into the 'hood.

Suddenly, the black American dream was being realized. Not from hard work, scholarships, or the access to the rungs of the corporate ladder that college offered, but through the street conglomerates that offered the good life to the common folks.

Graduating from school meant nothing. Why go through all of that hardship if your ultimate goal was to get out and make money? Why not make the money now? Start earning today.

What youths were viewing on the television, à la Blake and Alexis Carrington of *Dynasty,* and even J.R. of *Dallas* fame, was suddenly available to them for the meager price of blood and fearlessness. Jazzed-up Benzes and Beamers with tinted windows and flashy chrome rims cruised the streets of the 'hood in greater numbers than in Chevy Chase. Where the rich were afraid of appearing pretentious and ostentatious, the nouveau riche reveled in opulence.

Beepers migrated from the medical profession to the urban pharmaceutical industry. Once the trademark of the traveling salesman, they now identified the street-corner pushers.

Designer clothes descended from the racks of Lord & Taylor to downtown. Girls began styling and profiling in everything from Louis Vuitton to MCM to Fendi to Gucci. It didn't matter what it was, as long as it had a designer label on it.

These new roads to wealth found many avid travelers. You could go from feast to famine in a matter of days. From being a nobody to a somebody within a matter of weeks. From living to dead in the blink of an eye. The money brought the honeys and an escape from the bitter reality that the more things had changed, the more things had remained the same.

Through magazines like *Esquire* and *GQ*, Alex discovered a world free from the grit and grime he saw 24/7, a world where culture and legitimate business thrived and offered rewards. He dreamed the dreams that would one day become his reality, without the bloodshed and the blood money of life in drugs' fast lane.

There was one bright spot to Alex's visit home. Mrs. Marshall, fearing that he'd dropped out of school, offered him his old job back.

Chuckling, Alex replied, "No thank you, Mrs. Marshall." He clasped her hand and held it firmly. "But if I ever do, I'll be sure to come right back for it."

Mrs. Marshall hugged him warmly. "Chile, if you ever need it, don't be afraid to ask. You stay a good boy now, you hear? Don't you get caught up in a wrong crowd like so many of these others 'round here."

It was a comforting feeling to be missed. To be thought about fondly, as Alex was so often thinking about Tiffany.

EXHALING, ALEX BLEW his warm breath on the dirty bus window. Somehow he felt emancipated. As anticipated, Christmas had been miserable. There wasn't even a Christmas tree, or gifts. He'd bided most of his time at the Library of Congress until he could escape back to the sanctity of Hilliard.

Alex reclined in his seat in the comfort of the aging coach. The bus ride back to Tidewater was a relief. His dad had deposited him at the bus station a few hours earlier than his scheduled departure, but he hadn't minded.

Smiling privately, Alex massaged his breast pocket. Inside were his grades, six A's, and his dean's list citation. His scholarship was secure, and he looked forward to returning to the yard, where he could get a jump on his studies. By getting back early, Alex would be able to work for a few days, and purchase his books before the masses showed up. He'd even have the room to himself, because if Foody remained true to form, he wouldn't be back until the very last minute—and maybe later than that.

Alex shifted slightly in his seat, as the bus became jammed with overzealous travelers charging toward the rear of the bus, knocking over bags and other passengers as they rushed for the remaining empty seats. On that Greyhound bus Alex prayed. He was sure that he'd made the right decision about committing himself to getting out of Shaw and trying to get a college degree. Being a black man, he might not have completely eliminated the odds of being gunned down over a vial of crack cocaine, but he had reduced them dramatically.

RETURNING TO SCHOOL was Alex's nirvana. Unfortunately, many others, with the exception of the graduating seniors, were not of the same opinion. Foody being among them.

"So, how was home, Alex? You see my moms hooked me up. She even gave me more, to make sure you got some too." Foody rummaged through one of his goody bags. "Did your girl show up? I halfway expected to find you frozen to death and stuck to that wall you was leaning on when I got back here."

"Let's just say I got home." Alex shrugged and downplayed it. He still nursed his disillusionment with Tiffany. She was every man's dream, but knowing what he knew made it extremely bittersweet.

"I figured she didn't mean that bull about picking you up. But don't sweat it. She's just out of your league, that's all. You know, the little honey with all the hookups. She's got the big money, and the big frat guy, and he's frontin' for her daddy. We just ain't part of that crowd. Not yet, anyhow.

"She probably meant well, you know. But hey, she probably just forgot about you. It was probably that damned Sid, blowin' her mind." He looked at Alex with genuinely remorseful eyes.

"Yeah, man, whatever you say." Alex was relieved that Foody hadn't busted him out, but Foody was still suspect, notorious for lulling him into a false sense of security, then cracking on him hard. Alex wasn't about to get played that easily. He kept his face blank, covering his hold card.

"Come on, Alex. Let's go get something to eat. I'm hungrier than a mug." Foody extended his palm, as if he wanted Alex to slap him five, but Alex grabbed his hand and swiftly gave Foody the soul brother number-five handshake. They laughed at the unstated joke between them. Alex was finally getting cool.

CHAPTER 8

WITH the rush of spring, folks scrambled for summer internships, cabarets, graduation parties, summers abroad, and, oh yeah, finals. It seemed like the professors had forgotten the idleness of their youth, and were adhering to some unspoken edict that 10 percent had to fail. For the love of spring and all things good, there was promise, there was hope, and there was bitter reality.

By the middle of spring semester, Alex bravely departed from his comfort zone. He decided to incorporate real-life lessons with his academics. Learning the ways of the world, or at least of Hilliard, became his new challenge. Alex studied his peers and his environment with the same tenacity he devoured his textbooks. And he learned a lot, rapidly, hanging with his new friend Lisa.

Lisa Adams was a pretty, smart, well-endowed young lady Alex had partnered with in his basic-programming lab. Lisa was from Hot 'Lanta, where her parents owned a small yet thriving insurance company. She was an accounting major, and was really cool. Their friendship had blossomed out of the painfully long hours they spent working on problems and discussing life issues and their dreams and goals for the future. For the first time, he'd finally met a female he could relate to, and be himself with.

A real homegirl, Lisa was a slightly older sophomore, and worldly beyond her years. She absolutely loved giving him advice, and finally gave him honest insight into women. Except for the moments when she practiced her feminine wiles on him, she treated him like a kid brother. She schooled him on the feminine mystique in her own unique Atlanta-Georgian way. They were lessons Alex needed desperately.

Alex often wondered why Lisa took time with him, especially since she was one of the ones whose parents had gone to college. At H.I., that meant a lot. Your name got you far. You could be from an old family with lots of bank, or a son or daughter of the nouveau riche. Publishers of the only black paper in town eagerly sent their children to Hilliard. Businessmen, owners of janitorial companies or insurance companies, sent their children to the Southern Mecca. These children of the bourgeoisie were not standing in the financial aid line, or sweating over what their grades were. They knew they'd make it. But Lisa never carried herself like that.

"Alex, I'm nothing like these silver-spooned heifers around here," she said as they walked to Randolph Hall. "My folks humped for everything they have. My mother went to school at night, and my dad's self-taught. These folks act like this is some kind of secret damned society. Like their birthright gives them some kind of honorary degree. So what if Professor So-and-So taught their mother—do they have to casually mention it on the first day of class? They think it's a rite of passage to have gone to so many homecomings, that they already know all of the faculty before they're even admitted. The acceptance letter's just a formality. Big damned deal." Lisa sniffed and puffed on a cigarette as they strolled across the yard to check on their grades.

"You can say that, Lisa. At least your folks went to school. Plus they own an insurance company. I don't have any of that going for me."

Lisa cut her eyes at him and drew on her cigarette. "You have plenty going on. You just have to understand your position in the food chain, that's all. Now. You're not a legacy, your folks don't own their own business, and they don't have a corporate job. Sounds like you're S.O.L."

"S.O.L.?"

"Shit outta luck," Lisa said.

"Funny. Very funny."

"It is funny, Alex. You've just lucked out. You can't change who your parents are, but maybe you can get adopted by somebody that works for IBM. Then you'd have some guarantee of success. Nepotism is a real mother. Or better yet, you can buddy up with somebody whose parent has a white-collar job. They're the ones to be especially friendly towards. You never know who might be able to open the right doors for you, especially in the era of Reaganomics."

"Ha-ha. I get your point."

"A ha-ha hell. Now maybe you know how simple you sound. You can sit back and wallow in what you don't have, or capitalize on what you do have. Don't tell me all this good advice I've been giving you is all for naught?"

"No, you've hooked me up a lot. I think I'm getting into the groove now."

"Groove? You don't know the first thing about a groove. Without a love life, honey, there ain't no such thing as a groove."

Alex was still quite ignorant in the ways of *amore*. But he still had no time for that. Or so he convinced himself.

"You don't know what you're talking about," he said. "Just because I don't broadcast my business around doesn't mean I don't have something going on. Some things should be left between the two parties, don't you think?"

Lisa plunked her still-lit cigarette into the grass and smirked. "That might be the case, Alex. But you don't have two parties. You barely have one. And you can't count your hands."

Alex was increasingly bothered by his naïveté regarding the young ladies. Not that he wanted to know about just any young lady. Tiffany was the only one who had piqued his interest thus far, and that had proven to be a major disappointment. Still disillusioned over the events of the winter-break road trip, Alex ignored his thoughts and dreams about her and became even more focused on his goals and objectives. When he saw her, which was usually at a distance, he'd quickly wave, barely gaze her way, and hurry on in the opposite direction.

She probably didn't notice. She was completely immersed in her role of Ms. Hilliard Institute, and Alex was now probably just another face in the crowd to her. But he had to give her points for her competency in commanding her position. If Miss America were to come on the yard, she would probably have to check her tiara at the gate, and relegate herself to Tiffany's court.

Lisa was the only one who was even remotely aware of the attraction Alex had for Tiffany, and although she poked fun, she never cracked on him too hard. Even though he hadn't initially told Lisa about the Christmas break debacle, call it female intuition, when Lisa had caught him crossing the square to avoid Tiffany, she'd taken one look at him and asked him what had happened. Though they spoke only this once about his infatuation with Tiffany, that was enough for her to lock it into her memory. Lisa took a heartbeat to sum up just how much Alex, this painfully shy brother, thought about Tiffany. Lisa acted like that kind of saddened her.

THEY FINALLY REACHED Randolph Hall, and stood outside the lab where their grades were posted. The green-ruled sheet reflected everything from a D-minus to a few sparse A's. Some other students ventured forward, and either exited hurriedly or prayed to God for at least a passing grade.

Lisa collapsed dramatically against the wood door, successfully blocking his view.

"Oh, I just can't bear to look. If I get one more D in this man's class, my ass is going to be kicked to the curb. Word up."

Alex casually assisted her by pushing her shoulders to the side. Though not fashion-model size, Lisa was nice and firm, what they called "thick" in the South. Like a lip-smacking milk shake. Healthy. Alex had to admit that he liked brushing up against her womanly body. It was the first time he'd pressed a female's flesh, and it was nice.

"Well, step aside. Let me see what a righteous man gets on his exams." With butterflies bouncing in his stomach like intoxicated nightclub dancers, he bravely stepped up to examine his grades. Although he thought he'd performed well, he could never be too sure.

Not to be outdone, Lisa immediately broadsided him and pushed ahead to get hers first.

She immediately looked relieved. "It's not an A, but I'll take a B anytime." She rolled her head triumphantly, and peered sarcastically at him as he slowly perused the roll for his grade.

"Oh, you make me so sick, Alex. You act like you don't know what your damned social security number is," she fumed and walked away. "You know you got one of the A's, probably the only one."

Alex eyed his grade. As usual, she was right.

"I'll never tell," he said.

"You don't have to. I may not be a rocket scientist, nor do I know about the space program, but I think I can at least figure that one out." She rolled her eyes. "Now, don't think I forgot about what we were talking about. I haven't. You need to learn how to score out of the classroom."

She hurriedly lit up a barely used Newport before they even made it outside the chem building with its flammable gases, and received a dirty look from the janitor. Once outside, they strolled past the library, toward the Student Union. Posters announcing a PKO blast hung on the streetlights around the square.

"About your social life, please allow me to digress for a moment. You going to the PsiKOs' party? The big hoedown? Or should I say whoredown?" Pointing to the posters, Lisa was about to launch into one of her favorite tirades. How much she hated them and was a sworn PsiKO enemy. Kappa sweetheart to the bone, Delta in her heart, she scorned everyone else.

"Get real," he scoffed.

Dragging on the now stubby cigarette, Lisa savored it like fine wine. "You are such an old fuddy-duddy, boy. My goodness, you need to stop being so anal-retentive. Loosen up, get yourself some booty."

Many times Lisa had expressed those same sentiments to him. She had met Foody in their room, and ever since then the two had championed the effort of reminding Alex of his meager social existence. And between her and Foody, Alex knew just how much of a life he didn't have.

"Why do you care?" he said. "Isn't your old man coming down this weekend?" Brian, Lisa's boyfriend and one of her homeboys from Atlanta, was a linebacker for Virginia Tech's less-than-victorious football team. But that was okay with her. She liked the jock in him, plus she planned on prodding him into being a Kappa one day.

"For your information, Brian *is* coming down, and, no shit, Sherlock, I will not be at the PsiKOs' tired little function." She licked her red lips seductively. "You know we've got much better things to do. Maybe you should try it sometime." She poked his ribs mischievously.

He imagined Lisa and Brian entangled in a sweaty embrace. On more than one occasion Lisa had willingly provided the gory details of her lingerie and the various sex toys that she used. Lisa was too scandalous. He envisioned her clad in a skimpy Frederick's of Hollywood outfit, complete with "come f—— me" pumps, with cat-o'-nine-tails in hand. She hovered over the bed as Brian lay helplessly tied up. Alex snickered aloud.

Lisa continued smoking, oblivious. "You should go," she said "You know that your girl will probably be there. Then you can admire her from a shorter distance than afar. You can see her royal highness up close and personal with those puppy-dog eyes of yours."

"I knew I should've never mentioned Tiffany to you. I was wondering when you'd get around to that. I should've known something was up. You were always so merciful towards me, and so venomous towards everyone else. Now I guess I shouldn't feel special anymore."

"You *are* special, Alex. Special ed. You need a reality check. See, when I was growing up, I always saw that sick, sad, puppy-dog look on the faces of boys looking past me. Panting over those little frilly girls. They were teases, just like your girl. Little Southern belles, the kind whose parents doted on and groomed them to be Mrs. So-and-So. With their coming-out parties and balls and cotillions. They were always outfitted in fancy chemise dresses, with matching ribbons, while I was running around in hand-me-downs. They made me sick, perched on the front porch, their legs crossed with those little white anklet socks on. So prim and proper, they were scared to get dirty. While they were having their little fake tea parties, I was getting pushed around by my roughhousing older brothers and making mud pies at the playground.

"But I know the real deal. I don't have some pie-in-the-sky, white-picket-fence fantasy. I learned how to deal with little boys as they grew into bigger boys. And beat off the ones that tried to stick their hands in my pants. At least until they learned how to finesse me." She laughed softly, and turned away.

"I understand what you're saying, Lisa. But things aren't like that. I mean, Tiffany doesn't strike me as being like that."

"Yeah, like you know," Lisa said. "I remember when I first saw her sauntering around the yard like she's all that. She hadn't even been here a week. I don't mean to bust your bubble, but I bet she's the biggest freak going if she's dealing with that dog-assed Sid. She ought to kick his diminished-capacity ass to the curb, but she must like it like that."

Alex's face dropped, and he stopped walking. "I guess. But I hope not."

"Alex, you need to stop pining after that gal. You have a lot to offer; you're smart, and you're actually kind of handsome." She grabbed his chin and rubbed his cheek. "In a boyish kind of way. Look at you. You have beautiful eyes, and thick eyelashes. And a wonderful smile, when you do smile. All you need is just a big dose of self-confidence. Someone to bring you out of your shell. But face it, she is not the one. You are way too sweet and too innocent for the likes of her. Trust me."

Alex was a little taken aback by Lisa's comments, but he smiled slightly, and tried to swallow her words. She was on a roll.

"You need to spend less time looking in the books and more in the mirror," she said. "You just need to get out more. Going to the party might be good for you."

"Ah, you know I don't party too much. I probably couldn't even do the Smurf if I tried." Alex switched his overloaded knapsack from his left shoulder to his right.

She shrugged, exasperated. "You better get in the game, Alex. Hell, you better get in the stadium to get in the game. Act like you know. One day you'll realize that you've got a lot to offer, and then maybe one day you'll act like it." As they continued striding across the yard, Lisa rambled about the grades they'd just received. She'd let him win this battle, but the war was far from over.

Deep down, Alex knew Lisa was right, and that she probably had his best interests at heart, but somehow he couldn't force himself to join his peers in their zest for life. When Alex looked in the mirror, he didn't see a whole lot. He saw a short, slight, average-looking guy who could use a little help from GQ and Mother Nature. He knew that he ought to take Lisa's advice, but it definitely wouldn't be in time for tonight's party. Probably not in time for any party, anytime soon.

CLAD SCANTILY IN matching lace bra and underwear, she stood in front of her full-length mirror. Manicured hands on firm hips, she was a vision. She slid her hands down her curvaceous body, admiring every inch. She knew her body better than anyone. Less than 20 percent body fat.

She moved rhythmically to the house grooves playing on the "Saturday Night House Party" on WHIS. She was a spa girl long before there were franchised spas. She worked out in the family gym, where she had attended private ballet lessons, taken jazz and tap. She pliéd. Her body was a finely tuned instrument. She could block out anything for dance. This was first proven when she was six years old and about to perform her first solo for Madame

Toulouse, an instructor at the Duke Ellington Performing Arts School. Madame had wanted to cancel her performance, and the little debutante demanded to know why. Tiffany refused to obey instructions until given the reason, and Madame Toulouse had finally relented and said that her mother had been in an accident.

Little Tiffany had stood stoically, contemplating her fate. Then she had announced quietly that the show had to go on. Tears had welled in her eyes, but she blocked out everything except her dance, and at the end, the crowd, on their feet, sobbed with her. Little Tiffany Blake had grabbed the spotlight, and now, a mere twelve years later, she hadn't given it up.

She reached for her aloe plant and broke off a leaf, and smeared the juice in her palm. She gently rubbed it on her thigh. It kept her skin soft, just like a baby's bottom. Gingerly placing the leaf on her face, she recalled a poignant moment from her youth. Her personal governess, Mrs. Wellington, had said, "Push up-up and out-out. You must lift the skin on the face up, not down. You will get wrinkles." Imagine, a seven-year-old with wrinkles.

Tiffany hadn't done half bad to have been raised without her mother, Marjorie, who had died when she slammed into a parked car trying to avoid hitting a child. Tiffany had terrorized a whole host of nannies until the mercurial Mrs. Wellington had moved in. She was time enough for Tiffany.

She pulled her hair up into a flowing ponytail, then glided across the luxurious oceanfront condo her dad had purchased for her years before she came to Hilliard. Being the mayor's daughter could be a pain in the ass sometimes, but there were perks. The thick carpet zapped her with static electricity as she reached inside her expansive walk-in closet to choose an outfit for tonight's dance.

Tiffany tossed outfit after outfit onto her king-sized bed, but none captured her fancy. She wanted something that would match the frat's red and black, and there was little to choose from. Although most of the clothes still had the tags swinging, she was dissatisfied. She checked her Gucci timepiece where it sat daintily on her vanity. Eight-twenty. Time to get moving.

Though a first-year sweetheart, Tiffany was not required to do the grunt work and set up the ticket table and concession stand like the other girls. The older sweethearts, or "Baguettes," as they were called, allowed her to do what they did, which was to arrive fashionably late, look good, and get the party jumping.

Some of her girls, Holly and Taylor, were stopping by to pick her up, since she had let Sid borrow her car earlier that day. He was out and about, hosting some of his frat brothers who had driven down from Virginia State, and he wanted to make sure that he looked good. Sporting her ride would do the trick. Plus, a lot of the brothers thought it was his anyhow, and he was okay with letting them think that. Which subtly reminded Tiffany that she had to look good. It was *trés* important that she look good for her man in front of his frat.

Still frustrated about her inability to find a suitable outfit, Tiffany moved on to her makeup and accessories; she'd come back to the fashions later. PKO pins and a little eye shadow would do the trick. Sid liked to see her all made-up, looking hot, just so that he could flaunt her in everyone else's face. That was a little annoying sometimes, but that was Sid.

Sidney. Tiffany looked at his framed picture that sat on the corner of her vanity, and began moving seductively to the heart-thumping house beats. He was a good guy, someone she could possibly marry one day, she figured. Sure, he needed a little polishing, but who didn't? Not everyone was from her world, and she admired his rawness, his defiant nature. Their differences stoked the fire of their attraction, turned her on.

She'd heard that he turned a whole lot of other girls on too. Before she arrived at H.I., and even after they had gotten together. She discounted the rampant rumors as strictly petty jealousy. After all, Sid was *the* PKO on the yard, and he had chosen her, out of everyone else, to be his girl. The thought warmed Tiffany from her erogenous zones to her toes. Even her father liked him. Which was rare. Simon Blake rarely liked any of her suitors. Many times he would question their manhood, thinking that they had been too coddled to be a real man. Most of the time he would barely tolerate their presence, especially if they were from some of the DeeCee aristocracy.

This time, Tiffany had chosen a winner in Sid. True, her father probably liked Sid because he was his frat, but they seemed to have a genuine rapport. He liked Sid's toughness, and the way he was not intimidated by "Da Mayor." Mayor Blake also valued the way Sid protected Tiffany. It was immensely gratifying that she had finally connected with a guy who met her father's approval.

Tiffany felt she might have a chance at finally having a real family, and she couldn't think of a more desirable future husband. Tall, good-looking, and probably very virile. Tiffany could imagine herself married, raising a houseful of fine young kids with Sidney, à la the Brady Bunch.

Sid had a temper, and could be insanely jealous. He had gone off when he heard a Que had flirted with her at a step show at Norfolk State. Sid had jumped into her car and made a beeline for NSU. It had taken several of his frat brothers to contain him. Sid was a keg of dynamite, and a pass made at Tiffany was the match that lit it. From that point on, it was no secret that Tiffany was Sid's property, and one of the most desirable pieces of female flesh in all of colored Tidewater. She loved the attention that came with being so adored. She loved it almost as much as being crowned Miss Freshman.

And she loved Sid, despite his faults and occasional erratic behavior. Maybe he was a little too possessive at times, but she was just as possessive of him. It was a formidable relationship, and they both responded well to each other's needs. For all the quirks that Sid demonstrated publicly, she countered privately. Tiff had a few Achilles' heels that she took great pains to conceal, and which Sid protected with a vengeance.

Long before she hooked up with him, Tiffany had decided that she was not going to "give up the goods" before marriage. At first, Sid thought she was just playing hard to get, and relentlessly pursued her anyway. He enjoyed the challenge. But when he had realized that she was serious, he'd become increasingly frustrated. A

few times he'd got a little too rough with her about it, and even
bruised her wrists, but then he always seemed genuinely sorry af-
terward. During these times Sidney would be gentle and childlike.
She'd threaten to break up with him, he'd cry at the thought of
losing her. He'd apologize profusely, and show up at her door with
flowers and a half-cocked smile. It melted Tiffany's heart, and she
always forgave him. It touched her to see him being so emotional,
especially since he spent so much time being Mr. Macho. He'd
sworn not to do it again, and it had been a while since it had happened. Tiffany was content to blame it all on his childhood. Sidney had shared many stories of how he had suffered from abuse
and abandonment. All Sidney needed was her love, and a little polishing.

She felt especially close to him when he revealed his vulnera-
bilities. When no one was around, he really clung to her. She knew
he was just a little boy hiding behind this huge facade, and she
understood him. Except when the subject of sex arose. Their lack
of a sex life was always a trigger, the single issue that created the
few bad moments between them. But for Tiffany, it was tolerable.
She'd make Sid realize that there was more to a relationship than
sex, and that if he was patient, she would be worth the wait. She
knew that.

Yet, in her quiet moments, beneath her bravado, she was concerned. Lately he seemed to be a lot more argumentative about it,
but she tried to pooh-pooh her concern. He still seemed content
being her man; after all, he wouldn't let any other man get within
ten feet of her. He should be happy. Who wouldn't be? She was
fine, and everybody knew it.

She touched her small yet supple breasts, as she had sometimes
allowed Sid to do. He would try to be gentle, especially when they
were kissing, but it generally led up to the same thing: him wanting more. He would rub her breasts, fondling them as if they were
navel oranges. Then he would begin panting and grabbing her
hand, placing it on his crotch. She could feel his nature rise, and
she even felt a lustful urge or two between her thighs, but she was
adamant. No sex. Period. He would get upset, get up and leave,

and she wouldn't hear from him for a day or two. But he always came back, no matter what, sheepish and apologetic.

Tiffany laughed to herself. Once Sid had tried a different tactic to convince her to give up the goods. He had suggested that she take it up the butt, doggy-style. Therefore, he reasoned, she'd still be a virgin, and he'd be able to get his rocks off. Tiffany remembered laughing in his face, and promptly putting his ass out of her house. But she couldn't tell any of the Baguettes that one. She didn't want them to think that her man was some kind of freak or something.

She scanned her vast selection of perfumes, atomizers, oils, and powders, pondering what perfect scent to sprinkle her body with. It was a warm spring night, and of course the niggers would be creating a sweatbox in the multipurpose room, so nothing too heavy. But she needed a signature, something powerful yet alluring— something to separate her from the pack. She selected a bottle of French perfume that she had picked up a few years ago. No one else would smell like her tonight.

She lifted her flowing ponytail and released her tresses. Her sandy brown hair cascaded down over her shoulders. She tossed her luxurious locks, because Sid liked to see her do that. She did it again for good measure.

Tiffany dressed quickly and lingered by the mirror. She liked what she saw. She was together, she was fresh, and she'd turn the joint out. No bout a doubt it. She was a little peaked, though, and she needed a pick-me-up.

She grabbed a small crystal vial from under her vanity. Better than any No-Doz and faster than a Dexatrim, this white, powdery substance kept her on, fit and trim, and always at the head of the class. It also kept her entertained when she was bored. She had Sid and the girls from Bridgewell Friends to thank for her love affair with the 'caine.

Getting high and getting through school were almost synonymous. Her private-school teachers had used drugs recreationally, and the supply was endless. In a town where the children of the wealthy and elite did them for sport, drugs were not a big deal.

Every major party featured gobs of cocaine, served up in private rooms. Bring your own spoon. Fashionable, fourteen-karat-gold spoons were hung ceremoniously around many a Gold Coast diva's neck.

Tiffany's appetite for coke was nearly insatiable. Only she and a few of the more wealthy students shared her devotion, and Sid made sure she stayed stocked up. She could take a hit before class, go all day, and produce big results. She had energy, vibrancy, and personality to boot. It was so good to her.

She took a toot. As the chemicals tingled her nose, they entered her body on a mission. Suddenly she felt up, free, ready to take on the world. Or at least those hard-looking Que Pearls who were destined to be at the dance, and try to steal her thunder.

She wiped away all traces of the coke, then glanced at the clock. The hour of enchantment was approaching. She could almost imagine herself being out on the dance floor, working her tight body. She'd lead the sweetheart calls and perform all of the pseudo-fraternity steps. The spotlight awaited. Time to get the party started right.

CHAPTER 9

ALEX gingerly rubbed his aching eyes, heaved a sigh of relief, and wrapped up the last of his calculus problems. It was almost quarter to one, and he was getting his second wind. He'd just spent four and a half hours studying nonstop, without even a bathroom break. He needed to unwind, for the pea green walls were closing in on him. But he had to keep pushing. What was left to do? He reared back in the decrepit old desk chair and took a mental break.

Alex's desk was strewn with crib notes, books, and gum wrappers. He had finished all of his poli-sci crib notes during his tour of duty at the library earlier that day. All other possibilities exhausted, he figured that he could look over his chemistry lab work again. He suddenly realized that he'd left his lab notes in the top drawer of the library reference desk. A student had drawn him away from his studies to help him find some obscure book on medieval history. "Damn it," Alex cursed under his breath.

Exhausted, but too wired to consider sleeping, Alex figured that the best thing to do would be to jet over to the library and get it. It being after hours didn't faze him, because he had the keys. He could dash in, grab the papers, and still get in some productive study time. Then he wondered if it would even be worth it. Would he be too tired to be productive? He took a last swig of lukewarm coffee from his day-old convenience-store Styrofoam cup, and considered it on his way to the bathroom.

Foody was out, probably still throwin' down at the party. The dorm was quiet, except for a few partygoers who were drifting in solo. They were the unlucky ones. The ones who watched everybody else hook up after the dance, while they were left to go home and socialize with Hannah and her nine sisters.

He grabbed his keys and jacket, threw on his knapsack, and jetted. The sooner he got there, the sooner he'd be back in the safe haven of his dorm room.

"IT'S HOT IN here, it's hot in here. There must be some PsiKOs in the atmosphere."

The party was the bomb. The frat had drawn a crowd from all over, and the sweethearts were turning it out. As the crowd chanted *a-coo coo, coo-coo* to the beat of "Get Off," the PsiKOs gleefully flaunted their status of being the frat on the yard.

"Sid, why don't you slow down, baby?" Tiffany looked at him doing his wild fraternity steps and sweating up a storm. She was cool and precise, moving her body fluidly, and wondered why he was acting so out there.

"It's cool, Tiff. I'm just gettin' my high up," he said, hitting a joint and swilling Schlitz Malt Liquor Bull straight out of a paper bag. "I might need it for later." He winked at her, and started chanting.

"Well, I've had enough. I'm going to see what needs to be done before we get out of here."

Tiffany sauntered off the floor, wading through the crowd, hoping Sid would follow. She whirled around, and tempered her disgust as he continued his one-man step show.

The deejay spun the last record, the house lights came on, and the crowd reluctantly dispersed. The PKOs, high from the over-whelming success of the party, plotted their next challenge: who was going to zoom who.

"Where y'all headed tonight?" Gorgeous George asked the hodgepodge group of brothers, their dates, and the sweethearts. It was common practice for the brothers to have a set after a jam, and everyone would couple off and get into things. The goal was not to be alone.

Everyone knew that at fifteen past one, like clockwork, the se-curity guards would enter and start the process of emptying the area. You couldn't leave empty-handed.

The brothers answered that they had various plans, all about getting busy.

"Yeah, man, we down. We're going to chill at the frat house," Kold Krush Kyle said. He eyeballed his piece for the night, Keely, a nubile little sweetheart. He wrapped a protective arm around her, to indicate that he had sealed his evening's selection. This was also an indication that he would be willing to share his property, if necessary, in the most brotherly sense. As a frat, you had to make sure that every brother was taken care of.

"Well, we'll be there," Sid said, still sweating profusely. He en-thusiastically high-fived his brothers, and pulled Tiffany in the di-rection of the door.

"I guess we will," Tiffany said. "I'll see you all later."

"We'll meet you guys outside or either back at the crib. We've got to take care of a little something." Sid nodded his head confi-dently. Tiffany, brows furrowed, gave a brief sweetheart sign to her girls, and allowed Sid to lead her through the door and outside into the still night air.

Once they reached the nearly secluded area where the car was parked, Sid courteously opened the door for Tiffany. Once inside, he cracked the convertible's windows and laid the driver's seat back. His eyes were glazed and red from the weed. He leaned over toward her, breath reeking of stale malt liquor.

"Give me a kiss, baby. Let me taste a little bit of that tongue and those sweet lips." Hating to kiss him when his breath was so foul, Tiffany reluctantly obliged. She'd do anything not to start an argument with him. It would definitely bring down her high.

Sid continued talking to her up close and personal. Tiff placed her hand over her nose to block out the stench.

"Well, baby doll, you know what time it is." Sid's words were slurred. With his arm slumped over the wheel and worn PKO T-shirt emblazoned across his chest, he appeared menacing and larger than life. Tiffany blinked her eyes, which were beginning to tear from his halitosis. If only she had taken another hit of coke before the party.

Almost on cue, Sid produced a tiny yellow envelope. "You want some more, sweet thing?" He waved the package in front of her face.

Tiffany quickly put Sid's foul kiss out of her mind. Just thinking about how good she was going to feel after a hit of the nose candy made her giddy. One snort, she'd be beamed to another world. Suddenly, even his breath wasn't so bad anymore.

He carefully poured the white powder out onto Tiffany's compact mirror. After she inhaled the coke, she relaxed backward in her chair. Slowly, the world took on a different hue, and Sid was once again her man. Her main man. Her big baby who would hold and caress her in his overly developed arms. She sighed with pleasure at the thought.

"Baby, you know what's up for tonight? Right?" Sid licked his lips in anticipation.

Tiffany inhaled the remaining grains from the mirror and checked her reflection. She blew herself a kiss.

Sid caressed her arm with his tar-stained fingertips. "You know the bros are coming back to the crib. Just for a little set. Everybody's gonna be there, and I want you to stay with me, baby."

Tiffany, who was now brushing her locks, tossed her hair and ignored him.

He licked his lips and eyed her hungrily. "Look at you. You know that turns me on. But that's just not gonna work. It—it

just ain't gonna look right if you up and leave after everybody
gets there. Then they gonna know I ain't gettin' paid," he said,
frowning.

She tossed her hair once more for good measure. No way would
she spend the night over at that funky frat house. Plus, she'd gotten so coked up, she was thinking about getting one of her girls
to go with her to one of the dance clubs near the naval base.
She knew Holly was on the rag, and wouldn't be ho'ing at the frat
house tonight.

Tiffany grabbed her lipstick. "Si-id. You're smudging my makeup." She used her best little pouty voice, and brushed his cheek
with her fingertips. She shifted into her mode of taming the sav-
age beast. It was an act she utilized to calm him down when he was
after one thing: her panties.

She couldn't use her period again. She had just said that last
week.

"Okay, how about this?" she said. "Why don't we just go over to
the house, hang out for a little while, and then you can come over
to my place. Then your precious frat won't know what's up." She
plastered a smile on her face.

"Goddamn it, Tiffany. There's always a bunch of shit with you.
You got more excuses than a nigger on death row." He banged his
fist against the steering wheel, and the whole car vibrated from the
impact. Her arm shrank as he grabbed it with a powerful grasp.

She tried to pull away, but couldn't. "Stop it, Sid. You're hurting me. You know I bruise easily. Let go of my arm."

He loosened his grasp. "Come on, Tiff. Damn, what's a brother
got to do to get a little something from you? I give you the best shit
I got, try to keep you happy, and all I get is grief. You know how
much I care about you, and all you want to do is get me all horny,
then send me home. Come on now. I'm not going to hurt you. I
just want to love you."

He reached for her waist, and she recoiled. "Look, Sidney,
you've had a little too much, and I haven't had quite enough, at
least not yet. Why don't you just chill out, and—"

"Don't even try that 'Sidney' shit on me tonight. You don't give a fuck about me or my rep, do you, Tiff? You treat me like a little plaything. I'm a man, a real man. One hundred percent beef, baby, somethin' you wouldn't even know about. You're just a spoiled brat, but I got the answer for you."

Tiffany opted for the door. "This conversation is going nowhere. I'm not about to let you talk to me like—"

Sid reached over and locked her door. "You ain't going nowhere."

He grabbed his crotch, and began unzipping his sweaty shorts. "If I've got to fuck you right here, right now, in front of everybody, I'll do it. I swear I will. And you'll look like you're lovin' every minute of it." He lunged for her face and ripped her sweater, exposing a breast.

Tiffany swallowed a fist-sized lump in her throat. Could she get away? Her eyes darted around the deserted parking lot. Sid had parked so far from the Student Union that even the few departing partygoers wouldn't see them. The closest streetlight was off in the distance.

Sid became angrier and threatened to ravage her body in unspeakable ways.

"Sid—Sid," she said, but he ignored her. She had to be hallucinating. Things like this just didn't happen to someone like her. Maybe Sid had given her some bad stuff.

Someone she had trusted and loved was brutally attacking her. She had to do something. Anything. Suddenly, being Miss Freshman really didn't matter. Only her survival did.

She fumbled for the door lock. Sid pinned her arms with one of his powerful biceps.

"I'll do it, but please, let's just go home. To either your crib or mine." She thought it might work if she appealed to one of his senses. "Please, Sid. Don't make me do this out here. I don't want my first time to be in a car—not out here in a parking lot."

His grip relaxed, and she felt a spark of hope. "Come on, baby. We can go to my place; I can put on something sexy, you'll see. It'll be . . . it'll be fun." She made her speech low and alluring like he liked it. She squashed the fear and bile as it crept up her throat.

The vomit burned her esophagus as she fought to maintain her composure.

His grip loosened further, and he began playing with himself. Nodding, he considered it. Then suddenly, he grabbed her by the throat. "Don't try that psycho, psychological bullshit on me, girl. It ain't gonna work." He gripped her throat tightly, and her body jerked as breathing became more difficult. "Yeah, I almost believed that shit, but I know the deal." He squinted at her, as if he barely recognized her.

"You're gonna do me, nice and slow, and then I'm gonna flip that tight ass around and give it to you from behind. And—and then when I'm finished with you, I might pass you around at the set. Let me see how freaky you can get."

She grabbed his hands and tried to pry them from her neck. She desperately motioned her head toward the dance. "What if they see us?" she gasped, fighting back tears.

"I don't give a fuck if the whole damn party sees you. Ain't nobody in their right or left mind gonna try to stop me. They know better than to fuck with me."

ALEX'S LUCK WAS running exceptionally well. Slipping into the library had been a breeze, and he was able to get in and out without being seen by anyone.

Anxious to get back to the dorm before the overzealous partygoers arrived, Alex quickened his pace. He had no desire to get caught on the yard with a knapsack on. It would only reinforce his reputation as a nerd, and he'd never live it down. Who else but a nerd would be studying on a live party night like Saturday?

Approaching the side of the Student Union building, Alex heard the noise of the departing crowd. From the corner of his eye, he saw a few students milling around on the stairs. He desperately wanted to avoid being noticed by anyone, so he weighed his options. Cutting in front of the hall was an almost certain source of embarrassment. The only other alternative was sticking near the dark edge of the parking lot. This would lead him to a worn path in the bushes near the rear of the lot, then he could cut through and have a near perfect escape route to the dorm. Alex sighed with relief, until he noticed a lone car parked over by the bushes. But surely no one would be in there. They'd probably still be at the dance.

His pace quickened to the point that Alex was almost sprinting. His eyes were fixated on the pathway cut through the bushes, oblivious to everything, not wanting to see or hear anything else. He was focused on his getaway. He was free and clear until he noticed the bicentennial D.C. tags on the car. Then he realized that it was Tiffany's red Mustang.

The windows were slightly fogged and cracked, and Alex detected muffled sounds and saw movement in the car.

Maybe Sid and Tiffany were just having a little tête-à-tête in the parking lot. Alex changed his gait and moved farther away from the rocking car. It wasn't until he was nearly past it and home free that he heard what sounded like a scream, and then the sharp sound of a car horn, one that had been accidentally hit.

He froze. He glanced around, but there was no one else who could've made a sound. Assuming that Tiffany and Sid were just having a postcoital argument, Alex tried to force himself to ignore it.

But what if he was wrong? What if it wasn't Sid, and someone else was abusing Tiffany? The scream definitely had sounded as if it were not one of pleasure, but of desperation.

Instinct and stupidity led Alex to peer inside the car. Through the lowered window, he saw Tiffany crumpled in the passenger seat and struggling with Sid, who grabbed her and banged her head against the steering wheel. It was apparent that he was trying to force her to give him head.

Alex didn't know whether to run or yell. Some force drew his hand to the window, and he rapped on it. He had to be tripping.

Tiffany struggled to raise her head. Sid slapped her across the jaw, splitting her lip.

Seeing the blood spurting from Tiffany's lip, Alex became enraged. He banged on the glass again, bruising his hand and almost breaking the window.

"Get the fuck away from here, you punk-ass little bitch!" Sid snarled at Alex, then waved an accusatory finger in his direction. "Oh, so it's you. What are you, some kind of pervert or something?" Sid glared as if Alex had done something wrong.

Alex was in way over his head. Tiffany was clearly in danger, but what could he do? His common sense was telling him to haul ass, but his heart was telling him to do something. Adrenaline rushed as he tried to think of something ingenious to stop Sid from hurting her.

Sid reached over and smashed his large hand against the window, as if he were squashing Alex like a bug. Tiffany continued struggling with him, and managed to catch a glimpse of Alex.

The raw terror in her eyes infuriated him. Reason yielded to anger as Alex snatched at the door, only to find it locked. He kicked it in frustration. Desperately, he ran around to Sid's side of the car and flung the door open, causing Sid to jerk in his seat.

Sid lunged out of the car. By this time, some partygoers were milling around on the stairs. Someone took notice of what was occurring in the darkened corner of the parking lot, and alerted the others.

Tiffany, sweater ripped and lipstick smeared, used both hands to claw at Sid's arms. He slapped her senseless, reeling her backward into the car. She shrieked when her head banged against the steering wheel. Sid now focused his venom on Alex.

"What the fuck do you think you doing? Didn't nobody ever tell you to stay out of grown folks' business?"

Alex mustered as much courage as he could. "I—I th-think you should leave the lady alone."

Sid cocked his head like a dog and squinted. He stepped to Alex as if he were a disobedient child. "What you say?"

Alex smelled the liquor on Sid's breath, and realized he was in more trouble than he'd faced in his entire life. He was about to be made a public spectacle, and probably beaten to within an inch of his life, but somehow, Alex didn't care. He just wanted Tiffany out of there.

A crowd began to form, and murmurs of "Uh-oh" and "Who's that getting their ass kicked?" and "That's Tiffany, man" and "Aw, shit" filled the air. No one dared say anything, not even the handful of Greeks who stared with their mouths hanging open.

No PKOs were out yet, but a long, gangly kid frantically ran to get one.

Tiffany began screaming, "Leave him alone, Sid! Please, leave him alone!"

Sid never took his gaze off Alex. "Oh, so now you tryin' to front on me? Shut the fuck up, bitch. I ain't through with your ass yet."

The crowd gasped. Only a few of the girls in the crowd smirked, the ones who were probably jealous of Tiffany. But even they were visibly mortified by Sid's cutting words and physical violence.

Alex gulped and took a deep breath. "I—I—I said, leave the lady alone," he said, cold sweat popping out on his brow.

Sid laughed wickedly. "Ha! If you see a lady, well then, why don't you help a lady?"

Naïvely, Alex fell for the line, and reached for Tiffany's flailing arms. Sid balled up a massive fist and connected with a right cross to his jaw. "Dumb ass. She ain't no lady."

Alex's head snapped back like a rubber band, and his vision blurred and turned bloodred. Never before had he been punched, and he had no idea that it would hurt so badly. Blood filled his nostrils and trickled out. Still reeling from the blow, Alex kept reaching for Tiffany's arm through the blinding pain. The entire right side of his face was swelling like an overripe melon.

Sid wound his fist up, imitating Sugar Ray Leonard. He pranced around, snorting and beating on his chest. "Aw, shit. I'm gonna hurt you now. You sure you want some more of me, you little punk? Well, come on. Step to me, then!"

Tiffany noticed the rapid swelling of Alex's face, and her eyes filled with tears. "Why don't you just leave him alone, Sid," she said. "You're twice as big as he is. Please, just leave him alone."

But Sid swung again, this time connecting with Alex's sunken chest. The air rushed out of Alex's body as his lungs caved in, and he doubled over in pain and stumbled to the ground. His arms fell like dead weights by his side, and birds fluttered around his head, like in a cartoon.

"I—I s-said leave the lady alone!" Alex gasped, spitting blood as the effort drained his remaining strength.

Gorgeous George, with a whole bunch of frat brothers on his heels, ran over to the crowd. "Sid!" they yelled, but he remained fixated on Alex.

Tiffany ran over to Alex. She reached to help him up, and grabbed his limp shoulders.

"Wha-what do you think you're doing, girl? Oh, so you tryin' to help that little punk out, huh? Well, guess what, I got a little something for you too. I'm going to kick both of your asses, right here and right now. That's probably what you need, anyway. Somethin' your daddy never gave you. A good ass-whipping." He hawk-spat on the ground.

Light-headed from the blows to his head and crushed body, Alex sensed that the end was drawing near. It would have been a relief. His weakened arms were still virtually useless. But something wouldn't let him quit. Drawing on every ounce of his strength, Alex rose up on one knee. His heart was pounding, a loud, deafening thud of blood rushing to his brain, thumping and pouring through the gashes on his face where Sid's fists had torn through his flesh.

As Alex steadied himself against Tiffany's shaking arms, his hands brushed over his jacket pocket. Suddenly, he remembered Ivan's knife. He crawled to his unsteady feet.

Alex found the penlight, but kept it hidden, palmed in his right hand. "Look, Sid," he mumbled through bloodstained teeth. "Please leave her alone."

"Ha! Y'all hear that? 'Please' leave her alone. You're a proper little son of a bitch, ain't you?" He snorted in Alex's face, posturing, reveling in the spotlight. His hamlike fist swung wildly in the air. He took an unstable step in Alex's direction, but Alex didn't flinch.

By this time, most of Sid's frat brothers had formed a circle around them. "Come on, frat," they pleaded, Gorgeous George leading the pack. He cautiously approached Sid, hands up in a calming manner, but Sid hissed at him like a cobra.

"Stay outta this, man. It ain't got nothin' to do with you. Nobody but this little punk, and it's between me and him."

George stopped abruptly, cautiously extending a hand out to Sid. "I know, frat, but come on, Sid. Forget that little punk. That's Tiff, man. That's your girl, bro."

"Yeah, that's my girl, all right. And I've got some business to take care of with my girl, frat."

"Yeah, yeah, well, you got some business to take care of, but chill out, Sid. Chill, man." George reached for Sid's arm, but he violently jerked away.

Taking a cue from the respite George had provided, Alex, his eyes locked on Tiffany's, silently urged her to run away. But she held on tightly to his arm, squeezing it, conveying to him that they were in it together, no matter what happened. They both should have run, instead of standing there like two deer caught in the headlights of an oncoming car.

Aside from one scared onlooker, who rushed off to find some adult intervention, everyone else stood riveted, awaiting the next round of Goliath versus David.

Sid lunged, and Alex swiftly brought the penlight out from his side. Alex tried to shove Tiffany away from him, but she clung on. "Back off, Sid. I don't want to use this. But I will if I have to."

He looked at Alex strangely. "What are you gonna do, shine the light on me? What is that? Some kind of ray gun? You gonna beam me up somewhere, space boy?" He laughed cruelly at him. That was until Alex hit the button and released the blade.

A hush befell the crowd, and Tiffany tightened her grip on his free arm.

A wave of "Aw, shit"s filled the air. Alex's heart beat through his chest and drowned out the low roar of the crowd.

Sid halted in his tracks and eyed Alex with registered surprise. "I—I didn't think you had it in you." He backpedaled, trying to regain his composure.

The blade of the knife gleamed in the moonlit night, and Alex
raised it higher, aiming it at Sid's bulky chest. Alex wanted him to
get a good look at it.

Alex fought to keep his cool, his heart still racing as if he'd just
completed a ten-mile run. In the background, the rest of Sid's frat
implored Sid to drop it and go home.

"Let her go, Sid. It's over," Alex said, shaking his head slowly. "I
don't want to use this, but I will. I swear I will."

Sid raised his hands. "All right, all right, shorty. You know, I was
just illin'." He wiped his nose, apologized profusely, and extended
a hand in a remorseful gesture. "Come on, you got it. It's cool. No
need for all of this."

Alex hesitated. The Shaw in him doubted Sid's sincerity. But
Alex wanted it to be over. His immediate response was to accept
his apology, let it go, and get the hell out of there.

But the street came out of him. The street Alex never really
knew, or acknowledged, that he had inside him. His ghetto instincts told him that Sid wasn't quite right. They told him to stand
Sid down, that to save face, Sid would never give up. It was survival of the fittest. Tiffany pleaded in his ear not to do it, and tried
to stop him. But it was too late. As Sid extended his right hand,
Alex's peripheral vision caught Sid's left hand swinging toward his
face. Operating on sheer reflex alone, Alex shoved Tiffany aside
and thrust the knife down on Sid's arm, inflicting a deep slash
from his shoulder to his wrist.

Squealing, Sid let out a holler that would have shamed the biggest sissy. Blood spurted like a fountain from the gash, and he fell
back onto the ground, whining and grabbing his arm as if it were
falling off. The crowd stood around in awe, until finally the PKOs
swarmed around Sid. Although they gritted on Alex, no one came
up to further threaten him or to console Tiffany.

Gorgeous George spotted the trail of campus security cops rushing in their direction, and took action. "Come on, frat. We've got
to get him out of here. This is no joke. They catch us here, and this
may be it. Let's go." George eyed the knife still clutched in Alex's
hand and said, "I encourage you to do the same, guy."

A swarm of mute sweethearts surrounded Tiffany. Not knowing whether to go against Sid in defense of a sister sweetheart,
no one ventured to say anything. A PKO jacket was placed over
Tiffany's bare shoulders. Only whispers could be heard as they
whisked her away from the fray.

Holly offered a ride to Tiffany, who was now in a total state of
shock. She accepted, but she mumbled repeatedly that she wouldn't
leave without Alex. He had slumped to the ground, trying to
maintain consciousness. He groped around, seeking his precious
knapsack.

As the sweethearts helped Tiffany into the black Toyota Celica,
they hesitated, but made room for him. Alex grasped his tender
ribs, haphazardly gathered his meager belongings, and stumbled
into the backseat of the car. As they sped away from the scene
of the crime, he slipped into unconsciousness, still gripping the
knife.

IT MUST'VE BEEN a dream, Alex thought. Forget the dream. It
was a nightmare, reminiscent of the nightmares from his youth.
Except it wasn't a mental pain he awoke with, but the eye-water-
ing agony of severe physical pain. He struggled to open his eyes,
which seemed glued shut. His head throbbed with the beat of a
thousand drums, and he gasped. It was the first conscious breath
Alex had taken in a long time. When his eyes finally opened, he
was clueless as to where he was. The only thing he knew was that
he was lying flat on his back, staring up at an unfamiliar ceiling.

The faint scent of flowers and the sterile smell of antiseptic
hung in the air. There was also a distinct aroma, kind of a pleasant,
smoky fragrance that wafted into the room. Alex detected voices,
yet his hearing was slightly muffled, as if cotton filled his ears. He
attempted to raise his arm, but quit after sharp pains shot up his
shoulder.

Murmurs drifted into the room. Had he died? Was this heaven?
Or hell? Was he in the hospital? Where was he? Random thoughts
rolled around in his disoriented mind like marbles scattered on
the floor. His head ached even worse.

A slight, withered figure in a white coat entered the room, and stretched Alex's eyelids open and shone a light in his eyes, checking his pulse with a cold stethoscope. After commenting about how strong it was, he drifted away. Still groggy, Alex reasoned that whoever it was couldn't have been an angel, for angels don't need stethoscopes. The figure reappeared and promptly administered a needle into his throbbing arm. The injection crept up his arm in a cold wave.

Was this a hallucination? Alex still had no idea where he was, and he panicked. He had to get out of here. As he tried to move, his body writhed in pain. His ribs were like pieces of jagged glass that shredded his insides whenever he attempted to move or breathe.

Alex had to figure out where he was. The mattress he lay on was firm and comfortable. That definitely ruled out its being either dorm or hospital issue. The walls of the room were covered with designer wallpaper and matching shears. It looked like a showroom or something. As a huge figure slowly approached him, Alex immediately tensed. But then a calmness and a sense of security engulfed him. He suddenly felt safe, yet still slightly intimidated. Somehow he felt a sense of familiarity from this person, but he couldn't quite figure out who it was.

The deep, resonant baritone that spoke soothingly at his side was vaguely familiar, yet quite unknown. Was it God from on high? The voice had an air of mystique and authority, but Alex felt comforted by it. As the mysterious presence spoke, Alex slipped slowly into another deep slumber, cradled in the comfort of this omnipresence. His visitor was like a fairy godfather, an angel who had descended to protect him, part fantasy, part reality. Alex was too weak to know the difference. And for once in his logic-based life, he really didn't care.

CHAPTER 10

FTER the black sedan dropped him off in front of his dorm, Alex took the steps toward his room with a profound sense of uneasiness. He didn't know what to expect. Was someone going to leap out from the bushes and cold-conk him? Would Sidney finish him off? His sense of dread dissipated as his dorm mates met him with high fives and nods of approval.

By the time Alex reached his room, he was still ill at ease—not out of fear, but from the overwhelming attitude adjustment his dormies had when they saw him. It was nothing like before. He must have stepped into the Twilight Zone.

He was quickly brought back down to earth when he opened his door and saw Foody, Lisa, and several packages on his bed. "Well, well, well. If it isn't the Prince of Wales. Hello, Your Highness." Lisa fluffed his pillow and lay back on Alex's bed.

Foody shook one of the packages. "Word up. You do mean w-a-i-l-s, right? Yo, Alex. I wasn't sure if you'd be coming back here or not to hang out with us peasants."

Alex felt his tender ribs, and leaned against the doorway. "What's that supposed to mean? And to think I thought you were my friends."

"Oh, we *are* your friends, Alex. And we don't want you to forget that. See, everybody else might start treating you different, but Foody and I want to make sure your head doesn't get too big. We need to make sure you don't get too brand-new on us."

Foody tossed the package aside, and shook another. "Yeah, come on in, if your head'll still fit through the door." He smiled and gave him a bear hug. "Psych, we're just kidding. Welcome back, homey."

Alex grabbed his ribs and hugged Foody weakly. "Thanks, I was hoping you all wouldn't trip out on me too. I couldn't walk down the hall without somebody saying 'What's up' or trying to give me five. You know, I'm not used to all of this."

Lisa raised the window and lit a cigarette. "You okay? You look like you're still a little hurt. Well, I hope it was worth it, catching a beat-down like that. But whatever the case is, don't get too used to all this glorification. Your fifteen minutes of fame are almost up, but in the interim, you might as well milk it for all it's worth. But what I want to know is, what really happened? I've heard all kinds of wild shit. Like Sid had squabbled with Tiffany, and you had the nerve to jump in the middle of it. Then I heard you nearly killed him. Now, everybody's acting like nothing happened. Tell me. What's the four-one-one?"

"Yeah, we know something went down. Look at all these packages you got. And there's more in your closet." Foody lumbered back over to his bed and slouched down. "So, what's up?"

Alex sat down at his desk, dropping his knapsack by his feet. "To be completely honest with you, I don't remember much. I think I had a concussion or something. All I know is that I was walking home from the library, and the next thing I remembered was waking up in a room somewhere."

Lisa sucked her teeth. "Somewhere, right. You know it was Tiffany's house. You really don't remember anything other than that?"

"The only thing I know is that I was heavily sedated, and under even heavier security. It wasn't like I was at Club Med or something."

There was a bang on the door, and it flung open suddenly. In marched Kerry. "Foody? Is somebody smoking in here? You know the rules." Lisa eyed him seductively and blew her smoke out the window.

Kerry looked around the room and saw Alex. "Oh, Alex. I didn't know that you were here. What's up, man? Welcome back." Kerry shook Alex's hand and gritted on Lisa. "Well, I guess it's okay, if this is a friend of yours. Just try to keep the smoke out there, please."

Kerry headed out, then stopped. "Uh, Alex, once you get settled back in, come down to my room. I've got some more of your packages there." He waved his hand and said, "I'll see you later."

Foody watched the door close slowly behind Kerry, and shook his head.

"Damn, is this how it's gonna be? Kerry ain't gonna ride us no more? Man, you must've really done something somebody liked."

"And we all know who that was. Before everybody caught the vapors and clammed up, I heard Mayor Blake swept down here and hushed everything up. Just like it never happened. You know he'd never let any bad press creep about his little girl," Lisa said, her voice teeming with disgust.

"Well, I'll be glad when it's over. I'm ready to fade back into obscurity and anonymity."

Foody tossed Alex a package. "Well, be sure to open these before you fade back to black or get on the humble. I'm dying to know what's in them. I hope it's some of those delicacies or something. Whoever's sending them to you should know you got a roommate with a mighty healthy appetite."

WHATEVER ALEX ANTICIPATED, his notoriety didn't diminish. It only gained momentum. The incident revolutionized his life. He suddenly possessed a reputation that had soared to near mythical heights, and he was reeling from the fallout. Overnight, he'd been thrust from obscurity into the glaring limelight. The only one who stood up for Da Mayor's little girl was being handsomely recognized and rewarded for his efforts.

Since his return, large packages arrived for him almost daily. They appeared at the front desk, filled with designer clothes, shoes, and accessories. Everyone was highly impressed. Alex was embarrassed. He tried to keep it low-key, but Kerry took it upon himself to announce whenever a box arrived addressed to him. In addition, Foody made sure that everyone was gathered around their open door to survey the contents and provide the obligatory oohs and aahs.

Garments and fine accessories streamed in, from Woodies, Garfinkel's, Saks, and Lord & Taylor, the most chichi Washington clothing stores that before now he'd only heard about.

But that was only the beginning of his good fortune. Besides the transformation of his closet from played-out to fly, Alex was even promoted from his beloved library job. He didn't really want to leave, but he was made an offer he would've been a fool to refuse. He was named the student campus affairs liaison to the president, a specially created position. It gave him access to any organization or office on the yard. Alex could monitor registration, schedule campus activities, or recommend academic-process improvements. All the things that were once so difficult for him, he now practically controlled. He no longer had to worry about the ordeal of registration or getting into closed classes. Though tentative at first, Alex thought he could get used to having power and all that accompanied it.

Plus, the position paid almost $10 an hour, which made him rich by his previous standards. It didn't take a genius to figure out who was waving his magic wand. The position was sponsored by the alumni association, sanctioned by its vice chairman, Mayor Simon Blake.

Alex was dressed nattily on his first day back on the yard. The unfamiliar figures that once overlooked or bumped into him now greeted him with warm gestures and friendly words.

When he reached the registration office, the university comptroller, Mrs. Parker, greeted him.

"Good morning, Alex. It's great to make your acquaintance." She extended her hand. "I'm looking forward to working with you as our new liaison. Let me show you your office."

Alex fumbled with his knapsack, and shook her hand. "Thank you, Mrs. Parker. I'm looking forward to it also."

"Please call me Theresa." She led him down a hallway that was lined with gold-framed artwork and plaques to his richly appointed office. "This is it. I hope you'll like it."

Alex's eyes bulged at the poshness. The walls were painted subtle beige, with exquisite wood moldings at the ceiling and chair rail. The furnishings were an expensive-looking mahogany desk with matching file cabinets, an antique brass lamp, and leather desk accessories. There was a huge bouquet of lilies in a crystal vase on the center of his desk.

"You'll be on the honor system, so you can work your own hours, and you'll be paid for as many hours as you submit. You can use the office for studying, or whatever you desire. Simon Blake is a good friend of mine, and we have complete confidence that you'll excel in this position. I'm sure that a person of your esteem recognizes the high visibility of this position, and will always represent the university in the highest regard."

"Yes, um, I plan to do that, Mrs. Parker, I mean, there's no . . . I definitely won't disappoint you."

Alex was teetering between being grateful and scared witless. Sometimes, in his quiet moments, he couldn't help longing for his vastly unappreciated days of anonymity. Yet there was something intriguing about suddenly being one of the big people. It was a marvel, and a blessing. Alex had to thank God for what He had done for him.

He ran his fingers across the fine-wood-grained desk. In the air was a faint, familiar fragrance that tickled his nostrils. It was k d'Krizia, and seemed to come from a card nestled in the bouquet of flowers that graced his desk.

Opening the fragrant note, he read: *Thanks for being you—Tiff,* in near perfect cursive.

"I hope that didn't offend you." Alex raised his eyes from the card and saw Tiffany at his door. She was a vision of loveliness, standing with the elegance of a fashion model and smiling coyly. His face broke into a toothy grin.

"Offend me? How's that possible?"

Tiffany laughed softly. "You know how it is. Some guys don't like to get flowers." She walked toward the leather seat that faced his desk, and Alex stood as she gracefully took a seat.

"I don't think there's anything that you could do to offend me. But it's still early yet." The lightheartedness of their banter made him smile. He had gained a much higher level of comfort and ease around Tiffany than he ever would've imagined just a few short weeks ago.

But a lot had transpired since then. They had grown quite close during their mutual convalescence. While sequestered, they discovered many similar interests, including classic jazz and black art. More important, Alex was given a prime opportunity to see the real Tiffany, not the superficial one who was displayed on every Miss Freshman poster on the yard.

They had a lot of fun together. Although there was an almost endless stream of doctors, nurses, and plastic surgeons who shared their space, they had plenty of time to get to know each other. Many evenings they spent talking and gazing at the stars from her balcony. It was an invaluable time, one that Alex would cherish for a lifetime.

"You know that's not a problem for me, Tiffany. I'm secure in my masculinity. I'm in touch with my feminine side," Alex mugged, and fiddled with one of the sterling silver pens on his desk.

"Oh, so you remember that, huh? Wasn't that from Morton Downey, or one of those outrageous talk shows we watched during our rehabilitation?" She paused and then said quietly, "I know you were having problems with your memory. Has anything else come back yet?"

"Not really. I still can't remember what happened between the time I left the library and when I ended up at your house. Even that's still kind of hazy. But I remember stuff like Dr. Henry dropping my English homework by." He neglected to tell her that sometimes, when his memory failed him, he'd just laugh nervously. "So how are you doing?" He hoped the subject change was smooth.

"It's still kind of hard. I think I kind of blocked it all out, but I've been seeing a therapist. It's been helping, but it's going pretty slow. It was just too traumatic."

Alex sighed. "Yeah, I know. I guess I probably need to talk to a professional too. But I guess I'll just have to deal with it."

"Dealing with it. That's about what I'm doing, Alex. But I swear that before the ink dries on my last final, I'm going to be off to an exotic locale for some R and R." She tossed her hair, and leaned back in her chair. "You know, I actually hated the thought of coming back to campus, but I couldn't quit. I couldn't let something like, uh, what happened with Sidney change me." She paused and looked up to the ceiling. After a few moments, she said softly, "You know, that's the first time I've mentioned his name since it happened. I'm sure my therapist will consider that a breakthrough."

Alex clasped his hands and fidgeted in his chair. "We don't have to talk about it now, Tiffany. Especially if it's too painful for you. We never have to broach the topic of Sidney. It wouldn't bother me in the least." An unspoken bond had kept the subject of Sidney off-limits for them. Perhaps it was their way of dealing with the pain, and they never talked in depth about the events that had drawn them so close together. "But I have to be honest. Though he's pretty much vanished, I'm still haunted by him. And it's hard, because I think he might come after me one day."

Tiffany looked at Alex evenly, with her large eyes softening. "I don't think we have to worry about that. I'm sure that we'll never be bothered with him again. His memory's even been erased from the annals of PKO. They unceremoniously kicked him out for disgracing the organization and himself. His conduct was completely unbecoming."

It probably had more to do with disgracing the daughter of one of their most illustrious and beloved old heads. That was a line he should've never crossed. Alex forced the images of Sid out of his mind, and again marveled at how Tiffany looked. Coiffed hair, manicured nails, with just a hint of well-applied makeup, she was spectacular. Even casually dressed in linen shorts and a Polo knit shirt, she looked like a runway model.

"Well, anyway, enough about that. You're looking well, Ms. Blake."

"As are you, Mr. Baxter. So," she said, batting her lashes and looking around the office, "how do you like your new digs?"

Alex nodded in approval. "It's cool. It's a far cry from the library."

Tiffany laughed softly. "You know, I think that a nice Bibbs would look really fly right there." She pointed to the wall nearest the window, where there was a breathtaking view of the peninsula.

"Yeah, you know you're right." Then Alex caught himself. "Whoa. Hey, wait a minute. Please, Tiff, please, don't have your father send me one. I'm begging you." He didn't want to appear ungrateful, so when he noticed the smile creeping across her face, he knew it was cool. He raised his hands in the air, as if to assure her that he meant no offense.

"Don't take that the wrong way. I really, really appreciate all that he's done. I mean, look at me. I'm a different person." Alex patted down the crisp beige linen shirt and Calvin Klein tie he sported, compliments of Mayor Blake. "My wardrobe has improved one hundred percent, and he got me this great job. I mean, I don't want him to feel like he has to keep doing nice things for me. He's done enough already. Too much. If I worked one thousand years, I could never repay him for all the things he's done."

Tiffany's slightly amused expression didn't change. Alex searched her eyes for some kind of response, but she just continued to smile.

"Daddy doesn't want anything from you, Alex. It's just his way. When you've been a friend to him, he'll be a friend to you for life. Unconditionally. He survives because of loyalty. But when you make an enemy of him, you've got him as an enemy for life too. He means well, and I know he can go a little overboard, but it's only because he likes you, and he trusts you. He feels like he could never repay you for what you did, standing up to Sid when none of those other sorry bastards would. Bastards a whole lot bigger than you. It took a lot of guts, and face it, Daddy likes people who have guts." She reached over and patted him on the hand, and a warm sensation spread over him from head to toe.

"But don't worry. I understand. This can be very overwhelming. I'll make sure that he chills out a bit." She sounded sincere, yet a bit perplexed that someone would be uncomfortable receiving gifts.

Alex sighed with relief. "Thanks, Tiff. I'd really appreciate it. I've sent a ton of thank-you notes, but please make sure he knows that I appreciate everything he's done."

"He knows, Alex. And it means a lot to him, and to me. That's why I'm going to get it for you myself." Alex opened his mouth to protest, but she shook her head no. "Face it, Mr. Baxter, I'm a lot like my dad. Very persistent. I like getting what I want." She leaned over and lightly kissed him on his lips. Alex's eyes almost bulged out of their sockets. They had grown closer, closer than he'd ever imagined, but inhaling her perfume and being so near her made him weak. He shoved his hand between his knees to prevent the sound of them knocking, even though he was still sitting. His whole body was tingling.

Tiffany waved as she left, a slight smile etched on her lips. Alex couldn't utter a word, and barely raised a hand in response. For at least five minutes he was lost in a trance. Just dreaming. Pleasant dreams. Suddenly, Foody and some of the rowdy dorm crew awakened him.

"Yo, homey," Foody roared, barreling through his open door. "I thought I'd holler at you for a minute. I heard you stompin' with the big dogs these days. Carryin' a big clout card. How about ordering up a couple of pizzas from the café for some of your less fortunate brothers? Better yet, how about springing for some Domino's? You can afford it, big money."

Alex smiled, and tossed Foody the telephone receiver. This was going to be the start of something big. Really big.

DURING THE SUMMER, Alex's popularity continued to soar. He finally accepted the fact that this was not a fleeting moment, and that his fifteen minutes of fame had been exponentially extended. Most surprising to him was that he was actually getting comfortable with it. He finally knew what it felt like to be part of the "in" crowd.

Alex blossomed like a sapling tree after a nineteen-year incubation period. One fateful day, he pulled on a pair of his favorite khakis and realized that his pants legs were shorter and his waistband was a lot tighter. He anxiously whipped out a tape measure, and much to his surprise, he'd grown nearly five inches over the course of that hot, humid summer. What Ivan had told him years ago had come true: his genes had finally smiled on him with this unforeseen yet completely welcomed growth spurt. He only wished he had someone to share the good news with. Foody and Lisa had gone home for the summer, and Tiffany was traveling in Europe.

Remarkably, Alex now stood confidently at a sturdy six feet. The Alex of old was buried on that fateful night of the PKO dance. He still felt a mix of sadness and injustice when he recalled the trauma of being ridiculed in his childhood. Although his new height was a little late coming, it was definitely better late than never.

And also better late than never were the girls. Overnight, they found him utterly irresistible. It tripped him out, but didn't move him. Alex had no idea what to do; without Lisa or Foody around to school him, he was clueless. So as eyelashes fluttered when Alex passed, and brazen notes were left on his office door, he was flattered, but uneasy. Although he looked the part of a lover, he was far too insecure to ever act on anything. He tried to take the attention in stride, as difficult as it was. But the difficulty in dealing with all of these issues was tempered by the continuing generosity of Simon Blake.

After Tiffany mentioned that he was going overboard in his gift giving, Mayor Blake pointed his magic wand toward every other aspect of Alex's life. He was pivotal in steering the alumni board to bestow upon Alex an academic scholarship that included a generous living stipend. It enabled him to move off campus into a prime university apartment that was normally reserved for upperclassmen.

Despite all of the accoutrements, Alex was still a man on a mission. He kept his grades up and made the dean's list, and received several academic scholarships. Money flowed, and he finally had enough to open up a bank account and get a credit card. He counted his blessings, never forgetting where he came from; he didn't want to appear greedy. When even more scholarships were offered, he declined a few of the monetary awards so someone else could get the aid. As altruistic as he tried to be, he wasn't a saint. He made sure that he had a nice nest egg to get him through graduation, and enough to buy a fly little silver 1974 Datsun 260Z to sport around campus in. Tiffany was even kind enough to teach him how to drive.

One muggy July evening, Alex spent a few moments in the dorm joking around with some of the other summer-school casualties. They were laughing, and calling him *paisan,* or the "new Don." Alex was the man, not to be messed with. Not with Simon Blake backing him. But it was all in good fun.

"Yo, Alex, man," one of his fellow summer school refugees yelled from down the hallway. "Telephone!"

Not too anxious to desert the conversation he had just started, Alex continued talking, reluctantly heading toward the phone.

"Alex?" The caller's tone was deep and gravelly, and Alex knew instantly who it was.

"Yes, Mayor Blake." Alex automatically turned his back and lowered his voice to avoid being overheard by the many nosy students who passed by.

"Time is a valuable commodity, son. Don't waste it."

"I—I'm sorry, Mayor Blake. I was kind of in the middle of something, and it took me a while to get to the phone."

"I understand. I just want you to grasp the value of time. It'll be an important lesson to learn. Anyway, how are you doing, my boy?" Mayor Blake had a habit of asking rhetorical questions, and then going on before a person had an opportunity to answer.

He invited Alex to dinner, saying that he'd be in the area for a meeting and thought it would be nice to meet with him. Simon Blake had a persuasive nature that really didn't allow you to say no. Alex accepted the invitation, yet he was nervous as hell. He'd never gone one-on-one with the mayor before.

Mayor Blake chuckled softly. "I told you to call me Simon, son. Now, are you still in that godforsaken dorm, or have you moved out to your apartment?"

"I'm still here, sir. I have a few more weeks before the apartment is ready, but I'm really looking forward to moving out."

"I tell you what, Alex. I'll be by to pick you up around six-thirty. I'll meet you outside the dorm. Which one was it? Livingston, right? The old one that houses the freshmen? Okay, just be prompt, now. You know how much I value promptness. And if anything comes up, you be sure to give my secretary, Barbara, a call. She'll know how to get in touch with me. Always remember that."

The conversation soon ended. Simon had something pressing to attend to. Yet, what impressed Alex the most was that Simon always made time for him, that a man of his stature spent time with him on a regular basis. It was the same kind of feeling Alex had about Ivan. The mayor made him feel special, even though Alex was just a little peon.

Over the course of a few months, Alex learned a lot about the mayor. And the first thing Alex learned was that he'd better be ready by at least six-fifteen. Simon was a stickler, and sometimes refused to meet with anyone who had the audacity to be late. Even the most legitimate excuses for even the most minuscule tardiness could result in getting pushed so far off Simon's calendar that you'd practically have to wait until the next election year to see him. There were no exceptions to this rule, and Alex was smart enough to act accordingly.

A BROAD SMILE stretched across Simon's face as Barbara placed the wide, red-striped Express Mail envelope on his desk. "This was just delivered for you, Your Honor." Simon liked the way she always referred to him as "Your Honor." It was better than a hot cup of coffee first thing in the morning.

"Thanks, Barbara." He watched her wide hips swing toward his open office door and added, "Barbara, please hold my calls for the next half hour. That is unless Howard calls me. I've got to keep up with my PR. And please close the door."

Simon was intrigued. The initial reports he had received on Alexander Whitney Baxter were as clean as a whistle. It was as if the boy barely existed. But Simon knew better. He was always suspicious. Everyone had a skeleton or two in his closet, and he'd find it. As they said in the country, those bones probably had a little meat left on them.

Simon ripped open the envelope, and carefully placed its contents, a legal-sized file, on his desk. A quick call to a running buddy, a former special agent who was now working as a private dick, had set the wheels in motion.

He carefully perused each page. Each word fortified Simon's intuition, and the street in him was duly impressed. It was a rarity that a young black kid could grow up in Shaw devoid of a criminal record. It was amazing. An amazing opportunity. And Simon was known for his savvy ability to capitalize on an opportunity.

THE ATMOSPHERE IN the Captain's Table was noisy yet engaging. An aura of Southern hospitality greeted Simon and Alex at the door, and the large crowd of patrons looked and waved hello as they took their seats. Simon Blake was a well-known figure in these parts, one of the numerous Hilliard boys who had made good. He was recognized by most as Washington's incumbent mayor who was wearing Congress out with his relentless pursuit to make D.C. an independent state.

Alex was like an awestruck kid in his presence. A tall, stocky, stylish man, Simon Blake cut an impressive figure as he exercised his political prowess on the crowd. Witty and charming, he was larger than life, but still a man of the people. It was effortless for him to make small talk, sign autographs, take pictures, or kiss babies. It was all part of the political process. He was gracious as people came up to shake his hand or pat his back, even when he was elbow deep in Old Bay and cracking his crab claws. Alex took plenty of mental notes as he admired Simon's finesse.

Noticing Alex's not-too-subtle admiration, Simon downplayed his charisma. "It's all part of the job, son. But it's the part I love best." Simon gestured around the crowd in the room. "I love people, my people, anyway, and they sense that. I'm from the people. You know black folks can spot a phony a mile away."

Simon's precise diction was still haunted by a slight Southern accent every now and then. Alex smiled, and sipped his overly sweet iced tea.

"You can never get too big to sit amongst the little people. Always remember that."

During their frequent telephone conversations, Alex picked up that Simon had a tendency to end his sentences with that adage. "Always remember that" stuck in his mind throughout the evening. And Alex committed to memory everything Simon said.

"So tell me, Alex, what do you want to do when you grow up? Although you've done quite a bit of growing since I last saw you." Simon laughed at his own joke, an infectious laugh. Alex found himself laughing too.

"Well, Mayor, I mean Simon, I've been thinking a lot about law school when I get out of here."

Simon continued nibbling on his claw, while gesturing to the waitress to bring over some more water. "That's an excellent idea. You know Georgetown's good—that is, if you're thinking about coming home."

Alex nodded. He wanted to come home, and he was thinking about going straight through. But Alex was leaning toward Howard. There was something about going to Georgetown that unnerved him. When Alex mentioned it to Simon, he advised him to get a little work experience, to see how the real world operated.

"You can't rely one hundred percent on books to get you through life, my boy. You have to have some street smarts to survive too. Sometimes that'll get you further than those books. You know what I'm talking about. You're from Shaw. You know a book won't get you out of Ninth and T on a hot summer night if your car breaks down. Not unless it's made of concrete, and you can hit somebody over the head with it."

The advice sounded vaguely familiar, and it stuck in Alex's mind. Simon was right. Alex had learned a long time ago that book smarts and no common sense made you an easy target. He was awed by Simon's insight, and he clung to his every word.

Simon continued, occasionally searching Alex's face to ensure he was listening. He added that although he thought Howard was a good school, Alex should expand his horizons. "If you're going to do it, do it right. Howard's not going to buy you a whole lot. Now, it's a good school, and when I was coming along, we didn't have access to the white schools. We didn't have a choice—we had to go to Howard. But today, you have choices. One predominately black university is all right on a résumé, but you need balance. You need to get out there and find out what the white boys are doing. Get some contacts and some resources. Especially if you're trying to get into law. If you don't, you'll never get in the game with them. And it's their game. Always remember that.

"Just keep your nose clean, Alex. Keep your grades up, and you'll get into G-town. No problem. I'll even help you get that scholarship you're looking for, if that's what you need. Plus, you never know. Maybe you'll get into politics one day."

Simon polished off his seafood feast and settled back in his chair. Alex ate slowly, full now from the words of wisdom as much as the food.

Cradling his coffee cup, Simon shifted in the wooden captain's chair. "You know, you remind me a lot of myself when I was coming up." He sipped his coffee slowly. "I see a lot in you. And I'm going to try to help you as best as I can.

"But then again, you aren't really like me, because at least I knew how to have a little fun back then." He was amused by the memory. "Good old H.I. Boy, did I have some fun back in the day, and I still do. Every time I come back down, it's just like old times." Again he laughed that contagious laugh.

"Me and the frat, Alex. Those were some good times. Still are. Just like my brothers. Yes, sir. Do you have any?"

Alex winced, yet maintained his composure. He didn't want to let Simon know that even after all these years, it still hurt to speak of his only brother, who had been snatched from him.

"No—no, sir. My only brother was killed when I was young, around fourteen years old." Alex bit his lip and cursed himself for revealing his Achilles' heel, his nervous stutter.

Simon nodded sympathetically. "Really? I do understand, son. I know how it feels to lose someone you love. My wife was killed almost thirteen years ago, but it still pains me to talk about it today. That's why I generally don't.

"You may find that joining a fraternity would give you the brothers you've been missing all this time. I pledged years ago, and I can say that it was one of the best things that ever happened to me. I've had frat almost all of my adult life, and there's nothing like it. I've got a lot of family still in the South, but I don't see them. Not like frat. They're all over, and in my line of work, you need someone to watch your back, wherever you are. Always remember that."

Finally finished with his crab cakes, Alex gulped a mouthful of lemon-laced water. "Well, to be completely honest with you, Simon, I never really thought about it until I became the student liaison. And I must admit that it sounds a little intriguing. I was thinking about pledging Alpha. Do you have any particular fraternity you would recommend?" Alex joked.

Simon slapped the table and reared back in his seat, laughing loudly. "Is there any other fraternity than my beloved PKO?"

They continued laughing at their little inside joke, and Alex became more and more comfortable. Sitting in the shadow of the man who was fighting to bring statehood to the nation's capital had brought life and status to his little world. Although there was a large, red NO SMOKING sign posted on the wall, Simon pulled out his pipe and fired it up. It was obvious that no one was going to stop him. The pipe's distinct aroma tickled Alex's nose, and reminded him of the scent that welcomed him when he awakened

in Tiffany's apartment after the brawl. It was a pleasant reminder
of the man who also spoke to him during his drug-induced state
of euphoria. The man who promised to be there for him was there
now, live and in living color. Alex was seduced by and in awe of the
power he wielded.

Simon caught Alex glancing at the sign, and he again laughed
his contagious laugh. "Rule number one, son: There are always
rules. Rules are made not to be broken, but to be bent to the shape
that best serves your purpose. A weak man follows every rule, gets
nowhere. A strong man sees the rule, interprets it, and bends it
around his little finger. People admire the kind of strength it takes
to do that. The guts. Always remember that."

As Simon forced him to eat a piece of sweet-potato pie, more
admirers came over to shake his hand, or sat at other tables and
just gawked. There Alex was, Alex Baxter, having dinner with this
esteemed elder statesman, frequent White House guest, host of
diplomats and entertainers from around the world. And as Simon
laid his pipe down and continued to politic, he winked at Alex,
making him feel just as special as a head of state.

They walked out to the understated black Fleetwood Cadillac,
and Simon's burly bodyguard and chauffeur, Drew, automatically
opened the rear door. The humid Tidewater air fell heavily on
their brows, and both of them lumbered lazily into their seats.

Somehow, whether purposely or not, the conversation shifted
to Tiffany. Simon was still clearly disturbed by what had happened, and he seemed to partially blame himself.

"You know, I really don't get into Tiffany's business, but she's
my only child." Alex found that hard to believe. He wouldn't have
imagined any area to be off-limits to Simon, especially her. But
Alex sensed where this conversation was leading, and he listened
intently as Simon shared his thoughts.

"In fact, Tiffany really doesn't allow me to get in her business,
not really. She's kind of close to Giselle, my wife's sister, who
practically raised her, but it's always been kind of hard for her to
talk to me about inherently personal issues." He instructed Drew
to take the long way back to the campus, through the tunnel and

over the Great Neck Bridge, and then he raised the bulletproof privacy panel in the limo.

Simon rubbed his fist in his palm, and chose his words deliberately. "I love my little girl. She'll always be my little girl. She's all I have left. I don't think I'll have any other children anytime soon." He winked at Alex and continued. "And if I'd known that Sidney was such a loser, I would've—" Simon trailed off as the rage seeped through. He calmed down, and glanced toward Alex. "Well, let's just say, I don't want to see that happen to her again. Ever. In fact, I *won't* let that happen to her again. So, I'm asking you to do me a favor. Trust and believe, I don't ask too many folks for favors."

The pressure was mounting. Alex felt beads of perspiration forming on his upper lip. He wiped his mouth strategically and murmured, "Sure, Simon, anything."

"Look out for her. Now, I don't know what you two have going, friends or whatever. But if you're going to be her friend, be a friend. Watch her back for me."

Alex nodded, relieved. His heart raced a mile a minute, and he hoped that Simon couldn't hear it beating through his chest.

"And if you're going to be more than a friend, still be a friend. Always remember that."

THAT ONE EVENING with Simon, the first of many, left an indelible imprint on Alex, as well as on his future. Simon had a subtle way of getting his point across, and Alex had an innate understanding of what his mentor was saying. There was no direct pressure, but Simon had a way of finessing you into doing exactly what it was he wanted you to do. It was no wonder he was such a successful politician, and a pretty good father to a daughter Alex had come to know very well.

Mysteriously and miraculously, throughout the previous spring, Tiffany had become an integral part of his new life. She never kissed him again, or even remotely touched him in a personal manner, but they spent more and more time together. They were cautious about their budding friendship, but comfortable in the developing closeness. To him, the lip locking had just been Tiffany's way of saying thanks, and Alex tried not to read more into it than that. He knew she'd never go for him. He was completely under-developed. Literally.

So, Alex enjoyed the distinction of being her friend. As the days turned to weeks, they were quietly inseparable up until the time she went abroad with her friend Lily to practice her fluent French, relax, and do some seriously intense shopping for the upcoming fall semester. It was cool, perhaps because there were no hidden agendas, and he was so nonthreatening. They were able to relate to and accept each other for what they were, with no boundaries. They were even able to talk about some of the defining moments of their lives, and most of the underlying pain in Tiffany's life spilled out during one of their afternoon driving lessons. Alex had triumphantly parallel parked for the third time, and they cele-brated by sipping on some California Wine Coolers and strolling by the riverside.

"You know what. It's been really nice getting to know you. I don't know if you figured it out yet, but it's not that easy for me to get close to people, and I've never been this close to a guy before."

She squeezed his arm as they found a placid place to stop. "You're so easy to talk to, you know. You're so nonjudgmental. I almost tell you as much as I tell my therapist."

Alex smiled. "I'm glad you feel like that. You're easy to talk to too."

"Thanks. But I really mean it. And I want to share something with you. I've had to face a lot of truths about myself, and it hasn't been easy. I'm determined to keep myself together, now that I've got myself together."

"What do you mean? You've always been together."

"You're so sweet. But I've got to be real. I had to realize that I was partially to blame for what happened with Sid.

"In the back of my mind, I really used to wonder about him, Alex. He was a nice guy, and I know I was really into him, but maybe I liked him for all of the wrong reasons." She paused, as if she was having a revelation. The ripples in the water reflected in her eyes, and she lowered her lids thoughtfully. "He really had issues. The more I think about it, the coke was kind of skewing my judgment."

"Coke? You used to do drugs, Tiffany?"

Her brilliant eyes stayed downcast. "I did. It started in high school. It was, like, the thing to do. It was our coping mechanism, cocaine. It offered me refuge, a magical, mystical haven that made everything seem okay. My mother's death. And eventually, even Sid. Through my coke haze, he was the man of my dreams. I guess that's why I just ignored the truth."

"You mean, no one ever knew about it? You never told anyone about it? I would've never guessed."

"No, I never even told my aunt. I think she might have suspected something, but as long as I did what she expected me to do, she turned a blind eye to what was really going on. But I'm not blaming her or my father. He was busy, and I have to be responsible for my own actions."

What he'd sensed about Tiffany a while ago was true: although she seemed worldly, she was still a bit naïve. Inside there was a sheltered little girl whose father showered her with gifts and unbridled attention in the public eye, but didn't reach her on a personal level. Just as Alex's father couldn't reach out to Alex.

"And I guess I was just plain ignorant about men."

Tiffany's disclosure surprised Alex, but he wasn't shocked. It helped him understand how she had allowed a creature like Sid into her life. She fully accepted her role as a willing participant in the debacle, and admitted that coke had always been a crutch for her. He admired the strength that she showed just by opening up.

"But I've been doing a lot of thinking since that night. And you know what? I haven't had a hit of coke since then. I know if I hadn't been all high like that, I would have never let Sid get me in a position where I was so incredibly vulnerable. I think I was just a little numb, you know? I was so caught up in feeling good that by the time I realized I was in trouble, it was too late. Then all that stuff went down, and I feel like it was all my fault.

"Maybe Sidney wouldn't have gotten so brutal if I'd had more control. If I hadn't been so high. At least not to that degree. So, I've kind of gotten it out of my system, and I guess it's for the best. All the way around. Both coke and Sid are gone. Though, when all that stuff went down, and I was truly embarrassed, I so, so badly wanted to get high. It was a struggle, but I refused to give in."

They strolled a little farther down the riverbank, and Alex tried to listen as objectively as possible. It was hard, especially since he'd witnessed the type of destruction drugs could cause. But he sensed in her the resolve that she needed to kick her habit. She continued to talk openly. It was a rare, unguarded moment, and one that he'd forever cherish.

"Sidney was a lot like my dad, you know, a little rough around the edges, from the wrong side of the tracks. But he had a lot of personality, just like my dad does. I guess I saw us as my parents, and I just wanted that fairy-tale romance like they had. I guess I should thank Sid for smashing my rose-colored glasses, huh? I'm over my dream of being married with kids."

Tiffany had told Alex about her parents' union during one of their study sessions. It was a poignant love story, set against the backdrop of segregation and polarization, inside and outside of the black community, that kept Negroes in their place. Marjorie Newton, a light-skinned lawyer's daughter and debutante, was a fourth-generation denizen of the Sixteenth Street Gold Coast. Born of privilege, she wanted for nothing. Simon, on the other hand, was a mahogany-colored, hardworking, smart country boy. After months of courting, he made her fall in love with him. At first her family was hesitant about the differences in their backgrounds and their color, but her iron will convinced them that he was the one for her. Eventually, even they were swayed by his bravado and charm. The couple were married before the ink on their individual degrees dried, and moved to their new hometown of Washington. With the help of his in-laws, Simon earned his stripes as a noted attorney, and quickly became involved with local politics. The rest, as they say, was history.

"Plus, I know my dad really liked Sid. He was frat, and he looked out for him. I think he thought Sid was a lot like him, a guy from the wrong side of the tracks, trying to make good. I guess he was like the son he never had. Sidney liked my dad too. Sometimes I wondered if he liked me just because of my dad. . . ." Tiffany's words trailed off as she looked out over the water. The ripples edged closer to the bank, and Alex wanted to say something, but his thoughts were jumbled. So he listened.

"But I know I can't be my parents and relive the past, Alex. I have to live my own life, make my own decisions and my own mistakes." She smiled at him, that slight smile that Alex found ever so enchanting.

Unsure of what to say, Alex grabbed Tiffany's hand and held it firmly. "I understand what you're saying, Tiff. We all make bad decisions. But the key is to learn from them and grow. But I don't profess to be some sort of expert on love. That's probably the subject I know the least about. I've never even had a serious relationship."

Or any type of relationship. Love and emotions were still foreign to him. He could speak esoterically about it, but he quickly found that logic didn't always work when dealing with affairs of the heart. Part of him wanted to ask her if she was nuts, while the other part of him ached for her.

"Well, don't feel badly." She sipped on her drink. "I guess I've never been serious enough with anyone to really, really be involved with them, if you know what I mean." She searched his face, her eyes flashing.

"No, uh, I don't. Not unless you mean, um, what I think you mean." Alex became a little flushed, and he fidgeted with his nearly empty bottle.

"Yes, it's what you think. I'm still a virgin, contrary to popular belief. I know everybody thinks I'm out here slinging it, but I'm not. I kind of resigned myself to wait until I got married, but I actually thought about being with Sid. I'm so glad I didn't."

It was hard to believe her, but somehow Alex did. She had no reason to lie to him. He respected the fact that she was able to live life so fully without sharing that part of herself. Alex guessed she assumed he was a virgin too, but she never asked. He was positive that her female intuition told her he'd never been with a woman. That wasn't too hard to figure out.

Now he was even more attracted to her. Tiffany was truly beguiling. His heart and loins tremored when Alex thought about her, and she moved him in ways he never knew existed. But Alex had reconciled himself to the idea that he'd never have a chance with her, nor would he ever try. Even though he knew she was grateful for what he'd done, it didn't translate into a love connection. In his waking moments, he'd be content being her friend and confidant. But it didn't stop him from dreaming.

"I think that's commendable. Especially in women. But you know in men, we'd, I mean they'd, just be called nerds."

They laughed, and Alex enjoyed the break from the tension.

Tiffany continued talking, and Alex continued intensely listening. She really missed her mother, although her aunt Giselle had spent a lot of time with her. Being deeply affected by the absence of a mother was another innately personal experience that they shared. Although Tiffany didn't go into a lot of details, Alex detected that they were kindred spirits in their quest to mask the pain of loss. He retreated behind his books, while she hid behind a beautiful facade. A facade that came crashing down around her ankles the night Sidney humiliated her in front of the world. She had everyone believing that she was this strong, self-willed, confident woman, but inside she was tortured. Tortured by the things even being a mayor's daughter couldn't change. It was this reality that he came to know. And to care for.

Their walk ended and they headed back to the car. Alex was still in a state of disbelief that he was the guy strolling on the riverbank with the one and only Tiffany Blake. If only she wasn't going away to Paris for the summer. He longed to get to know her even better, but now she seemed to pull back, as if she had revealed too much about herself. For all of her growth and the reality checks she had faced, she was still the debutante. She still had to keep up appearances.

Nevertheless, Alex was elated. He'd caught glimpses of the real Tiffany, and he liked what he saw. Not only on the outside, but on the inside. She had a depth of character that was more beautiful than the eye could see. Probably even more beautiful than she ever saw when she looked in the mirror.

Saying good-bye was bittersweet. Although they agreed to stay in touch, Alex knew that she'd go overseas and meet a count or some other celebrity and fall madly in love. Alex figured that he'd open *Jet* magazine and see the announcement of her pending nuptials. When he watched her drive off on her way home, he never imagined that they'd keep in touch.

THOUGH SHE WAS gone for only three months, they talked often. Too often. Most of his hefty summer paychecks should have been made payable to AT&T. But it was worth it. Alex would be bleary-eyed during his early-morning chats, but the six-hour time difference made no difference to him. He loved talking to her, whether it was four o'clock in the morning or not.

One early morning toward the end of July, he settled in with a hot cup of coffee and waited for Tiffany's call. Like clockwork, around 3:45 A.M. the telephone rang.

"Good morning, sleepyhead," Tiffany's velvety voice chirped with glee.

Alex suppressed a yawn, and cracked his blinds to see the still-black sky. "Yeah, I guess you can say that. At least the sun's shining where you are."

"Oh, pooh. Not only is the sun shining, but I have a fabulous view of the Champs Élysées, and I'm eating a buttery croissant with fresh boysenberry marmalade. Not to make you jealous, mind you."

Alex grunted, and stirred his instant coffee. "I'm not, thank you very much."

"Oh, Alex, this place is absolutely wonderful. I came here once when I was in eighth grade, but I have a whole new appreciation for it. The shopping is just primo. I've gotten such great outfits, no one will ever look like me this fall.

"And it's so romantic too. Paris is just so beautiful and so full of culture. It's the perfect place to honeymoon."

Tiffany's words immediately awakened Alex. "Oh, you mean you've met somebody that's got you thinking about honeymoons? Just yesterday, you were talking about how pretentious the men were over there."

"Don't be silly. I'm just making an observation, that's all. Paris is a beautiful city, but that's it. All of the guys I've met are either wanna-be Casanovas, broke, or just too old. Lily hasn't had much better luck either. But we're going to train over to Venice this afternoon. Maybe our luck'll change." She chewed loudly, enough to make Alex's stomach grumble. He decided to get a bowl of cereal.

"So, what about you, Mr. Man? How's your love life doing? Have you taken any of my advice yet?"

Alex nearly dropped his cereal bowl. "Let's just say I'm still a work in progress."

"You should listen to me. Don't try to be suave bolla. Be confident, but not too cocky. Try to be cool, and fun to be around, but most important, be sincere. Just be yourself."

"I'll try to do just that. I'll let you know how it goes. I did get an invitation to one of the summer socials. One of your sweethearts asked me about it."

There was an immediate chill in the air. "Who?"

"Kelly. I don't remember her last name. You know her?"

There was another pregnant pause. "I guess. Oh yeah. Kelly Brown. She's the one with the disproportionate chest and the big feet. They look like flippers."

Alex chuckled to himself. "Well, I hadn't noticed all of that. Anyway, do you have any helpful hints?" There was a definite tinge of jealousy. Or maybe it was true that women really didn't want to know about other women. It was kind of fun, believing that Tiffany was affected by anything he was doing. It was almost flattering.

Tiffany sucked her teeth. "Try to listen to the girl, but not too close. I hope you have some tic tacs on you, because I think she's got some wicked breath. And try to make eye contact. Don't stare at her chest. Although I know that'll be difficult."

"Was that some kind of crack about my height? Well, you'd be pleasantly surprised to know that I've actually grown a bit since you last saw me."

"You're lying. How much?"

"Enough to make a difference," Alex said, slurping on his Cap'n Crunch.

THE SUMMER FLEW by, with the assistance of their now nearly twice-a-day phone calls. With the exception of other women, no topic was off-limits. Over time, Alex opened up to Tiffany, a long, seamless process that seemed to take both of them by surprise. By the end of summer, they realized that feelings had developed that weren't there before. Tiffany actually cared for him and about him. It was so easy for Alex to feel that way about her; he was relieved to know that the feeling was now mutual.

Tiffany was happily surprised to learn about his physical transformation. During several conversations, she had commented about how his voice had gotten deeper, but Alex never told her the full extent. He waited until their last shore-to-shore conversation, the morning of the day she was scheduled to catch her flight home.

"You've got to be kidding, Alex. You never told me you had grown that much," she said when he sprang the news on her.

"Can you believe it? I went to the gym yesterday evening and checked. I'm about six feet tall now, and I gained about thirty-five pounds." Alex caught a glimpse of himself in the mirror, and was almost astonished by what he saw. He had a fly haircut, razor sharp, and his teenage acne had vanished. Completely filled out, he even had a slight mustache growing in, and his mocha-colored skin looked toned and buffed.

"Thirty-five pounds? What have you been eating? Everything? Has Foody been around you or something?"

"Funny. I'm solid, though. You know I've been trying to work out. And I jumped almost two full shoe sizes."

Tiffany was speechless. "Why, wow. That's great. But why did you wait until the last minute to tell me? I think I'm having a heart attack."

"I wanted to surprise you. Surprise!"

The phone rustled, and Tiffany called out to Lily in the background. "Well, I've got to go. But I'm going to call you later."

"Why are you rushing? Your flight's not until later."

"Never mind. Let's just say that I'm glad you told me about your little growth spurt. I've got to try to exchange all of these shoes and Italian silks I got for you. Now, I'll call you with my flight information. I'm going to fly into Norfolk, and I want you to pick me up from the airport."

ALEX WAITED AT the terminal for her return, his heart palpitating. She was absolutely breathtaking. As she strolled out of the declaration area in her Chanel lime green sleeveless minidress, heads whipped around. Her three-inch matching pumps clicked on the tiled floor. She wore big black Jackie O. sunglasses propped on her head, and her full-bodied hair bounced on her shoulders as if it were on springs. She looked more like a supermodel on a runway than someone deplaning from a transatlantic flight.

The dozen yellow roses Alex held in his hand fell carelessly to his side when their eyes locked. Sparks flew. Porters fought over who was going to transport her full set of Louis Vuitton luggage, yet she and Alex were lost in the moment. She just stared at him with an incredulous expression and rubbed his muscular arms. She'd draw him nearer, then shake her head in disbelief.

"Look at you, Alex. I can't believe it's you," she said. Then they held each other tightly, and a passion rose inside Alex's soul. He remembered how soft Tiffany's lips were, and he longed to feel them again. This time he'd be ready. Their lips met passionately, kissing until the crowd around them began to clap and whistle.

"Let's get out of here," Alex said, his voice deep and confident, filled with an urgency he'd never felt or expressed before.

She looked longingly into his eyes, and nodded her head slowly. Intuitively, he knew that whatever they'd had before had definitely changed. And all for the better.

CHAPTER 11

M ANY changes had occurred by the fall of the year. Alex was still evolving and learning to do things in a different manner. He felt brand-new, yet challenged to deal with life without the support of his two closest friends. Foody had dropped out after blowing his tuition money over the summer. He had made a hasty decision to go into the service, and had been shipped off to Fort Bragg in North Carolina.

Alex rarely saw Lisa. She'd gone home for the summer and barely recognized him when she returned. She was stunned, and Alex was amused. "Too bad I've got a new boyfriend," she said, in a self-deprecating manner. He was a local navy guy, and she was plenty busy with him. When they found time to talk, she didn't try to hide the fact that she was mega-disappointed that Alex was now seeing Tiffany. But she seemed genuinely happy that *he* was finally happy.

Tiffany and Alex were a couple. They had the run of the yard, and she carried it off with style and grace, while he was still adjusting. Wherever they went, people treated them like royalty, and it took him a while to get used to the lingering looks they received. Alex often attributed his burgeoning self-esteem to Tiffany. She was so calm and cool that it eventually rubbed off on him. After a while, he chilled out about all of the notoriety.

Even as they sat at the café, with Tiffany at the PKO table and him across at the Student Union's, they were completely into each other. In a crowded room, she was all Alex ever saw. She made his heart sing, and he had no problem letting her know it. All of the changes they'd gone through had made them stronger, and confident in their relationship. Tiffany had gotten over her cold feet, and Alex was comfortable in his very first relationship. Only they knew the true depth of their bond, which was forged on that fateful summer night when she returned from Europe.

Despite their passionate meeting at the airport, and the scorching moments that ensued once they reached her apartment, they had both cooled down and agreed to wait. As aroused as Alex had been, he didn't want her or his first time to happen so quickly. What if something happened that turned her off? Their relationship would be over before it had a chance to grow. It was a chance neither one of them was willing to take. Difficult as it was to calm the raging fires that burned in their hearts and between their legs, consummating their feelings would have to wait.

That night he had held Tiffany in his arms and watched her as she slept. They were both anxious and exhausted from freeing their emotions, admitting their love and squelching their burning desires. They knew that what they were feeling was real, not just gnawing lust. Alex honestly felt good about himself. She felt good to him, and she felt right. He was aroused when he felt her soft yet firm body pressing against him. She rubbed him tenderly, with those long, slender fingers, and he felt such a rush. It was a sensation that was invoked every time he laid eyes on her, or when he inhaled her sensual perfume. He was content to hear her breathing and feel her warm, sweet breath on his face. Eventually, he had drifted off to sleep.

"I'VE GOT SOMETHING to tell you," Tiffany leaned forward and whispered excitedly. Alex caught a whiff of one of her favorite fragrances, Obsession, and it immediately turned him on.

"I don't want to jinx my luck, but I think I made line."

Making line, or being accepted into the AKAs' pledge club, had topped Tiffany's list of priorities for the fall. Her excitement was obvious, and Alex was happy that she was so elated. He loved to see her smile, even if it meant that their time together would be scarce.

Alex grabbed her freshly manicured hands. He adored the way they looked, and she enjoyed keeping them meticulous and attractive. Her freshly coiffed hair was neat and trimmed in the latest asymmetric style, and her outfit perfectly accentuated her figure. Every time Alex looked at her, it seemed like she became more beautiful. If that were possible.

"Jinx your luck? You can't be jinxed. I think that's great, love. Any word on when it's going to start?"

"I'm not sure. Since the AKAs haven't had a line in a year, they're anxious. But nobody knows for real. I just hope that we'll go soon. This waiting is driving me nuts."

Alex had decided to take a huge step and consider pledging. His roommate Morgan had persuaded him to attend the PKO rush. He was a little leery that Sid's frat brothers would hold grudges against him.

"I haven't heard anything. Morgan asked me about it the other day, but who knows, they might not even accept me. I'll come home and find Morgan on line, and my face'll be cracked."

"Don't be silly. Of course they'll accept you. Now, since their rush was held on the same Sunday as the AKAs', you'll probably hear something soon. With homecoming coming up, all of the frats and sororities usually have their lines on. It's just a matter of time. Let's just hope that we'll both be ready."

"I hope so." Alex's words were hollow, since he didn't know if he'd ever be ready. Pledging was a time of self-sacrifice, a grueling indoctrination into the fraternities and sororities. Mere mortals were selected to be under the tutelage of the big brothers or big sisters and shaped and molded into the ideal member. Pledging was designed to build character and dedication to serve the community and the organization. It was the stuff dreams and night-mares were made of.

Tiffany rubbed his cheek with her deftly polished fingertips. "Don't worry about it, Alex. You should be excited, not wringing your hands. You know, I hope we'll be on line at the same time. I'd hate not to be able to see you while I'm pledging, and then you not be able to see me if you go on line later."

Alex nodded. Two of Tiffany's future line sisters, Melanie and Edie, rushed over to where they were seated. They uttered a cursory hello to him, and guardedly bent over to whisper in Tiffany's ear. Though their voices were muffled, he overheard them discussing the intricate details of pledging. It was kind of humorous, watching them plot and plan their covert activities like secret agents. But this was just the beginning, and Alex realized that he'd better get used to it. He casually whisked his history book from his knapsack and read, oblivious to the elevated noise level in the café.

Suddenly, Tiffany uttered a terse good-bye, kissed his cheek, lovingly wiped off the lipstick, and trotted off with her future line sisters. Alex watched that sexy image vanish down the café's corridor and smiled. How did he ever get so lucky?

Pondering the thought with a gleam in his eye, Alex failed to notice that George, Gorgeous George, had placed a greasy tray of curly fries, a double cheeseburger, and a bottle of Pepsi on the table and sat down beside him. Alex was still sitting there with a silly look on his face.

"What's so funny, man? Care to share? I could use a little humor today," George said.

Alex wasn't stupid. He knew George already knew the answer, and he realized that it frosted George that Tiffany was going with him and hadn't given anybody else a chance. Even though he and Sid had been the tightest of tight, George wouldn't have hesitated one minute if Tiffany had given him some time.

George was always standoffish, which Alex readily attributed to his friendship with Sid, and George always gritted on him. When

Alex found out George had been named the assistant dean of pledges, he almost decided not to rush PKO. But he hand-carried his letter of intent to them anyway. It wasn't like he'd never faced rejection before.

"Nothing's funny, George. Nothing at all," Alex said, his eyes still locked on Tiffany.

Stuffing a handful of ketchup-laden fries into his mouth, George sized him up carefully. "Look, homeboy. I know you got a lot of things going for you right now. You got it going on. Everything's real nice and easy for you. But you can rest assured, you won't get in my frat like that. Not PKO. You won't get it handed to you on a silver platter. I'm going to see to that. Me and a whole lot of other brothers feel the same way. Ones that are here, and ones that aren't."

Alex couldn't tell from his tone if he was just doing some pre-underground hazing, or if he was dead serious. The thought of this man being someone he was supposed to depend on made his head ache. He prayed that pledging wouldn't cause his childhood nightmares to reoccur.

"George," Alex said, trying to sound confident. He refused to let him think that he was afraid of him, at least not yet. "I'm aware that you and some of your brothers may not like me very much. You probably think that I *do* expect to have PKO handed to me on a silver platter, but you're wrong. I know you think I don't value your fraternity as much as you think I should, but trust me. If I get accepted to the line, I'm prepared to work for it." Alex watched George as he consumed his burger.

"Smart boy, Alex. They said you were kind of intelligent," George said, completely unfazed. "But you don't know the definition of work, at least not until some of the brothers get a hold of you." He slammed his half-eaten burger down on the tray, and looked him up and down.

In the midst of their conversation, a group of PKOs, lunch trays in hand, surrounded the table where they were sitting. Their faces were shaded in mischief. "Come on, frat. What you doing sitting with him? Come on over to our table, bro."

George stared Alex down and pointed a narrow finger in his face. "I'll be seeing you around," he said. "Believe that."

Alex breathed deeply, and tried to ignore the intimidation. His head pounded. Knowing that most of the PKOs deeply resented him, he wondered if it would be worth even trying to join them.

But as Alex saw the numerous fraternities filling the cafeteria, doing their secret handshakes and private calls, he envied their camaraderie. Even though he was now a popular campus figure, with Foody gone, he missed the semblance of brotherly closeness in his life. Simon was right. These frats were just like brothers.

At that moment, Alex felt the loneliness he had when Ivan died, and a twinge of guilt, for he knew that he didn't think of Ivan as often as he should.

Alex wondered what Ivan would be if he were alive. He would have graduated from college and either be playing pro ball or working with kids. He loved kids. Alex smiled at the thought of his six-foot-plus brother towering over a group of tiny schoolkids. He really missed him, and made a mental note to try to stay on track with his plan to honor his memory. These unforeseen yet wondrous events had thrown him a little off course in meeting his goals, but he couldn't allow himself to forget about Ivan.

Alex was jarred from his daydream by the noise of the PKOs joking and laughing as they ate. Their closeness and affection seemed genuine. Alex knew pledging would be a hell he could hardly imagine, but he had to do it.

BARELY TWO DAYS later, a note mysteriously appeared under his office door, instructing him to pick up several articles of clothing and shoes. Three days later, at the stroke of one o'clock on a Friday morning, he and Morgan were roused from sleep by the ringing of the security buzzer.

On the intercom were Gorgeous George and Trent, barking out strict instructions to join them in the parking lot, appropriately dressed, in three scant minutes.

Once they arrived in the parking lot, they were harassed and harangued into learning the proper way to speak, address their elders, dress, etc. From that moment on, they were no longer just college students. They were members of the secret society. They were getting their first taste of being pledges.

Morgan and Alex stood shivering in the damp fall air, listening to Trent and George rattle off a laundry list of orders. They were instructed to round up the other potentials and meet at the fraternity house. All in the matter of twenty-nine minutes.

Trent and George walked off. Trent stopped when he reached his shiny Black Jeep and offered one more word of advice. "Oh yeah, guys. I just remembered. On our table in the café, there's an envelope with everyone's name and address. That may help. And Alex, don't worry about it. I heard you know how to get into places after hours. And this time, be sure not to have a knife on you."

That chilly Indian-summer night marked the first night that Alex and nineteen other sophomores, juniors, and seniors went underground. Underground was a term used to describe being accepted informally into a fraternity or sorority without officially being on line. Pledging was conducted in the open, usually from four to six weeks, but being underground meant that you could be hazed for four to six weeks prior to anyone being informed that you were officially on line. And you were sworn to secrecy, although every other fraternal organization on the yard knew the deal.

Alex had never experienced anything like this before in his life. That night, he got "wood broken," or paddled, for the first time. Being tall, Alex was near the end of the line, number eighteen. He and the other potentials had been taken into a darkened room and quizzed, harassed, and abused by a group of big brothers, and no matter what Alex said or did, he was always wrong. And the ringleader of the big brothers was none other than the ADP, Gorgeous George. Even Trent offered no support as the dean of pledges.

Whoever the potentials had been before they entered that room did not matter. They were merely grids, or PKO pledges, hoping to survive long enough to be elevated to probate Axes. They would be led to the brink of the burning sands to their crowning glory—

to become full-fledged PKOs. Like made men of Italian mob lore, "going over," or finally completing the arduous pledge program, meant rewards and recognition of mythical proportions. Or at least that's what motivated most to seek the elusive prize of being Greek.

It was dawn before they were released. By the time they made it home, students were hustling off to their eight o'clock classes. Alex yawned and said a prayer, for he knew that this was the beginning of what would prove to be the longest season of his life. He didn't even have the energy to phone Tiffany, but she'd been out all night too. The AKAs had officially started their fall 1983 pledge club.

For the next six grueling weeks, Alex experienced more about living than he ever imagined. He learned about humility, something he thought he was familiar with, and the extent of depravity you reach when you are constantly controlled.

It was a learning process. The PKO evolution plan required that the pledges be stripped of everything and retaught to eat, think, breathe. Alex's life was no longer his own, but he was determined to embrace this new, exciting, emotionally and physically draining wonder. Even when he received the first C of his academic career, he was further motivated. He refused to bow to the constant challenges placed before him.

If he could only endure. Though motivated for different reasons, his line brothers and Alex shared a common goal: survival. Alex longed for the lifelong bonds that they'd forge, and the feeling of achievement and association he'd have with this great fraternity.

Another struggle Alex faced was the lack of contact with Tiff. Their talks were sporadic at best. They couldn't even leave messages on their answering machines for fear of some big brother or big sister intercepting them, and hazing them a little extra. Pledges weren't allowed a social life. They weren't entitled.

Alex would spot Tiffany only in passing, and she was catching hell. Hurrying to class, he'd see her, carrying her pledge ivy plant in hand, also rushing across the yard. A lurking big sister would catch her, and command that she recite something, do a step, or just bow down. Tiffany wasn't used to being humiliated, and he wondered just how she was handling it.

But she hung in there. It was a humbling experience for her too, but she finally hit her stride. She came into her own as one of the leading ivies on the line. All those years of cheerleading and aerobics had come in handy. She was the best stepper, and the few times Alex had seen her on the yard, she boldly entertained her big sisters with the intricate steps that she had mastered. And she was loving the obvious attention the position of "ivy shine" was bringing her.

Meanwhile, Alex felt like a complete failure. He had never learned how to dance, and was having a hard time learning the challenging steps the PKO pledges were being taught for their probate show. Many a night he got wood for fumbling over his feet or being off on one of the chants. It might have been silly, but he began questioning his ability to continue, especially as homecoming approached and it didn't seem like he was going to be able to carry his weight.

Alex was a whiz at learning the frat's history, reciting fraternity lines, and remembering details about each big brother. But combining intricate hand movements and dance steps with detailed chants was nearly impossible for him. He had no rhythm. Everyone was amused at first, but now even his line brothers were getting a little impatient with his inability to grasp the steps. Even number one, Sean the lunchbox, could step. Alex never told them that he'd never danced before, and at that point, there was no way he ever would.

ADP Gorgeous George was especially hard on him, riding him like a horse. But Alex learned that what doesn't kill you makes you stronger. Every opportunity, George mocked and ridiculed him for his mistakes, and it was clear he had a vendetta against him. But Alex took it. Even when George threatened him with the one thing that a pledge never wants to hear: that he had told an "old head," one of the elder members of the frat, that Alex was a major fuck-up, and then told Alex this old head couldn't wait to get his hands on him.

"The Deliverer" was his name. Someone from the old school who had gotten the reputation for making pledges drop line on hell night so viciously that it was as if they had never pledged. It was a common occurrence for these revered brothers to see the pledges before they crossed, especially during homecoming. However, this big brother, with the company of his line brothers, took greater pleasure in drawing blood from everyone who pledged and crossed at the Beta Chapter.

"If you think I've been riding your ass, wait till the real deals get down here. These are the masters. These are the bros that made us." George pointed a long finger in Alex's unblinking face, grazing his nose. "They are going to chew your little soft asses right on up." He walked down the line, swiftly kicking any combat boot that was not precisely aligned with the others.

The group of big brothers, high from the beer they had brought for the pledge session and exhausted from the energy they had exerted in hazing them, grunted in agreement.

"You best be ready," George continued, eyeing Alex intensely. "All y'all best be ready. 'Cause if one of y'all drop, all of y'all gonna drop. I don't want my frat to think that we put a bunch of candy asses on line." He took a big, thick, wooden, red-and-black paddle from one of his bros and swung it in the air. "Best get to steppin'. And I mean correctly too."

For the next three hours that night, the grids stopped for their lives. Alex continued to mess up, but he persevered. Homecoming was only a few days away, and they were far from ready. The few hours of sleep they'd grown accustomed to dwindled down to nearly minutes. It was almost three-thirty in the morning. Alex dragged home, feet and butt swollen, almost too incoherent to hear the phone ringing.

"Alex?" The female voice on the phone was meek, barely recognizable.

"Tiffany?" Alex said. He coughed and tried to clear the cobwebs in his voice.

"Yes, baby. I was so afraid to call. I thought maybe one of your big brothers would be there."

The lack of physical and emotional contact had gotten the best of them. They had barely spoken, and could never acknowledge each other's presence on the yard. It had been torture. The rare occasions when they'd been able to speak were brief and intense.

"I need to see you, Alex. I really do." Tiffany's words cracked with emotion, in a way Alex had never heard before. His heart tugged. How could they possibly meet? It was too dangerous. There was no safe place. He was physically drained, too frightened to go out, and too frightened to stay in. But he couldn't let her know just how bad off he was.

"I need to see you too, Tiff. But it's so dangerous." Alex rubbed his eyes as he glanced at the wall clock. The time made him cringe.

"I'll be careful. I just dropped off one of my line sisters, and I'm just down the street from your apartment. I'll be there in a few minutes."

HE OPENED THE door, and Tiffany melted in his arms. She had arrived before Alex had a chance to take off his funky T-shirt, fatigues, and combat boots. She didn't seem to notice as their lips locked forcefully. Tiffany's vigor nearly knocked him over. Explaining that she and her line sisters had been kidnapped by their big sister "specials," Tiffany's "spec" Jeannie had given her the evening off. She knew that Tiffany hadn't seen Alex in weeks, and she advised her to use the time wisely.

"I'm just so glad to see you." She cupped his closely cropped head in her hands, exposing her unpolished nails. Alex grasped her hands, enjoying their softness in his hardened palms. It was the only time he had ever seen her nails unpolished.

Embarrassed, she quickly snatched her hands away. "I know I look bad, Alex, but it's just so hard. We can't have our nails done, at least not until our probate show. Then they all have to match."

Alex nodded. The last thing he cared about was her fingernails.

He just wanted to know that she was okay. "Don't worry about it, baby. I'm just glad to see you, nail polish or not."

Looking deeply in his eyes, she bit her bottom lip. "I really missed you too. You just don't know how much. I've been so lonely without you."

"I know the feeling. I missed you so much." A warmth radiated through Alex's body as he held her close. He thought about the time they'd spent apart, and how strong the feelings were now that she was here. Alex never wanted to let her go. An urgency crept down his leg, and he was embarrassed by his arousal. He loosened his grasp on her so that she wouldn't notice his bulging erection.

She grasped him tighter, and gently touched his rising nature. "I—I know we talked about it, and I know we said that we'd wait until we were sure. But I'm sure. I need you. I want you to hold me so badly. I know how it's going to be once all of this is over. I don't want you being with those sweethearts just because we haven't been together."

Alex tried to assure her that that wasn't the case, and that he had no interest in anyone else. But she placed her soft lips forcefully over his mouth, kissing him passionately. "I'm ready—more than ever before. I want you. Not just now, but always. And I trust you. I know you won't ever be like Sid."

Tiffany's words unnerved him, but Alex quickly recovered. Though he hadn't thought about an "always," somehow it felt right. Though a lot of time had passed, he could remember all that they had been through as if it were yesterday. He vividly recalled how Sid had nearly raped her, and the agony she had suffered because of it. Alex wanted to protect her, to have her, totally and completely, always. He wanted to dispel her fears. He wanted to kiss away her hurt and pain, and commit to their love for each other. Alex pulled her tightly against his chest and gently caressed her back. "You know I'd never hurt you like that. I care for you too much. I love you, Tiffany."

His tongue explored her mouth deeply, the scent of their bodies mixing heavily in the air. They had kissed before, but never to this degree.

"I want you too, Tiffany. But are you sure? I need to tell you something. You know, I've never been with anyone before. And I don't want you to ever regret this—" She responded by stripping off her trench coat and leading him into the bathroom.

"We can teach each other," she said breathlessly.

Alex, at first a little shy about his body, soon relaxed. Tiffany was so comfortable with hers that she made him feel completely uninhibited. Together they showered, washing each other tenderly. He was in total awe of her body, so curvaceous and tight. It was everything he could have wanted, and more. Her breasts were soft and full, and her nipples hardened as he lathered her with the papaya-scented shower gel Morgan's girlfriend Daria had left on the side of the bathtub.

Together, under the stream of hot water that danced on their bodies, they reveled in the beauty of the moment. Kissing deeply, they caressed each other; the months of anticipation had not adequately prepared them for what was in store.

Wrapped only in towels, they dashed from the bathroom to Alex's room, careful to avoid running into Morgan or Daria. They fell, entangled, on the double bed. Alex fumbled with the ministereo system on his nightstand, and turned on the Luther Vandross tape he usually studied by.

Trembling, Alex marveled at the beauty of Tiffany's sleek dancer's body. Her smooth, honey brown skin was moist and supple, and he silently thanked God for the opportunity to go where no man had gone before. She nuzzled under his chin, and he outlined her body with his tongue, tasting every delightful inch of her. Controlling his excitement, he slowly licked the soles of her feet, sucking gently on each toe, wiggling his tongue up her leg to her moist inner thighs. Call it instinct, but he discovered making love to someone you loved wasn't too difficult.

Yet, as Alex found himself becoming overcome with desire, a paralyzing fear gripped him. Suddenly he was ashamed of his nakedness. What if he wasn't big enough? What if he wasn't able to satisfy her? Alex froze and clung to her, burying his head by her side, too frightened to move.

"What's wrong, baby?" Tiffany lifted his face and looked deeply into his eyes.

Alex looked away and said nothing. Here he was with the most beautiful woman in the world, and he was tripping.

She gently rubbed his head. "Don't be afraid, Alex. It'll be okay. Take your time, baby. I'm not going anywhere."

Her encouraging words and probing fingertips slowly prodded him back into action. Lovingly rolling her over onto her stomach, Alex massaged her back, and lightly blew kisses up and down her spine. Tiffany writhed in pleasure when he gently touched her love area, feeling her wetness form to the point of dripping. She gripped the ransacked sheets as he slowly explored the intoxicating mysteries of her secret garden. His mouth had taken on a life of its own.

Her body trembled in a series of orgasmic convulsions, and she moaned in pleasure, digging her nails deeply into his back.

As he worked her body into a heated frenzy once more, she weakened, and, unable to resist, opened up to him. He strained to be cautious, not knowing what to expect. Afraid of being too rough or too fast, they slowly built a passionate rhythm. From the arching of their backs, to the frantic grasps of their fingers, to the uncontrollable force of flesh meeting flesh, lips hungrily exploring uncharted territory, their bodies became one in the depths of a passion neither had ever experienced before. Together they made love, urgently and patiently, all night long, until their dual virginity disintegrated in eruptions of new sensuality.

They lay in each other's arms, too breathless to speak, emotionally and physically drained. The sun peeked from behind the venetian blinds, and as they greeted daybreak, they discovered that they were once again aroused, and began another heated encounter. For the moment, nothing else mattered. Classes, homework, and even pledging were forgotten in their newfound passion.

THE NEXT NIGHT at probate-show step practice, there was a noticeable difference in Alex's movements, providing a rare moment of comedic relief. Pledges and big brothers alike joked about his overnight transformation. Though they might have suspected, they never knew the real reason. Somehow, Alex had found his rhythm.

IT WAS THE Friday night before homecoming, and it was rumored that all of the sororities were crossing that night, after the Death Marches, and would be out in full regalia for the homecoming festivities. But now the gymnasium, packed to the rafters with students, alumni, well-wishers, Greeks and non-Greeks, was riding an emotional high as the probates from all of the Greek organizations stepped and chanted their way into what they hoped would be the final hours of their servitude.

The PKO grids, now completely transformed into baldheaded probates, or axes, finished their show with the audience clamoring for more. Now the smallest pledge group on the yard, they had dropped five more over the last week, yet they had outperformed the thirty-two Que Lampados, and even the twenty-five cane-twirling Kappa Scrollers. The last to perform, the PKOs commandeered the floor, dressed in gangster-style clothing and gear, where they stepped and sang their hearts out. They crooned a stirring rendition of "PKO, With You I'm Born Again" that almost brought tears to everyone's eyes.

As they triumphantly marched off the floor, their big brothers lit up the gym with their frat calls. They were especially proud, for the grids had done them right. The big brothers had threatened them within an inch of their lives to do so.

"You guys did all right!" Trent high-fived them all as they entered the locker room. The other big brothers crowded in, giving their trademark frat call, and rubbing each of the grids' heads.

The grids finally relaxed, taking a break from the hell they had lived through so far. Praying silently and aloud, they hugged, slapping backs and wrapping their legs around each other's waists, as they'd seen their big brothers do so often.

Even George was impressed. "I'm glad to see you all pulled it together. You know, if a line can't step, that's a reflection on us." He flipped his thumb toward Trent. "But don't get too happy. It ain't over till it's over."

Reveling in their sweet victory over the arrogant Lamps, they cherished the moment. The smell of sweet success overrode the funk of sweaty bodies and the corn-chip odor of combat boots that filled the air. They had proven that they could hang in the PKOs' steep stepping tradition, and even if they did nothing else right, that couldn't be taken away from them.

Then George instructed them to line up and march outside. The Death March began with the pledges from all of the organizations holding candles in the center of the yard. The mood was solemn, eerie; it appeared as if this were truly a march of death. Big brothers and big sisters huddled around their prey, and some mumbled words of strength and encouragement, while others foretold of the agony they were about to experience.

There were sobs and moans from the girls and the guys. Ivies must protect their ivy plants. Scrollers better not drop those bricks. There was a muffled roar as pledges were commanded about and verbally assaulted, and spectators stood around in awesome wonder as they witnessed this time-honored tradition.

As each of the groups filed out to their undetermined destinies, Alex did the unthinkable: he looked for Tiffany. His heart leaped when he saw her, leaning back at an unbelievable angle, holding both plant and her line sister in the front up. Alex's line of sight was broken by the piercing eyes of his ADP, who had witnessed the whole thing. Suddenly he was paralyzed with fear.

George slid up to his ear and whispered low and strong, "Yeah, number thirteen, you about to find out just how unlucky your number is. I got something really special for you. You better look, and look good, 'cause you ain't gonna see that for a long time. And after tonight, you might not ever want to see her again. Remember that."

As soon as they marched over to the frat house and were blindfolded, cruel reality set in. They were corralled into a van, tossed in on top of each other. The pledges tried to comfort themselves, urging one another to be strong, to hold on tightly to each other, so the wayward swings from fists and paddles wouldn't injure anyone specifically. Yet, from the cab of the van, they overheard covert plans being whispered, and when they finally took off, it seemed as if they rode for hours. When they arrived at their destination, the pledges were flung out of the van and ordered to line up, even though they were blindfolded.

Trent's familiar voice rang out in the chilly autumn night. The smell of damp night air, fresh-cut grass, and manure indicated that they must have been out on a farm somewhere in southern Virginia. There was a peculiar stillness that intensified the spookiness of the hour. "You lowlife pieces of shit are about to live a moment in your lives you will never forget. You better hang on to each other, because if you get separated, you will only be a memory. We won't remember you, and your line brothers will forget you. You are one body. The Fall 1983 Pledge Line, the Fourteen Step Program. One of you goes, all of you go. Tonight."

Clearly, they were supposed to hang on, no matter what. This was the final test to see how much they really wanted, or deserved, PKO.

Alex knew he was in trouble. He felt his line brother Evans hyperventilating behind him, and he heard someone gagging. The blindfold around his eyes seemed to be pressing into the back of his skull, and he felt weak because he hadn't eaten all day.

A force from out of nowhere mowed them over like a bowling ball rolling over pins. They were scattered, and left with nothing but the shreds of their closest line brothers' clothing as they were ripped apart.

Alex groped around, calling out for his front and back, who were nowhere to be found or heard. Voices rose, those of the big brothers blending with the muffled cries of the axes.

Alex walked aimlessly, tripping over feet and bodies. George's acidic voice burned his ear: "Told you I had something special for you, Boy Wonder. And you're going to get it tonight. We're about to get medieval on your ass." His fist landed on Alex's unguarded chest, and Alex crumpled. Alex awkwardly threw an arm up to block any more punches, and used the other to reach for his line brothers.

"What's the matter with you, thirteen? Too good to ask for

help?" A foot found his knee, and Alex immediately fell to the ground, flat on his face. George continued his tirade, now joined by several other big brothers, each taking their time to swing mercilessly at Alex's defenseless body. Franklin, his spec, finally found him, and persuaded his brothers to step back while he helped him up. Franklin pointed him in the direction of nearby moans and hollers, rubbed his back, and encouraged him to be strong.

Before Alex took a step, a strong hand gripped his shirt and hung a heavy chain around his neck. A big brother said with pointed authority, "I'll take him, frat. He's got somewhere special to go."

Over Franklin's cautious objections, Alex was dragged away by the chain, its weight cutting into his neck, slowing his circulation. Alex again yelled for his line brothers, but he was repeatedly greeted with a familiar voice. The same menacing one that he'd heard since day one, warning him his time had finally come.

It was George. "Yeah, yeah. They got him. Get him, frat. Your time is up, Boy Wonder," he exclaimed. A hush fell over the crowd.

Panicking, Alex lunged at the person dragging the chain. "Big— big brother. The chain. The chain is too tight. I—I'm choking." He tried in vain to breathe and keep up with the dizzying pace.

"Shut up and hurry up." The frat's tone was gravelly and agitated, unyielding to Alex's obvious pain. He dragged Alex along, over the muddy ground, not even pausing when Alex stumbled.

His air intake was almost completely blocked, and Alex felt his head getting lighter. Though his eyes were blindfolded, he began to see a bright, searing light.

Alex passed out, falling with a loud thud on the marshy terrain.

"GET UP." THE command was muffled and low, almost in a whisper. It sounded altered, as if by some kind of device used to distort voices beyond recognition. The voice was almost comedic, a cross between Darth Vader's and Pee-wee Herman's. Alex's blindfold had been loosened, but still covered his eyes. Instinctively, he reached for it.

"Leave it alone. Don't think for one moment that just because you passed out you're going to get any kind of break."

Cold water splashed across his face, and Alex jerked from the sensation.

"What's wrong? I'm just trying to revive you." Muffled voices carried on a covert conversation in the background.

"Axis Alex, meet The Deliverer."

His first impulse was to beg for his life, but Alex immediately realized that it wouldn't make any difference. Instead, he tried to greet his maker as he should be greeted. "Good evening, big brother, The Deliverer, of the Beta Chapter of the Psi Kappa Omicron Fraternity, Incorporated, sir."

"Quit pandering. I want to see how much heart you have."

Alex began reciting the PKO pledge, but The Deliverer stopped him abruptly.

"I'm not talking about something you memorize. I can get a damned parrot to do that. I'm talking about what you feel. I'm talking about what's inside of you. What's in your heart."

A round object was pushed against his mouth. "Bite it. Bite it like you want it," he instructed through the distortion.

Confused because his lack of sight had affected his sense of smell, Alex reluctantly opened his mouth. He had no choice, so he bit down, and immediately retched. It was an onion.

"Swallow it. Don't you dare spit it out. If you do, then you're spitting on my fraternity. And you won't do that." There were jeers and mockery at Alex's dry heaves.

Alex continued eating the slick vegetable, gagging with every bite. Tears filled his eyes. He tried to block out all of the voices except the one, the only one that seemed to matter, that of The Deliverer.

For what seemed like eternity, it taunted him. Question after question was fired at him, but somehow Alex found the answers. If he was too slow, he was forced to eat more of the Greek meal, a wretched combination of food that made his stomach convulse. He was beaten mercilessly, but he couldn't cry. The big brothers were vocally upset that Alex hadn't shed PKO tears.

After The Deliverer was assured that Alex knew his history, he was finally allowed to stand. Alex overheard that most of the PKOs were impressed with him, and satisfied that he knew his stuff. But he was still worried. Although he was physically and mentally exhausted, Alex knew in his heart it wasn't over.

Alex was shoved from behind, and caught by two large hands that grabbed him by the chain. He could hear the big brother breathing, and felt his hot breath on his face. He also smelled a familiar scent on this person. Cologne? Reefer? He couldn't tell.

"So I hear you like knives?" The warbling voice was right in his face, and the hum from the voice alterer vibrated off Alex's cheeks. The hairs stood straight up on the back of his sweaty, crusty neck.

"Answer me. Answer me now." The air was dead silent, and fear blocked out his surroundings.

Every fiber in his body cried out for him to either punch The Deliverer with all of his might or run for his life. But Alex knew that he'd come too far to jeopardize his chances of going over and becoming a PKO.

"No—no—no, big brother. I don't like knives," Alex said meekly. His voice sounded like that of an ashamed child who'd been caught doing something wrong.

"Oh. So you don't like knives? What are you trying to do, make me out a liar? Hey, bros. This piece of trash is calling me a liar. That's not what I heard. I hear you're into slicing up PKOs. Is that true?"

"N-n-no, well, yes, big brother. Not really, big brother. It was an accident. Just an error in judgment. A big mistake, big brother." Alex must've rattled off "big brother" a hundred times in two minutes. He grasped for words, hoping to key in on something that would satisfy The Deliverer and preempt what he knew could be a very painful experience.

"An error in judgment? A mistake? How can taking a knife to somebody be a mistake? Especially if that somebody is one of my dear frat brothers?"

A chorus of big brothers chimed in. This was the moment they'd been salivating for. Sweat poured down Alex's forehead, soaking his bandanna. The salt from the perspiration stung his eyes. Before he could respond, he felt the cold sensation of a sharp metal object pressing against his throat. His Adam's apple bobbed up against it, and he gasped for air, trying to prevent it from penetrating his skin.

"Let me tell you something," the voice commanded. The Deliverer grabbed Alex by the forehead and snapped his head back, pressing what felt like a knife against his neck. He nearly fainted. "The next time you draw down on somebody, you better be ready to follow through."

The blood rushed from Alex's head, and his body went limp. Passing out into an abyss of darkness, the chilling final words of The Deliverer rang in his ears, and would haunt him for the rest of his life. "The next time you pull a knife on someone, you better know why. It's not a toy. It's not a plaything. You either be prepared to use it for real or have it used on you. For real. You either kill or be killed. Always remember that."

CHAPTER 12

TRAFFIC was murderous during the waning days of the summer tourist season. D.C.'s notoriously stifling heat never deterred any of the Hawaiian shirt–wearing visitors from flocking there every summer. Alex tooled down the crowded street in his shiny black-on-black 525i BMW and honked his horn at the creeping car in front. The driver, an obvious tourist, clutched a map and had a dazed and confused expression on his face. The blare of the horn startled him, and he jerked the car out of the lane. The luxurious Beamer was a wedding present from Simon, and Alex loved the way it handled. He was usually cautious, but right now he was in a hurry. His years in D.C. had turned him into an extremely aggressive driver. In fact, he cut people off at will. It was one of the perks of having D.C. government tags.

Stuck at a traffic light, Alex daydreamed about his carefree days back at Hilliard, which now seemed so long ago. Though he'd started off on a rocky path, there were some really good memories. Especially after he pledged and got to see how the other half lived.

He sorely missed his friends, and made a mental note to get in touch with Lisa, Foody, and Morgan.

Lisa had returned to Atlanta to work for a new black magazine based there. After it met an untimely demise, she reluctantly took a job at her family's insurance agency. Always the one to keep up with the gossip, she usually contacted Alex at least twice a month, but she'd never gotten over her disdain for Tiffany. Lisa's visits with him were limited because of it. That and the fact that Alex was so busy. Lisa and her last boyfriend had broken up a while ago, and she had entered into a string of meaningless relationships. Lisa always wanted him to hook her up with somebody, even one of his frat. She was definitely like the sister he never had, and the thought of their quasi–sibling rivalry and her unsolicited advice still made him smile.

Foody had been booted out of boot camp and was living in New York, still trying to make it in the rap music field. He had many near successes, but was most recently working as a bouncer in one of the underground dance clubs. Alex would see him from time to time when he traveled to New York, but their worlds were drifting apart. Foody was falling in with some rough crowds, and the Big Apple was making him quite a schemer. Alex was most concerned about him. Foody had stuck by him, even when he was a social outcast. Foody would always be a friend, and Alex would be there for him no matter what. Even when Foody called collect to hit him up for a couple of bucks.

Morgan was one of the few frat brothers Alex stayed close to. He lived a few hours away in Richmond, successfully working in his family's textile business, and they talked at least once a week. He and Daria had gotten married and were living the cushy life. They had land and a sprawling house, and many times Morgan said he wouldn't move to save his life. He was a Southern boy, and he and Alex enjoyed sparring with each other over the differences in their lifestyles. They had planned to take a vacation to the Caymans together, but Daria had gotten pregnant, much to Tiffany's chagrin. A dedicated career woman now, children were not high on her list of priorities. Since their plans had been put on hold, Morgan and Alex had a lot of catching up to do.

Maneuvering from Georgetown to Capitol Hill was hell, especially trying to traverse Rock Creek Parkway, past Hains Point, and up Independence Avenue. Alex glanced at his watch and grimaced. Twelve-fifteen, the hands on the gold Presidential Roléx indicated.

"Damn." He had a twelve-thirty meeting with Simon, and he knew better than to be late. Alex pictured Simon sitting in his high-back chair, back to the door, flicking a sleek Mont Blanc pen between his fingers. At the meeting's hour, Barbara, like clockwork, would shut his door and insist that the latecomer knock first. And Simon wouldn't even turn around in his chair. Such a grievous act against his time was a cardinal sin, and he was not above letting anyone know it. Your first offense became your only offense if you hoped to continue doing business with His Honor. The only person Alex had seen get away with being late was Howard, Simon's public relations man, who seemed to hold the key to Simon's very existence.

Perspiration built up around Alex's forehead, a despicable tendency he'd picked up from pledging. Whenever he became nervous, in addition to that annoying stutter, beads of sweat would now pop out on his brow. Alex wiped the sweat away with his initialed handkerchief. Thank God those days were over.

Alex never looked back on that hellacious pledge program, except when he'd become nervous and start profusely sweating. His frat brothers would joke and say that the only way he'd find out who The Deliverer was, was on another Hell Night. But Alex never got an opportunity. The national office placed a moratorium on pledging for three years, based on a hazing incident at one of the schools in the South, and the Beta chapter of their fraternity never pledged another line while he was there. But he really didn't mind. The thought of witnessing such cruel behavior under such macabre circumstances was a little more than Alex could stomach, literally. He became nauseated at his own memories, and usually had to focus on the present until they vanished.

The hell of pledging had been worth it, though. With fraternity life, Alex flourished. He worked diligently on the yard, and erased the blemishes from his encounter with Sid. Alex was a true, red-and-black PKO. He became well respected and loved by his brothers, and even George came around. Simon was especially proud of him. Alex had proved himself. It also didn't hurt that his GPA helped save the frat from the threat of academic probation that had been hovering over them. He let bygones be bygones, but he never forgot those eleven weeks of pure hell.

After Alex completed Hilliard, Simon placed him in a prestigious position on his staff, circumventing the approval of the nine district board members. The new position, urban affairs liaison, was specially created to manage the housing and urban development offices. This placed Alex directly above all of the figureheads of those departments, none of whom really minded, for they saw him as Simon's glorified gopher. It wasn't a big deal if Simon wanted to place his daughter's boyfriend in a cushy position while Alex struggled through Georgetown Law. No one even grumbled. It wasn't like it was any money out of their pockets, only those of the unsuspecting taxpayers.

Alex knew his assignment to the position was nepotism, but he couldn't complain. For the next year, Simon groomed him for even higher heights. Tiffany and Alex attended all of the right social functions and became prominent figures on D.C.'s social and political scene; Alex had become comfortable hobnobbing with the social elite. His relationship with Tiffany flourished. Monogamy was his strong suit, and although Alex was getting more attention from more women than he'd ever had in his life, he wouldn't bow. Not even with the constant ribbing of the few friends and frat brothers he hung out with in the city.

Their third year out of Hilliard, however, it became evident that Tiffany was getting restless with the status of their relationship. She had a reasonably good job as a marketing coordinator at the United Care Fund, one of the nation's foremost charitable organizations, and her side business of event planning was taking off. But it wasn't enough to keep her content. The hints were coming fast and furious that something was missing from her life. After the third soror in her chapter got married, she couldn't suppress her hostility any longer. The time had come for a showdown.

They usually met for dinner on Thursday nights, the only night Alex didn't have class. Due to some last-minute work he had to do for Simon, and heavy traffic due to bad weather, Alex was about fifteen minutes late getting to the restaurant. They had agreed to meet at one of the trendy waterside eateries, Hogates. By the time he arrived, Tiffany was laughing and joking with a brother in a Brooks Brothers suit at the bar. Alex was immediately guarded.

"Hey, love, sorry I'm late." Alex reached to kiss her.

Tiffany, colder than the late November skies outside, barely acknowledged his presence. Dressed in a mauve mini-suit, displaying those gorgeous legs, she had every man's eye and every woman's ire. She continued smiling and talking to Brooks Brothers.

Alex motioned for the bartender, and ordered a gin and tonic. Nothing too heavy. He had to study later.

"Would you like something, Tiff?"

Tiffany pointed toward a partially filled glass of wine. "In case you hadn't noticed, I've had time to drink a couple of glasses of wine." She emphasized "couple," and the brother smirked.

Seething, Alex grabbed his drink with one hand and Tiffany's arm with the other. "Come on. Our table's ready."

She shot him a look and collected her purse. "I'll talk to you soon, Niles."

Niles leered. "Yeah, Tiffany. I'll look forward to it." Alex gritted on him with a "don't start none, won't be none," straight-out-of-Shaw look.

Once they were seated, Alex's anger boiled over. "What was that all about?"

"That what?"

Clasping his hands, Alex calmly brought them down on the glass table. He didn't want to make a scene. One of the first things Simon had taught him flashed in his mind: Never air your dirty laundry.

"Don't play innocent with me, Tiffany. You know what I'm talking about." Alex nodded in the direction of the bar. The spot where she and Niles had been sitting was now vacant.

"Oh, you mean Niles? Surely you can't be referring to that. I was just drumming up some business. He and some of his business associates are going to throw a little soiree, and he was interested in my services."

Alex grunted. "It seemed like he was interested in a little more than your services."

"Well, Alex, I didn't notice all that. It could be just a figment of your imagination."

"I don't think I could imagine something so obvious."

"Well, at least you're using something with regards to me. It's a shame that it's your imagination."

Alex braced himself for the inevitable. They had been down this road before, and he knew how it was going to play out. Let the games begin, he thought, as he calculated his next move. Play dumb. It was the first offense in round one of the game they had perfected: the game of love. More precisely, the battle of the sexes. Alex had become quite savvy in this, his one and only relationship. Dealing with Tiffany had taught him a lot. So he responded in the way he learned would buy him the most time. "What are you talking about, Tiff?" His expression was blank.

After checking her nails, Tiffany stared him frostily in the eye. "I'm saying that you're wrong about Niles's intentions. But if it were true that he was interested in more than my services, then I wouldn't be concerned if I were you. That's a whole lot more than I can say about you lately."

Alex immediately got on the defensive. "What do you mean, more than you can say about me lately? You act like you don't know what I have on my plate these days. Between work and school, there isn't a whole lot of time for fun." His patience was wearing thin. Playing this game could truly be work, and he was a bit tired of it.

Tiffany zeroed in. "Fun? Is that all I am? Well, guess what, Alex. This is not fun for me. I'm tired of being an afterthought, someone you fall into bed with and screw after a busy day. If you're not too 'tired' to do that. Think about it. I'm not getting any younger, and I do not want to spend some of the best years of my life watching you do what you have to do, with no promise or guarantees."

Alex was caught off guard. He wasn't prepared to discuss their relationship. And he certainly didn't want to discuss it in public. But he was losing big-time, and had to say something that would keep him in the game. "I thought you understood that I wanted to go to school. I thought you understood what it would require, and you were cool with that."

Tiffany's roll wasn't slowed for a moment. She had the upper hand, and she was ready to use it. She motioned for the waiter, and promptly ordered another Chardonnay. "That excuse is just so passé, Alex. Don't think that I don't understand. I have a life too, you know. I have things that are important to me. And if you're too busy to understand that, then maybe you don't know enough about me. Maybe you just don't love me as much as you profess to. And maybe you just need to find your fun elsewhere."

Alex sweated. She had him completely baffled, like one of Ali's opponents caught up in his infamous rope-a-dope. She was working him brilliantly. Maybe he hadn't been paying enough attention to Tiffany, but he never thought she'd question his love for her.

It had been almost three years since they graduated, and he guessed he *had* kind of taken her for granted. Maybe he just assumed that she would always be there for him. But as he looked at her across the table, it was as if he were seeing her for the very first time. The way the candlelight caught the twinkle in her eyes, her beauty still made him weak. From her perfectly coiffed hair, to the meticulous makeup, to the tailored clothing, she was flawless. How could he have been so blind?

Alex remembered that even before they had gotten together, Tiffany told him about the fairy-tale dream she had of being like her parents and marrying her college sweetheart. After they fell in love, they never really talked about it. There was an unspoken, implied agreement that they'd be together forever. Now reality was upon them. Tiffany was a grown woman, and she still wanted the white picket fence. But what could he do?

Alex wasn't ready to get married. He had a perfect vision of how he wanted his life to be after law school: to get a nice house and good job. And although he had a good job, he wasn't where he wanted to be. At age twenty-four, it was a lot to consider. So like any cornered man, he played with his drink, played dumb, and hedged.

"What are you saying? What do you want me to do?"

"I don't want you to do anything, Alex. Do what you want to do. But I'm telling you, I'm not waiting anymore. I will not be put on hold." She placed the goblet to her lips and poured the wine down her throat.

Then she stood up. "I've lost my appetite." She waved her hand around the room. "Oh, that's right, I forgot. This is your designated evening for fun, so let's see. Hmmm. I'm sure someone here would love to have some 'fun' with you. That way you can cross it off your little to-do list as completed. I'd hate to be the cause of you not doing something you've flagged on your schedule."

Alex sat calmly, trying not to make a scene, but he was cracking under the pressure. "Look, Tiffany. Please sit back down. I'm sure we can talk about this rationally."

"Are you calling me irrational?" The Oscar was hers for an award-winning performance.

"No, I'm just saying that this isn't the time or the place to discuss this. I mean, I—I'm not prepared."

"Alex, this isn't one of your law courses. You can't pick up a book that's going to tell you how to live your life. You don't prepare for life, you just live it." She pirouetted on her pumps and stormed across the floor. Alex fumbled for the money to pay for the drinks, then ran after her.

By the time he reached the restaurant entrance, a cab was pulling away from the curb. She had already disappeared into the arctic night.

Alex was too through. He snatched his keys from the valet and furiously drove home over the icy streets, constantly talking himself out of trailing her to her place. After driving around his block a couple of times, he selfishly parked in front of a hydrant and slapped a bright orange OFFICIAL BUSINESS sticker on his window. He normally didn't exploit his position, but tonight he was too pissed off to care.

Approaching the staircase that led to his English basement apartment, Alex stopped short at a body sprawled out on the stairs. Vacillating between calling the cops and pouncing on the bum himself, Alex angrily, and stupidly, stepped to him. Balling up his fist, he took his foot and nudged the body. The heap rolled over, and to his surprise, it was Foody.

"Yo, what's up?" he said, that irreverent smile plastered on his face.

Alex reached down to help him up. "What in the hell are you doing on my steps? You were about to catch a serious beat-down, Rudy. Not to mention the fact that if I hadn't come home, you would've froze to death."

"In case you haven't noticed, I got enough here to keep me warm," Foody said.

Within moments they were inside, laughing about Foody's sidewalk lounge act. They popped open a couple of brews, and Foody made himself at home while Alex peeled off his business attire.

Alex was glad to see him, but his timing couldn't have been worse. He had work to do, Tiffany to deal with, and professors breathing down his neck. By the time Alex had changed into some jeans and a T-shirt, Foody had transformed his cramped apartment into a Fritos-smelling brewery. Alex was instantly taken back to his college days, and it momentarily took his mind off his troubles.

"Yo, Al. What's up? You seem a little down in the mouth," Foody shouted over the blaring television as he raided the refrigerator, and rattled pots and pans.

Alex sucked on the lime-laden rim of his Corona and played it off. He turned down the TV's volume and flipped through a couple of channels.

"Nothing, man. I should ask you that. After all, you were the one stretched out on my stoop, looking like the last bum." As cool as Foody was, Alex wasn't sure how he'd respond. Alex kept flipping, hoping to find something Foody'd want to watch instead of grilling him.

"I heard that. But you can expect something like that out of me. You just looked like you were a little pissed about something else besides me being on your stoop." Foody went on to say that he was in town trying to get a gig as a roadie for one of the rap groups at the upcoming Budweiser Superfest. And due to another snafu, he really needed to get out of New York for a couple of days.

Foody had had so many jobs since he left school that Alex wasn't too surprised by this turn of events. He was like a Headley from *In Living Color,* always working somewhere different. Alex was even less surprised that Foody had had to leave town quickly. Alex started to ask why, or who had hastened his departure, but then decided not to. If he didn't press Foody, Foody wouldn't press him. So Alex kept mindlessly changing channels, until he came across some hard-core pornography.

"What the hell?" Alex wondered aloud. He hadn't subscribed to any sex channels. He didn't have time to watch the regular ones. "Foody, did you order up some of these pay-per-view porn channels?"

Foody laughed, as he started building a couple of Dagwoods. "No, Alex. You worry too much. I didn't order nothing. In fact, it won't cost you a dime. Here, let me show you what's up."

Alex squinted at Foody as he whipped out a laptop computer and a set of tools. He showed him how, in a matter of moments, he had cracked the code on his cable box, descrambled the signal, and reprogrammed it to give him every available channel. Alex had never dreamed that Foody had skills like that, but evidently he was a computer whiz.

"It's no big deal, man. I been fooling around with computers and programming and shit for years," he said, sliding a sandwich in front of Alex and munching on his own.

"I'm impressed," Alex said seriously.

"Yeah, well, I'd be impressed if you told me what was up with you. I know something's up. How your girl doing?"

He looked at Alex searchingly, so Alex turned away. As he nibbled on his sandwich, Alex prayed that Foody had washed his hands first. "She's all right."

"That was mighty tired. Oh, I get it. It's baby girl giving you the blues."

It didn't take too long or too many beers before Alex spilled his guts.

Foody was uncharacteristically quiet. "Well, old boy, I guess your time is up. You knew that it was gonna happen. Y'all been hanging for years now, and I guess she's about ready to *clank-clank*." He simulated being handcuffed, his wide eyes twinkling mischievously.

Alex gritted on him and took another bite of his sandwich. He was surprised that Foody thought of marriage as a natural progression.

"Yo, face it, man. It don't get no better than what you got. Tiffany is fine, and she's always had your back. Even before you was cool, remember? If she ain't the one, then there ain't one."

Alex kept playing with his food. "Yeah, Foody, I know she's the one. But I'm just not ready yet."

Foody rolled his eyes. "Boy, you been ready since I've known you. What the hell else you got to do? I know she's sexing you up right. You couldn't possibly be trying to get with no other freak, are you?"

"No, it's not like that. I just don't know if I'm ready to settle down."

Gobbling down his sandwich, Foody headed back to the refrigerator, where he pulled out the beer carton. "Well, whatever, man. But you need to recognize you got a good thing, and think about what it was like before you got that good thing, Mr. Lonely Man."

Alex knew he was right, but somehow taking advice from Foody wasn't high on his list of priorities. He was more concerned with how long Foody was going to be there, and how he could keep him out of trouble until then. The topic of Tiffany was closed, and they moved on to more benign matters, like getting some more beer. As they sat around and talked, Alex blew off studying for some harmless fun. He wasn't sure what was going to happen tomorrow, but for tonight he was going to chill.

FOODY'S COUPLE OF days wound up being a couple of weeks. When the roadie job fell through, he spent much of his time crammed in Alex's old Z, bumming gas money from him and trying to find work in the entertainment venues. Things were kind of slow since the Christmas holiday season was approaching, and Alex found Foody's company comforting. He filled the void from Tiffany's self-imposed absence, and lessened the possibility that Alex would have to spend his Christmas alone for the first time. Tiffany refused his calls on a daily basis, and thwarted any attempt Alex made to contact her.

The gaping hole Tiffany left and the angst Alex was going through made him reexamine his life. Maybe Foody had a point. Alex was being a hypocrite, of sorts. He didn't seem too appreciative of where he was, or how far he'd come. He was basically sitting on top of the world, yet he was still unsure of himself. It was time to come together. His relationship with his father had deteriorated to the point where it didn't exist. And it had been months since Alex had visited the cemetery. Yet he was finally in a position where he could do something he'd talked about for years: he could finally find a way to honor Ivan. With all of the resources he had within his reach, he might even be able to find out what had actually happened to him.

But he'd have to be careful. Even though he and Simon were close, Alex was still uncomfortable, maybe even a little ashamed, about discussing his personal business with him. Especially Ivan. Until Alex was able to vindicate his name, he wanted to keep his memory as far away from Simon as possible.

An idea struck him. He closed the door to his office, then picked up the phone and dialed Lisa. She'd know how to help him.

"Hey, boy," she said. She was still working as a manager in her family's insurance agency, and actually enjoying it. "To what honor do I deserve this call, you fortuitous flunky? You got a few minutes to slum with us little people or something?"

"Ha-ha-ha. You know I can't go too long without talking to you, Lisa-Lisa."

"Bullshit, Alex. I call you to shoot the breeze. You're the one always uptight about something."

Her remark was a dig at Tiffany. Alex dared not mention those woes to her.

"Well, you got me, sis. I've got a little something I want to talk to you about. I, uh—"

"Listen, Alex. Don't say anything right now. If it can wait, I'll be in town next Tuesday. Let's get together then."

Lisa's paranoia was probably driven by the fact that she was now working with insurance investigators, and although it gave her more gossip than she could handle, it also made her extremely distrustful of people. Alex figured that she could put him in touch with a private investigator or something, but he never figured that she'd be this 'noid.

"Okay, Christy Love. Or should I say Foxy Brown," Alex said, and switched the conversation to something she felt comfortable discussing. He didn't mention Foody, for Alex knew she'd get too much pleasure from his latest escapades. So he let her catch him up on her love life and gossip about their old H.I. cronies.

They talked for at least half an hour, as Alex fought back the urge to call Tiffany. Before he could hang up, there was an urgent rap on his door. It was Sheila, his secretary, insisting he take another call.

Alex clicked over, hoping it was Tiffany, but was wrecked to find out it wasn't. Instead it was Foody. He had been stopped in Alex's car, and was being held at the First Precinct. "I need for you to come and get me, Alex. Please," Foody said, his voice trembling.

Foody had done a lot of things in his life, but he wasn't a jailbird. The tone of his voice sent chills through Alex's body. "What's going on, Foody? Why did they stop you?" Alex said, scrambling in his desk drawer to get his keys. He stood up and grabbed his coat, the telephone still plastered to his ear.

Foody sighed deeply. "It's not my fault, Alex. I swear."

"Why won't you tell me what happened, Foody? Did you hit somebody?" Alex stretched the cord on the phone and cursed as the phone nearly fell to the floor.

"Alex, I'll explain it when you get here, I promise. Just come and get me, man."

Alex dropped everything and ran out, giving Sheila some made-up excuse for his hasty departure. He was speeding, literally and figuratively, trying to figure out what had happened, and why Foody refused to give him any details. When Alex reached the booking area, a stout, plainclothes detective met him. After looking him up and down, he checked Alex's credentials, then ushered him into a holding area where Foody was pacing the floor.

When he saw Alex, Foody rushed over to the bars and reached for his arm. "Alex, man, I don't know what's up, man. I swear I didn't do nothing, man." His eyes were red and glistening, as if he were about to cry.

Alex tried to calm him down, but Foody was becoming more and more upset. "Will you tell me what happened? Did you have an accident? Just explain to me what happened, Rudy."

Foody grabbed the bars and looked down. "I was stopped for running a yellow light."

"You can't be arrested for that, Rudy. You don't have any warrants, do you?" Alex asked.

Rudy stared at the floor. "No, I don't have any warrants, Alex. You know I do a whole lotta dumb shit, but I don't break the law. It all happened so fast. Some undercover cops or them jump-out boys found something in the car and impounded it. And locked me up."

"Foody, look at me. Right here," Alex said, pointing two fingers toward his eyes. "What did they find?"

"Two rocks and a wad of bills," Foody said, his eyes filling with water.

Alex stared at him in disbelief. "What do you mean, rocks? You had crack in my car, Rudy? What the hell. And where'd you get the money from?"

"I didn't, I swear. I ain't have that stuff. You know I don't do drugs. And I ain't got no ends."

Alex tore way from the bars and shook his head. He couldn't believe what he was hearing. "What do you mean, it wasn't yours? It damn sure wasn't mine. Oh, I get it. Were you riding somebody around with you today or something?"

Foody paused, then sheepishly replied, "Yeah, but he don't do no drugs or nothing either. Least I don't think so. He's just a rapper."

Alex folded his arms and rolled his eyes to the ceiling. What the hell was he supposed to do? Here was his friend, driving his car, and about to be charged with narcotics possession. He glared at Foody with disgust and disappointment. "Foody, how could you?"

"Alex, I—I swear. I wouldn't go out like that."

"Just skip it. I've got to try to figure out what to do now." Alex paced the floor, fuming at Foody's proclamation of innocence.

He couldn't call Simon, so Alex's options were few. He buzzed out of the area, and went to find the detective who had shown him in. The detective whisked him into a side room, where Alex tried to plead Foody's case. After several excruciating minutes, they agreed not to charge him. It was a favor they'd do for him, given his position, as long as Alex could vouch for Foody and guarantee that he'd stay out of trouble.

A grateful Foody practically kissed his feet after Alex negotiated his release. Foody didn't completely understand that he was now Alex's dirty little secret, and that he'd practically sold his soul for his freedom.

"Man, I'm so sorry. But I swear I didn't do it. I wouldn't do that to you."

As they drove away from the station, Alex was drawing his own conclusions. He wanted to believe him, but he was too incensed. As if he didn't have enough drama going on in his own life, here was Foody parking his grief on him too. Alex was beginning to feel a little tired of what seemed to be an endless series of lows and disappointments. Foody's childish and impetuous actions had jeopardized everything Alex had worked for, all in a matter of a few weeks. If this was the best that single life had to offer, it wasn't too appealing.

"I hate to tell you, Foody, but the only way I was able to get you off was to make sure you didn't get into any more trouble. And I can't watch you twenty-four/seven, so, you're, uh, you're going to have to go."

Foody looked at Alex, his big puppy dog eyes filling with water. "Man, I'm sorry, Alex. But I understand. You gotta do what you gotta do," he said, choking back tears.

CHAPTER 13

ALEX was extremely bummed out after Foody left. He felt as if he'd turned his back on his best friend. It was difficult to forget how pitiful Foody looked getting on the bus, yet Alex had to let him go. It was best, at least until things settled down.

Loneliness had a chokehold on him. Alex tried calling Tiffany a few more times, but as the days turned into another week, he eventually stopped dialing the numbers. The rejection didn't bother him as much as his still not knowing what to say. He was still walking around in a zombielike state when Lisa called. She was in town for a midyear job fair at Howard, and anxious to recruit a young tenderoni or two. They agreed to meet at her favorite restaurant, Houston's, for dinner.

Lisa looked great, as voluptuous as ever. She was wearing her success well. By the time he reached her, she was on her second Jack and Coke. They air-kissed, and Alex slid into the booth next to her. Before he had ordered his first drink, he told her about Foody.

"Alex, when will you learn? Foody needs to grow up and quit

tripping. He can be such a lunch box sometimes. If his happy ass didn't know anything about it, he shouldn't have had that thug up in your car. So stop beating yourself up about it. He's just trifling, and you had to protect your shit. Case closed."

She wasn't being too hard on Foody, because she was right. Alex couldn't argue with her. By the time they had eaten appetizers and finished off their third drink, he'd asked her to help investigate Ivan's death.

Lisa shrank back in her seat. "Alex, I never knew that about you. I never knew that about your brother."

"I never really talk about it, but it's something I want to do. I need to do it."

She pondered briefly. "I can help you. You know that's what we do, investigate false claims and stuff with surveillance. But I want to do this myself, just to make sure it gets done right. You'd be surprised at the amount of information that's available through public records, but I'm going to need some specifics."

Even though so many years had passed, it was still painful to dredge up the memory. But Alex had to. He recounted the whole story as he knew it, and Lisa took copious notes: the dates, what Alex had seen, what the cops had told his father, and how Fortune was the only link to the truth. That was, if he was still alive. But at least Lisa could help in clearing Ivan's name. Alex reiterated that this was something he wanted to remain confidential, until they had some good news to publicize.

By the time the food had arrived, Lisa felt she had enough to get started with. But Alex had to ask her why she had been so cautious on the phone the other day. He didn't want her to take this conspiracy thing too far.

She lowered her voice and glanced around. "I know you think I'm tripping, but I'm not. Alex, you don't know who is watching, listening, or whatever. And especially in your position. Politics is mad scandalous, and from what I've learned about the information flow and Big Brother, you can never be too careful. You never know who's zooming who. I suggest that if you really want to keep this on the d.l., you get a separate phone, like a mobile phone, with a scrambling device on it. I'll contact this brother I know and have him send you one. That way you know your stuff'll be tight. I'll probably have something for you in a couple of weeks, so when you get the phone, call me from it."

For all of Lisa's suspicions, she made sense. By the time dinner was over, they were both blitzed, and plenty festive. Hanging out with Lisa had lifted Alex's spirits, and he was feeling upbeat and ready to go forward with his life. But beneath all the laughing and cutting up, Alex knew the real deal. He was still unsure of what to do with the smoking ashes of his love life, and it bothered him to no end.

TIFFANY STILL REFUSED his phone calls. For the next week or so, her secretary took his every message with a smug tone. At home, Tiffany's answering machine did the task. But Alex persisted, leaving message after message, until one day Simon overheard his conversation with the machine and burst into peals of laughter.

"Son, she's really got you going, doesn't she? You are truly p-whipped. Your nose is so wide open I can see your thoughts."

Alex had purposely not discussed Tiffany with him. Throughout the years, Alex had sought Simon's advice about a lot of things, but never her. It was inconceivable that he could be impartial when it came to his little girl.

"Come on, let's go get a drink," Simon said.

"But, Simon, it's the middle of the afternoon and I've got class tonight. My finals are next week."

"Like you'd be able to concentrate? Loosen up a little bit. Blowing a class every now and then won't kill you. You're dying slowly now anyway."

They walked down the street to one of the city's favorite watering holes, a place where many government workers, lobbyists, and wanna-bes hung out for long business lunches and tête-à-têtes.

Over a few Tanqueray and tonics, Alex explained what had transpired between him and Tiffany.

"Well, it was bound to happen. Let's see. Let's examine this situation. Tiffany's almost twenty-five now, and I guess she's ready to settle down. Think about it. All of the sorority sisters are getting married. Having a career is nice, but she can't show pictures of her job when everyone else is showing honeymoon and wedding pictures, you know.

"If she's anything like her mother, which I know she is, she's invested a lot of time with you. I'm sure that it's somewhere in the back of her mind that you might get all you can get, and then up and leave her. So, she's getting you while the getting's good. The love is there, and she knows she has you by the balls."

Alex contemplated this over his drink, which instead of getting watered down seemed to be getting stronger and stronger as he sipped. He hadn't noticed Simon motion for the bartender to keep his glass topped off. "But I don't have much to offer her, Simon. I know that I don't want anyone else, but what do I have to give her? I want to be in a better position than what I'm in now."

Simon's pager went off, and he pulled it out of his pocket. He examined the number, then swallowed his drink in one gulp.

"Listen, Alex, I hate to leave you in this quandry, but I've got to run. Let me put it to you like this: the time has come for you to put up or shut up. Let her go, and she might stay gone. Make the decision to be with her, but work out the issues up front. She's too much like her dad not to be reasonable."

Simon patted him on the back. "Be strong, son. I've taught you well. I'm sure you'll make the right decision."

As Simon departed, Alex checked his watch and fumed. He'd already missed his night class, so he decided to have another drink. Before he could order it, someone tapped him on his shoulder.

"Chip? Chip? Is that you?"

Before him stood a familiar face, but he couldn't place the name. It had been so long since anyone had called him Chip, so she must have been from his past. She appeared to be slightly older than he was, but he still couldn't think of anyone from his childhood who might look so good. She was attractive, of medium height and build, with a very full chest. She gazed into his eyes as if she was prodding him to remember her.

"You don't remember me, do you?" She smiled, and sat down on Simon's vacated bar stool.

Alex hated not remembering someone, and politely shook his head. "I'm afraid I don't. It's been a while since someone called me Chip."

"God, you look just like Ivan. You're so fine, I can't believe it. Maybe you were too young. It has been a long time. You really don't remember? It's me. Stacey."

His jaw fell and hung down in surprise. "Stacey?" Alex hugged her warmly. He couldn't believe it. It was Ivan's old girlfriend.

The years had served her well. No longer the little cheerleader, she looked great for someone who'd had such a rough life. She'd had a daughter, Mya, shortly after Ivan was killed, and subsequently married and divorced. She was working for one of the government agencies, and was putting herself through school. In fact, she was on her way to catch the subway to school when she stopped in the bar to get change for the token machine.

Over the next four hours, Alex allowed himself to do something that he'd never been able to do: mourn for Ivan, and heal the wounds he'd never acknowledged in the process.

They talked in depth about how Ivan's death had impacted their lives. The hurt, the pain, the unanswered questions shrouding his loss. They talked about how Alex had transformed from being little Chip to the talk of the town. They talked about his father. He never thought about just how much Stacey really loved his brother, and she never knew how much Ivan's death had affected his life.

They talked, they shared, and they bonded. Ivan's death had left a gaping hole that they both had tried to fill with methods that failed to console. Stacey had filled hers with self-destructive relationships, and Alex by becoming driven and emotionally detached. Not until they came face-to-face did they realize that. And finally understand it. Now that void was finally being filled.

When the bartender yelled, "Last call," it took them both by surprise. Their chance encounter had been so cathartic that time had slipped by. The happy-hour crew had transformed into the dinner crowd, and the barflies had assumed their positions. Alex, so relieved at having shared so much with Stacey, was too emotionally high to realize how exhausted he was. Seeing her had been a bright spot in an otherwise dismal day, and he wanted to let her know how much he'd enjoyed it.

"I didn't realize it was so late. I better check on Mya. She's at my mother's, and she can be quite a handful." Stacey rushed over to the phone, and it occurred to Alex just how removed he was from the reality Stacey was facing as a single mother. He was such a part of the well-oiled political machine that he was clueless about the toils of everyday life. This was the only time he'd been close to the issue, and it was difficult to contemplate. Stacey led a hard life.

This thought brought him to a more profound realization. Stacey's child could have been Ivan's if he had lived. And Alex would have been an uncle, something he'd never have the opportunity to be. Not to his brother's child or to anyone else's. Because he had been stripped of that opportunity. He suddenly felt melancholy, and even more exhausted. He wanted to be alone.

Stone sober and ready to make a graceful exit, Alex stood up when Stacey arrived back at the bar. As he paid the tab, she confirmed that her mother would keep her daughter for the night. He was relieved that she'd have one less concern, at least for this evening.

Even after the doors closed behind them, Alex could tell that she didn't want to leave. He felt a little guilty for having kept her out so late, and it was too cold to catch the bus, so he offered her a ride home. It was the least that he could do, considering he'd probably never see her again. Although he was glad to see her, he felt a sadness too. The sadness of regret. Alex felt like apologizing for her life being the way that it was.

They walked toward the mayor's office, where his car was

parked. Alex waved for Percy, District Building's reserved-parking-lot guard, to retrieve his car. Alex was too tired and too distracted to notice the side glance Percy made when he saw Stacey. Percy pulled the car up, opened the door for Stacey to get in, and winked at Alex slyly.

"Good ev'ning, Mr. Baxter," he said.

Alex igged him, uttering his standard, cursory hello.

As they drove the short distance up Pennsylvania Avenue to Forestville, where Stacey lived, they continued reminiscing about the old days.

"This is the only thing Ivan and I never really got a chance to do," Stacey said, looking out over the Southeast Bridge as they crossed the Anacostia River. "Take drives. You know he had just gotten his license, but he didn't really have a car to drive."

Alex smiled at the memory. He remembered Ivan being embarrassed to practice on their dad's cab, and would only drive around the stadium armory parking lot at night.

"I remember," he said quietly.

When they reached Oakcrest Towers, Stacey offered him a drink.

Alex checked his watch. It was almost one-thirty. "I think I've had enough to drink for one night."

"How about a cup of coffee?" Stacey clearly didn't want him to leave. She paused, then half-smiled. "I'm sorry, Alex. I guess it's just been so long since I've had a chance to talk, I mean really talk, about Ivan, and it's meant a lot to me. No one's around that really remembers. Or that really cares. And you brought it all back. At least let me fix you a cup of coffee. I'll make it to go."

But after they got inside, Stacey brought out the old yearbook and the offer of coffee never came to fruition. As she flipped the pages, a dried rose fell from the bindings, and she fell apart. It was the rose from her and Ivan's junior prom.

Alex tried to console her. He hugged her and placed her head on his shoulder. She sobbed, sinking her head onto his chest, smearing her makeup on his shirt. Alex felt inept and awkward. This level of emotional depth was difficult for him, but cathartic. The more she sobbed, the more he tried to comfort her, until she clung to him in a suggestive manner that made him uncomfortable.

She nuzzled her face into his neck, and before Alex realized it, she was kissing him through her tears. Shocked, but not wanting to reject her, he tried pushing her gently away.

"Stace—Stacey, I can't do this. This isn't right."

"Please, Alex, don't turn me away. It's been so long. Too long. I need you. I need you tonight."

Alex tried to convince her to stop, but as his heart and mind were saying no, his body and soul gave way. She needed him and somehow Alex needed her. To bridge a gap, to fill a void. For the only time in his life, he made love without love being part of the equation.

Stacey yielded to him in an unimaginable manner, while he felt removed, as if he were having an out-of-body experience. She was driven to release the pain the years had burdened her with, and he fully understood the depth of her anguish. Alex was the vessel for her to reach Ivan, to satisfy a need that transcended the sexual. It was metaphysical. When she cried and repeatedly called him Ivan, Alex realized that his purpose was to channel him for her. To bring her closure.

Alex left her quietly sleeping. He placed the dried rose from the yearbook beside her head. And as he drove home, he knew where his future lay. Though he'd taken his brother's place this once, it was with mixed emotions. He felt regret for having slept with another woman, and that he'd betrayed Tiffany. Sex without love, no matter what the reason, meant nothing to him. But he also felt relief and confirmation: relief knowing that he had provided Stacey with the opportunity to close a chapter in her life, and confirmation that without a doubt, he knew where his heart and his love were. He was not about to lose Tiffany, for anyone or anything.

AFTER WEARING OUT the knees of several pairs of expensive Polo khakis, all of Alex's crawling paid off. The announcement was made in *The Washington Post*'s Style section on Christmas Day, the fol-

lowing week. Alexander Whitney Baxter and Tiffany Renee Blake
were engaged to be married the following spring.

ALEX GEARED HIMSELF up for the future. He planned to graduate and ace the bar exam, and then his life would be in order. Lisa
kept to her word, sending him the mobile phone and the bill
within a few weeks of their meeting. She was about the business
of investigating the mystery surrounding Ivan's death, and Alex
was encouraged that he might be getting closer to bringing closure
to that painful part of his life.

Tiffany was busy planning the wedding, and their relationship
couldn't have been more solid. The only area he couldn't seem to
make any headway with was the broken relationship with his father. The more Alex thought about it, the less inclined he was to
reach out to him. He wanted to wait until he had something tan-
gible to offer, like bringing Ivan's killers to trial, but that was a long
way off. It allowed him to avoid doing what he knew only he could
do: bridge that gap.

Professionally speaking, life couldn't have been sweeter. Simon
wanted him to assume greater responsibilities working with the
city's legal staff too, and he had a way of getting what he wanted.
Alex was going to sit for the D.C. bar, and he'd be prepared, with
Simon greasing the skids for him. Simon convinced him that he'd
have a great future with the city, and becoming a licensed attorney
was great training for the rigors of political life.

Alex had never given politics a lot of thought. He enjoyed his
position working with the housing department, but he figured
that there were a number of options he could consider. In Simon's
less-than-humble opinion, politics was the only choice. It was
a natural transition. The court of public opinion had charged
lawyers and politicians with being one and the same, white-collar
criminals, so there was no great distinction. Alex discussed it with
Tiffany, and she agreed that politics was probably his best career
path. After all, not everyone had a future-father-in-law/godfather
like Simon. Plus, from Tiffany's point of view, the thought of
being a politician's wife was rather appealing. She'd be follow-

ing in her mother's footsteps, a role she'd practiced for all her life. But Alex was worried about measuring up. Eventually, after many conversations and several of her special hot-oil massages, he saw the merits of Simon's plans. Somehow he always saw the merits of Simon's advice. And as always, his advice proved to be infallible.

TODAY TIME TICKED away. The thought of being late still made him nervous. Running a red light, Alex zoomed up C Street, a narrow, one-way street, hoping to avoid the bottleneck guaranteed on Constitution Ave. He always seemed to be in a rush. Rushing here, rushing there. There was always something to do. Screeching to a halt for a tour bus, he seized a moment to take a well-deserved mental break. For the first time that day, he noticed the sunshine.

It shone on his face, and he gazed upon the sky. The warm rays tingled on his skin and made him smile. It was as if his mother and brother were sending down the sunshine from the heavens above, just for him. To remind him where his strength came from. It was subtle, but forceful. Enveloped in the comfort and solitude of his plush vehicle, Alex allowed himself to feel. He caught his image in the mirror and saw regret, gratitude, and longing etched on his face.

He reminisced over the years of his life, and said a silent prayer to God. Things were going great. He was healthy, the few months of his marriage were blissful, yet suddenly, he felt selfish. It had been too long since he'd thanked God. Was he too busy being a rising political power broker to be grateful? But God knew he was truly thankful. Just too busy to stop and say so.

Alex was too busy being too many things. Alex the lawyer, Alex the big shot, Alex the husband, Alex the lover, Alex, Simon's protégé. Rarely was he just Alex, the scrawny little boy who grew up to live a life beyond his wildest imagination.

Despite all that he was, he knew what he wasn't. Sometimes the image he caught in the mirror disturbed him. Outwardly, he was together. But inside, he knew the real deal. He was one step out of Shaw, and never could deny that. He was the success story, but he couldn't forget the brothers who hadn't made it. In D.C., their failure was all around him. The ones who'd given up. The ones who hitched their dreams on selling drugs, or fathering children without responsibility. The ones who used their wives as punching bags for their frustration. The ones who viewed life through a crack pipe, or a needle, or a joint. Whatever this failure was, he vowed never to fall victim to it. He owed his mother and Ivan too much.

Lost in thought, Alex was jarred back into reality by the honking horn of another irate driver. The tour bus had pulled off, and Alex was blocking traffic. Back to the real world, he thought, conveniently filing his loved ones and renewed commitments in his mental to-do list. He grabbed the car phone mounted conveniently in the console, deftly punched in seven digits, and hit the "send" button.

"Yel-low?" Percy, the parking-lot guard with the scratchy voice, yelled into the phone. He was slightly hard of hearing, at least when it was advantageous for him to be.

Alex identified himself, and Percy instantly chuckled. "Oh, yes, Mr. Baxter. I was wondering if I'd hear from you today."

"I'm on my way. I'm running late, but I should be there in about five, make that ten, minutes. You know the drill. I'll leave the keys in the car." Alex often just dumped the car by the guard's desk, engine still running.

Percy chuckled loudly. "Yes, Mr. Baxter. I'll be here. Just like always." Percy kept on talking, and Alex sighed. Once Percy got started, it was almost impossible to get a word in edgewise. He'd talk to him from the moment Alex stepped foot out of the car until the time that the keyed security-elevator doors closed. He hated to be rude, but he had no time for Percy today.

THE MEETING WAS short and to the point. Simon's PR man, Howard, was in Simon's office, going over some upcoming political strategies, and smiling that sly, wicked smile of his.

Alex often wondered about Simon's association with Howard Norman. Howard was smooth, articulate, but there was something shady about him. He had a demeanor that made you feel he couldn't wait for you to leave so he could talk about you. He was calculating, but he had managed to keep Simon crisis- and scandal-free for over twenty years, and Simon was obviously grateful. Howard was the only one Simon allowed to come to a meeting late without severe repercussions.

"Hello, Alex," Howard said, with that look on his face that made Alex think he'd just been talking about him.

"Hello, Howard." Alex prepared to sit down, but Simon indicated that he wanted him to stand. It was a signal that he used whenever he didn't want anyone, including Alex, to linger.

"Please get to the point, Alex. Howard and I have some very pressing business to attend to regarding this upcoming election."

Public relations was the only area Simon handled exclusively with Howard. It really didn't bother Alex, since his plate was so full with other things, but Howard knew how to annoy him. It was as if he were vying for Simon's attention, needed to have it wholly for himself. Howard shot Alex an "I thought you knew" look, and ruffled papers in his expensive briefcase. Alex gnashed his teeth to keep from saying something to him.

Howard was the only person Simon allowed to disrespect Alex, no matter how subtly. It took a lot of nerve, but Howard was never short on that. Flamboyant and pushy, he had a well-earned reputation for being a top-notch PR person. Simon was known for being surrounded by excellence, and letting few people into his inner circle. Simon even allowed Howard to hear proprietary, mayoral-related information.

"Just brief me on the stadium. Is Winnie still wreaking havoc or what?" Simon leaned over on his chair and placed his head on his fist, his jaws tight.

Its progress was being held up by one of the area's board members, Winnie Sutton, much to Simon's chagrin. Winnie was acutely sensitive to development in the city. From homeless to

battered-women's shelters, she was a valiant fighter, and Simon
was often at odds with her, for her social agenda often overshad-
owed any commerce efforts or enterprise development in that
area. Whereas privately he would sometimes applaud her efforts,
publicly they fought tooth and nail.

"Winnie's still at it. She's against every site that's been proposed," Alex said. "She's said in no uncertain terms that she will
fight any attempts to build a new stadium in her district, or anywhere near it. She's afraid that if it's in her district, her constituents will be displaced, and if it's too close to her district, she'll get
the overflow of the people that'll be displaced from that district.
I've been thinking about how to handle it, but—"

"But what? Winnie's in Southeast, she doesn't control the whole
city. That's my job. Everything's not about her and what happens
to her area."

"I know, Simon. But the bottom line is that she wields a lot of
influence, and the board will be at an impasse until she's satisfied.
She can hold the stadium hostage, and her ransom demand will
be the guarantee of shelters in the displaced district. That's her
main concern. She made it clear that this was one fight she had no
intention of losing." With her scarves and chunk jewelry flying,
Winnie was like a Gucci-outfitted matador. And the stadium was
her bull.

Simon swore under his breath. "Well, look, Alex. We can't keep
pussyfooting around this. Time is short, and my patience is even
shorter. I want you to make finding a site top priority. Nothing else
takes precedence, because it's too important to my campaign, you
hear me? Find me a good square mile, and we'll be in business.
Get a plan together, and we'll discuss it over dinner. I'll be there at
seven." Simon waved a hand in the air and shooed Alex out of the
office. "Now, go make something happen. I've got a golf date with
Mayor Nash from Richmond at one o'clock, and I don't want to
be late."

"Okay, Simon. I'll get right on it." Alex gave Simon and
Howard firm handshakes. "I'll see you later. And Howard—have

a pleasant day." Alex paused to close the door behind him, but Howard, with a smug look, swiftly shut it in his face.

THEIR HOME WAS a quaint yet regal four-bedroom Tudor off Sixteenth Street. Simon had helped them purchase it as yet another extravagant wedding present he lavished upon them. Despite the fact that Alex was making good money as the liaison, Simon was concerned that Tiffany was struggling with a "paltry" salary at the United Care Fund and juggling event planning on the side.

They were both overwhelmed with gratitude at Simon's generosity, but Alex was also uncomfortable with Simon's propensity for surprises. Simon was just like a kid sometimes. The night before the wedding, at Alex's bachelor party, Simon had astounded him with another unique gift.

The party was held at their fraternity house in Northwest. The mood was festive and light. Many of the Hilliard bros had shown up in full regalia and ready to throw down. Morgan was going to be his best man, and Alex had a full contingency of his frat brothers as groomsmen. But something was missing. Alex wanted Foody in the wedding, couldn't marry without him, but he knew Foody was unreliable. Even getting him there posed a problem.

After several frantic weeks, Alex had tracked him down and sent him a plane ticket. Foody was elated to hear from him, and he made it, although he had cashed in the ticket and caught the Greyhound bus. But it didn't matter. He was there, and that's what was important. He almost devoured the entire buffet, and was generally his unabashed self, but Alex was delighted that his friend was there, and that Foody was working sound and lights at a hot new dance club. He was proud of Foody, and glad that he was finally getting his life together.

Simon's chest had protruded a mile that night. Puffing on one of his favorite PKO pipes he'd had especially made for himself while on a diplomatic excursion to South Africa, he made numerous toasts to his future son-in-law. Slightly intoxicated from the cognacs he had been drinking, Simon raised his snifter. As some of the frat hoisted him above their shoulders, Simon toasted "the son

I never had; I couldn't have asked for a better one," and the bros cheered heartily.

Alex had bawled. Although Simon's actions always made him feel special, it was the first time he'd publicly proclaimed his affection. Having no blood family at the affair really bothered Alex. He had invited his father, and had hoped against hope that he would come celebrate with him. But he was a no-show. Uncharacteristically, though, he left a message on Alex's answering service that he wouldn't be able to make it. His voice sounded sincere, as if he genuinely couldn't come. For once, Alex felt, his father had done something not out of disinterest, but out of the fear of the unknown, the unfamiliarity of being around people in a social setting. It was odd for Alex to think of his father being afraid. Gerald Baxter wasn't afraid of anything.

Masking his disappointment, Alex had tried a different approach. He enlisted the help of Mrs. Owens to ensure that his father would come to the wedding. Alex finally got him to commit, and take his proper place at the front of the huge Metropolitan Baptist Church. Alex even made sure that the tailor went by his father's apartment to custom-fit the tuxedo for him, and arranged for a car to pick him up that Saturday morning.

But Alex couldn't keep hoping to get something from the man who had all but ignored him his entire life. From his best man, Morgan, to fourteen fraternity brothers he'd chosen as groomsmen, Alex felt like he finally had family. He could barely contain the joy he felt when he thought about his life. He thanked God for all of his many blessings.

Amid all the chaos of the female strippers and Playboy-bunny waitresses, Simon pulled him aside and sequestered him in one of the private meeting rooms.

"I've got a special little gift for you, son. Something I didn't want to share in front of the bros." He closed the door behind them. As Alex eased down in one of the oversized chairs, Simon pulled a small box out from behind the desk.

"Really, Simon, you didn't have to get me anything. You've already done enough. I should be giving you something." Simon had paid for the entire wedding, which was going to be held at one of the grandest churches in the area, and a reception for five hundred people by one of the area's most exclusive and expensive caterers. In addition, he paid for their honeymoon, which was one glorious week in Paris and a seven-day Mediterranean cruise. How could Alex possibly accept anything more from him?

Simon chuckled with that infectious laugh. Propped up on the edge of the desk, he seemed relaxed, his blue seersucker suit draped gracefully on his body.

He extended the red wrapped box to Alex, and he took it reluctantly. "Oh, but you have given me something, Alex. You gave me a son, someone I can be proud of. Someone I know will make my girl a good husband. Not some little knucklehead, or a blue blood who's clueless about life. Yes, you've already given me a whole lot."

"I—I don't know what to say, Simon." Alex shook the box cautiously, but it didn't betray its contents.

Simon puffed on his pipe and winked. "Go ahead, boy. It won't bite, unless you provoke it."

Alex could feel beads of nervous perspiration forming on his forehead. Even as close as they had become, Simon still unnerved him at times. Alex cautiously opened the box. Inside the satin-lined box was Ivan's knife, the blade still ejected, still splashed with Sid's blood. Alex's guts convulsed as Simon roared, his chest heaving with glee.

"Come on, Alex, this is a good one, don't you think?" He slapped his shoulder and whooped it up.

Alex had thought the knife was long gone. In the course of everything that had happened, it was the last thing that he thought about. Even after all the time that had passed. Alex was happy to be reunited with his only physical connection to Ivan, but it was rather disgusting. Alex didn't want to seem ungrateful, nor could he explain to Simon just how important this knife was to him. Somehow Simon had found the one thing that could catch him completely off guard. He carefully deliberated, seeking the right words. "Well, I—I guess I kind of wondered whatever happened to it."

Simon let out one final guffaw, and then sighed deeply. "You had gripped that knife so tightly that even by the time I got down to Hilliard, it was still there. Even though you'd passed out."

Simon looked him squarely in the face. "That knife is your turning point, son. It represents the first day of the rest of your life. Without that, you might have been just another little grease spot out there in that parking lot.

"But you used your head, and your resources. That knife should mean a lot to you, Alex. Hold it, cherish it. I left that blood on it just to remind you of that. Of what you fought to have, of where you were and where you are today. Always remember that."

Alex tried to comprehend Simon's words. Somehow, what he'd said about this profoundly disgusting object was correct. Alex began to understand Simon's point of view. He twirled the knife around in his hands, and began to draw strength from the memory. Alex silently nodded his head in agreement.

"You've got to remember where you came from, and have the common sense to realize that you don't want to go back there. I had it rough too, but I never forget my humble beginnings."

Simon tamped his pipe against the rosewood desk, stood up, and stretched, shaking his nearly empty snifter. "I need a refill. Now let's get back out there and have some fun."

TIFFANY GREETED HIM in her usual flirtatious manner, with a come-hither look. She knew exactly how to turn him on. Hand slipping under his waistband, she teasingly undid his suspenders. This was their routine. Every evening, they made it a point to be home by five-thirty, unless he had class, so they could have one intense hour of quality time before their seven o'clock dinner. Their part-time housekeeper and cook, Trish, would have dinner prepared and candles lit when they arrived, which usually signaled her time to leave for the day. This titillating custom was an appetizer to the all-night sessions they'd indulge in after the evening's events were completed.

Starting at the front door, they would begin kissing passionately, giggling and disrobing as they made their way upstairs. Tonight, Tiffany teased him and his long, thick love handle, which she'd fondly nicknamed Derrick. She lovingly seduced him, blowing feathery kisses on every part of his body. Alex rubbed her succulent breasts gently, and held on to the handrail as he carried her, and crawled up the stairs.

Falling urgently on the massive king-sized Egyptian post bed, Tiffany slowly stripped him. She stood and began her seductive, private dance, which rendered him completely weak and panting.

Her gyrations drove him wild. She refused to let him touch her. She had devoured every book on how to please her man, and she put the knowledge to good use. The years of formal dance training paid off—she could *work* that body. And oh, what a body. She gingerly removed each article of clothing, teasing him with every fluid motion. Stripping down to her red push-up bra and matching panties, she seductively removed her panty hose, draping each sheer, nylon leg over his beckoning face. Alex was being worked beyond control, and she straddled him hungrily.

Unable to withstand any more, he grabbed her shoulders, and together they rode a wave of pleasure. Moments seemed like hours, as she scraped her manicured nails across his heaving chest, draping her sweat-soaked hair over his face. They made love until they were mutually exhausted, and totally satisfied.

Tiffany slumped over on top of him, tossing her tangled hair out of her face. Alex held her close, rubbing her sweat-glistening arms. They both enjoyed the afterglow, the afterplay, the cuddling, the caressing, that they shared after one of their strenuous quickies. They lay there, restless and giddy, sucking down air as if they needed oxygen tanks. Their toned, brown bodies were entangled in the comforter, the image of a modern sculpture.

Alex smiled down at her, absorbing her ravishing beauty. "You—you are too much, Mrs. Baxter," he said.

She kissed him lightly on the lips, allowing her flowing brown hair to brush him.

"And you," she giggled, fingering the comforter, touching the damp spot where the remnants of their joy lingered, "have ruined yet another comforter." She smiled at him, her full red lips revealing perfect white teeth. Wiping the moistness from her face, she shattered their euphoria with a dose of reality. "Come on, lover boy. We need to get up and get cleaned up. We need to burn some incense or something. Daddy'll be here at seven, and I don't want him looking at me sideways." Tiffany motioned toward the digital clock, which read 5:57 P.M.

"Why?" Alex joked. "He knows you keep me satisfied, woman."

Tiffany crinkled her face. "Ill, don't talk like that. I don't want to think about my father when I'm in this state. Now," she said, pointing at the clock, "get up, baby."

Alex moaned, and begged for five more minutes.

"I can't give you any more time, Alex. You think you're slick, but you're just greedy. You don't know when to stop. Before you know it, we'll be all in the mix, and then the doorbell will be ringing. And then we'll be embarrassed."

Replaying the numerous times that they'd nearly been interrupted by Simon, they both snickered. Alex jumped up, butt naked, and raced toward the master bath. "I'll race you to the shower!" he shouted as she threw a huge white down pillow at him.

"THAT WOMAN IS just plain obtuse," Simon said. "She can't see the forest for the trees. I've had it up to here with all of her bleeding-heart rhetoric. She's still singing 'We Shall Overcome' and getting nowhere fast. This new stadium is for the betterment of everyone, but she just won't give an inch. I don't get it. She's worse than one of those—what do you call those dogs? Pit bulls. Yeah, that's right. Once she sinks those ill-fitting dentures into something, she won't let it go. Even after you shoot her. Hey, maybe that's not such a bad idea." Simon smirked at the thought, then walked around on the terra-cotta patio, fanning himself in the clinging mid-September air.

Alex nursed his lemonade, relaxing comfortably on the chaise lounge. Tiffany sat upright in her high-back wicker chair, playing with the glowing citronella candle with a vacant expression on her face. She looked a little bored with the political conversation, but continued to nod at the appropriate times.

Alex flicked off a wandering gnat and wondered when and how she'd plot her escape. "Well, it's the stadium thing I'm concerned about. I'll keep looking for those alternative sites, Simon. There's got to be a location somewhere in this city that is acceptable to her. Something's got to surface soon."

They were working under the constant threat of having the Redskins whisked out of D.C. to the suburbs. It was practically extortion by the owner, but the ploy was gaining energy. Counteracting it had quickly become the focus of Alex's life, forcing aside everything else.

"All of this would have to happen just as I'm trying to gear this city towards statehood. But don't think that this is by happenstance. It's all part of the plan to keep us in the fields." Simon continued pacing, and pulled out his pipe. He became annoyed as his pipe lighter failed to work.

"Daddy, I think we've got one of yours inside. I'll get it for you," Tiffany said.

She sauntered off the patio, her backless sundress flowing around her ankles, and carefully closed the sliding glass door. Alex realized that they probably wouldn't see her again. He checked his watch. It was precisely nine minutes from the time he had first observed her restlessness. He smiled at the subtle way Tiffany had of diverting their attention and escaping their boring conversations. He had to give it to her, she was smooth. She had mastered that craft a while ago.

Guiding D.C. to statehood was one of Simon's primary goals. He was sick of the federal government controlling his city, and this stadium thing was just another wrinkle in that quest. His time frame was close, reelection was coming up next year, and he needed a strong platform to run on. If he could score with the stadium, it would place him one step closer to obtaining the sought-after statehood. It would be his legacy, his crowning glory. And he wasn't about to let an age-old nemesis stop him.

The federally appointed drug czar had targeted D.C. as one of the areas to be cleaned up. Interstate 95 had been dubbed the Cocaine Freeway. From Florida to New York, drugs ran rampant up the coast, with D.C. being a major distribution stop for points west. The czar's goal was to put a chokehold on I-95 and the Beltway, and harass anyone who fit his proposed profile: a young black male driving a late-model import car with D.C., New York, or Florida tags. Simon was simply livid about it.

"Who do they think they are? Harassing my folks like that? Attaching some stigma to D.C. that makes it seem like we're some mini–Colombian cartel or something. They're trying to make an example out of us, and I won't let them. They're staking out ninety-five like it's a war zone. I can't believe it. The next thing you know they'll be rolling the National Guard in, and giving us the bill for it. I swear, if it's the last thing that I do, we're going to get statehood."

"I see your point," Alex said. "The feds are coming down hard, too hard on us, and it doesn't seem fair. None of the other cities seems to be catching fever like we are. If they can put the real criminals away, well then, more power to them. But their method of accosting everyone is just foul." He shook his head. "If I didn't have those official tags on my car, they'd stop me every time I went around the block."

"Don't get too comfortable with those, either. They could start gunning for us at any moment." Simon sighed and glanced down at his gleaming Rolex. He made a quick turn, signaling his abrupt departure. "It's nine o'clock. I've got to run. I'm expecting a phone call from one of our constituents over in Korea; you know Joey Cavanaugh. He's over there trying to form some sort of joint venture with one of their electronics companies, Stargold. Especially in Anacostia it could mean jobs, you know.

"But I've got to pull young Joey's coattail. I don't want his mouth writing a check his behind can't cash and have them pounding on my door with a list of demands from the city. That's not going to happen." He extended his hand to Alex as he walked toward the driveway.

"Tell my baby girl I said good-bye. And you, Alex, beat those bushes tomorrow. We've got to get a location soon—my future depends on it. Your future and our future depend on it. Always remember that."

STRETCHED OUT ON the ice-white chaise lounge in their bedroom, Tiffany was polishing her toenails with a deep-red nail polish. The shiny black pipe lighter lay next to her on the floor. She'd probably found it within two minutes of looking for it, and refused to come back outside. Alex mischievously toed it with his leather loafers. "You know your dad is still trying to light that pipe of his."

"Oh, I'm sorry, babe." Tiffany looked up innocently at him. "I was going to bring it down when I noticed that my toes were a little mussed. So, well, you know . . . one thing led to another." She smiled at him, that award-winning grin. "Plus, I figured that if you or he really wanted it that badly, someone would eventually come for it. And, voilà, here you are. Tell me I don't know the men in my life."

Alex reached down and swiped the lighter. "And tell me I don't know the woman in my life." He loved her feet, long and slender and perfectly shaped, and had developed quite a foot fetish. He fumbled with the lighter, passing it back and forth between his hands, trying to conceal his noticeably growing arousal.

"And speaking of the men in my life, just where is the other man in my life?"

Alex began rubbing her shoulders seductively. "Does it matter, Tiff? You are making me so hot with all that foot action—I can't take it anymore. So what if Da Mayor is around." He fondled her hair, something that really got him excited.

"Oh no, Alexander Baxter, you will not do this. Stop it, you're going to make me mess my nails up again. And we will not do the wild thing over my father's head."

He kissed her neck, and planted passionate bites. "Come on, Tiff. Just a quickie. Simon's taking a long-distance call, and he won't miss us," he lied, to see how she'd react.

Tiffany had the presence of mind to close the bottle of nail polish. "Alex, Alex. We-we can't. I can't do this with my father down there."

Alex slid his hands lower. "Yes, baby. Your father may be downstairs, but your man is right here." Tiffany looked at him as if she were in a daze. She nodded, kissing him with reckless abandon. For the first time, they both realized just which man was more important to her.

CHAPTER 14

FALL gradually turned to winter, and the search for suitable sites for the stadium was a tedious, time-consuming process. Alex was sinking fast. He was trying to complete his third year in law school, with deadlines approaching for numerous papers. He was on the accelerated track at Georgetown Law, and would graduate in just a few months. Then, he was battling Winnie over potential sites, and trying to meet the constant demands of Simon and his liaison position, as well as Tiffany's needs. Alex was juggling too many balls, yet he couldn't let one drop.

Myriad problems confronted him as he tried to find a suitable location for the Redskins. He had engaged every available resource, but between meetings and more meetings, he wasn't getting very far. The fear of failure was eating him alive. But why was he so concerned about disappointing Simon, especially with everything else on his plate?

It was a real wake-up call. Alex was trying to do everything for everyone, yet he was clueless as to his own satisfaction. Extrinsically, he had it going on. Everything Alex did was for some external gratification, and in that sense he was a major success. Internally, when it came to what was really important, he was a miserable failure. He hadn't been to place flowers on his mother's grave in months, he still had no relationship with his father, and he hadn't even followed up with Lisa on her investigation. He felt like a sham.

He was blessed but wasn't acting like it. Alex had all the trappings of success, but wasn't happy. His priorities were screwed up. He had to come through for Simon, for all that he had done for him, but Alex had to be true to himself too.

Alex made himself a promise, though he'd made it before. He wrote it down in his daily planner. He was going to complete his mission and find a site. He was going to finish school. And he was going to get himself together. Mentally and spiritually. He was going to heal those old wounds with as much gusto as he brought to everything else. As soon as he finished what he had to do.

Alex called Lisa on his private mobile phone and left her a message. He hadn't heard from her in a while, and he wanted to find out how the work on Ivan's case was coming.

Tiffany called while he was leaving Lisa's message. After he told Tiff he probably wouldn't be home until after nine, she just slammed the receiver down in his ear. He had noticed that she'd been increasingly cranky over the last few weeks. He wasn't sure why, except that they hadn't been spending enough quality time together. Sure, he'd been coming home late, between working in the office, meeting with his study groups, and trying to complete his papers. Alex knew they were both sorely in need. As the winter winds howled against his windows, he thought about how nice it would be to be wrapped up in a blanket in front of a roaring fire with Tiffany. He made a mental note to try to make some time this weekend for that specific purpose.

IT WAS EIGHT-THIRTY Friday night, and instead of going home to have an enjoyable evening with his wife, Alex had opted to swing back by the office to tap into some of the research databases to support a paper he was working on for his labor relations course. He scurried through the deserted hallways, entered his office, and quickly found the data he was looking for. Relieved, he thumbed through the reams of paper and thick folders that were stacked up on his desk.

Then Alex had an epiphany. Why not run a check of the abandoned or condemned housing in the city? That might come up with a potential area that could be used to build the stadium. As he entered the parameters into the database, the computer hummed as it retrieved the matching information. He realized this search might take a little longer than he anticipated, so he ventured down the vacant hallway to the dusty executive snack room for a Coke and maybe a bag of something salty.

The cleaning people had gone hours ago, and the hallway was completely empty. The silence in the building was strange, nothing like during the day when radios played softly, and there was the constant rise and fall of voices. Alex walked wearily down the hall, passing by Simon's unlit office and several stairwells, toward the snack room.

He selected a Coke, and debated whether to get a bag of chips or a candy bar. Alex stared at the vending machine. It was fast approaching nine o'clock. If he drank the Coke and ate chocolate, he might never get to sleep. He decided to go for the salt.

On his way back, as Alex approached one of the rear stairwells, he was startled as someone slowly cracked the door and stepped into the hall.

It was a short, stocky guy, dressed casually in a cap, slacks, and a dark green windbreaker. He had rain rolling down his sleeves, and seemed startled to see him.

"May I help you?" Alex eyed the man suspiciously. What in the world was anybody doing in this building at this time of night?

"I—I, uh—well, I'm with the maint-maintenance company. I—I was just doing a quality check on the condition of the floors." The man shifted uneasily, and he was evidently very nervous, for his eyes blinked rapidly as they darted around the hallway.

Alex's mind clicked. He'd run across most of the contracts for the building services department, and this was unheard of. Nobody worked more than they were contracted to do. They didn't want to do even the work they were contracted to do, in most cases.

"Oh, I see. That's very interesting. I feel honored to meet a man who's so diligent about his job. Your name is—?"

"Blanks, Edwin Blanks."

"And you're with what company?"

"AB—ABC Janitorial."

Alex vaguely remembered ABC. "Okay, I'm sorry, Mr. Blanks. Just checking. This is supposed to be a secured building, and I just wanted to make sure you were legit. You know you can never be too sure." Alex extended the bag of chips. "Would you care for some?"

Mr. Blanks calmed down considerably. "No thanks, son. I've got to watch my pressure. Can't do too much salt these days." He looked around. "I'll only be a few minutes. I want to make sure the place is being cleaned properly. We've gotten a few complaints from some of the people down on the fifth floor, and I just wanted to make sure that everything was okay."

Alex shook Mr. Blanks's hand firmly. "Sorry for the mix-up. I'll let you get back to your work."

He walked back into his office, and closed the door slightly. Maybe he should call security, but maybe Mr. Blanks was just a harmless old man. Everyone needed access cards for the building, so he must've been legit. Alex blew off the idea of notifying the guards as the database cranked out a list of properties. He anxiously hit the "print" button and ran off five pages of addresses. It was only a start, but it was better than what he was previously working from, which was nothing.

When the pages completed printing, Alex hastily shut the printer and PC off, grabbed his belongings, and headed for the door. The smell of victory was in the air regarding the stadium, but he knew he had a losing battle to fight once he got home.

"I'M PREGNANT."

Tiffany's announcement hit Alex like a tackle from a 350-pound linebacker. As she sat on the edge of the sofa, he sat next to

her, crossing and uncrossing his arms. He swallowed deeply and
loosened his tie.

"Aren't you going to say anything?" She put her hands on her
hips. "Didn't you hear me? How can you just sit there with that
dumb look on your face and say nothing? I mean, what is up with
you?"

Alex rubbed his mustache, biding his time. He was a mixed bag
of emotions, but he knew that Tiffany was a lit fuse. He felt tight-
ness in his chest, and hoped he wasn't having a heart attack. "We
never really talked about this. I mean, we're still practically honey-
mooners. We're still a few months away from our first anniver-
sary."

"So what, you want to talk about it now? What's to talk about?
I'm pregnant, and it's not like you didn't have anything to do with
it."

Alex searched for the right words. He definitely didn't want to
set her off by saying the wrong thing. Then it dawned on him. No
wonder Tiffany had been so emotionally charged lately. But how?
How could it have happened? She was on the pill, and took it re-
ligiously.

He reached for her, and she jerked away, tears running down
her face. "How dare you, Alex Baxter! This should be one of the
most joyous moments of our lives, and you're sitting there in a
daze. Like you're calculating something. Like this isn't registering
with you."

She was right. Alex *was* calculating something. It must have occurred around Labor Day, when they had spent a long weekend
jet-skiing and frolicking in the mountains. Between the bubbly
and the outdoor hot tub, she had slipped on taking her pills, and
he, feeling his oats, couldn't wait. "I'll pull out," he'd vowed, anxious to capture the heat of the moment. Oh well, he figured that
he hadn't pulled out soon enough. Alex rubbed his eyes wearily.

But there was a bright spot. This was his wife, the woman he
loved. It was kind of exciting thinking that there might be a cute little Tiffany running around, a real daddy's girl. Alex glanced over to

one of Tiffany's baby pictures that adorned the mantel and smiled. Or, it could be a bouncing little boy. Maybe he'd even look like him. Suddenly, he realized that it was important to him to be a better father to his child than his father was to him. Despite his misgivings and concerns, Alex actually liked the thought of being a father.

Alex knelt down in front of her, and grabbed her with a force he hadn't demonstrated in a long time. He drew her close to him, tears welling in his eyes.

"I'm so sorry, sweetheart. I love you so very much. I really do. This just caught me completely by surprise. But you know, this is so exciting, Tiff. I guess I was just overwhelmed. I mean, I haven't done this before. You mean I'm actually going to be a father?" He cautiously placed his hand on her stomach.

Tiffany's tears turned from anger to joy. "Oh, yes, baby. Isn't it something? I can't explain it. I just found out on Monday, and I wanted to wait until the right time to tell you, but our schedules have just been so screwed up lately. That's why I got so angry with you today when you said you wouldn't be in until late tonight. I wanted it to be nice when I told you, but I didn't know if it was a good time, or if there would ever be a good time. I did know I had to tell you."

Tiffany rattled on and on about the pregnancy. She was excited, and so was he. She was just more vocal about it. "I've got to call Aunt Giselle. And Lily. And my sorors. I have to make sure they start planning the baby shower. Oh, I know they're going to be so surprised."

She went on about what exercises she could do to maintain that dancer's body. What steps she had to take nutritionally, and the outline of the prenatal classes they would have to take. She wondered what kind of sex they could have, if she felt up to it, of course. She'd have to ask the doctor about that. Would she require bed rest? Oh, she was going to need a full-time maid, or nanny, or both.

Alex rested his reeling head on her chest; his information bank was on overload. His neat list of priorities had just been flipped upside down.

"Oh, yeah. I think that Lily should be their godmother. Maybe Trent and Daria can also be their godparents."

"Their?" Alex asked.

"Oh, that's right. Honey, I forgot to tell you. You're going to be a daddy twice over. We're having twins."

SIMON TOOK THE news in his normal stride. He promptly threatened to have specially designed pink and blue cigars flown in from Cuba. He immediately picked up the phone and left a message for Howard to do a press release, announcing his pending grandfatherhood. "That ought to win me some votes with the senior citizens," he said.

"Well, you'll retain my vote if you can give me some counsel and advice on how to be a good father, Simon," Alex said on the unseasonably warm February afternoon.

"Just take it easy, son. It'll come naturally. No one is ever one hundred precent ready, especially if you have no previous on-the-job training under your belt. Which you don't, do you? You don't have any little bastards running around here, do you?" Simon chuckled. "Although Marjorie, God rest her soul, and I had been married a little while longer than you two, it was still a bit unsettling for us, the prospect of being parents. You're used to your time being your own, socializing and climbing up that ladder of success. But with the proper resources, you find that you adjust.

"You two will work it out. You'll be out of school soon, and making enough to ensure that the kids will have a good nanny, I'll see to it. So if that's what you're worried about, don't. You know that their grandfather will make certain that they're okay. In fact, I'm already planning to set up a trust fund for the little ones, and you know that they'll always be taken care of."

Alex was at a loss for words, as he usually was when Simon sprang one of his extravagant gifts on them.

"But, Simon, you don't have to do all of that. I know I probably can't count on my dad being there, but we'll be okay. Trust me, you just being a grandfather to them and an active part of their lives will be enough."

Simon leaned back in his seat and ran his fingers through his salt-and-pepper hair. "In case you haven't noticed, Alex, I'm not getting any younger. I don't have a lot of dreams and goals to realize. Hey, I'm living them already. I'm about ready to slow down now. Relax for a little while. Abdicate my office. In fact, I'm making plans to do just that. I've decided to get that little boat I've been looking at for a while."

So Simon had finally decided to get the boat. An eighty-foot Lazzara yacht that would be custom-built down in Florida. He had mentioned it a long time ago, but hadn't brought it up recently. It was a lifelong dream of Simon's, to sail and to fish at will. But Alex should have known that with Simon, there was no such thing as a fleeting thought.

"But before I can go sailing off down the Potomac, I want to make sure all of my ducks are in a row. And more importantly, I have to make sure that you're ready."

"Me? Ready for what?"

"The changing of the guard. Ready for you to become the next mayor. You're my legacy, son. Come on now, don't try to make the old man out a fool today. You can't say that the thought hadn't crossed your mind a time or two. Get out of law school, get some courtroom experience, remain my right-hand man. It's a natural progression from liaison to deputy mayor. I can do that for you.

"The last thing I want to do, besides getting this stadium, would be to provide the farewell gift to the city of getting us the statehood we deserve. Get one hundred percent control of our existence, so we don't have to keep going to Congress, hat in hand, begging for what our taxes pay for. Then I'll step down, and you'll be a shoo-in. At that point, I can sit back and be John Q. Citizen and enjoy the fruits of my hard labor. All you have to do is just keep right on doing what you're doing, living right, keeping your nose clean, and it'll happen. I can make it happen."

"That never occurred to me, Simon. I would've never thought about being mayor. Plus, you're supposed to be mayor for life, remember?" Alex had to admit it was intriguing. The offer was too phenomenal not to consider, and Alex knew he could never say no to Simon. "I'm flattered, but I'm, uh, far too inexperienced."

"Time's on your side. You've got at least a term or two to prepare yourself. Plus, you have the benefit of having me as a resource. You can always hire me back as some high-paid political spin doctor or something."

They both laughed at the prospect of Simon working for anyone. He was a self-made man, one who marched to his own beat. And in his parade, Alex had learned, you either join in the revelry or get run over by the ornate floats.

Impending fatherhood prompted Alex to reach out to his dad once again. They were so close in proximity, yet so far apart. Alex had seen his father only a few times since he had married, once at a cab commission hearing, and when Tiffany had invited him and Mrs. Owens over for dinner. Their relationship was still strained, and the two adult male Baxters had reached an impasse. Gerald Baxter seemed too uneasy in Alex's world.

The dinner had been uncomfortable. Mrs. Owens had been pleasant, and she and Tiffany had hit it off; it was the first opportunity the ladies had to chat since Tiffany and Alex had married, and it was nice being around Mrs. Owen. However, Alex's father was a different story. He was ill at ease, sitting out on the patio, nursing an iced tea and marveling at the manicured lawn. He'd commented several times that he had driven through this neighborhood, but this was the only time he'd actually been inside one of the homes. Alex had tried talking to his father, but the conversation went nowhere.

Still, Alex wanted to share the good news with his father and get more than a detached response. Alex accepted the fact that Gerald Baxter would never be Simon, but he *was* his father. He mentally fortified himself for the inevitable disappointment.

Alex dialed Yellow Cab, and requested number 241, his father's cab. He had the presence of mind to request a trip uptown, knowing his father wouldn't cross the Anacostia Bridge, no matter who wanted to go.

When Alex entered the cab, his father didn't even notice that it was him. The years on the street had taught him to read the body language of his riders, not the faces. And Alex, stylishly attired in one of his best Italian suits, posed no potential threat.

"Where uptown you going?" Gerald Baxter hadn't lost his refined social skills.

Alex barely heard him. He was running his fingers along the cracked vinyl seams of the backseat, absorbing the surroundings. He hadn't been in his dad's old Pontiac cab since he'd dropped Alex off at school freshmen year. It hadn't changed very much, and he wondered how his father had dealt with this same old, same old, for most of his life.

"Dad, don't you even recognize me?"

Gerald Baxter slammed on the brakes. Cars screeched behind him, then roared by, the drivers vigorously giving him the finger.

"Alex? Son, I'm sorry. You're about the last person I'd expect to see. What you doing catching a cab?" His dad continued driving, squinting in the rearview mirror as he headed up Connecticut Avenue.

"Well, Dad, I—I figured this might be the only way I'd get to see you. And I wanted to talk to you about something, at least before you read it in the paper." Alex shrank back in his seat, feeling like the stuttering little boy who never measured up.

His dad remained silent, alternating his glance between the rearview mirror and the road ahead.

"I just wanted to let you know that Tiffany and I are expecting. Twins."

For the first time in a very long time, Gerald Baxter grinned. He actually showed teeth. He swung the cab over to the curb of the busy street, shifted the gear into park, and whirled around.

"You don't say. You mean I'm actually going to be a grandfather?" A look of bewilderment and happiness filled the contours of his aging face.

Alex had no idea that his father would be happy. "Yeah, Dad. You're going to be a grandfather. In about six months."

His father shook his head, and looked at Alex as if he'd never

seen him before. That afternoon, they talked and talked. What
started off as a doomed cab ride turned into a prescription for res-
urrection. They put away old pains and past hurts to talk about
something they had never spoken of before, the future.

THINGS WERE FINALLY coming together in Alex's personal life.
He was glad he'd taken the steps to bring his father into his life,
and Lisa was garnering some success in their secret mission. It had
taken her a while, since she was nursing the wounds of yet another
failed relationship. She caught him late one night as Alex was
working in his home office, and shared the good news.

"What's up, Money Man?" She always had a new nickname for
him.

"What's going on, Big Easy?" Alex could now give as good as he
could get.

"I've got some good news for you," she said, popping gum in
his ear.

"Great. And I've got some news for you too." Alex refrained
from saying "good." He had avoided mentioning Tiffany's pregnancy before, but now he had to. It was only a matter of time before Lisa found out, and he hoped that she'd be happy, or at least
act like it. "You're going to be an auntie."

Lisa paused. "That's cool, Alex. So, you're going to be a daddy.
Hmph. Well, I'm sure things'll work out. Just don't leave your
wife alone with those babies. You know she might just trip out
with some postpartum depression and whatnot. You know how
high-maintenance she is."

Alex gave Lisa her morbid dig without responding. As expected,
she wasn't thrilled, but she was at least civil about it, and that
was enough for right now. Eventually she'd warm up, as she had
in accepting his and Tiff's relationship. He just hoped the kids
wouldn't be about to graduate from high school by then.

But she took it in stride, and even talked about it before changing subjects. "Anyway, I got some info on Ivan's death. It appears
that he was killed with a twenty-two, and within a week's time
from his shooting, there were three other unsolved murders. Right

now, we're looking into who the victims were, and if there was any connection to your brother.

"And regarding his friend, who shall remain nameless, we haven't been able to find anything. He never had a social security number, never applied for one, and seems to have just vanished. We're going to look into any reported deaths of John Does that might've shown up in the metro area during at least three months after that time."

"I am so impressed," Alex said. "I always knew you were smart, and listening to you rattling off that P.I. jargon, I know you've found your niche. I owe you big-time. I just can't tell you how much this means to me."

She laughed, and came back with one of her usual razor-sharp retorts. "Well, I can tell you how much it means to me. I'm going to send you my big fat bill. But in the interim, just hook a sister up with an eligible brother, will you? Sister's lonely."

THE NEXT FEW months flew by, and Alex busied himself trying to keep Tiffany in the house during the winter months. Washington was notorious for its inability to clean and salt the roads in a timely fashion, and Alex was bent on keeping Tiffany and their babies safe. It was a difficult task, but someone had to do it.

Alex hadn't heard from Lisa, nor had he any success in locating a site for the stadium, partially due to the bad weather, but also because of the lack of time he had to devote to the cause. Another reason was the fact that Winnie's husband, Jake, had been seriously wounded in a botched attempted robbery outside of his office. The incident prompted Winnie to clear her calendar indefinitely, and table a number of issues. Although she had an aide, this stadium thing was not one of the items she had delegated her to follow up on. Alex kept the short list of addresses, ever on his mind, in his breast pocket.

He finished his coursework, and would graduate early, with honors, from Georgetown. Alex's plan was to promptly sit for the D.C. bar, which was held in late May. He wanted to get it out of the way before the birth of the twins, who were due in June, if

Tiffany went full-term. Needless to say, Tiffany was furious that
he wouldn't be home more often to share in her misery. He tried
to get her to understand that it was better if he got the bar exam
over. This way he'd have more time after the twins were born. Yet
her emotions prevailed. She refused to acquiesce.

The next few months of Tiffany's pregnancy were extremely
trying for both of them. She continued to blow up, both in size
and in attitude, and Alex learned there was no pacifying her. She
was overly obsessed with her body, which had swollen to what
seemed twice its normal size, and despite all of the exercising she
did, those nightly cravings for pizza and hot fudge sundaes got the
best of her.

Because this was her first pregnancy and she had such a small
frame, her OB/GYN, Dr. Collier, had recommended bed rest at
the end of her sixth month. Neither she nor Alex looked forward
to that. Tiffany was inconsolable most of the time, except when
she was eating, entertaining a constant flow of guests and sooth-
sayers, or ordering around the interior decorator who was design-
ing the nursery. She was even so evil that she made Alex twenty
minutes late to his graduation because she threw a major tantrum,
and threatened to destroy his bar review course documents.

FOR THE FIRST time since Alex graduated, he had a little time
on his hands. Enough time to realize how absolutely miserable
Tiffany was. Unable to work, she was dedicating herself to making
his life as miserable as hers. And she was succeeding.

With her hormones raging, she'd be angry one minute, and crying
the next. Alex had never witnessed such a volatile shifting of emotions. Her taste buds also swung back and forth, from not wanting to eat anything, to wanting to consume the entire refrigerator.
Sometimes he'd take the video camera out to record Tiffany's
moods, but that wasn't such a good idea. Especially after she threw
water at it, and Alex had to get another one. At a couple thousand
bucks a pop, he couldn't justify spending the cash, given her emotional extremes.

Simon allowed him to work from home, which had multiple

purposes. He could work, study for the bar, and it amused Simon that Alex was baby-sitting Tiffany. Although Alex felt that he'd be much more productive in the office, Simon wouldn't hear of it. Alex was sent back home to be at his daughter's beck and call. Each day Alex had a list of mundane tasks to perform, from reviewing, ad nauseam, the myriad baby names, to providing the daily foot massages she demanded, to constantly running to gourmet restaurants for takeout. The only reprieve, he discovered, was to make these excursions armed with his pager and mobile phone. It provided a breather from Tiffany and her constant requests, and it offered him the perfect opportunity to finally review that list of abandoned buildings.

He automatically scratched off locations that were too inaccessible to the masses, upper Northwest, outer Southeast. His list dwindled down to some key spots in the Anacostia area of Southeast.

Paused at a traffic light near the corner of Martin Luther King Boulevard and Southern Avenue, the heart of Anacostia, Alex reviewed the addresses of what seemed to be nearly an entire block of vacant row houses. On this unseasonably warm early May day, his tinted windows were completely closed, with the air-conditioning blasting. WHUR's Quiet Storm caressed his ears in quadraphonic sound, and Alex was caught up in the memory of times when he could actually enjoy this music, times when he and his wife were still making white-hot love. The memories were so intense that Alex was startled by the honking of angry horns behind him. The light had turned green, and he'd slept through it.

He pulled over and continued perusing the list. He was interrupted by one of D.C.'s "squeegee men," already sponging down his front window with one side of the squeegee. Like lightning, the guy was preparing to swipe it clean with the nylon blade on the other side of the tool.

Proper street etiquette taught you to wave the person away before he or she wet your window, for then you would be expected to pay for the service. The squeegees and the filthy water almost always made the windows dirtier than they were before. However, if you got the service and did not ante up, or did not ante up enough, you would be subjected to profanity, violence, or both.

Stuck, Alex fished for some change. Cursing under his breath, he cracked the side window and passed a wrinkled dollar through it. The squeegee man gripped the bill with long, thin, dirt-encrusted fingers. They fit snugly through the small slit in the window, and he held on long after Alex had let go. The putrid scent of body odor and cheap cologne wafted through the tiny opening, and it was becoming unbearable. Although Alex couldn't see the guy's face, there was something eerie about the encounter. The hairs on the back of his neck began to prickle, and a chilly sensation crept down his spine. Maybe he might get carjacked. Alex shoved the money out the window and took the light as it was changing to green. Those government tags sure came in handy.

Safely away from the squeegee man, Alex's mind ran rampant over the menacing encounter. That cold wave of fear clung to his body and made him shudder, even in the warm spring weather. There had been a rash of carjackings in the area, with people sometimes meeting fatal encounters. Folks were getting blasted, in broad daylight sometimes, even if they didn't try to resist. Alex made a mental note to remind Tiffany to keep her doors locked and windows rolled up tight, and not to resist if anyone approached.

Alex didn't realize that he was in the area of the abandoned buildings until he looked up. The buildings seemed to extend into both wards, where Southeast and Southwest met. This might not be a bad thing, since this would mean he'd have to garner the support of Southwest Councilman Montgomery, who was inclined to support the stadium and the potential windfall it might bring. Plus, Montgomery had a good rapport with Winnie, and could be the one to get her to agree to the location.

Surveying the street, Alex checked for what Simon had coined "the obvious Winnie showstoppers." There was a mix of commercial and residential properties on the street, but no shelters or other Winnie-cause-related holdouts. The property had access to the park and the Potomac River, two of Simon's favorite spots. Alex felt a warm, comforting feeling growing in the pit of his stomach, so much so that he could almost hear the sports announcers broadcasting a game from the new stadium. Relief was turning into triumph. For the first time in a very long time, Alex finally thought that he might've actually found a winner.

He checked the time—it was approaching six o'clock—and his pager vibrated in his pocket. Tiffany paged him so much that although Alex had just gotten the thing, the low-battery message was already indicated. He knew there was no need to check the number, for he knew who it was. It was notice to get the Macadamia Nut Surprise ice cream to her quickly, or either incite World War III.

ALEX WAS PLEASANTLY surprised when he arrived home. Tiffany and Aunt Giselle were engrossed in conversation in the den. Tiffany was lounging, fully coordinated in her latest maternity outfit, running through her baby registry, and inundating her helpless aunt with her list of pregnancy-related problems.

He presented her with the ice cream, stayed just long enough to kiss them both hello, and slipped off into his office. He was intent on getting away before she could shout another order at him. Before he could make his escape, Tiffany flung a small padded envelope at him, mentioning that it had arrived a few moments ago by courier. She casually mentioned that she had almost opened it, because it was left on the doorstep with some other packages for her.

Once safely inside his office, Alex closed the door and breathed a sigh of relief. He fingered the envelope, not overly anxious to open it. It was probably something from the mayor's office, another item to add to his to-do list, or some tickets to a political event Simon wanted him to attend. It couldn't have been anything too urgent, so he let his mind drift back to the events of the afternoon.

Still hyped by his earlier discovery, Alex decided to rest on it until he could at least make a foot patrol of the area himself, wrap up his findings in a nice little package, and present it to Simon. He'd have it all together, leaving no stone unturned, and the accomplishment would set him on his way. As the November election was pending, any good news would be welcomed by Simon, just as another wild-goose chase would probably set him completely off. Alex decided to try to contact Winnie tomorrow, and see if she would accompany him on this excursion.

Out of nowhere, Alex was reminded of that putrid scent from the squeegee man, and he grabbed his stomach to suppress the feeling of nausea that engulfed him. The feeling passed, but he made a mental note to remind Tiff to be careful.

Exhausted, Alex figured now might be a good time to chill out and catch a nap while Aunt Giselle was tending to Tiffany. That way he'd be refreshed for the midnight shift Tiffany was sure to put on him. His mind drifted back to the midnight shifts he preferred, the ones from their pre-pregnancy days. He sighed at the thought of just how long it had been since he and Tiffany had worked each other until the wee hours of the morning.

The queasiness subsided. Alex decided to treat himself to an icy-cold Corona with a slice of lime. His mouth was watering as he rose from his desk. He recalled the sealed envelope Tiffany had given him, and debated whether or not to open it. Part of him said to chuck it, and get the brew. Whatever it was could wait. The other part of him, the one Alex hated sometimes, said to open it. This way, he'd have a jump on whatever it was.

The pragmatic side won. Vowing only to read the contents, and wait until tomorrow to work on it, Alex ripped open the envelope. The contents spilled onto the desk, and he gasped. There were pictures of him and Stacey, obviously taken that night at the bar.

It had been so long ago; Stacey had never crossed his mind after their clandestine encounter. He picked up a note that read, "THE NEXT SET WILL BE FOR YOUR WIFE, IF YOU DON'T KEEP YOUR NOSE CLEAN."

Alex stared at the photos, and immediately flopped back in his chair. How could he have been so stupid? There were shots of him and Stacey driving away, pulling up to her apartment, going in, and a few hazy, yet scandalous snapshots of them getting busy. Finally, there were two snapshots of him alone. One as he exited the building with a sheepish look on his face, at daybreak. The last one, with him in his car with an extremely guilty look on his face, and date/time stamps in the corner. As his mind raced back to that ominous night, Alex tried to remember how anyone could have snapped the pictures. Someone must have followed them, and then looked at them through the blinds in Stacey's ground-floor window.

Suddenly, Alex felt sick to his stomach again, but now he also felt violated. Who would do something like this? He tried to calm down, and he thanked God that Tiffany hadn't opened the envelope. It would have sent her off the deep end.

Alex squeezed his eyes shut. Who could be behind the pictures? He'd always been so aboveboard, but he knew politics was lowdown, and now someone had dirt on him. His world was wrecked, but what could he do? He couldn't tell Simon about his indiscretion, and he definitely couldn't tell Lisa. He was in a jam, with no clear motive or culprit.

Then it dawned on him. It had to be the stadium. So many people were fighting to get in on the deal that someone, anyone, could be motivated to compromise Simon. There was really nothing else Alex was involved in that could dredge up such a treacherous assault. Could this stadium be such a volatile thing that Simon's political future was endangered by Alex's involvement? Suddenly, Alex was nervous, and more jittery than ever. The thought of being watched sickened and incensed him. If this was what politics was really about, they could have it.

His nervousness slowly turned to fury. Alex was not about to be run off so easily. He had worked too hard to get where he was. He again scanned his memory to see if he could remember angering anyone to this degree. Nothing and no one came to mind.

Alex slipped the pictures into his briefcase. He would destroy them when he went out the next day. He knew he had to do something, and quickly. Alex had to figure out who was behind it, and, in the interim, find Simon's stadium. If that was the motivation behind the pictures, he'd soon find out. The stadium would be the one thing he would be able to give back to Simon, and there was no way he was going to be stopped.

CHAPTER 15

ALEX destroyed the pictures, but within a week, all of his other plans went awry. Tiffany went into premature labor after arguing with the interior decorator over the color of the nursery walls. Alex's pager was going off repeatedly. When he got the message from Lily that Tiffany's water had broken, he rushed to the hospital.

By the time he arrived at the Columbia Hospital for Women, Tiffany had the place in an uproar. The nurses halted their conversations when they noticed he had arrived. They pointed nervously in the direction of Tiffany's room, as if they were divulging some horrible secret. As soon as Alex passed their station, they immediately resumed their whispering in hushed tones.

Alex ran into Tiffany's doctor in the hallway, but he was only a little better than the jumpy nurses. Dr. Collier tried to assure him that everything would be okay, although he didn't look too well himself. Despite his numerous years of practice, with all of the babies he had delivered, it was obvious that Tiffany Blake Baxter had struck a nerve no other mother had before. He implored Alex to try to calm Tiffany down, because the birth would be a lot easier: for her, the babies, and him.

Trying not to be alarmed, Alex assured him that he'd try to get her to relax. His confidence vanished quickly as he noticed Dr. Collier shaking his head and talking to himself as he walked away. Obviously, Tiffany was working everybody's nerves.

Alex took a deep breath and slowly pushed the door to his wife's hospital room open, fully expecting to see Tiffany levitating above the bed like Regan in *The Exorcist.* Instead, she was pressing on the nurse's call button, demanding an epidural. For the next ten hours, Tiffany fussed and Alex sweated until Alexander Whitney Baxter II and Anya Simone Baxter were born, six pounds each. Anya had forced herself out of the womb first. Though they were premature, there was nothing underdeveloped about their lungs.

When Alex saw them, he was so proud he wanted to hoist them up high above his head and proclaim, "Behold! The only thing greater than yourself!" just as Kunte Kinte had in *Roots.* The moment was nearly perfect, with one exception: Simon was not present. Alex had sent word for him to be paged, but no one could find him.

Simon was the first visitor to arrive after the birth, rushing in with the paparazzi on his heels. His arms were filled with packages, and his chauffeur, Drew, carried a huge bouquet of blue and pink balloons. He had been sailing on the Potomac on his new yacht. It was his desire not to be reached when he was on the newly christened *Masquerade,* which was equipped with no ship-to-shore communication. He could not be contacted, except through maritime radio channels, until he returned. No mobile phone, no pager. In an emergency, the only way to reach him would be to take a speedboat out to catch him.

Simon spent the morning of May 12 making jokes about Tiffany's birth. As promised, Simon had established trust funds for the kids, and had their social security number application forms for Alex to complete at the hospital.

Cards, telegrams, flowers, and balloons filled Tiffany's private room. Congratulations flooded in from all over the country. Even Mrs. Owens and his father visited, and his father remarked that little Alex looked a lot like Ivan, and Anya resembled Elizabeth. Maybe life had come full circle.

It was truly a different time for the Baxters, and for the second time in his life, Alex felt like he had a real family. It was as if the disconnection he felt throughout his life had finally come together. And as he looked into the faces of his two little jewels, there was a tie that bound him to them that was stronger than anything he had ever felt.

IT TOOK A month for Tiff and Alex to get adjusted to parenthood, with the help of their live-in nanny, Mrs. Stiles. She made it a lot easier for them, but they always made it a point to get up for the babies' midnight feedings. After a few weeks, it became routine. Tiffany was working frantically to get her hourglass figure back, and Alex was able to ease back into his office. Although he'd become quite comfortable working from home, he decided to go into the office a few times a week. It was great spending time with his family, but work was still heavy on his mind.

After six weeks of being at home, on his first day back in the office, Alex was presented with the kids' social security cards from their grandpop. Leave it to Simon to leave no stone unturned, Alex thought. He was also greeted with myriad congratulations, greetings, cards, and projects to complete. The most prevalent being the stadium conundrum. How could Alex have forgotten? On his to-do list, it became priority one.

Alex made it a point to catch up with Winnie the next day. After calling her office, he confirmed that she was at one of her favorite haunts, the Julian Weston Homeless Shelter at the corner of Martin Luther King and Southern Ave., so he went there. He was taken aback by the decrepit building. The heat inside was stifling, reminiscent of his Shaw days, but what else could you expect for a late June day in D.C.?

Alex was overwhelmed. Against a backdrop of crying babies, youngsters ran around, playing with broken toys, jumping double-

Dutch, and cracking jokes. Old and young men alike wandered aimlessly, scheming for the next bottle or the next hit. Thin, wispy figures walked alone and talked alone, hungering for the fix the shelter's food could not quench. The sight was truly sobering. Congregated in a corner, watching a floor-model black-and-white television with one rabbit ear, was a group of young mothers too absorbed in their soaps to mind their children. Alex felt depressed over the misery he saw. He made a mental note to make sure his children felt loved every day.

If there was a federal government War on Drugs, it wasn't apparent here. Evidently just saying no was not cutting it. Drugs were running rampant in the city, and this was only one of the many fallout shelters attending to the casualties. Folks were evicted because of drug use, families ripped apart over the increased number of crimes drug-running caused. It was such a sad, vicious cycle. Even in his childhood, Alex had not witnessed such madness.

Alex spotted Winnie, who was in the middle of reviewing some paperwork for the shelter. She looked up, and smiled like a spider that had noticed a fly in her web. A tall, beautiful, brown-skinned woman, she was radiant, yet visibly weary. Though it had been a while since her husband's near fatality, she had taken the full responsibility of managing his recovery, and it had exacted a toll on her. She may have been tired, but she was never slow.

"Well, well, well, Mr. Baxter. It sure is a pleasure to see you. I don't think I've ever seen you in my neck of the woods. Tell me, to what do I owe this great honor? I'm sure Simon didn't send you down here to bring me any heartfelt condolences." She continued working, while members of the staff and some of the residents muffled their laughter.

Winnie was their hero. A native D.C. resident who had risen up the civil rights ranks, she was a woman of raw intensity who helped her husband cultivate a lucrative mortgage-lending business. The business put plenty back into the community, and received many commendations from the government. Becoming involved in politics was a natural next step for her. No matter how

much she acquired, she never left the 'hood. Never even considered it. She was never too high to speak to the lowest, and they
loved her for it.

Alex smiled at the invitation to joust. Actually, he was the one
who felt honored. For Winnie Sutton to come after you meant
that you had to be a worthy adversary. Yet he was just a little peon.
Maybe he had underestimated himself. Evidently, he was making
a name in D.C., even if it was as Simon's son-in-law.

"Mrs. Sutton, it's always a pleasure to see you. On behalf of
Simon and myself, we would like to extend our condolences over
your recent troubles. I trust that your husband is recovering well?"

Winnie nodded slowly, contemplative. "Thank you, but you
can call me Winnie. Now, let's get down to business. I'm sure
that's not why you're here, so please continue."

"Actually, I've been spending time here in your neck of the
woods, and I think I might have something that is a win-win for
all parties concerned." Alex motioned toward a table with a few
empty chairs set away from listening ears. "Do you mind if we sit
for a moment?"

Winnie handed her clipboard and papers to an eager assistant
and stood. She wore her business uniform, a bright orange linen
pantsuit, and one of her trademark scarves knotted around her
neck. It seemed out of place amid the sea of poverty.

Sitting down, Winnie continued to eye him suspiciously. She
listened to him without interrupting, taking copious notes, and
only pausing to manage a crisis or two as they erupted. Content
with the overview Alex provided, Winnie gave him her blessings
on checking out the sites.

"I don't believe there are any agency buildings over there. To
tell you the truth, I don't get over there very often. There aren't a
lot of residences there either, and the businesses—well, let's just
say that any type of commerce would revitalize that area. And if
Monty—Councilman Montgomery, that is—and I can manage
this little plan, it might be beneficial to the both of us.

"I like the fact that you are willing to do a foot patrol. I'd join you, but I must get home to make sure that my husband gets to physical therapy on time. I do think that it's good that you, representing the mayor, would take the time to do that." Winnie could barely enunciate, her tongue was so deeply plastered in her cheek.

She motioned to another assistant who was waiting anxiously. Alex marveled at her ability to deal with distractions. He knew that this scene would have plucked his nerves on a daily basis.

"But, if I were you, I think I'd go home and change first." She smiled at him, nattily attired in his power suit. "You may want to blend a little bit better. You know, we folks here in Southeast can spot a foreigner a mile away." Summoning up a solicitous smile, Alex reached for her hand.

"Thank you for your time, Mrs. Sutton, I mean Winnie. And if you wouldn't mind, could we keep this under our hats until we reach an agreement? I'd like to present something airtight to Simon."

"I understand, and I'll keep it under my hat. I'm just like you. I think we shouldn't get too excited too soon. Look around you. This area is changing, but not for the better. My husband worked right down the street for over thirty years, and never as much as had a flat tire outside of his building. But someone comes along and decides to rob him. It's just heartless. The drugs are ravaging our community, and it's causing people to do just about anything. Sell themselves and their babies. Rob people, stick a gun in your face for five dollars. Cripple a man that never hurt anybody before in his life." She paused, catching herself from becoming too emotional. "So if you think you can help this district, then I'm all for it. But if it means that you're just going to bring more crime and depravation here, forget about it.

"I do appreciate your interest, Alex. You strike me as someone who may actually have a heart behind that high-priced suit." She smiled, and clasping his hand with hers, she drew him closer. "And by the way, son, exactly where are you from?"

Alex knew she was being facetious. He was certain she had read his dossier a long time ago. It was standard operating procedure in the world of politics. Everyone knew everything. They just wanted to see how you responded to the questions. "I'm surprised you asked me that, Mrs. Sutton. I'm from here, from Shaw."

She clasped his hand warmly, as if she recognized a long-lost friend. "I know it's probably been a long time, but you should feel right at home. Welcome back."

ALEX HAD SPENT the next morning taking Tiffany and the babies to the doctors and was getting a late start at assessing the properties. He tried to get away earlier, but Tiffany was not having it. She made it clear that these were their babies, not just hers, and that he would do his fair share to take care of them. Eventually, it appeared that Mrs. Stiles was there more for support, not to work, since they themselves did so much for the babies. But Alex reveled in his role as proud papa, for the twins were as cute as they were demanding.

Elaine Bidwell, one of Simon's frequent escorts, was hosting a fund-raiser for him on the *Masquerade* at nine-thirty that evening. It was a black-tie affair, and was expected to generate at least $10,000 toward Simon's reelection coffers. Alex was driven. He wanted to present Simon with the stadium information as a great way to kick off the campaign.

The drive back from the doctors was upbeat. The kids were healthy, growing, and progressing well. Tiffany was looking forward to getting back into the working ranks, and spoke optimistically about their future.

"You know, Alex, this is almost like a dream come true." She patted his hand as he maneuvered the gearshift. She was dressed like a knockout, outfit coordinated down to her matching sandals.

Alex smiled warmly as he glanced at his wife and peeked into the rearview mirror at his two precious jewels snoring in their car seats.

"I can't believe this is me and you. It's hard for me to believe that all of this is ours. I was so young when my mother died, and although my father raised me very well, I always missed being part of a family unit, you know?" She sat silently, a thoughtful expression on her face.

"I've been thinking. I'd like to get some portraits made of our mothers. You know, since they aren't here, I'd like to commission an artist to do paintings of them so that the kids can see them and know who they are. What do you think?"

"I think that's a great idea, Tiff."

Tiffany sighed. "Becoming a mother has really made me start thinking about life differently. Motherhood really means a lot to me. I want to be there for my kids. I want to be a good mother to Anya and Alex. I know I never mentioned this to you before, but you know, I've always had this fear that I'd be just like my mother and not live very long into my children's lives."

Alex sought words, but could think of none. He then realized that she wasn't asking for feedback.

"I knew that I always wanted to have kids, but I never knew how I'd be as a mother, or even if I'd get the chance to become one. Then I was afraid of getting out of shape. But, really, I always had this deep-seated fear of dying tragically like my mother. You probably think that's silly."

"I don't think it's silly, Tiff. I mean, I've had the same thoughts. But you have to believe that you'll be different. That things will be different for you. God has given you the opportunity to have children, and you'll be here for them. These two, and a few more."

Tiffany laughed, her moment of self-exploration passing. "Oh, no you don't, Alex Baxter. Not after I've struggled to get this body back together. And you know I'm still trying to tighten it back up for you." She grabbed his hand and rubbed her thighs with it. "Seriously, though, promise me something. Promise that if anything ever happens to me, you'll take good care of the kids, no matter what."

"Nothing's going to happen to you, baby. I'm not going to let it. But if it does, you know that I will. You promise me the same."

Tiffany leaned over and kissed his cheek. Caressing his ear with her tongue, she whispered, "Deal."

BACK AT HOME, Alex's nostrils were greeted with the aroma of mouthwatering barbecue. Coming from his own backyard. He cautiously approached the side yard, thinking that it was a stretch for their housekeeper to fire up the grill, especially in the middle of the day.

To his surprise, it was Foody, beer in hand, apron stretched across his broad belly, and wearing a cheerful grin. Even Tiffany was amused.

"Yo, cuz, what's up?" Foody grinned, stabbing at what appeared to be a slab of ribs, then rushed over and hoisted both babies onto his sides. "I was just in town and thought I'd drop by. Man, this grill is the bomb. Y'all must not ever use it."

Tiffany shook her head, and went over to inspect the contents of the grill. "Foody, you never cease to amaze me. I hope you plan on preparing some fish or chicken, because you know I don't eat anything that oinks or moos."

Ever since Foody's near arrest, Alex's interactions with him had been limited. Foody was still ashamed, and unnerved by the way Alex had treated him, but the distance seemed to have done both of them some good. Foody was working steadily, and shifting into adult mode.

Tiff's growing fondness for Foody made Alex smile. The kids loved him, which made her come around even more. Alex was astonished that she wasn't the least bit upset that he had arrived unannounced. He took his fist and jabbed at Foody's arm.

"Welcome back, my brother."

After dining on Foody's sumptuous lunch and catching up with him, Alex was less than enthusiastic about going down to Southeast. But he knew he had to. With the evening already planned, time was of the essence. He tried to entice Foody to come with him, but he declined, choosing to nap with the kids laid out on his jelly belly, a comedic picture.

Alex glanced at his runner's watch, for he'd already taken the precaution of removing the Rolex. It was almost three o'clock. A little late to be venturing down to Southeast, but he was tired of putting it off, and wanted to move on this issue as quickly as possible. Simon had not been pressuring him about it—he was too caught up in grandparenting, his yacht, and the election—but Alex still wanted to present the stadium idea to him in a tight package.

Arriving in Southeast, Alex decided it was best not to park the eye-catching Beamer on the street, and parked in the lot of one of the few service stations in the area. Walking quickly, he soon arrived in the multiblock riverfront area, which was desolate.

Armed with a notepad and his list, he began checking the addresses. Vagrants and addicts hung about, and Winnie was right, there were no viable businesses around. Storefront properties were boarded up, as were the old row houses. Homes were now used as flophouses for the bums and crack houses for the druggies. Alex felt as if he were walking through a ghost town, or an area that had been emptied by the plague. He passed a few multiple-story buildings with shattered windows, and graffiti sprayed all over them. They were the remnants of businesses gone by, when Anacostia was a mainstay for black-owned stores and businesses. Now they were chained up with fences and huge padlocks.

But Alex had to be thorough. He checked for electric or gas meters, most of which had been removed. He jiggled door handles and peered in windows for any signs of habitation. He cautiously checked down the alleys to the backs and sides of the buildings. D.C. was known for its numerous alleys, as if Benjamin Banneker, with a slave's mentality, had designed the city to have as many escape routes as possible.

With the exception of only a few addresses, the area was vacant. The wind blew and debris scattered in the air, and Alex was reminded that this was a place that time and change had evidently bypassed.

Satisfied that he'd found the prime location for the stadium, Alex headed back to his car as dusk was settling. On the way there, he happened across a few more abandoned warehouses. He quickly scanned his paperwork, and became concerned when he found that one of the buildings was curiously not included on the condemned-buildings list. Even more strangely, it wasn't on the list of properties that the city maintained.

Against his better judgment, Alex felt compelled to know why. After all, he'd come so close; he didn't want to slip up now and overlook an obvious problem. He glanced around, then made a quick decision to check the rear of the anonymous warehouse.

Alex cautiously ventured down the alley. The building backed up to the river, with a rickety little dock that looked like it hadn't been used in years. The alley fed into another narrow alley that ran parallel to it. Rats rustled behind dumpsters, and he began to think maybe this wasn't such a great idea.

At the rear of the building, Alex happened upon a rusted steel door. Impulsively, he tried the door. It gave way and opened. Suppressing the urge to ask if anyone was there, he went inside, careful to leave the door ajar.

Alex crept down a deserted hallway. He was surprised to find that the building had lights. Only occupied buildings had power, usually the first thing to go when they were abandoned. Few vagrants ventured to jerry-rig power off the poles.

A working elevator further disturbed Alex. Maybe he should turn back, and do some further research; but he couldn't stop. He was too curious. He pressed the elevator "up" button, the doors opened, and he went in. The engine hummed like a finely tuned piece of machinery, and although the floor buttons were marked, he pressed them all, only to have the elevator speed up to the tenth floor.

Alex's mouth dropped in shock when the doors opened onto a carpeted hallway of brightly painted doors. Beads of sweat popped out on his brow. Was he suddenly caught up in an episode of *The Twilight Zone*?

Driven by instinct, Alex tried the first door, only to find it securely locked. He walked the distance of the hall, down to the very last door, which was slightly open. He resisted the urge to knock; after all, he was a city official conducting official business. Alex slowly pushed the door open.

There was something strangely familiar about the room, including the faint scent in the air. It was a plush office. A large, European-style desk sat in the middle of the room, with a wingback leather chair facing a window that overlooked the river and the city. Equipped with the latest computers, telephones, fax machines, and coffee machines, it appeared to be the office of someone important. But in the middle of Southeast? It made no sense whatsoever.

There was no indication of whose office it was, or what the business could be. Alex checked the desk: no nameplate, no company letterhead, not even a stapler. There was no number on the phone, yet there was a switchboard blinking in one of the adjoining rooms, which appeared to be a war room. Color-coded maps of the city adorned the walls, while maps of waterways and streets were strewn across a table, with notes scribbled across strategic locations. The smell of coffee hit his nose as Alex stuck his head in the doorway.

Alex had obviously stumbled onto something that he shouldn't have. He was torn between the urge to run and the urge to find out what the hell was going on. Back inside the office, he tried the desk drawer. Locked tight. There were rows of file cabinets. He tried the handle on one of them. It too was locked. Trying drawer after drawer, he realized they were all locked tight. Until he came to the bottom drawer of the last file cabinet; it wasn't completely closed.

Alex leaned down to open the drawer and found several folders, tightly bound, with his name on them. Stunned, he had to know what was in them. As he bent over and reached to pull them out, he felt an agonizing blow to the back of his neck, and then the world spun into darkness.

CHAPTER 16

Wᴴᴱᴺ Alex awakened, he was behind the wheel of his car. Head reeling and neck aching, he was at any moment about to heave his guts up. Not because of the blow to his head, but because of the stench filling his nostrils. It was a stank mixture of funk, stale cigarettes, and cheap liquor.

Through his fog, Alex sensed that there was someone in the passenger seat. He attempted to move, but a hand restrained him.

Alex shook his head to try to gain some clarity on the situation. "Wha-wha-what the hell . . ." His voice trailed off as he noticed a steel pipe in the man's hand.

The stranger held his finger against his chapped lips. He then motioned for Alex to drive.

Alex swallowed deeply, trying to get his bearings together. Okay, okay, he thought, afraid to even mumble. He looked for the keys, which had been jammed in the ignition. Alex got the feeling he was about to experience one of his worst nightmares. He was being carjacked. The silent criminal motioned to the right with his dirty hand.

As Alex slowly drove to an unknown destination, his captor

continued to motion left and right. Weaving in and out of traffic, Alex tried to piece together an escape plan. As they approached the on-ramp to I-395, they passed an isolated strip of highway under an overpass. The captor jerked the wheel over to the shoulder and left the car running. He tapped the lead pipe, and motioned for Alex to get out of the car.

This might be his only chance to run, so Alex complied. His kidnapper must have read his mind. Before Alex's feet touched the ground, he hovered dangerously close to him, twirling the lead pipe in his hands in a threatening manner. Alex fell against the car in frustration.

But he was quickly encouraged. The area where they had stopped was pretty empty, and he figured he could make a run for it. He couldn't overpower the jerk, not with the lead pipe in the guy's hand, so he had to think. He tried using his well-honed negotiation skills. "Look, guy. If it's the car you want, take it. I won't even try to get it back. But don't hurt me. I've got a wife and kids."

The man laughed, a loud sneer. "You such a little smart-ass, ain't you? I don't want your tired-ass car. I don't drive no sticks. I bet it's so wired up, I couldn't get down the street before five-oh pulled my ass over."

"Look, you want money? Take it." Alex began reaching for his wallet, when his captor pushed the pipe into his chest.

Even in Alex's stupor, the thought of a carjacker stealing a car that he couldn't drive was beyond ludicrous. But this whole deal was ludicrous. Alex strained to remember what had happened, but kept drawing a blank as his head throbbed with every thought.

He had followed the man's instructions, and now he panicked. This deranged man was going to kill him, and leave him in the bushes where he wouldn't be discovered for weeks. Alex wasn't going out like that. His mind was racing, but his thoughts were jumbled. Looking down, Alex suddenly realized that he was wearing a filthy old overcoat, one that he'd never seen before. It was repulsive. What was it doing on him?

After what seemed to be an eternity, the man spoke.

"So tell me, you still tryin' to be Thurgood Marshall?"

Thurgood Marshall? The name made Alex impulsively ball his fist and connect a right cross squarely to the man's jaw. Anger drove the fear from his heart. Alex lunged for the man and grabbed his grungy collar, oblivious to the lead pipe, and commenced to punch him repeatedly. The only person who had ever called him that was Fortune. Fortune Reed.

"What in the hell? Is that you, Fortune? How dare you, you sorry-ass coward. How dare you show your face now!" Glaring at him, Alex shook him violently and uncontrollably.

He kicked Fortune's ass for taking away his brother. For lying. For running. The years of pent-up frustration were finally released. Alex's fists were the outlets, and each blow became stronger and stronger. Alex swung until he fell exhausted to the ground, hot tears stinging his eyes.

Standing and not flinching, Fortune took his whipping like a man. Like it was his punishment, and he'd been waiting to receive it as long as Alex had waited to give it to him. After Alex had whaled on him, and finally bloodied his nose, he dropped the pipe by his side. "I guess I deserve that, Chip."

Alex angrily wiped the tears from his eyes and mucous ran from his nose. "Don't call me that," he ranted. "I haven't been that since you killed my brother."

Fortune stared at him squarely. "You know I ain't kill Ivan. He was like my brother too."

Alex spit on the ground, barely missing Fortune's holey shoe. "That's what I care about what you think. Your trifling, gutless ass ran away and let Ivan's memory lie in shame. You didn't care then, so don't act like you care now. I ought to kill your sorry ass."

Fortune licked his chapped lips and shrugged. "Go head. I'm already a ghost, man." He paused and looked away. He murmured, "I know you mad, but you don't know a whole lotta shit. We can't talk about this here. We gots to roll. We can't stay here no more. Calm yo' ass down, else you gonna get us killed. If you ain't already done that shit."

Alex dusted himself off, his gaze fixed on Fortune. "I don't care what you say. I'm leaving you and this behind. As soon as I get somewhere, I'm going to call the cops and tell them to come and get you. Maybe you'll tell them what happened to my brother."

Fortune scratched his head and shook it fiercely. He looked at him suspiciously. "Boy, is you stupid or what? You can't be that damned dumb. I'm telling you, we need to get up outta here. Now. You can call the pigs later, if you still think it's wise." Fortune reached for him and smiled that crooked, mischievous smile. Although now he was a lot older, and his teeth were stained and in bad need of dental attention.

Alex snatched himself away, a thought suddenly crossing his mind. "Hold up, wait a damned minute. Wait, wait a minute. You, I saw you. Aren't you—?"

"No shit. You not quite as dumb as you act sometimes."

"You were the one with the squeegee. About a month ago. Not too far from here. You tried to rip me off. I remember now."

"Just calm down, Chip, I mean, whatever your name is. It's all right. I ain't try to rip you off. I told you, I can't drive no stick. Otherwise, we'da been outta here long time ago. Now, let's go. I'll explain it to you later. But now, get this thing in gear and let's roll."

It took a minute for Alex to gather his thoughts. "Wai-wait a minute. What happened? What's going on? Where did you come from? Where did I get this coat? Where on earth are we going?"

Fortune pulled out an old Newport cigarette butt and promptly fired it up. "Look, I'll tell you when we get where we goin'. We gotta break camp. Right now. I don't know if they caught your ass on that video camera or not. Don't know who saw and who ain't seen shit, so let's go. But we can't go back to your booby-trapped-assed house. That place got so many bugs that a damn exterminator couldn't kill 'em all. And for God's sake, when we get back in this fancy ride of yours, don't say a goddamned thing. It's bugged too. Now, let's get over to your pop's place. If they did see you, that'll be the last place they look."

Before Alex could ask who, Fortune slapped him across the chest, yelling, "Let's go!" and looking up to the heavens. "Eye, you know I'm really trying to help this boy, but I swear it ain't easy."

BY THE TIME Fortune picked the lock to Alex's father's apartment, Alex had peeled off the reeking overcoat. He found some
ice for his neck and for Fortune's bloody nose. Through the haze,
Alex was able to remember being in the abandoned building, or at
least the one that was supposed to be abandoned. He remembered
finding a suite of offices, and looking into the file cabinets. That
was it.

"Your pops ain't got no liquor here?" Fortune blurted out, searching in the kitchen cabinets for some unknown stash. "Some things
don't never change. Good thing I carry my own these days."

Staring at the figure that called himself Fortune, Alex couldn't
help but feel a bit sorry for him. Time had taken its toll on him.
He was no longer simply wiry; now he was a shell of a man, and
his limp was even more pronounced. It had worsened through the
years on the streets of D.C. The years of probably sleeping out in
the harsh elements. He was pitiful. Once so fly and so hip, now he
was just a cruddy bum. The years of degradation had punished
him more than Alex ever could. The man he held personally responsible for the death of his brother was now rambling through
his father's cabinets, just like he and Ivan used to do every day after
school. It was tragic.

Fortune's face looked aged beyond his years, but Alex couldn't
tell if that was from the dirt, or living the life of a bum or an alcoholic. Alex had little time to further waste on wondering about
Fortune's life. He had gotten what he deserved. This was not
about Fortune or the old homestead. He had to find out what had
happened, and after he told Fortune not to ever call him Chip
again, Alex pressed him for answers.

Flopping down on the sofa beside him, Fortune raised a stink
that made Alex's eyes water. He watched impatiently as Fortune
pulled out a half-empty unlabeled bottle from one of his coat
pockets. And then he began to talk.

It was Fortune who had whacked him on the neck. "It was the
only way I could get you outta there. If I'd told you who I was
then, you'd have probably gone off on me. They was on they way,

coming 'round the block, and if you had got caught, you would of been dead right about now.

"See, you stumbled up on something that you shouldn't have. I made a promise to Ivan on his grave that I would look out for you, 'cause I didn't want your blood on my hands too. And then you go and get your ass all caught up in this shit."

"What are you saying?"

"Only you could say that and really mean it. You don't have a clue to the shit you walked in on, do you?" Fortune shook his head.

Alex shook his head no. After all these years, and although they were living in two distinctly different worlds, Fortune still had his way of making Alex feel like the pesky, know-nothing little brother. Here he sat with a world of education, and he was about to be taught more in one evening than he'd learned in a lifetime. Alex motioned for him to continue.

"You know, Chip, uh, I mean Alex, we made amends, me and Ivan. That was my boy, you know what I'm sayin'. And his blood was on my hands. I messed with the wrong one, and Ivan got taken out 'cause of it. As his boy, I couldn't even stand up for him, when everybody spread all them lies 'bout him. I had to live with that shit every day." Fortune took another swig from his bottle of no-name liquor.

"Then you grow up, go to college, and then you come back here and get into more treacherous shit than I could've ever imagined."

Alex jumped up, holding his aching neck. "Look, Fortune, I'm not that snot-nosed little boy you used to push around all the time. Look at me. I'm all grown up now, and I'm running out of patience for this game you're playing. Stop messing around and tell me what's going on."

Fortune seemed surprised at his outburst. "Got some balls now, huh, Alex?" He looked up to the heavens for confirmation. "Maybe you were right, Ivan. The kid does have a little heart."

Alex figured that Fortune spoke often to Ivan in this way,

through his drunken yet semicoherent stupor. Alex couldn't tell if it was just the liquor or maybe drugs that had turned him out. But guilt and grief had certainly played a large part.

"Get to the point, Fortune."

Easing backward, Fortune planted his dusty feet on the coffee table. "See, I have been out on these streets a long time. Running numbers, petty boosting, anything to get by. Word came out that they was lookin' for someone with a little youth to do a job one night, and I volunteered. I knew it was the best way to get noticed.

"All I had to do was run 'cross the street in front of this big ole Lincoln, try not to get hurt, and then split. I got clipped a little bit, but I was able to run off. 'Course I didn't split. I ran 'round down one of the alleys and watched. The Lincoln had jumped the curb, but the driver was okay. She was gettin' out of the car when *bam*—the next thing I knew, about four guys had her, beating her all up'side the head. Then they took the car and smashed it into a parked car.

"What's that got to do with anything?"

"That's how I started into this life of crime. I figured I seen something I wasn't supposed to see, and I was gonna get mines. And my reward was my own thing. That's when I started selling drugs."

"So, you had something on somebody and started selling drugs. Big damn deal."

"Yeah, big deal, all right. I was hooked up. Makin' bank. I was doing damn good. Till I got greedy and shit. I decided to break off on my own. The HNIC found out about it, and that's when they decided to smoke me."

Alex was getting impatient. What Fortune was saying still made no sense to him. "I hear you, Fortune. I understand all of that— I'm not stupid. I know that Ivan was shot by accident. I knew they wanted you, not him. But what in the hell does that have to do with me now?"

"It has everything to do with you now. That office you walked into belongs to the biggest drug dealer on the East Coast. And his boys was on they way back, and if yo' ass had got caught, your ass woulda been new-mown grass."

This news hit him hard. Was his life suddenly in jeopardy because he walked into the wrong building?

"Okay, okay. I got that. But did you have to almost break my neck in the process?"

Finally, there was a bit of comic relief. Fortune snickered again. "No, I didn't have to, but let's just say that was a bonus. You know, one for ole times' sake. Alex, don't you get it? I had to get you out of there. The only way I made it happen was to make it like you was one of the fellas. It was evening. Miller time! You could pass for a dude having his evening highball, know what I mean?

"I threw a paper bag up on that damned security camera they got out there, made it look like the wind blew it up. Then I snuck in. You had left the door halfway open, anyhow. So when I seen you up in the office, I knew I had to tag you. I slipped my coat on you, and dragged your ass all the way down them steps, up the street till we got to your ride. One of my buddies faked a fit in the middle of the street to take the attention off us. By the way, I gave him your pager in return for the favor. He needed a coupla bucks."

Alex felt for the pager on his belt, only to find it missing. He stared at Fortune in disbelief. No wonder Tiffany hadn't paged him all evening. Luckily, he had a spare mobile phone and pager under his seat. "But how'd you know I was there?"

"How you think? I been shadowing you since way back in the day. You see, when you a bum, nobody sees you. You invisible. 'Less you get too close. That's when all hell breaks loose. But we bums got a network, from the winos to the crack heads to the squeegee men. All I had to do was put the word out to look out fo' you, and they let me know what was up. That's how I know everything that you've been doing. It's as simple as that.

"I saw you down at the shelter, and I saw you tryin' to play I Spy at the gas station. Walking around the 'hood tryin' to act like you lived there. I thought it was cool, until you just had to go to that building. Of all places."

"But you've been tailing me all this time? Why? What do I have to do with this guy? Who is this guy anyway, and what was he doing with files on me? What about my wife? Oh shit, what about Simon?" Alex cringed at the notion that this dealer, whoever he was, was someone powerful enough to hurt not only him but his family. "I've got to get to Simon. He'll know what to do."

Fortune began laughing, a raucous laugh that penetrated the walls. Then he gulped down the corner of liquor and finally spoke.

"You ever heard the old saying 'dancing with the devil'?"

"Yes, I know what you mean. But what are you talking about? I'm not dancing with the devil."

"Ha! Negro, you not only danced with the devil, you even mated with him."

Dropping his ice pack, Alex grabbed Fortune by his dirty collar and shook him violently. "Stop playing with me, Fortune. I keep telling you, I'll break your neck if you don't tell me what you're talking about."

Fortune snatched away from him, cold sober. The old street rose up in him. "Don't ever touch me again, Alex. I mean it. I let you get that shit outta your system because I deserved it. But don't try it again. You so fucking stupid. How could anybody from Shaw be so green? You one stupid-ass nigga to have all them pieces of paper hanging on your wall.

"You really think anything goes down in this city that your daddy-in-law don't know about? Come on, fool, think! Use your head. Not no book sense, but some street sense. I know it's in there somewhere. Now, I done told you that the biggest drug dealer on the East Coast is holed up here in D.C., and you want to believe that Da Mayor don't know about it? Right under his greedy nose? Nigga, please. Stop being so simple and think!"

Alex was numb. "That's ridiculous. Simon's never showed any signs of dealing with any criminals. He's clean. His record's immaculate. Even after the feds went through his garbage cans looking for dirt years ago, they turned up nothing."

Fortune looked at him curiously. "You ever heard of the name Moses before? In all of your high-falutin', big-time wheelings and dealings, you mean to tell me you ain't never run across nothing with a Moses associated with it?"

Shaking his head when Alex stared back with a blank face, Fortune mumbled under his breath. "Man, that nigga is good. Too damn good. He got the black Opie to cover his ass, an honest-to-goodness choirboy. You so legit it's sicknin'. To think I doubted you there for a while. Ain't life a bitch."

Moments passed before Fortune's words sank in. "What are you talking about, you doubted me? Quit all this cryptic nonsense and get to the point."

"The point is the one person I tried to keep you furthest away from and the one person that caused you the most harm is the one person you turn around and worship. The point is that I used to hump for Moses. And now you do. My boy Moses is your boy Simon."

The news hit him like a crash-test dummy hitting a brick wall. Fortune's words spun over and over in his mind. Moses was the biggest gangster in the city. Yet Moses was Simon. Simon? Alex started yelling at the top of his lungs at Fortune, who sat calmly on the sofa. This man had drifted like a ghost back into his life. After more than ten years, Fortune had found another way to destroy his life in a matter of minutes. Alex wanted to curse him out for lying through his rotten teeth.

"Look, young buck. You best be quiet. They might've caught your ass on camera, and we don't know who might've seen you tonight. So, until we know, you gotta lay low."

"You're lying, Fortune. You're just a lying son of a bitch." Alex spat the words out halfheartedly.

"If I'm lying, I'm flying." Fortune sipped from his bottle.

Why should Alex listen to some old bum, a guy so morally corrupt that he let an innocent boy, his best friend, die in shame? A smelly, unkempt bum who had waltzed into his life after all this time, professing to be some type of gutter guardian angel.

"What do you really want, Fortune? Are you trying to blackmail me? Tired of living like you're living? You want some cash? Well, you can forget it. You're wasting your time. Take this garbage someplace else. I don't believe it. I can't. The man has been too good to me for too long. It just can't be true. I won't believe it. I'd take his word over yours in a heartbeat."

Fortune laughed in Alex's face, and his breath nearly knocked Alex out. "So don't believe it. Go running off to him with this and he'll rub yo' ass out. You'll be real close to Ivan then, if they ever find yo' ass." Fortune stared at him with vacant eyes. "I ain't trying to blackmail you, Alex. For what? You ain't got nothing I want. I told you, I made Ivan a promise, and that was to look out for you 'cause it was obvious that you couldn't do it yourself. You ain't gotta believe me, man. If you'd seen what was in them files, you'd know for real."

"So are you saying Simon, or this Moses person, is responsible for Ivan's death?"

Fortune flung his arms to the sky and yelled, "Ding-ding-ding! You get the prize!"

Alex tried some attorney tactics, in hopes of finding some subtle inconsistencies in Fortune's story. "You're insinuating that he pulled the trigger. Don't even try it. Remember, I was there when it happened."

"Look, kid. I might be on the streets, but I ain't lunching. No, that nigga ain't pull the trigger. He's the grand pooh-bah. He had some of his boys do that shit. Those same stickup boys that was knockin' over the stores in our neighborhood. They was the ones that did that People's Drug job you saw."

"What? You're lying. So where are they now?"

"Cracked out. Like they tried to do me. But I wasn't fallin' for that nonsense. I knew too damned much."

"If you knew so damned much, how come you never said anything to anyone?" Alex was grasping for straws now.

Fortune's eyes rolled up. "Alex, you been around them politicians too long. You beginning to talk out both sides of your mouth. Case you forgot, and just in case this smell don't remind you, I was strung out, remember? But I wasn't no fool. I knew the deal. Who woulda believed me? I can see the headlines now. 'Crack Head Spills Guts: Mayor Major Drug Dealer.' Film at eleven. Yeah, right.

"So I did the next best thing: I watched yo' back. It wasn't easy, though. Followed yo' ass through good old Cardonza, down to Hilliard, and whatnot. But then you turn around and hook up with his daughter, marry her, and move up in a house his blood money bought. He picked it out for you so he can watch you like a hawk day and night. He's got so many bugs and cameras up in there that I know he made some good damn home videos. I bet he was just zooming in and out on you waxing that ass. Man, I know that big-time freak be getting his jollies.

"I figured you was hip to what was going on. There was just too much shit flying around for you not to be. But then," he said, pointing up to the ceiling, "Ivan and I figured it out. Naw, maybe not. Moses could best use you dumb and clean. It would be more legit. He molded yo' ass into what he needed most, a good cover. And you played the role perfectly, 'cause you really a good kid, you know, to the bone. A good little yassa boy. Like a damned puppet. He had your head so far up his ass, he had to tell you when it was daylight. Watchin' you was just like watchin' that game Simon Says. Simon says do this, and you did it. Simon says do that, and you jumped to it. Damn, you was a sucka. And it worked fo' him and fo' you too. Till you had the bright idea to start thinking for yourself, and go down Southeast. You really done it now. But hey, I guess it's worth it, right? You sell your soul to the devil, but in return you get taken care of. You was over like a fat rat. Hell, he even serves up his girl. Man, that's one ole gal you got." Fortune carved out an hourglass with his hands. "Boom. Baby girl got a body on her. Built like a brick shit house. And if she's half the woman her momma was, I know she know how to work it."

"What do you mean? What the hell do you know about her mother?" Alex's head was spinning.

Fortune continued his yarn, with intricate details about how Simon's wife had taken up with another man who was more in keeping with her standard, and with her family's approval.

"Her folks was gonna run Simon's country ass outta town. She was a tough broad, and she ain't care if Simon knew about it or not. She had the cash, and the old family name, and she was just 'bout to do it. The only thing she wanted was a divorce and that baby girl of hers, which Simon started thinking wasn't his anyway. So, he really ain't care too much, but he wasn't about to let her divorce him. He'd lose too much. Old boy decided it wouldn't be good for his career. You know, he wanted to get in politics and shit. He wanted to be Mr. Big Stuff, but back in them days, no one would have that. A divorced black mayor? Naw, no way. That would have been political suicide. It wasn't cool. But he figured that being a widowed mayor would work. So, before she could dump him, he worked his magic. And *poof,* I was running out in front of that Lincoln, and old girl was on her way to glory."

Alex jumped to his feet and paced. "I don't believe you. Tiffany's not Simon's daughter? Simon's responsible for his own wife's death? That's crazy. It's preposterous. You want me to believe that he's been invading my privacy all of this time? That's bullshit, Fortune."

"Face it. You ain't nothing but a puppet on a freaking string. They say that the truth'll set you free, so flap, flap." Fortune fluttered his hands like a bird.

Alex banged his fist on the coffee table, and grabbed a book and flung it into the wall. "This whole thing makes me sick. You mean to tell me that every conversation, every phone call, every time I touched my wife has been monitored by him or one of his wretched henchmen?"

Fortune nodded his head. "You're damned skipping. Right back in that high-rise building in Anacostia."

"I could take that damned building down brick by brick with my bare hands."

Suddenly, Alex was cast into a void of doubt. How could he deny what Fortune had said, yet how could he believe that Simon was the monster Fortune described? Had he been that gullible? Or was he just so ambitious and self-centered that he had ignored the obvious? Had he turned a blind eye and a deaf ear because he was getting what he wanted? They were tough questions with even tougher answers.

Alex mentally inventoried his life. Everything he had was somehow connected to Simon, and hinged on how he would react to this newfound knowledge. Part of him wished Fortune would just disappear again, and then he could act like this had never happened, while another part wanted to run screaming from the building. Was he the stand-up man he professed to be, or was he just a sham?

Whatever else Alex was, he was livid. He was enraged at Simon and himself for his ignorant descent into this heinous situation. After moments of uncomfortable silence, and vacillating between what he wanted and what he was dealing with, Alex realized there was no choice. He might have been a fool, but now he wouldn't be foolish. Moreover, Alex wouldn't be played by Simon anymore.

Alex wanted to scream, but reached deep inside and found a quiet voice. "This is just too much," he said. "Too damned much. If what you're telling me is even partially correct, then I'm in a world of trouble. If Simon's boys saw me, they're going to come for me. I've got to get my family out of there." Alex's words were barely coherent.

Fortune shrugged his thin shoulders. "You best chill out, boy. They ain't see you. I know that. Otherwise, we wouldn't even be having this convo. He would've smoked us by now. So just calm down a minute and think about what you sayin'. Damn. I'm the one with the substance-abuse problem, not you. You can't get crazy and flip the fuck out on me."

The irony of listening to Fortune being rational slowly calmed Alex down. "I can't digest all of this information, Fortune." He began pacing the floor. "I just can't comprehend this. It makes no sense. Why would the mayor push drugs? Why would he run the risk of getting caught? He's got too much going for himself."

"It's simple. Moola. Money. Ducketts. Greenbacks. Whatever. Plus, it's in his nature. The man got game in him from way back. You see, his wife and all her money and connections got him in the door politically, but it wasn't enough for him. Her family never really accepted him. He was too black, but for they little girl's sake, they let them get married. He got a taste of the good life, and he wanted more. He was greedy. He wanted mo' money.

And he knew the kind of money drugs was bringing in. So he went back to what he knew best. Hustlin'. The man is just straight-up greedy.

"See, when I was coming up, we pushed herb. No harm intended. Get a little high, but it wasn't killing nobody back then. Then came dust. It was cool, but folks acted real crazy with that shit. A few black folks might've been doin' a little heroin, mostly the musicians and shit, but that was way too expensive to mass distribute. Plus that required all that shooting up and shit, and you know how we black folks is about needles. Then you had cocaine; well, that was the white folks' drug of choice. And some of the rich black folks started doing it recreationally.

"See, Moses had it goin' on. He was the lawyer representing all them thugs. He hit the big time when this big dealer name Julius asked him to represent him on a petty traffic ticket. Well, Simon was about that. He did everything but shine Julius's shoes. Julius liked that he had a connected nigga licking his boots, so he started usin' Simon to sell nose candy to the bougee black folks that ain't wanna deal with Julius and his boys because they was too ghetto."

Fortune lit another butt and kept talking. "Simon made a mint selling drugs to black folks while still under Julius's organization. Simon had the perfect plan. He'd represent thugs in court, and once he got them released, they'd show up on his payroll. So, you do the math. Simon got large while Julius met an untimely death. Go figure. And guess who was, like, in charge of Julius's estate?"

"Simon."

"You got it. And part of his estate included a large parcel from Colombia. Some heavy shit, and it had to be moved. It was crack, baby. Nothing like it had ever hit these streets before. Simon was reborn into Moses, and it was on. He pushed that shit as a party for the poor folks, do you hear me? Party down for a rock of crack cocaine. He dealt that shit to the people, and that's some ugly stuff. Folk'll sell they souls for a hit of the pipe.

"So, the kingdom kind of fell into his little lap, not to say he ain't had nothing to do with it. But he did that shit to the community. He ain't give a rat's ass. By being Da Mayor, he was regulating all that. Distribution, manufacturing, everything. He was running that shit up and down the East Coast like UPS and gettin' paid. Till the feds started cracking down, and now Ninety-five's like a war zone."

Alex folded his arms and sighed. "So that's why he's pushing for statehood. I guess since the highways are practically on lockdown, that's why he got that boat. He had to get control of the city again."

"You know a nigga's always got a back door. Old boy is smart, he's always got a plan. See, drugs is a powerful tool. It took all I had not to get strung out on that shit, 'cause I knew I couldn't watch you like I was supposed to. But I will admit, I do like my drink." Fortune patted the empty bottle. "Face it, kid. Your boy is fuckin' ruthless. He'll eliminate anyone and anything that gets in his way, believe that," Fortune said. "Dig this. When that damned councilwoman started givin' him too much static, he took her husband out."

"You mean?"

"Yeah, that's exactly what I mean. Simon had the old boy all shot up, just so he could get the wife out the way."

"Jesus Christ," Alex said. "Well, at least he didn't kill him."

"At least. But that's how your boy is. Everything he does is with a threefold purpose. And sometimes it's so heavy, the shit happens so far down the line, that you don't even see it coming. You know what I mean?"

"Damn." Alex felt like a fool. He had been the simplest little pawn in the biggest chess game in town. Yet he still sought to understand. "Well, why did he choose me?"

"You just happened. You was like a gift. See, something happened with that boy your girl was going with before. What's-his-name. He was one of Moses's boys. He found out the boy was giving, uh, her the 'caine, and he wanted him out. Poof. He was not about to get tripped up by some scandalous shit like that. But you came along and did it for him. All he had to do was clean up your leftovers."

"Sidney?" It was a name Alex hadn't thought of in years.

"Yeah, whatever. I heard Simon turned him out. Got him strung out, and gave him to some pimp who owed him a favor. Now I hear he's some crack-head trick living up in New York."

"Trick? What do you mean?"

Fortune smirked. "Trick, as in a ho', faggot. You know, sellin' his worm up there in the Big Apple. Do anything for a hit of that pipe. Sucks it like a dick." He made irritating sucking noises with his crusty lips.

Alex was repulsed. Big Sidney, a gay prostitute? Alex could only remember how gigantic and strong the brother had been, and now this? He couldn't imagine the sight of Sidney bending over for somebody, not the way he used to bully folks. No wonder not even frat had heard from him since he left H.I.

"Dropped him to his knees. For real."

"Well, at least he didn't kill him. Or have him killed."

"Yeah, um-hum. But is it worth living? I'd rather be dead."

Alex glanced over at the clock. It was almost six-thirty. "Man, I've got to do something. I just can't act like I don't know. I'll never look at Simon the same way, that dirty bastard. I've got this damned fund-raiser to go to tonight. I don't have a choice. But I have to do something. I can't let this go on. Too much has happened. Too damned much and he needs to pay."

"Well," Fortune said, resting comfortably back on the sofa. "That's on you. They ain't see you, but it was Lady Luck that got your ass up in there today. Normally, that place is like Fort Knox. I guess that damned cockeyed Blinky is getting lax in his old age."

"I have to go back. I don't have any proof. If what you're saying is true, I still can't say jack. But I know he's got something on me, just for insurance. If all else fails, he can always hurt my family."

"No doubt."

"I've got to get some proof. Without that, I'm just pissing in the wind." Alex mulled over his options. Who could he trust? He didn't know who knew and who didn't. He couldn't even trust frat. But then he remembered Foody was staying at his house. Alex was sure he could help out. In some kind of way. Then there was Fortune. The skid-row, alcoholic bum. Damn.

The jiggling of a doorknob interrupted his thoughts. Alex and Fortune glanced at each other in panic. Instinctively, they jumped to their feet, and began reaching for anything they could find to defend themselves.

"What in the hell is going on here?"

CHAPTER 17

HEARING voices coming from his supposedly empty apartment, Gerald Baxter came in strapped. He pointed a .45 at them, and kept moving it from side to side, keeping both of them within his range. Barely recognizing Alex, his father fixed his gaze on Fortune.

"Dad, Dad. Put the gun down, Dad. Please. It's me, Alex." Alex was relieved that it was his father, but how would he react seeing Fortune? Alex figured he'd shoot first and ask questions later.

"Alex?" His father stared down the barrel of the gun.

Fortune shifted uneasily, looking like a trapped wild animal. The odds weren't in his favor. There was only one way out, and that was on the other side of the gun.

"Please, Dad. Calm down."

After a few agonizing moments, his father finally brought the gun down to his side. Alex heaved a sigh of relief, and Fortune reached for his bottle.

"Hell of a time for a visit. I could have blown you away." His father tapped the gun against his leg and pointed a crooked finger at Fortune. "What kind of company you keeping these days, son?"

Alex slowly took the gun away from his father. "Le-let me explain, Dad." He clicked the safety back on, and placed the gun on the kitchen table. "Dad, you need to sit down. This is Fortune."

His father immediately leaped over the coffee table and grabbed Fortune by the neck. "Give me my gun, Alex. Give it to me." The pain of losing his son surfaced on Gerald Baxter's face and in his powerful grip. As Alex broke them up, Fortune dove toward the kitchen table and grabbed the gun.

"Back up off me, old man. I didn't come here for this shit. It's just the same ole, same ole. I'm outta here," Fortune heaved as he backed off toward the door.

"You're going to have to kill me now, then. Just like you killed my son. 'Cause if you walk out that door, I'm gonna find you. If I ever see your lame ass again, I will kill you. I'll shoot you like a dog in the street." His father spewed the angry words, still tussling with Alex to get to Fortune.

"Well, you must be one sorry-ass cabdriver if you've been driving around all this time and never seen me," Fortune said with a sneer on his face.

Gerald Baxter glared at Fortune as Alex restrained him. "I'm still your elder, boy. You better realize that I ain't on the street like you."

This was not how it was going to be. Alex had been devastated, and the only person who could help him was getting ready to vanish into the night. If Fortune went, he'd never see him again.

"You can't go, Fortune. You gotta help me with this." Alex loosened his grip on his father.

His dad never took his eyes off Fortune, but spoke to Alex. "I know you might not think very much of me, Alex, but let me tell you something. If you think I'd ever welcome this killer into my house, you're wrong. Dead wrong. I want him out of here. Right now."

"Dad, I understand how you feel. I felt the same way. But the truth is, Fortune didn't kill Ivan, but he knows who did. I finally see that it was a horrible mistake. And he saved my life tonight."

He looked at Alex curiously, but didn't utter a word. Fortune continued pointing the gun at him.

"It's true, Dad. And if you never listened to me before, you've got to listen to me now. We're running out of time, and Fortune's the only one who can help. He's the only one who can bring Ivan's killers to justice."

AFTER ALEX disarmed Fortune, the two men stared each other down as Alex replayed the evening's events. At first, as he recounted each detail, his father showed no signs of softening. But Gerald Baxter came to understand that the future of his only son and grandchildren depended on the one person he despised the most; he had no choice but to accept Fortune. Finally a truce was declared.

"I don't like this one bit, Alex. You think you can really trust this thing?" He eyed Fortune with contempt.

"I don't have a choice." And before Alex knew it, he was saying words that he couldn't recall ever speaking before. "And Dad, I'm going to need your help."

His words sliced through the dense air like a knife. For once, his father's concentration was focused on the words and actions of his living son, and not those of his deceased son.

He shook his head reluctantly, accepting Alex at his word. "Whatever you need, son. But I'm telling you, I'm not working under these conditions. He reeks and is funking up my house. This boy better go wash his ass with some lye before I agree to anything."

FORTUNE EMERGED FROM the shower a different man. Since Alex's dad had left the place just as it had been twelve years earlier, Fortune was able to find a pair of Ivan's old jeans, shirt, and jacket from his closet. While Fortune transformed himself, Alex and his father huddled around the dining room table, mapping out a plan. They had it all figured out, with the exception of how to get back into the office.

"Fortune, my primary concern is my family," Alex said. "I think we've got a plan to get me and Tiffany out of going to that party tonight without arousing suspicion. I've already called Tiffany, and she didn't sound like anything out of the ordinary was going on. I told her I was running late because I got into a little fender bender. My buddy Foody's still there, so when I get there, I'll get him outside and tell him the deal. Dad'll pick him up, with the kids, and Foody'll meet us at the building."

Fortune asked, "What the hell is a Foody? And how you know you can trust him?"

Alex igged him and continued. "I'm going to get a rental car and leave that bugged one here."

"We'll go down to the boat, and then Dad is going to call me on the mobile phone, just before we get on the boat. I'll act like it's a call from our nanny, saying that one of the kids got violently sick. That way both Tiffany and I can get away. Then I'll tell her just enough to keep her calm, once we get back in the rental car. In the interim, Dad will have picked up the kids and Foody, and he'll meet us near the Fourteenth Street Bridge. That way I'll know they'll be safe.

"We just bought tickets to four different destinations. We purchased a couple train tickets and two airline tickets. I called my friend Lisa and told her that I need her help too. She's in Atlanta, and said she could cover us for as long as we needed it.

"If something happens to me, it'll take a while for them to figure out how to get to Tiff. But what I haven't figured out is how to get back in that office tonight. I've got to get the evidence I need, then call the feds and have them take that place down. It's beyond the cops, plus they're probably on the take too. And I've got to do this before I do anything else. Otherwise, it won't even be worth it. I can't risk waiting another minute."

"Alex, dumb luck got you in that joint today. Trust me, that door is sealed up tighter than a nun's twat. It's never open. Never." Fortune settled onto the sofa and promptly put his feet up, which now sported a pair of Ivan's barely worn Converse sneakers.

"Take your feet off my table, boy. This ain't no flophouse," Alex's father hissed, yet Fortune just ignored him.

"But I have to get in there," Alex said.

"It ain't gonna be easy. What you think you gonna do? Bang on the door and say 'Domino's Pizza'? What, you Avon calling or you gonna be a Jehovah Witness?"

Alex's father cracked his knuckles and looked at Fortune like he wanted to swing on him. "Come on, man. You're a career criminal. This should be right up your alley. You picked the lock to get in here, didn't you? Why can't you pick that lock, or is talking all you can do?" he asked, his nose wrinkled.

"Yeah, real funny, old man."

"You know your mouth always got you in trouble. I see you never learned to respect your elders, boy. Some things never change."

Fortune scratched his face, sizing up Gerald Baxter. "Yeah, I see some things don't ever change. Least I been on the streets all this time. What's your excuse?"

Alex shot both of them an "I've had enough" look. He spoke firmly, and they both knew he meant business. "That's enough, now. We don't have time for all this. You can pick back up on this later. For now, let it go. We've got to get down to business."

But the two men started bickering again. Alex lifted a bowl of plastic fruit from the credenza and heaved it at the wall. The veins in his neck bulged, and he yelled, "Will you two shut the hell up!"

The room was immediately silenced. Both men looked away warily, avoiding eye contact. Finally, Fortune spoke.

"Awright. I'm sorry. But this ain't no plaything. It ain't that easy. I can pick the lock, but there ain't no guarantees. They got security cameras all over outside. Plus we ain't got enough time to even find out who's up in there. You damn sure can't bum-rush the place. See, they got the labs going on one floor, distribution on another. At any time, there could be a whole bunch of people up in there. We might be walking in on an army of folks. And trust me, if it's an army, they gonna be packin'."

Alex paced. "Who can get us in there? Foody's really good with electronics, but if he disables the security system, it's going to be noticed. We've got to be able to get in there without a whole lot of confusion. We need someone who can get us up to that office without drawing any attention."

Fortune scratched in unmentionable places. "Look, I need a drink or a smoke or something. Face it, the only nigga that can get you up in there is Blinky. He's Simon's eyes and ears on the street. He runs the shit.

"See, they got a night shift over there that works from ten to seven. Got security badges and everything. Blinky is always there at the stroke of ten. His ass be like clockwork. Sometimes he bring a prospective client there. But he works solo. He always sits over by the dock, 'cause he don't trust nobody. He know how cutthroat Moses is. He'll be there. His greedy ass'll be eating a fish sandwich he gets from up the street, till the last worker goes in, and then he follows them in."

"So you're saying that the only way we can get in there is with this guy Blinky?"

Fortune nodded.

Alex grabbed the .45 that was on the center of the table and said, "At this juncture, don't worry about it. I'll take great pleasure in taking care of Blinky's rotten ass."

ALEX SHUT HIS eyes and prayed for strength. They had gone over the plan a million times; it had to run flawlessly. Fortune, armed with the extra phone, ventured back to man the streets of Anacostia. Alex and his father picked up the rental car and set the plan into motion.

Driving home, Alex wondered if he was doing the right thing. Was he being too hasty? Was it too late to bail? Everyone he knew and cared about was involved, and they were vulnerable. Alex had to keep his head straight and do what needed to be done. If Simon wasn't who Fortune said he was, or if there was some simple explanation for all of this, no one would get hurt. Even Simon. Everything had to work out. Just like his life had, at least up until this point.

When he arrived home, he lured Foody to the car to get a

bushel of nonexistent crabs. Alex knew he'd jump at that opportunity. Once outside, Alex quickly gave him the abridged plan,
refraining from mentioning Simon. Foody quickly got over his
disappointment regarding the crab ruse, and listened intently.

"I got it, Alex. Whatever you need. I'm there," Foody said, his
voice flooding with optimism.

"I know you're swift, Foody. But this is serious. A lot's on the
line, and I can't say that it won't be kind of dangerous. I don't want
you to do anything that you might regret."

"Look, it's cool. You know I'm always down for a little excitement."

"Just remember not to say anything in the house. From what
I've been told, it's bugged, and I don't want to take any chances,
okay? So let's get back inside. We've got a tight time frame, and we
need to get going."

"Are you okay?" Tiffany asked, as she looked at Alex's disheveled
appearance. "You look horrible. What happened to your clothes?"

"I'm okay. I just had to change a tire, that's all," Alex said.

He hurried through the door. He grabbed his babies, and kissed
and held them like he'd never seen them before.

"What is up with you, Alex?" Tiffany glanced at him sideways.
He set the children down, and threw his arms around her and
kissed her deeply. The more she tried to speak, the harder his lips
smothered her mouth. He had to keep her quiet. The kisses caught
her by surprise and were enough to keep her from questioning
him.

"I'm fine, babe. Now, I know we're running late, so let me
jump into the shower."

Tiffany wiped her mouth, a pleasant look on her face. "Okay. I
laid your tux out for you."

Standing in the marble shower stall, Alex could barely wash
himself. With every scrub, his eyes surveyed the room, wondering
where the cameras were. He shut the water off after only a few
moments, disgusted that he was being watched. He wanted to just
pack up his family and run, but he couldn't. He couldn't pretend

that he didn't know about Simon, and he couldn't be a coward. He didn't know how many people had died because of Simon, but he knew one, and that was Ivan. Alex knew in his heart that he couldn't let Simon get away with it any longer. Emerging from the shower, Alex dressed quickly, making sure they'd get to the boat before it sailed. He said a silent prayer, asking God for His divine intervention.

Tiffany looked exquisite as usual. She was more than excited at her first real social outing since the twins' birth. She stood proudly primping in the mirror. She had gotten that spectacular body back together in less than a couple of months, and was anxious to show it off.

The boat was to be docked until nine-thirty, when it would promptly cast off, per Simon's strict instructions. Again Alex silently prayed, begging the Lord to make sure his father called at nine-twenty sharp. It was approaching nine o'clock, and they both hurriedly kissed and held the babies. Alex made sure to tell Mrs. Stiles to page him if anything happened, and he winked at Foody as they scurried out the door.

There was valet parking at pier 7, where Simon's yacht was docked. Alex was surprised to see Percy coordinating the cars. But then again, maybe not. Everyone was suspect tonight and no one could be trusted.

Alex checked his watch. It was almost twenty past nine, and they were still strolling down the pier. He tried to hurry Tiffany along, but she was back in her glory, chatting and smiling with the social elite. He was tensing up, but he knew he had to play it cool. That phone could not ring until they were near the boat. He wanted to make sure this performance was held in front of Simon, because Alex knew how inquisitive he was. It had to be played perfectly.

Alex approached the boat, his nervous energy crackling like static electricity. Especially when he saw Simon and Mrs. Bidwell standing at the end of the plank, greeting all the finely dressed guests. Alex held his breath and summoned up all of the courage he had. Simon's smile widened when he saw two of his prized possessions nearing, although it was dangerously close to nine-thirty.

"Well, well, well. I was beginning to get worried about you two," Simon's voice carried across the pier. "I was getting afraid you weren't going to make it. I thought I'd have to call the National Guard out for you two." His laughter now made Alex's skin crawl.

As Alex assisted Tiffany up the stairs, his mobile phone rang. Trying not to appear overly anxious, he calmly opened up his jacket and took the call.

"Oh my goodness, Tiffany. Alex just got sick, and Mrs. Stiles isn't sure if he needs to go to the hospital." He grabbed Tiffany's arm to stop her from continuing up the stairs.

"What do you mean, she's not sure?" Simon asked. "As much as that woman is getting paid, she ought to know everything. Don't worry, kids get little bugs all the time."

Tiffany stopped abruptly in her tracks. "What did she say was wrong? He was fine when we left him."

"She said he vomited a yellowish substance and hasn't stopped. She's afraid he might get dehydrated or hurt himself. So she doesn't want to make that decision." Alex took the opportunity to manipulate the situation a bit. "Well, you know how we new parents are, Simon. We worry a lot. I guess we'll have to take a rain check on this one. I don't want to be too far away from my child if something happens."

"Alex is right, Dad. We have to find out what's wrong with the baby. I wouldn't have a good time anyhow," Tiffany said as she tried to mask her disappointment at missing the event.

Simon offered up a suggestion. "Well, it doesn't take both of you to make the decision. Alex, you go and see about my grandson. When you find out what's what, call me back on my boat's private number. I'll make sure that Scotty answers the phone. Tiffany, if you feel like you need to go be with little Alex, I'll have Scotty drop anchor. He'll use the smaller motorboat to take you back to the pier. If you get things under control, and you want to come back, Alex, I'll have Scotty come pick you up. Is that fair?"

Alex gnashed his teeth, but tried to remain calm. This was not how it was supposed to go down, but he couldn't argue with Simon. It would arouse suspicion, and Alex couldn't risk it. He'd have to pray that Tiffany would be all right until he could get back to the boat. His mind raced a thousand miles a minute.

As Simon handed him the number, he said, "Now, after tonight, lose this number. It's private, you know. I'm not supposed to be reached out here on my little oasis."

Conjuring up a weak smile, Alex grabbed Tiffany and kissed her gently. "I'll call you as soon as I know something for sure, okay?"

Tiffany seemed happy to see that Alex was holding up his end of parenting. "Try to give me a call by ten-thirty. Otherwise, you know I'll be worried about you."

Alex waved quickly as he turned and jogged back down the pier. He was really under the gun now. Leave it to Simon to screw up the plan. He had a lot to do in very little time, without a moment to lose.

HIS FATHER WAS in the park by the Fourteenth Street Bridge at nine-forty on the dot. Alex and Anya gurgled and squirmed in their car seats, while Alex's father and Foody sat looking around.

"Boy, where's your wife?" his father questioned loudly as Alex recklessly careened up to the cab. Foody fumbled out of the cab and lumbered over to Alex's car.

"There's been a change of plan. I don't know if Simon suspects anything or not, but he wouldn't let her leave the party. Did you get Mrs. Stiles out?" Alex craned his neck to see his kids. "How are my kids doing?"

"The kids are fine. And I got that woman out the house. I told her that I decided to take the kids for the evening, and that she could have the evening off. You might need to watch her too, boy. She was out of there before I could get the babies in the car good."

Alex checked his watch again. "Dad, you've got to get my babies out of here. Can you get Mrs. Owens to watch them for me until we can get back? She's the only person I'd trust."

"What about Lisa?" Foody inquired, digging in his PC bag and pulling out a Krispy Kreme doughnut.

"No time," Alex said, narrowing his eyes.

His father waved his arm. "No problem. I'll get them right over there. Then what you want me to do?"

Alex rubbed his temples, hoping that his plan wouldn't completely fall apart. "I need for you to be back at pier seven at eleven o'clock. I'm going to call the boat at ten-thirty to have them bring Tiff back by eleven. Then I want you to get her, take her to the babies, and get them the hell out of town."

"Got it. Anything else?"

"At precisely ten thirty-five, I want you to call D.C. Cellular and have them take this number out of service," Alex said as he handed his father Simon's private telephone number. "I want to make sure no one else can get through, and I don't want Simon to be able to make any calls. I definitely don't want to raise his suspicions any further."

Foody perked up. "Yo, Alex, give me the number. I can hack that joint in a second, and make it so it won't never ring."

"You sure?" Then Alex realized who he was talking to.

"Yeah, I'm sure." Foody nodded with a half-cocked grin.

"Ten thirty-five, Foody. And not a moment later."

Alex turned back to his dad and told him to make sure he picked up Tiffany. Alex was confident that Foody could handle the technical stuff.

"Got it, son."

"And Dad?"

His father looked up pensively as he made notations in his cabbie's log. "Yeah?"

"Thanks."

DRIVING LIKE A maniac, Alex tried to reach the warehouse before ten o'clock. He filled Foody in as much as possible, and Foody became more enthralled with every detail. By the time Alex ditched the car behind an abandoned building and pulled on an overcoat to disguise his tux, he was ready. He grabbed his father's .45 from the glove compartment, crammed a piece of rope in his pocket, and then he and Foody hurried over to the warehouse.

Fortune had a curious expression on his face when he saw them, Alex walking fast, and Foody huffing and puffing, coming down the block.

"Man, I can't believe you came down in that tux. They'll shoot you just for lookin' wrong. And who's this? Fat Albert?" He flicked a thumb in Foody's direction.

"I got your Fat Albert, you crack head," Foody snarled.

Alex struggled to untie the bow tie and opened his shirt collar. "All right, all right, you two. Look, they can't see it under this coat. Anyhow, where is Blinky?"

"Where I said he'd be. Over there stuffing his face. A few minutes later, you woulda missed his ass. Look, it's almost ten, and he's sitting over there picking fish bones out his teeth, gettin' ready to book."

Alex looked from the shadows of the darkened alley and saw a man sitting by the dock, just as Fortune said. He was alternating his glances between the activities of the harbor and the back door of the building.

"Okay, Fortune. I've got it from here. You and Foody stay out here and watch my back. Make sure nothing goes down. I'm going to waltz in there with Mr. Blinky, get what I need, and waltz him back out. Once I have him back here, you tie him up and call the feds."

Fortune wrinkled his nose. "Waltz over there? All you gonna do is go get some lead in yo' ass. You know you should let me do that, Alex. After all, I ain't got nothing to lose. You go up in there, get smoked, that's it. They'll make you the bad guy and Moses will still walk, and be the hero."

"Yeah, Alex, let him go. He really ain't got nothing to lose," Foody said.

"I've got to do it. I've got to make sure I get what I need, and only I can do that."

"When a man's back is against the wall, and you know who put it there, it's personal." Fortune nodded, accepting the code of the street. "But at least let me help you with this one."

Before Alex could say no, Fortune was stumbling over toward Blinky.

"Yo, Blink. Is that you? Well, you old son of a bitch!" Fortune acted like he was drunk, stumbling and stammering.

Blinky looked up, astonished, and demanded, "Who the fuck is that?" He dropped his greasy sandwich on the ground and immediately reached for his pocket.

"Yo, it's me. Me, man. You know, Fortune. Used to be one of your hardest workers."

Blinky stood. "Well, you little son of a bitch," he said, walking toward Fortune. "Long time no see. You know, we've been looking for you."

Fortune raved with drunken laughter. "Well, Blinky, I always knew your eyes was bad, but damn. You must not've been looking too tough."

As Blinky reached to pull out his gun, Alex jammed his gun barrel deep in his back. Fortune straightened up immediately.

"I'll take that," Alex said as he reached in Blinky's pocket and tossed Fortune the .38.

"Who the fuck . . . ?" Blinky stammered as he tried to turn around.

"I wouldn't do that if I were you," Alex warned with a ferocity he'd never before displayed. The nervousness had dissipated. He was working on raw nerve.

"Hold up. I bet there's more where that came from," Fortune said. He patted Blinky down and immediately dispensed a pager, mobile phone, and two other guns.

"May-maybe we can talk, fellas. I—I ain't trying to cause you no problems. But I don't think you know what you're doing." Blinky held his arms out to the sides.

"We know enough. Enough to know that I'm an interested businessman tonight, and I want you to take me to your office. Now, what I want you to do is walk nice and slowly over to the door and get me upstairs. Act calm, let me get what I came here to get, and you won't get harmed."

"Hey," Blinky said. "I know you."

Swinging the old man around, Alex pointed the barrel of the gun at his temple. "Now you know the face."

Both Blinky's and Alex's faces registered surprise. "Well, go figure. This is the man that I happened upon one night at work. He was supposed to be the cleaning man."

"Aw, shit. You done gone and done it now, little rich boy. You've dug a hole yo' ass can't get out of. You don't know what you're doing here. You better get yo' ass back uptown and forget you ever saw me here," Blinky warned, his red eyes blinking.

"I know enough, and if you ever want to know anything else, you'll do as I say, or otherwise I'll put you out of your misery now."

Blinky clutched his chest. "You—you know, I—I got this condition. Heart condition. I—I can't take a lot of stress. See, I—I got this Medic Alert button hanging around my neck just in case I feel an attack coming on. In fact, I—I feel one coming on now." He tried to press the button, but Alex cocked the gun.

"If the years of dealing drugs and killing folks hasn't stressed you out, tonight sure as hell won't. But just in case, if I see you reaching for it again, I'll make sure you won't die from a heart attack. It'll be from a gunshot wound right between those crossed eyes."

Fortune stared at his protégé, then looked up into the darkened sky and gave Ivan the thumbs up. "Well, awright, little brother. Now that's how you handle yo' bidness."

Blinky reluctantly did as he was instructed. As Fortune stood watch, Blinky led Alex and Foody past the myriad security guards to the elevator. Finally, they were on the same floor where Alex had been earlier. All the while Blinky kept warning Alex under his breath to quit now before it was too late. Alex refused to listen to a word he said. Instead, he checked his watch, which read 10:05.

Tonight, almost every door on the floor was open. The floor was abuzz with noise from faxes, and as they walked by the rooms with the video monitors and the sound of machines humming, Alex was unsettled; he knew these were the people who had recorded his every step.

The few people in the corridor barely acknowledged their presence. It was as if they were conditioned to avert all eye contact, blend into the background, and it suited them just fine.

When they reached the office, Blinky pretended he couldn't get in. "You—you know, I can't find my keys. I really don't think I have them."

Alex nudged him in the back with the gun, which was still in his pocket. "Better find them quickly, Blinky. Or that won't be the only thing you lose tonight. You won't have those eyes to blink with anymore."

Blinky reluctantly opened the door, and they walked into the office. Alex took the gun out of his pocket and pointed it at Blinky. "Check to make sure no one's in there," Alex said as he motioned toward the door where the maps were located. In the meantime, he tried to lock the office door behind them.

Blinky stuck his head in and mumbled, "It's clean."

Alex pointed Foody in the direction of the war room. "Get as much info as you can," Alex said.

"Got it, dude." Foody whipped the laptop off of his shoulder.

Motioning for Blinky to sit, Alex took a piece of rope from his pocket. He proficiently bound Blinky's hands behind his back, staring at him with contempt.

"I swear, boy. You better quit now. Cut your losses before it's too late."

Alex grabbed the gun again and placed it near Blinky's mouth. "Shut up, old man. I don't want to hear another word from you, except where the keys are to these file cabinets."

Blinky defied him, pressing his lips together until they turned white. He remained silent as Alex roughly frisked him, and snatched a set of keys from his breast pocket. "Well, don't tell me, then. I'm sure that'll get some brownie points for you from Simon. They might do you some good once you get to prison."

Alex grabbed the keys and tried several before the file cabinet he'd searched earlier that day opened. He kept eyeing Blinky, uncertain if he'd try anything.

What Alex saw inside rendered him speechless. There were files on everyone Simon had ever been in contact with. His own file was at least two inches thick, and there was even one on Alex II and Anya. It figured that Simon, the quintessential planner, would have everything on file, in addition to the computer.

Increasingly aware that he was running out of time, Alex was still drawn to the files. He couldn't resist looking to see what Simon could have on his newborn children.

Simon had established Swiss and Grand Cayman bank accounts in both of their names. Obviously, he was using their social security numbers to hide his ill-gotten gains. There was over three million dollars funneled into their accounts.

Outraged, Alex slammed the drawer closed. There was too much information here. As he slipped as many files as he could under his coat, he knew he'd never get the computer files out as well, and it would be a waste of time trying to get any information out of Blinky.

So Alex did the next best thing. Between pointing the gun at Blinky and checking the door, he pried open the covering of the computer with a pair of scissors and hastily ripped out the hard drive.

Then, he noticed the time. Ten-twenty. He had to call Tiffany before she got too worried. He slipped the hard drive into his pocket, pulled out his mobile phone, and called the ship. Just like Simon said, Scotty answered.

Alex made every effort to sound calm and controlled, with a rehearsed inflection of concern. "Yeah, Scotty, this is Alex. Um, my baby boy's really sick, and I think his mother should come on back. How far out are you? Can you have her back around eleven o'clock?"

"Don't worry, Alex. I'll be sure to have her back by then. You want to talk to her?" Scotty asked.

"No, it's okay. I'll just see you then."

Before Alex could click over, Blinky tried yelling out, and Alex punched him in his face.

Suddenly the door opened, and two of Simon's henchmen came in, guns drawn.

"Hold up. Drop the piece, brother. What's up with this shit?" one of them yelled as he pointed a gun at Alex.

Blinky glared at them. "I'm glad you boys showed up. We got us a situation here. Now, somebody help me untie this rope."

Alex laid the gun on the desk and held his arms up. Just as one of the henchmen turned to help Blinky loosen the rope, a lead pipe appeared from nowhere, and landed on his head. The pipe continued swinging, striking the other gunman, and knocking him down to the floor. They were both out cold. Fortune stood in the doorway, grinning.

"I told you, your blood wasn't goin' to be on my hands too."

Blinky groaned and threw his hands up in the air, then slumped back down in the chair.

Foody reappeared, a puzzled look on his face. "What's going on?" He surveyed the two bodies on the floor. "Anyway, every-thing's cool. I tapped into their mainframe and I'm sending the files to, well, you know where," he said, his voice low and dra-matic, as if he were in some spy movie. "It's gonna take a little while. But I didn't forget. At ten thirty-five, I'll send the code in to the telly."

Fortune picked the guns up from the floor and tossed one to Foody. "Come on, big boy, make yourself useful. Find some duct tape or something and tie these knuckleheads up." He turned to Alex and said, "Now, go on, get out of here, Alex. We got it un-der control. If Blinky tries something, I'll stomp a mud hole in his ass. Now, go down the stairs. It'll put you out right by the door. The guard won't see you. And don't worry, we got these bastards covered."

Alex looked at the two of them, both holding guns and looking like something out of a blaxploitation movie. But it was an exhila-rating moment, and Alex felt great love for them. "Okay, Fortune.

And thank you, Foody. I owe you, man. But I've got to run. Don't forget to call the feds. Call them now. Tell them to get their asses over here, pronto. There's a whole lot of shit here they can use, but I can't wait for them. I've got to go get Tiffany."

"Don' sweat it, partner. It's cool. Now, quit lollygagging and get yo' ass outta here!" Fortune said.

AS FORTUNE HELD the mobile phone, dialed 411, and asked for the FBI, Blinky broke into peals of laughter. "Ain't this a sight. A damned drug-addict, pipe-head, skid-row bum calling the FBI. I bet they'll take this shit very seriously."

"Shut up, Blinky. I'm 'bout tireda all yo' noise. One mo' peep outta you, and that's it," Fortune said, dragging his finger across his throat. "I still ought to break my foot off in yo' ass, just for old times' sake." Waiting impatiently, Fortune soon realized that the wheels of justice grinded pretty slowly. He was put on hold, and listened to mind-numbing music as he waited for a live person to answer the phone. After a few agitated minutes, someone finally answered, and he tried fervently to get directed to the right department.

Blinky acted quickly and pushed the Medic Alert button around his neck. Foody caught his eye as he whispered into the mike. He ran over and snatched the alert from around Blinky's neck, his reaction seconds too late.

Fortune, entangled in the conversation with the dense operator, dropped the receiver and ran over and shoved the gun in Blinky's mouth, hissing, "Tell me what you just did! Tell me, you son of a bitch!"

Fearing nothing, Blinky pushed the gun from his mouth. "Go 'head, Fortune. Do me. It don't matter. In fact, don't even worry about it. 'Cause in ten minutes, there won't be a damned thing left here for them to find," he said as he twirled the Medic Alert around. "Not me, and damn sure not you two."

Emergency lights started flashing in the building, and a high-pitched alarm sounded. Murmurs of voices and footsteps filled the hallways, and Fortune panicked.

Snatching the alarm from Foody's hand, Fortune hurled it against the wall. Cocking the trigger, he swore. "Damn you, Blinky. What the fuck did you just do? I should've killed your ass when I had a chance."

"Could've, would've, should've. Go ahead, pull it. 'Cause if your black ass ain't outta here in ten, we'll both be dead." Blinky laughed wickedly.

Fortune glanced over at Foody. "If this fool says we got ten minutes, then that mean we got a whole lot less than that. Oh shit—"

Blinky cracked up, his voice resonating like that of a madman.

CHAPTER 18

SIMON'S beeper vibrated and he quietly excused himself from his guests. Scotty had just told him that Alex called to say he wanted Tiffany home, and that he planned on anchoring the yacht, and taking her back on the small motorboat.

Simon headed to the bridge, where Scotty was slowing the boat down. "We'll all head back, Scotty. Make an announcement, giving them my regrets, but tell them that we're going back to shore because one of my grandchildren is sick."

The vibration was Blinky's code that something bad had gone down, and Simon had to find out what was up. He went down to his bedroom and checked the communication station in his bureau. The red light was flashing. The ultimate disaster had occurred. But who?

When Simon pressed the audio button, he immediately knew something was wrong. Someone had cracked his code, and now code blue was in effect. His mind ticked like a bomb. Who could've been the trigger? The feds? Couldn't be. The CIA? One of his competitors? When he heard Blinky's message, he reached into the hidden compartment over his bed and pulled out a shiny nine-millimeter gun.

WHEN ALEX ARRIVED at the pier, it was deserted. There was no Scotty, no motorboat, and no Tiffany. He tried not to be alarmed, and reasoned that they were probably still en route. The documents and hard drive were safely hidden in the rental car, and he was prepared for the unknown. The darkening sky overhead indicated that a storm was on the horizon. Alex shook off the dreariness of the night with resolve. He could not break down now, even as the beads of sweat popped out on his brow. There was no way Alex was turning back. Fortified by the .45 tucked in the small of his back, he ran down the pier and began looking up and down the harbor for signs of the boat.

It was then that Alex saw the *Masquerade* charging up the harbor. He was relieved, yet nervous. Why would Simon have turned the boat back? He couldn't flip out. If Scotty promised to bring Tiffany back, he would. Maybe Tiffany didn't want to ride the smaller boat back to the harbor.

Alex stayed focused on the boat, watching intently as it maneuvered the channel. Suddenly, out of nowhere, there was a thunderous bang that made him cover his ears. As a red fireball shot in the air, Alex could see a horrifying blaze illuminate the sky. The flames roared across the harbor in Anacostia, but he quickly dismissed it as just one of those things. There was always something going on over there.

Before Alex could glance back toward the boat, it was pulling up to the dock. There were blaring noises landside, as it seemed that every fire truck in the city was turning on its ear-piercing sirens and heading over to Anacostia. After a few moments of negotiating the slip, Scotty shut off the boat's engines and tossed out one of the lines. He tied down the boat, and opened up the gangway. Simon was on deck, offering his sincere apologies to everyone for cutting the evening short, and promising them a nice long ride in the near future.

Alex approached the boat cautiously, and as the departing guests filed past, they assured him that the babies would be okay. Two of the last guests to leave were Howard and Mrs. Bidwell. She hugged Alex warmly and uttered words of support that fell on deaf ears. Even Howard managed to muster up a few comforting words as he breezed by. Alex played it cool.

"Simon, where's Tiffany?"

Simon continued shaking hands and saying good-bye. "Well, she's suddenly not feeling too well either. One of the doctors on board gave her something, and now she's lying down in one of the staterooms."

As the last partygoer left, Scotty walked over to Simon and their heads met. They whispered briefly, then Scotty grabbed his bags and walked off into the night.

Alex trailed Scotty's disappearing figure for a few moments, and then turned back to Simon. "Listen, Simon. I know that Tiffany might not be feeling too well, but we need, I mean *I* need to get her home."

Simon pursed his lips, and he drew on his pipe. "What's going on, Alex? Why so tense? You're looking a little disheveled. Come on, you haven't even had a drink with me tonight. Haven't even anted up any money for my reelection. If I didn't know better, I'd swear you didn't want me to win." He placed a strong arm around his shoulder, and guided him toward the bridge. "You're not secretly plugging my opponent, are you, son? You're not out to sabotage my campaign, are you?" Simon winked at him playfully. "I'm just kidding. Come, have a drink with me."

Simon's grip tightened on Alex's shoulder, and he tensed up. There's no way that Simon could know anything, Alex told himself. He knew that Fortune would have taken care of Blinky and the operation, so he had to calm down. He was totally repulsed at Simon's touch, and could almost visualize Ivan's blood on Simon's outstretched palms. Alex wanted to pull away, but he calmly yielded to Simon's request.

"Just a quick one, Simon. Then Tiff and I must get back to the kids. Plus, it looks like the weather is getting bad," Alex said, pointing to the sky.

Simon led him out to the upper deck, then began helping himself to the crystal glassware behind one of the many serving stations. The blaze Alex heard and saw across the water must have been upgraded to a three-alarm, for the sound of the sirens was now almost deafening.

"Must be some kind of blaze going on over there," Alex said, attempting to sound casual.

"Well, you know how it is. The natives must be restless tonight."

Simon filled the snifters with aromatic cognac, and grandly presented one to Alex. "Drink up, my boy. Here's to a successful election year." Simon extended his snifter to toast, and after their glasses clinked, he took a large gulp of the vintage cognac. Alex hesitated.

"What's the matter, son? Not in a drinking mood tonight?"

Alex thought fast. "Well, Simon, the baby is really on my mind right now. I'm trying to keep my head straight. I guess I'm just a little tired and worn out from it all. You know how fatherhood is."

"Oh, come on. One little sip won't hurt you."

Alex sipped the cognac, wincing slightly at its bitter taste. Not a habitual cognac drinker, he'd thought this top-shelf liquor would have been a lot smoother.

They stood by the rail, absorbing the warm summer evening. The water rippled below them in the lights of the boat. But the clouds overhead looked threatening. Alex poured some cognac over the side of the boat when Simon wasn't looking.

"So tell me, Alex. I was trying to reach you this afternoon. Where might you have been hiding?"

"I was out scouting places for the new stadium. I think I just may have a spot, but I want to do some more research." He fingered the rim of the snifter nervously, hoping that his decision to tell the truth wouldn't trip him up later.

"Well, I hope it wasn't over in Anacostia." Simon pointed across the harbor. "It looks like it's going up in smoke. Looks worse than the riots in the sixties."

Alex followed Simon's arm, and realized that the fire was in the same vicinity as the warehouse was located. A feeling of overwhelming heat began raging in the pit of his stomach, hitting him so intensely that he knew something was terribly wrong. He had to get Tiffany out of there.

"Uh, uh, Simon, Tiff and I really need to go. . . ." His voice trailed off as his head began to reel. The boat rocked and swayed, and Alex felt himself spiraling downward.

Simon casually whisked the snifter from him and set it on the bar. "Careful, there. Don't want to break the Waterford. I think you better sit down, Alex. Looks like you're coming down with the same thing as your wife."

Alex's head was spinning. He groped around for the bench near the rail as Simon looked down on him, his face a montage of amusement and contempt. Alex tried to talk, but his windpipe seemed to be closing, and it was becoming difficult to breathe.

Simon continued to stare at him, playing with a gadget that was sticking out of his pocket. He pulled it up and placed it on his throat. When he finally spoke, it was as if he were a ghost from the past. This was the voice Alex had buried so deeply in his mind, when he heard it now, it made his heart stop.

"So why don't you tell me what you really did this afternoon. I didn't want to believe it, but I hear you've been a very bad boy." Simon stood motionless and expressionless.

Alex instantaneously recognized that the person speaking was the vicious, sadistic Deliverer from his college days.

It was all coming back to him now, all of the things that he had blocked. Hell Night rushed to the forefront. He remembered the smell. The pipe smoke. He remembered that suffocating feeling. He remembered him. Simon was Moses and the Deliverer.

"I can't believe this, Simon. Why didn't you ever tell me you were The Deliverer?"

Simon glanced away, and stared out over the water. It slowly began to drizzle.

"Answer me, damn it. Why didn't you tell me who you were?" Alex demanded, his voice cracking.

Simon turned to stare at him silently. He continued to ignore him, like a parent would an unruly child.

"What have you done to me, Simon? What are you talking

about, I've been a bad boy? What kind of foolishness is this? Just tell me where Tiffany is so we can go."

There was a dangerous edge to Simon's tone. "Don't worry about her, Alex. She'll be fine. If I were you, I'd be worried about my damned self."

Alex tried to move, but his body was not responding to the commands from his brain. His vision was blurring, and he began to panic as his heart raced. Clearly Simon had slipped something in his drink. Alex thanked God that he hadn't consumed it all. His mind traveled back to his college health course, and he tried to think of what to do to get this substance out of his system, quickly. It had to be some type of mind-altering drug. The harder he tried to force his body to react, the more it refused to respond even slightly.

"Relax, son. Don't try to fight it. Based on the amount of my little concoction that you swallowed, it'll all be over soon anyhow." Simon leered at him from the corner of his eye.

Alex grabbed the snifter from the bar and ran his finger around the inside. It was slightly oily. He smashed the crystal on the deck, while Simon laughed diabolically. Alex's stomach dropped.

"Poor little Alex. And I thought you were such a goody two-shoes. Tsk, tsk. What a pity. You could have had it all, you know. We could have really made this thing work."

Simon spread his arms out toward the city. "What made you think that you could take me down? Don't you know bigger, more worthy men than you have tried? You're just a little nothing that I picked up out of the gutter. Ungrateful little bastard, don't you know I made you? You of all people want to betray me? Drop a dime on me? I thought you were a lot smarter than that."

Simon snatched him up and shoved him against the railing. He pointed Alex's head toward the fire.

"You see that, you little punk? That's my shit. Don't pretend you don't know what I'm talking about. See that fire? Smell that smoke? How dare you! You ought to know me better than that. My people know how to protect me. Unlike you. Right after you left, I got the call. And guess what? Boom! Anything you might've seen is gone." Simon laughed evilly. "You're such a good lawyer. What's a case without evidence? Eh? Dismissed."

Alex's plans and dreams were going up in that smoke. What the hell happened after he left? What could've gone wrong?

"What a stupid move, Alex. I needed an heir to all of this, but you were just too damned smart for your own good. But if you think you owed me before, you really owe me now. You're in my pocket, boy. You cost me a lot of money."

Suddenly, Alex's legs began to tingle; he was regaining the feeling in them. Yet he had to convince Simon that he was still completely drugged.

Alex slurred his words for effect. "Wha, wha, wha you, are you talkin', talking about? I don-don't what you're talking about."

"You know damned well what I'm talking about. You think you know the deal. But let me tell you the real deal.

"You see, I have ruled this city for years. Then I let you into my life, and you think that you can teach the master. I brought you out of Hilliard and made you somebody. But did you appreciate it? Hell, no. The moment you get the opportunity to prove your loyalty, you fail. So you've failed me, now I'm going to fail you."

Simon shoved him back on the seat, which was slippery from the now pouring rain. "My own little Judas. I raised you like a son, and then you try something like this. Well, I guess I shouldn't be surprised. After all, betrayal is part of you, isn't it? Tell me something, O pious one. Did you ever tell Tiffany about that little one-night stand you had?" Simon peered into Alex's hapless face. "Didn't think so. But I'm sure she'd love to know now. Better late than never. I think I have another set of those pictures around here somewhere. To think my little choirboy is really just a low-down dog. Oh well, I guess neither one of us is perfect, are we, boy?"

"You-you have a lot of damn n-nerve, Simon. I should've known you—you sent those pictures to my house. That cheap, that was so, so cheap. Why didn't you just st-step to me with them, instead of nearly ruining Tiffany's preg-pregnancy?" It was difficult to slur his words when his anger made him quite lucid.

Simon smirked. "It wasn't about ruining Tiffany's anything. It was about you sticking your nose where it didn't belong. When you ran across my business associate, Mr. Blanks, I had to make sure you didn't think too much about it."

"You-you're a lying, murderous, evil son of a bitch. You're n-not so big and bad. You—you're a coward, Simon, sitting around watching people's lives that you've des-destroyed. You-you're just a common per-pervert. How dare you compare me to you. There was a time when I would've been—been proud to be like you, but not now."

"I suggest you shut up and take a seat, because you, me, and that pretty wife of yours are going to take a little ride. The only thing better would've been to have those two little ones of yours here. Oh well. I can play the grieving grandfather later, because you won't be coming back. Tragic, isn't it? Whatever you saw will be lost at the bottom of the Potomac with you. But that's okay, I'll play the mourning-father-slash-father-in-law. I'll be a shoo-in for reelection, if I can overcome my grief."

He shuffled around the slippery deck, oblivious to the rain and just sipping his cognac. "It'll make great press. Howard'll love this. 'Mayor's Daughter and Beloved Son-in-Law Perish in Freak Boating Accident.' Who knows, maybe I'll keep the little orphans. I need to keep them alive at least until I retire."

The blood rushed to Alex's head. "You bas-bastard. Leave, leave my children alone!" He lunged for Simon.

Simon grabbed him by the collar and snapped his head back. "Boy, don't be a fool." He caught Alex's jaw with a right cross, and knocked him to the deck. Alex lay there and pretended to be unconscious.

Straightening his tux, Simon gingerly placed the voice box back into his pocket. Kicking Alex with the stub of his patent-leather toe, he congratulated himself. "You still got it, Simon. You can still keep these punks in check." He gingerly lifted the anchor before going up to the bridge to begin the ominous voyage down the river.

ASSURED THAT SIMON was busy gearing up the boat for departure, Alex went searching for Tiffany. He stumbled in the darkened staircase that led into what appeared to be a lounge area under the upper deck. Its walnut-finished walls were handsome and refined, all the things Simon took great pains to be. Alex thought about the thug Simon really was, and wanted to kick himself for being so gullible. But he had no time to waste. He had to find Tiffany.

After opening several doors, Alex finally found her sprawled out in a very un-Tiffany-like position. He knew instantly something was wrong. He grabbed her and shook her furiously, hoping to revive her. Her pulse was weak. She was nearly comatose.

"Tiffany, wake up, baby. Tiffany." Alex wanted to yell, but didn't want to make too much noise.

Tiffany remained lifeless. Spotting a flower-filled vase, Alex tossed the flowers on the floor and splashed the water in her face. She barely responded. He kept shaking her, each moment becoming more and more frightened, wondering whether she'd ever awaken. After what seemed like an eternity, Tiffany opened her eyes, and he exhaled with relief.

"Wake up, baby. Oh, Tiffany. Get up. You've got to stay awake."

"Alex, is that you? Wha-what happened?" Tiffany's eyes were bloodred, and she was limp.

"Tiff, you've got to stay awake. You need to throw up now. Did you drink something your father gave you?"

Tiffany babbled incoherently. "I—I don't know. I think so, Alex. Oh, I don't know. I can't remember." She slumped back on the soggy bed.

"Tiffany, I'm going to stick my finger down your throat. It's the only way we can buy some time until I can get you to a hospital. But you've got to stay awake." Alex felt the boat pulling away from the pier. He figured that Simon would head toward Maryland and the Woodrow Wilson Bridge. He'd never steer the boat down by Virginia—too many white folks.

Alex estimated that he only had a few minutes before Simon would have the boat far enough beyond the bridge that he could drop anchor and toss them both over the side. Then he'd get on the marine radio, page the coast guard, and begin his stage act.

Alex rolled Tiffany over onto her stomach. Positioning her head off the bed, he helped her vomit. When she finished, he checked to see that her throat passage was clear, and then kept her on her stomach. Tiffany was still too groggy to move.

"Please don't leave me down here, Alex. I want to know what the hell is going on. Where's my father?"

Alex wiped his hands on the bedspread, then rubbed the back of her head. "Tiffany, I love you, but you're in no shape to move right now. I'm not leaving you; I've got to get you to a hospital, as soon as we get the boat back to shore. Just try to stay calm, sweetheart, and I'll be back to get you. Soon. Right now, Simon and I have some unfinished business."

THE SPRING SHOWER was nearly over, and Simon had killed the lights on the boat, and was maneuvering down the channel, past the seafood restaurants and crab houses. His chest stuck out as he looked out over the Fourteenth Street Bridge. The boat veered southward toward the Wilson Bridge. He jerked the wheel as a cold piece of steel pressed into his back.

"Raise your hands, Simon. And don't try anything. I want you to turn this boat around, nice and slow. Take it back to the pier. Right now." Alex pushed the barrel of the .45 into Simon's spine.

"Well, I don't believe it. Is that a gun, Alex, or are you just glad to see me?" Simon eased up on the throttle, but continued staring straight ahead.

"Turn the boat back. Back over there by the pier." Glaring, Alex stepped to Simon's side and tried to keep his hands from shaking.

"You disappoint me, Alex. We can talk about this, can't we?" Simon used his best politically savvy voice.

"Just turn it around. There's nothing more to talk about. A few minutes ago, you had no problem plotting my death, and now you want to talk. No way."

For once in all the time since Alex knew him, Simon took an order. He turned the wheel around in a deliberate manner.

"Why, Simon? Why'd you do it?" Alex gritted his teeth, and tried desperately to hide the fear that rattled his soul.

Simon continued maneuvering the boat through the calm waters. "You're just so naïve, Alex. If I didn't know any better, I'd
swear you were never from Shaw."

"Evidently, you didn't know any better, Simon. After all, it never
occurred to you that you'd murdered my own brother."

Simon swerved the wheel, causing the boat to skid. "What the
hell are you talking about?"

"Quit jerking this boat and take it back to the pier. I don't want
to have to hurt you, even though you've had no problem hurting
other people. But I will if I have to. You really don't remember,
do you? That's a pretty sad commentary. You've probably had so
many people killed that you don't even bother to remember. To
think that you were at the funeral, acting like you really cared."

"Funeral? What funeral? I've been to hundreds in my line of
work."

With balls of steel, Alex shoved the gun in Simon's face. "Back
in 1978, a kid, a promising basketball player from Cardonza, got
gunned down. He was blown away, right in front of my eyes, because somebody thought he was Fortune. Fortune Reed. One of
your little street hustlers."

Simon suddenly jerked the wheel and slammed the throttle
down. Alex, still slightly wobbly, stumbled, and the gun flew from
his hand. The boat careened toward the rocky coastline of Hains
Point. They fought for the gun, and it fired, blowing a hole in the
roof of the bridge.

They struggled on the slippery deck as the boat gained speed. It
was heading directly for the sandy embankment of the recreational
park; the light of the Washington Monument stood out against the
dark backdrop.

Alex shoved Simon closer to the deck's edge. "You know me
better than this. I'm not going out like this, Alex. I'll never let a
piece of ghetto trash take me down. Never."

"I've been out of the ghetto for a long time, Simon. And if I'm
trash, then you made me in your image. It's too late. I'm not about
to let you get away with anything else. Give it up. It's over. Stop
this boat before we all get killed."

Alex freed a hand and tried to grab Simon's arm, which was reaching for the gun, but Simon was too strong. After a renewed struggle, Alex finally wrestled the gun free, but it fell and slid off the deck as the boat, tilting sideways, sped toward land.

Simon stood. "Now what are you going to do, Alex? Now that you have no steel to help you? Boy, I ought to whip your ass for dirtying my clothes." Simon smoothed his tux and pulled out the 9-millimeter from his ankle strap. "Always come prepared. Always remember that."

"Daddy? Daddy? What's going on? Why do you have that gun on Alex?" Tiffany stood near the stairs, still groggy. Her face was wrinkled and perplexed.

Simon swung the gun in her direction. He instantly altered his demeanor. "Now, Princess, don't ask so many questions. Just come over here and get next to your good-for-nothing husband."

Alex lunged for the gun just as the boat collided with the embankment of the park, tossing them across the deck like limp rags. The acrid smell of fuel hung in the air. They had only moments to get off the boat before it burst into flames.

Simon furiously scrambled overboard. He leaped over the embankment wall, running like a thief into the pitch-black night, yelling, "I told you you'd never catch me!"

Bleeding from a cut on his arm, Alex struggled to help the semiconscious Tiffany off the burning boat. He carried her with all of his remaining strength, and barely made it as the boat became engulfed in flames.

His father's cab raced up from out of nowhere.

"What in the hell is going on here?" he hollered from the open car window.

Alex couldn't remember the last time he was so glad to see his father. "Dad! How'd you know where we were?"

Huffing and puffing, his father hotfooted it over to them. "I had just gotten to the pier when the boat pulled off. When there was no Tiffany, and no you, and I saw the boat moving, I knew something was wrong. So I followed it. It wasn't easy, but I followed it."

Alex eased Tiffany into his father's arms. "Dad, you've got to get Tiffany to the hospital. She's been poisoned, and she needs her stomach pumped."

"What about your arm? You need to get that checked too." He reached in his pocket and pulled out a handkerchief. "Tie that around your arm, son."

Alex grabbed the handkerchief and knotted it over the cut. "Look, Dad, you've got to hurry. The police, the coast guard, and every reporter in town will be here soon, and now is not the time to answer a whole lot of questions. Just get her there fast, okay?"

"I'll get her there. Don't worry. But where's Simon, or Moses, or whoever? If he's run off into these woods, you'll never find him. That country boy could probably crawl up a gnat's ass if he had too." He helped the confused Tiffany into the car.

"I don't know where he is, but I bet I know where he's going. He's got to get his stuff together, and try to leave town. I don't know what happened over at the warehouse, or what happened to Fortune or Foody, but I've got to stop Simon before he gets away."

A weak Tiffany struggled to talk. "I love you, Alex."

Alex put on a brave face. "I love you too, Tiff."

With immense effort, she grabbed his hand. "Alex, whatever you do, please don't forget what we talked about earlier."

Alex's bottom lip trembled as the anger swirled in him like a raging storm. If Simon had done her permanent damage, Alex silently swore that he'd kill him. At that moment, there was nothing and no one more important to him than she was.

"Don't worry, baby," he said, struggling for confidence. "Nothing's going to happen to you or to me. I promise."

Alex sprinted off in the direction he'd last seen Simon. The words he had spoken to Tiffany rang in his ears with each thud of his feet hitting the ground. He would never forgive himself if something happened to her. He had to find Simon and make him pay for what he'd done.

Alex's mind raced almost as fast as his feet. Simon wasn't in great shape, and he couldn't have been prepared to escape on foot. As Alex ran, he tried to think of the places he'd go to regroup and get whatever he needed to make his getaway. The warehouse had gone up in smoke, but Alex knew that Simon was resourceful enough to have a plan B.

There were a few cars parked out around the water, with couples in various stages of lovemaking. Alex scoured the area with his eyes, never breaking stride, looking for any sign of his fleeing former mentor.

It was a good half mile to Rock Creek Parkway, where Simon might be able to stop a passing car or hail a cab. Alex had to move faster, and as he approached the Lincoln Memorial, he saw Simon's shadowy figure trying to cross the busy thoroughfare.

Spotting Alex, Simon frantically tried to flag down a car. The driver took one look at him, clothes dirty and mangled, waving his arms like a lunatic, and sped away. As Alex got closer, Simon ran off in the direction of the memorial.

"Give it up, Simon. It's no use," Alex yelled, trailing after him.

Simon glanced back at Alex and headed toward the river. He crossed the darkened trails that led down to the piers, where a few motorboats were docked. Alex poured it on. He knew Simon would try to get away by boat, and now there were only a few yards between him and freedom. Alex stretched his leg muscles to the point of ripping.

Chest heaving, Alex closed in on Simon, then lunged for his back, bringing him down.

"Get off me, you fool." Simon scrambled to get away, yelling, "You just couldn't leave well enough alone, could you? You just couldn't let well enough alone."

Using all of his strength to try to hold Simon, Alex was practically out of breath when he tried to speak. Gasping, he begged, "Give it up, Simon. Just let it go. You had it good long enough, but it's over."

Simon kneed him in the groin, forcing Alex to lose his grip. He doubled over in pain.

"You just won't quit, will you? Always have to be so self-righteous. Well, come on, let's see what you're made of. I'm just going to have to get rid of you once and for all."

Struggling to his feet, Alex glared at Simon. "So you want to get rid of me, huh? Like you did your wife? Like you tried to do to your own daughter? You're just a cowardly bastard."

"I don't know what you're talking about."

"You have a very selective memory, don't you, Simon? Or should I just call you Moses?"

Simon swung so hard, he temporarily lost his footing. Alex grabbed him and clung to his midsection. "Listen, enough is enough. Too many people know about you and what you've done."

Breaking Alex's grip, Simon swung at him like Ali. His fist landed on Alex's throat, and sent him tumbling to the ground. "They can't prove a thing. It's hearsay. Inadmissible in a court of law."

Winded, Alex said, "If something happens to me, it'll be all over tomorrow's headlines. I—I took precautions, just in case. If I don't show up by tomorrow morning, your stuff is in the wind. Your whole story will be told on every television and radio broadcast in the country. You won't be able to hide under a rock without a TV camera shoved in your face."

Gasping for air, Alex kept talking. "I have enough information from your little hideaway to put your lying ass away for life. And don't think they'll set you up in one of those country club joints, either." The bluffing gave him enough time to get up on one knee. He'd be a dead man if he didn't get up quickly.

"They'll have to catch me first," Simon said with his usual bravado. "This ain't new to me. Don't think I'm going down that easy."

Alex shook his head in disgust. "You know, you make me sick. I finally see you for what you really are. Callous and evil."

Simon circled him and said, "I've been running for a long time. Maybe not forty years, but damn near. That's how I got my name. Just like Moses the Deliverer. He couldn't be stopped, and neither can I. Always remember that."

"They could have never called you Moses and meant it. Some damned deliverer you turned out to be. Delivering your people to crack. You got a lot of balls, Simon."

Simon grabbed his neck and squeezed. Alex's head wobbled as Simon shook him. The air escaped his lungs. Alex was getting dizzy. Breaking Simon's grip was nearly impossible; he was too exhausted. The drugs were still in his system, and his energy was sapped. He tried scrambling on the ground, anything he could, but his body was failing. As his oxygen supply was cut, he began to fade quickly. He was about to let go of life as he knew it.

Then, he was struck by a force greater than himself. Images of his mother and Ivan flashed in his mind. They begged him not to let go. Their voices, and the voices of all of Simon's faceless victims, called out to him. He was their last hope. Alex couldn't let them down. If he gave up, Simon would win. He'd slink off into the night, and no one would ever know the twisted truth. Once again, a Baxter would be left to die in shame.

Alex pushed himself beyond all limitations as the images of his mother and brother drifted off into the night. He fought for his life. Thinking about Tiffany and his children, he bulged with rage. He clutched his fist and swung his elbow into Simon's gut, causing him to double over.

The two men exchanged powerful blows. Simon charged him again, pinning his arms at his sides. Alex tried pushing Simon off him, but he was like lead draped on Alex's worn body. Simon struggled to throw him down the embankment. Alex stretched his hands and felt in his pocket. There it was, his saving grace, Ivan's old knife that Simon had returned to him.

They continued to viciously grapple, slipping on the muddy terrain. As they rolled down toward the edge of the water, Alex struggled with all of his might to reach the knife. Finally, he was able to grasp the handle. He pulled the knife out and waved the blade defiantly in Simon's face.

"Get off of me, Simon. I'll use it, I swear I will. I'll stick it so deep into you that they won't be able to remove it."

Simon's eyes shone brilliantly in the midnight air, his face proud yet surprised. "I don't believe it. You actually listened to what I've said."

"That was the problem. I always listened to what you said. I never exercised my better judgment. I should've seen you for what you were years ago."

Simon jerked away. "Don't even try it. You don't have the heart, you never did. You couldn't hurt me if you tried."

Alex stood, holding the knife on Simon. He shook the ringing words from his ears, and steadied his nerves. "Simon, it's over. Don't make me prove it, because I will hurt you. In fact, I'll stop at nothing, even if I have to kill you. I should kill you for what you've done, but I want to be the one you face in court. I'd love to personally prosecute you and send your ass to prison."

Simon laughed in his face. "You think you're that good, eh? Well, you haven't learned a damn thing, have you? I told you, I'll never go to prison. I don't belong in prison, Alex." Simon tried to sucker-punch him, swinging wildly and missing by a mile. Simon quickly grabbed for the knife.

Reacting swiftly, Alex blocked Simon's hands. Simon continued lunging for him, and lost his footing. His hulking frame went tumbling into the now choppy water.

"Alex, help me! Help me, son. Something's caught my pants leg, and it's pulling me down. Help! Don't let me die like this!"

Impulsively, Alex shoved the knife into his pocket and reached for Simon before he was able to secure himself to the shore. "Grab my arm!" he yelled.

Simon grabbed his arm, and immediately laughed that sinister laugh. "Sucker," he said as he snatched Alex into the water. "I knew you'd fall for that old line. You caved like a house of cards."

They thrashed in the water as the undercurrent began pulling them out into the channel. Alex scrapped like he'd never scrapped before, violently pounding Simon with his fists, exhausting every ounce of power.

"If you're man enough to take me out of here, then do it. Talk is cheap and who knows that better than me: I'm a politician. Just do what you gotta do." Simon laughed, sloshing water.

As Alex's mouth and nostrils filled with the disgusting Potomac River water, reality hit him with its final blow. It was do or die.

He pulled out the knife. It empowered him as his legs and arms weakened. With immense effort, he raised it out of the water, high enough so Simon could see his fate.

Simon grabbed his arm, but Alex resisted. The more Simon struggled against him, the more powerful Alex became. Alex held Simon's fate in his hands, and it showed in his eyes. The blade inched closer and closer to Simon's chest. Knowing he had no alternative, Alex closed his eyes and plunged the knife down deep into Simon's chest, shouting, "This is for you, Ivan!" as he dealt the lethal blow. Alex released the anger that permeated his soul, and repeatedly drove the knife into Simon's chest. The knife made a sucking noise as Alex pulled it out. Still struggling, Simon fought and cursed him until his grasp slipped, his strength fled. Finally, he gave way. Alex snatched himself from Simon's clutches, only to face the suction of the undercurrent. A large wave crashed over their heads. Finally able to breathe, and free from Simon, Alex struggled to keep his head above water.

Off in the distance, approaching sirens blared, and Alex prayed for a miracle. He fought with every tired muscle in his body to swim against the tide and get back to shore. He glanced back briefly, still clutching the knife. That battle was over. Alex was now fighting the river for his life, and it was a much more formidable adversary.

CHAPTER 19

SQUINTING as the bright lights burned his bloodshot eyes, Alex could barely lift his aching head. He caught a glimpse of himself in the mirrored wall behind Tiffany's hospital bed and cringed. He looked a wreck. Deep purple rings circled his eyes, and a fist print was embedded on his cheek. His clothes were ripped and dirty, and he felt like he'd been run over by a freight train. Every breath he took racked his body with pain. He rested his head on the bed rail.

Alex caught a cramp in his neck. He struggled cautiously to work the stiffness out and unkink the muscles, but he couldn't. It was too damned excruciating. Hot, agonizing tears singed his racoonish eyes as fiery spasms shot down his spine, and he writhed. *"Damn,"* he moaned, shutting his eyes in anguish. With his eyes closed, he blocked out the tortuous hospital lights and hoped to get relief from the searing pain.

The cover of darkness from his eyelids provided little solace. The pain and rampant thoughts in his mind made it impossible to concentrate, but he had to regroup. His left arm was jacked up, and he could barely maneuver his right. He carefully rested his throbbing head in his palm. He had lost track of precious time. An eternity seemed to have elapsed since he'd passed out on the cold metal railing surrounding the bed.

His mind wandered aimlessly, his thoughts garbled. Get a grip, he commanded himself. Sighing laboriously, Alex forced the fog from his brain, only to be reminded again of the hell he'd suffered the night before. Recounting the events, bitter words rang in his ears, and he tried to block them out. But they continued with a vengeance. Snippets of violence and mayhem merged and diverged, creating a vivid, painful collage on the canvas of his mind. The images cut like jagged pieces of broken stained glass, and Alex cursed under his breath at the pain that ravaged his thoughts. The entire bloody night replayed itself, and repulsion forced his stinging eyes open.

It had been such an extremely long night. Alex was still groggy from the painkillers the doctors had forced into him. When they dragged him into the hospital, he had been almost beaten to death, but he didn't want anything that would alter his state of mind. He vowed never to take another drug, not even alcohol. Being under the influence weakens you. Slows your roll. So, after arguing and threatening him with restraints, the doctors had conceded and agreed to give him the bare minimum, a tetanus shot and Tylenol 3. Maintaining a stream of thought was still difficult. Over the course of the last twenty-four hours, his whole world had flipped upside down, crumbling right before his very eyes. The only world Alex had known in his adult life was gone.

Alex opened his palms and cringed. His lifelines were shriveled, and there was still a trace of blood on his cuffs, the blood of Simon. The blood of the man Alex had loved like a father. The man who had helped mold and make him. The same man who had taken a shy, young boy and made him a man who would grow up and fight Simon for his life. The same man who would grow up to take Simon's life.

Swearing under his breath, Alex cursed Simon for all that he had done. The pain, the lies, the deception, the crimes. He felt like a fool for having accepted everything Simon had said or done without question. He should have known better, he was an attorney, for Christ's sake. Frustrated, Alex banged his leg with his one good hand, and felt the rigid sensation of metal in his pants pocket. Carefully leaning to reach into his pocket, he slowly pulled out the knife that he'd used to stab Simon.

Alex couldn't remember shoving the knife back into his pocket, the way he did again now, but he must have. It was the only evidence that linked him to Simon's death, and Alex contemplated what to do about it. By law, he was required to submit the knife into evidence, but maybe all of the years of working under Simon had gotten the best of him. Although he had only defended himself, did he really want the risk of criminal charges?

Wrestling with his conscience, Alex continued sitting patiently at the side of Tiffany's bed. Her breathing was shallow as she slept in a heavily sedated state. The sight of her made him wince. Her once gorgeous face was now swollen and puffy from the poison Simon had given her. Burning tears again sprang to his bloodshot eyes as he wondered if she would ever recover, physically and mentally, from the trauma she had endured the night before. He said a silent prayer, grateful that she was alive. It had all happened so quickly, and he had almost lost her. As unbearable as it was seeing her lying in that hospital bed, the alternative was worse. He could not live without this woman.

Alex sighed heavily, fighting back feelings of rage and helplessness. Deep down he knew he was to blame for her condition, and he hated himself. He should've known better. He traced her exposed arm with his fingers, and said another prayer for her recovery. Alex hoped that God and Tiffany would forgive him and that someday he would forgive himself. Her condition was serious but stable, upgraded since his dad had rushed her in. According to her doctors, the prognosis was favorable.

Alex reached for her hand. He thought about the conversation they'd had the day before, and how close he'd come to losing her, and how close their kids had come to being orphaned. Simon deserved to die, not only for this, but for all of the other heinous things he had done during his miserable life.

Alex prayed for the strength to tell her the truth. He wondered just how he was going to explain it all to her when she awoke. He remembered rushing out of the back of the ambulance, pushing past the cops to find Tiffany. Although his father had tried to calm him down, Alex refused to leave Tiffany's bedside, and the doctors treated him for minor injuries as he sat in a state of shock. He rubbed the sling that held his left arm tightly to his chest, the same arm Simon had pummeled over and over when they fought.

All of this was just too much to digest. It could not have happened, although Alex had the wounds and the bandages as evidence. He wished it were all a dream. But it wasn't. It was reality, and the dreams of hope and promise that he'd built his life around had been destroyed.

As the sun peeked through the closed window blinds, Alex rested his head on Tiffany's thigh. Suddenly Howard burst through the armed security that guarded Tiffany's door. He had that gleam in his eye, like the cat that had swallowed the canary. Alex wearily looked up, and placed his head back near Tiffany's side.

Howard threw the June 27, 1992, edition of the *Post* into his lap, and waited with anticipation. Alex was unsure just how much Howard knew, but at this point, he really didn't care. Howard would weasel out of it, no matter what. Plus, Simon probably had told Howard nothing, keeping the Moses part of his life separate and distinct from his persona as Simon.

"I'll have you to know that I've done a magnificent job of keeping the press at bay, and spent the morning attending press conferences and media blitzes," Howard said. "I'm sure you'll find my services invaluable."

As Alex read the headlines, he was astonished. They provided a stunning version of the events that had led up to Simon's presumed death, for the coast guard was dredging the channel even as Alex read. The reports merely indicated that there had been a mechanical failure on the boat, which had caused it to crash, seriously injuring Tiffany, while Alex had received minor wounds. Simon had been thrown from the boat on impact and was presumed dead. There was no mention of the warehouse, federal agents, the big fire, nothing. It was as if the events of the night had never happened.

Alex jumped up and shoved the paper into Howard's chest. Trying to keep his voice low, he said, "Get out of here with this bogus bullshit. How dare you come in here with this."

Howard took the paper, folded it nice and neatly, and laid it on the foot of the hospital bed. "I suggest you read this carefully, Alex. You may want to know what you said, since I no longer have a job. You may want to rethink that decision. Who knows, you just may be the next mayor and need a good PR man."

Alex stared him squarely in the eyes. "Look, Howard, Simon is dead. I don't take orders from him anymore, and I damn sure won't start taking them from you. Now, do I have to call security or what?"

Howard held his hands up in jest. "Okay, okay. I was just trying to help. I know you're a little upset right now. Calm down a little bit, and get your thoughts collected. After a day or so, you'll want to call me. You have the number." Howard glided over to the door, a cocky smirk on his face.

The door suddenly opened. "What's up, youngblood? This slick, candy-ass nigga givin' you a hard time? Just say the word. I got somethin' for his ass." It was Fortune, dressed like an orderly, and holding a package. Alex had never been so happy to see him.

"Fortune, man, I—I didn't know what had happened to you. I thought, well, I just knew you got it. Man, am I glad to see you. Hey, where's Foody, man?"

Fortune shook his head, never taking his eyes off Howard. "Now, you know I'm like an old alley cat. I still got about four lives left. A man that's been playing dead long as I have ain't ready to die just yet. Now, what about three-piece over here?" He stepped brazenly in Howard's face.

Howard, always one step ahead of the game, hastened his

departure. "I'll be talking to you real soon, Alex," he said, as he briskly walked out the door. Turning back, he added, "And by the way. If I were you, I'd really be a little more careful around knives from now on."

Alex tried to respond, but Howard darted out the door into the swarm of police officers and press. Alex stared at the closing door, rushing to slam it shut.

"What he mean by that?" Fortune asked.

"That smug bastard. He's probably just fishing for something. He always acts like he knows everything, and I guess he wants me to play his game. But I'm not." Alex swung his head back in Fortune's direction. "Man, where did you get that outfit?"

A smile cracked Fortune's lips, and before he could respond, Alex threw a hand up in the air. "Never mind. Don't answer."

"Now, you know how resourceful I am. I knew it'd be harder than a mug to get up in here, so I had to prepare myself. You know what I'm sayin'?

"But, Alex, I got some bad news. Your boy ain't make it. I tried to get him outta there, but he wouldn't go. He kept saying that he ain't wanna let you down no more, said he was trying to get those files sent. I swear, I really tried, but he stayed up in there. He said he was gonna stay till he got you what you needed."

Alex leaned against Tiffany's bed and massaged his temples. Tears burned his eyes. "No way. You mean Foody didn't make it out?" Alex turned his head so Fortune couldn't see the tears forming.

"Naw, I ain't see him. But I know that cat hooked you up, though. He said he wasn't gonna let you down no more. He was gonna make sure he sent that stuff to you through that computer or something."

Alex blinked, thinking that Foody's death was just another one that could be accredited to Simon. He suddenly understood how Fortune felt having Ivan's blood on his hands. Now Alex had Foody's on his.

Alex felt numbed by it all. He motioned with his sling at Tiffany, who was still sleeping peacefully. "That damned Simon. He's taken away almost everyone that I cared for. Now I don't even know what happened to him."

Fortune looked at him strangely. "Yeah, well, it looks like old boy got some of you, with your arm all messed up and shit. But, what you mean? What happened to Moses?"

Alex shrugged, then rubbed his aching shoulders. "I stabbed him, Fortune. I didn't have a choice. I stabbed him with that same damned knife that has haunted me from my days at Hilliard. I stabbed him dead in his chest, over and over. It was like déjà vu."

"Day-jah who?"

"Like it had happened before. Like when I fought Sidney, except I know Sidney lived. All I can remember is fighting that under-current trying to get back to shore and him slipping out of my hands as he was being pulled under. So I don't know what happened to him. I don't like to think that I killed a man."

Fortune stroked his chin. "It was either you or him, right?"

Alex nodded, and sighed slowly.

"You ain't have no choice, Alex. It be like that sometimes. Plus, his ass deserved to die."

Fortune's words of comfort failed to soothe Alex's tortured mind. "It bothers me, Fortune. In fact, it kind of unnerves me. I was right there, but I swear I don't remember shit. I don't even re-member how this knife got in my pocket." Alex revealed it to him.

Fortune's brows knitted, and he bit his chapped lower lip. "That's some weird shit. But, if you was drinking some of that river water, you bound to be hallucinating for days. You better ax them for something to take care of that shit."

They chuckled, a welcome yet brief reprieve from the gloomy air that surrounded them. Fortune sighed. "I don't know, Alex. I just don't know. That dude ain't like a cat, he's like a damned mountain lion. If a cat's got nine lives, his ass got about ten. I'm goin' to put the word out, but, man, there ain't no way he could've survived all of that. Not in that nasty-ass Potomac. He was a mean son o' a bitch, but he was human, I guess. If you stabbed the brother in his chest like that," he made a powerful, overly animated gesture, "that oughtta have done it. I don't know what else to tell you, 'cept you know I got your back."

Alex said nothing, but mulled Fortune's words over and over in his mind. Maybe Fortune was right.

Fortune handed him the package. "Anyways, this is for you."

Alex took it and opened it slowly. Inside was Ivan's old letterman's jacket, neatly preserved in a plastic dry-cleaning bag, and the stack of letters his father had tossed into Ivan's grave.

"I don't believe this. How'd you keep this all of these years?" Alex rifled through the correspondence and ripped the plastic off and held the jacket up. It was in remarkable condition, just like it was in 1978.

"I ain't even gonna front, it ain't been easy. Many a time I thought about hocking this bitch, but I promised Ivan that—"

"I don't know what to say. This is too unreal. It's unbelievable." Alex's eyes filled, and he choked back tears. "Thanks, man. I'm going to treasure this for the rest of my life. I feel like I owe you so damned much."

"Now, don't you go gettin' all jelly on me and shit." Fortune winced.

"Naw, man. It's just the painkillers wearing off," Alex said, not missing a beat.

The men smiled at each other. Alex finally broke the silence. "But for real, Fortune. I owe you so much, I can't ever repay you. I haven't seen you for years, then, overnight, it's like you never left."

"It's like Ivan and me ain't never leave."

Alex wiped his eyes. His guard was down, and he was okay with it. He finally understood the closeness between Fortune and Ivan. Alex could feel it. A calmness washed over him as he realized their bond had only gotten stronger over the years. The only change was that now he was finally a part of it. He wanted to lift his head and talk to Ivan too.

"I know what you mean, man. I know that my big brother is watching out for me, and I need the both of you to help me through this. I've got some serious cleaning up to do. I've got my family to be concerned about, and even though none of that shit showed up in the papers, I'm worried. I don't know who knows what, who may be out to finish us off, or whatever. Simon had to have left a lot of enemies out there, and folks are going to be looking to me for answers. Answers that I just don't have."

"The answers to what, baby?" Tiffany's voice was weak, still groggy from the sedation.

Alex beamed. She had finally awakened, and she recognized him. He couldn't wait to hold her in his arms. He walked back over to her bedside, praying that the answer to her question would come. So many other questions remained; this was only the beginning.

Alex suddenly realized he was well prepared to deal with them. He'd been taught by the master. The master of the silver tongue, the master of deceit and deception. And Alex had been an outstanding student. He had always listened to exactly what Simon said.

Acknowledgments

I would like to first thank my Lord and Savior, Jesus Christ. Thank You for giving me a "second chance." To my mother, Frances, thanks for instilling in me a profound sense of being. Your love, spirituality, and support are immeasurable. To my father, Leonard, thanks for making me believe that nothing is impossible, as long as I'm willing to work for it. To Grandma Susie, my "hush-buddy," I can't imagine my life without you. To Lynette, thanks for being more than a sister, you've been my friend. To Linda, thanks for always giving me a different perspective on things, and for looking out for Chad. To my nephews and nieces, Brandon, Mickey, Morgan, and Portia, always remember to follow your dreams. To Mary and Yolande, my favorite cousins, your love and support have helped in more ways than you'll ever know. Y.B., thanks for being more than just my "bottle buddy." To Twanda and Crystal, you're like my eldest and youngest sisters. Take care and thanks for always looking out for me and mine.

To my family: the Palmers, the Lakins, the Browns, the Mumfords, the McIvers, the Applewhites, the Campbells, the Woods, the Savages, and the Fishers. Thanks for making the fabric of my life stronger. To my best friend, Greg Parrish, thanks for hanging with a sister for over twenty years. To Mrs. Gaunt and Ida Hutchison, thanks for always looking out for me.

To my partner in crime, Dywane Birch, thanks for making this journey so incredibly fun and interesting. I can't tell you how important you are to me.

And to my boyz: Brian Garland, Gene Lowe, Rodney Akers, Don Johnson, Louis Thomas, DuJuan Brown, Mike Walker, Toney Monroe, Mike Graham, Will Smith, Reggie Oliver, Darrell Morgan, Quentin Peterson, Darnell Carpenter, Mario Scribner, and

Emile Brown. And to my girlz: Ros Murphy, Barbara Coles, To-mika Reid, Loreen Williamson, Tanya Mena, Brenda Brown, Leola Thompson, Tinya Coles, Pat Sugick, Yolanda Ezell, Kim Montgomery, Sandy Watson, Lisa Jeffress, Val Robertson, Tina Dowhite, Brenda Miller, Sandi Holly, and Colyn Chege. You've been my special friends for more than a minute, and there would not be a whole me without you.

And finally, to Pastor Gilmore, Sharon, and Carlyn. Your courage is awe-inspiring. You are living testimonies to His healing power. Keep making me believe in miracles.

To my Shero, Zane. I can't thank you enough for your inspiration, support, and encouragement. Thanks for hooking a sister up. You are a very special person, and I'm glad to call you my friend. You're who I want to be when I grow up!

To my agent, Sara Camilli. Thanks so much for welcoming me into your fold. I truly feel honored, and really appreciate your support and motivation.

To my editor, Melody Guy. Thanks for taking me into the Random House family. You're great to work with, and I'm looking forward to a long and successful future with you.

To the many bookstores and book clubs that took a chance on an unknown author and showed your love and support. Thanks so much. I'll never forget the kindness and words of encouragement.

To all my family, friends, sorors, and acquaintances. I appreciate all that you've been in my life. I wish I could name each of you individually, but space limits me. Any omissions, please charge to my head and not my heart.

In memory of Auntie (Margaret Palmer), Aunt Mildred Lakins, my uncles Alphonso, Chris, Lonnie, LeCoste, Americus, and Frank McIver, Scott Haulcey, Joel Harrell, Judge Sylvania Woods, Mr. Ernest Ferguson, Mr. Jim Butler, Mr. William Cabbagestalk, Darryl Tolson, and the Johnson Family. I miss you all very much. You've left a footprint in my life and a little bit of all of you will live on in my words. Rest in eternal peace.

Q: You originally self-published Simon Says. *What drove you to write this story and then market it on your own? What was the most challenging part of this process?*

A: I had read John Grisham's *The Firm,* and was completely captivated by the story. After seeing the movie and reading a few more of his books, I was really drawn into the whole thriller genre. I really like Mr. Grisham's flair for developing characters and storylines, and I thought that it would be nice to read books like his that had African-American characters. I wondered why no one was really writing books like those. I decided that instead of complaining about the lack of diversity in the genre, I'd try to write one myself. I was always an avid reader, and a decent writer, so I figured that writing a novel wouldn't be too difficult. Boy, was I wrong! Reading well and writing well are distinctly different. The most challenging part of this process was learning the craft of writing through self-paced courses, and practice, practice, practice.

Q: Simon Blake is a charismatic mayor involved in illicit activities. Is he modeled after anyone in particular? Are any parts of the story modeled after events in your life?

A: Simon is a composite of a lot of people. A lot of people ask me if he was modeled after Marion Barry, the former mayor of D.C., but he really isn't. Simon is a very complex, multifaceted character, with very good and, at the same time, inherently bad, characteristics.

Q: Why did you decide to make Alex's mother a civil rights activist?

A: I thought that it was important to have his mother be a person of substance, and since Alex was born during that era, and she was a woman ahead of her time, I thought that it would be a realistic thing for her to do. An additional reason was that oftentimes we hear about the more famous people who participated in the movement but nothing about the everyday people whose contributions were just as significant.

Q: Who are your favorite novelists?

A: I actually read a lot of nonfiction, but my favorite novelists are John Grisham, Valerie Wilson Wesley, James Baldwin, and Gloria Naylor.

Q: What is next for you? Are you working on another novel?

A: The sequel, *Every Shut Eye . . . ,* is underway. I promise to tie up all the loose ends from *Simon Says,* and perhaps develop some of the characters for future books. I really like the role of Lisa, Alex's friend and insurance investigator. I think that she would be a good character for another thriller, especially since I've developed an interest in forensic science and autopsy reports.

The questions and discussion topics that follow are intended to enhance your group's reading of Collen Dixon's thrilling debut, *Simon Says*.

1. Tiffany has her pick of the men on Hilliard's campus, but even from the start she seems drawn to Alex. Does she choose him just because he saved her from Sid? What does Alex offer Tiffany that other men do not?

2. Alex experiences two life-changing events in his youth—the death of his brother and saving Tiffany from her attacker. How do these two events shape the direction his life takes and his attitude toward life?

3. Simon seems purely evil. Is he? Does he really love his daughter?

4. Alex's father is nearly destroyed by the death of his wife, and then his son. Why can't he recover? What is instrumental in bringing him back into Alex's life?

5. Much of Alex's success after college is due to the influence of Simon. Would Alex have been as successful without Simon's help? Where would he have been without it?

To print out copies of this or other Strivers Row Reading Group Guides, visit us at www.atrandom.com/rgg.

6. Tiffany is the queen of the Hilliard campus and seems to have it all. Does she? What affect did her mother's death have on her? Does she have any suspicions about her father's activities?

7. Without the protection of Fortune, Alex might never have survived his discovery of Simon's secret. Has Fortune redeemed himself? Is this enough payback for his role in Ivan's death?

8. *Simon Says* is a story of loss and coming-of-age in a world of drugs and violence. How is this theme explored in the lives of the main characters, Alex, Tiffany, Ivan, and Fortune? What is Ivan's legacy?

9. Growing up, Alex shrugs off his Shaw background and hopes to leave it behind forever. However, in the end, he finds it may be the one thing that can save him. What does he finally come to realize about Shaw and Washington, D.C.?

10. Alex's last confrontation with Simon is, in some sense, the completion of a cycle that began with his brother's death. Does Alex finally avenge his brother?

COLLEN DIXON is a native of Washington, D.C., and *Simon Says* is her debut novel. She recently completed her second novel, *Behind Closed Doors . . . In My Father's House,* and she is hard at work on her third, *Every Shut Eye.* Collen has worked in corporate America, as a consultant, and in management and sales. She enjoys feng shui, tending to her bonsai trees, and collecting art and automobiles. She also enjoys "viewing the world from two wheels," skiing, traveling, and entertaining. A huge movie buff, she recently successfully underwent treatment for an addiction to online auctions. She and Chadwick, her fur-faced little dog, currently reside in Mitchellville, Maryland. Her motto is, "Always be grateful, never be satisfied."